PRINCE OF DECEIT

DAWN OF RAGNAROK BOOK 3

ALIANNE DONNELLY

PRINCE DECEIT

And from the icy mist rose, like a great beast of Shadows deep, a new world, wrought of the blood and bones of the old. Fragmented, deformed, its first cry was one for war; its first thought one of hatred and fear. And so the Bringer of Light shaped his world—with a fury of steel and flame that consumed all that was into all that was left.

PROLOGUE

"The Son is rising. I can see the light."

"The sun has risen long ago, My Queen," replied one of her holy knights.

He will expect to find a powerful kingdom to rule.

"Yes, and He shall have a kingdom worthy of His glory." She let the heavy curtain fall back into place and turned away from the window. As beautiful as the light was to behold, it hurt her eyes.

"Your Majesty?" the knight questioned. Jonah was his name. One of the First, the five knights who'd journeyed to the land of heathens and brought her the Cup of Eternal Life.

Such tales they'd told upon their triumphant return. They'd awed and entertained the court with fables about a land filled with magic, and a powerful witch seated at the right hand of its king—a woman who had his ear in all things. A woman who'd led the knights to the hermit's cave for the Cup they'd sworn would restore Queen Genevieve's youth.

It hadn't worked, of course. These things never did—unless one was worthy of them. The knights had all fallen under the heathen witch's thrall, and with their fall from Grace tainted the Cup before it'd reached Queen Genevieve's hands.

For many years thereafter, she had prayed to her God for guidance, seeking to become worthy. She'd purged the disbelievers and heathen heretics from her lands. She'd established order with laws to purify the soul and safeguarded her kingdom against the evil of pride and the temptation of sin in all its forms.

Still, the glory of God, His guiding voice, had been denied to her for all these years until one day, in her despair, she'd sought to purify her withered body with boiling water. No pain had been too great for the majesty of her God. No sacrifice too much for the promise of eternal life in His all-encompassing embrace.

And as the scalding waves had lapped at her knees, His voice had spoken to her from the shadows. In His mercy, He'd declared her devotion divine. He'd named her His prophet and shared with her a glimpse of His power. At once, the water had cooled to soothe her burns. Her pain had disappeared. And when she'd managed to tear her gaze away from the miracle, He'd shown her another—the briefest glimpse into her just reward. For a few moments, her youth had been restored, and she'd looked and felt as she had in her prime.

A glimpse, but a promise, as well. "Serve me well, and I shall give you youth eternal, and you will dwell in my kingdom for all time."

Awed by His power, Queen Genevieve had prostrated herself at once and sworn fealty to Him and no other.

His counsel had never left her side since.

Her court might think her mad, but Genevieve now knew the Holy Truth. She was its bearer, her God's chosen messenger in this world until He came to speak for Himself. Until He deigned them all worthy of His presence.

Your knights grow suspicious. Send them away.

Genevieve nodded and allowed the knights to help her to her seat by the hearth. Her weary bones creaked as she lowered herself into it. She held her gnarled, twisted fingers up to the fire's warmth.

After so many wars, so many villains slain, so many glorious victories won, age had turned out to be the one enemy she couldn't defeat. Once, she'd walked with her head held high, her thick, black hair draping over her shoulders like a veil. Now, her hunched, dried out husk of a figure curled in on itself so much she had to tilt her head up to look straight ahead. Men who would have been of a height with her in her youth towered over her and made her feel weaker still. And her once beautiful hair had been reduced to a few wiry white strands she hid beneath a silken veil held in place by a golden circlet.

The crown she hadn't worn in years sat on a pedestal against the far wall, a symbol of her political power and her physical weakness. Were she to don it now, her neck would break beneath its weight.

Her frail form failed her more and more every day. She no longer possessed the strength to hold court in her grand throne room as was expected. She could only walk the distance from her bedchamber to this sitting room, with its plain wooden floors and sparse tapestries. Her servants had draped it in gold and filled it with plush seats and dozens of candles, but it was still a paltry substitute, and a hateful inconvenience she tolerated because she had no other choice. "Leave me now," she ordered. "Find me Sir Arnaud. He is summoned before the queen."

The knights complied at once, closing the heavy wooden door behind them, but not before it admitted a chill breeze to sneak underneath her thick robe and make her shiver.

Yes, well done.

"Why him? There are hundreds of them now, and more flock to the Holy Order every day. Any of them could carry out Your commands better than the traitor."

It is not service I require. It is knowledge. He alone has spoken to the heathen queen.

Not so. There were others—Frederick and Lucca. Oh, but yes, yes. Her weary mind remembered. Frederick was dead, long years ago now. And Lucca, the heretic, had been made an example to the rest of them. He'd screamed his dead wife's name as he'd been pulled apart, a final affront against their God.

Bearing witness, Sir Arnaud had sworn himself into silence and solitude. His ominous words that day had sent a chill down Genevieve's spine. "The next time you hear me speak will be my last. But my words will live on long after my death!"

Of the five knights who'd braved the heathen lands to bring her the Cup, only Arnaud and Jonah remained. And Arnaud alone refused to obey her royal orders, yet suffered no consequence.

As an elder of the Holy Order, he ranked highest among them, save for Genevieve herself. Sequestered in his cell, shrouded in silence, he placed himself at the mercy of others. Younger knights cared for him, provided food, water, and clean robes. Genevieve questioned them often about Sir Arnaud's condition. They always replied the same, "He prays in silence and never speaks a word."

For twenty years, he had done this. For the strength of his conviction alone, she ought to have him executed—his piety surpassed her own.

She stayed her hand for one reason. With all his devotion, piety, and silence, God still hadn't chosen him. He'd chosen the queen of Synealee instead. As long as Arnaud remained silent and didn't publicly oppose her will, Genevieve was content to leave him to his barren cell to rot.

When the knights returned with Sir Arnaud, she stood once more to face him. Age had left its mark on the former knight, as it had on Genevieve herself. What a pair they made, the queen hunched at the shoulders, and the knight whose legs no longer straightened all the way. But at least Genevieve still took pains to ensure her looks befitted her station. Sir Arnaud did not. His hair was white, grown past his shoulders in shameful disarray. His beard, too, reached past his chest. The plain linen robes he wore were as clean as she'd ever seen them, save for the two dark spots that would forever stain it where his knees pressed into the ground during endless prayer. This was one of his nicer robes. She'd seen him before in ones with holes worn through.

But none of that mattered when she stepped close and looked into his eyes. Such unusual eyes he had, so steady and serene, filled with utter peace. It was said he never faltered in his routine, never displayed a hint of fear or doubt. It was said he was the silent prophet, and any who sought him with questions found answers in those eyes.

It was said…

Genevieve despised him for every scandalous whisper bearing his name. The queen had defied death. She was by far the oldest regent ever to sit the throne of Synealee. She was God's chosen, His instrument and herald.

Yet her people—her knights—spoke of only *him*. In their whispers, he was no longer Sir Arnaud. He was Saint Arnaud the Silent.

No audience, God decreed.

"Leave us," she ordered.

Arnaud showed no reaction to her command.

"I am told you speak to the heathen queen of the north."

The witch who'd sat by her king had staked her claim most thoroughly by stealing his heart along with his reason. Rumors traveled far and wide about Wilderheim and its king and queen. It was a land of faeries, elves, trolls, and all manner of inhuman creatures never meant to be seen by human eyes. The people of Wilderheim called them Other. Genevieve called them what they were—demon spawn crawled up from the deepest pits of Hell to corrupt the righteous.

Their king had broken royal protocol and defied the laws of his ancestors by taking the witch to wife. Genevieve had prayed for dissent among his nobles to finally bring Wilderheim to its knees, but she'd been denied. Wielding untold power of their own, the heathen monarchs had calmed the unrest and bewitched their people to love them.

"What is said between you?"

Not a word or a twitch in answer. Arnaud didn't blink an eye.

"What would your acolytes think if they knew their Silent One wasn't so silent after all?"

The knight stared at her.

"You've drunk from the Cup, haven't you? All of you must have. The pride of men hath no limits. Nor does their irreverence. But it did not work. Here you are, as old and decrepit as time itself, no better than you would have been without it. Worse, for knowing your prayers went unanswered. And do you know why? None of you were worthy."

A slow blink.

"You will tell me what was said between you and Nialei the Whore."

He remained silent.

"Your queen orders you to speak."

He will not part with his secrets so easily. Perhaps he needs a little incentive.

Arnaud's gaze darted to the side and back to Genevieve. As if he'd heard.

She rushed him. Her hand raised of its own accord and struck him across the face. She felt tainted by that brief contact, her palm stinging with the coolness of his flesh. "I can make you speak. The dungeons have no shortage of clever devices and implements to unravel even the most tangled of tongues."

No, God said from his shadow. *Do not give your knights cause to doubt your judgment. They must not witness him suffering unduly on your order.*

Sir Arnaud tilted his head in the direction of the voice, his mouth twisting in displeasure, and oh, how she wanted to defy God's will and make the knight suffer for his insolence.

God, too, seemed to notice. When He spoke again, His question was directed to the silent knight. *Has she found the song?*

The knight dismissed the voice of God as if it meant nothing to him, turning back to Genevieve.

"Answer Him," she wheezed, feeling heat rise up her neck as her heart thrummed in her chest. She knew nothing of this song, but if it was important to God, it had to be a powerful thing, indeed. She would get the answer out of Arnaud one way or another.

Sir Arnaud leaned down to match her stoop and dared to meet her gaze with a stare so direct Genevieve felt herself falling forward.

Shadows closed in around Arnaud, then swallowed all but those cursed, knowing eyes of his. She lost herself in them. Her aged heart thrashed, and her lungs labored to keep up as visions took shape before her. A woman with golden hair and magic in her eyes. An endless winter. A dark cave, and inside, a hermit older than time itself, yet possessing youth eternal. And the Cup. She sensed no pride in what she saw. Only humility, awe, and love.

Genevieve whimpered, broke away, and turned her back on him, suddenly cold and weary. So weary...

Enough. You tire yourself needlessly. I have all the answers I need.

Then His will was done, and Genevieve was free to deal with the heretic as she must. Sir Arnaud had the power to induce visions with nothing but his stare. He was tainted with heathen sorcery, and still, his acolytes worshipped him. He was a threat to everything Synealee stood for. She couldn't allow such a man to live. "Guards!"

Seven knights rushed in, swords drawn in readiness.

"Take him to the stake."

They hesitated.

"I said take him! He is accused of practicing witchcraft and consorting with demons. In the name of God, burn the heretic!"

Two of the knights seized Arnaud with obvious reluctance. God's guiding voice said nothing, yet she still felt His presence. Surely He wasn't displeased with her.

Arnaud stayed his guards with a simple look. "You dare invoke the name of God," he rasped, "and accuse me of witchcraft when the Devil himself whispers in your ear."

The knights gasped, drew away in shock.

"I know what you seek. You think to earn God's favor by tearing down those who oppose Him, but you are wrong. Queen Nialei's world is not yours to conquer. She has her own gods to obey and has little care for ours. I have glimpsed the future, False Prophet—yours and hers."

"Silence!"

No, let him speak.

Genevieve flushed.

"You will fail," Arnaud prophesied. "Your armies will march into Wilderheim, waving your banner with pride, and they will find nothing but snow and death. Thousands will fall and none by the Queen's order. Her progeny will be the ones to raze your armies to the ground. Her son will be your undoing, and his cause will be just. And you, *My Queen*, will not live to see this come to pass."

His ominous words fell like physical blows on Genevieve's shoulders, driving her to hunch lower. She couldn't catch her breath to speak.

But her guards did. Into the shocked silence following Arnaud's prophecy, one of them found voice enough to say the only word that mattered. "Treason."

"Burn him," she ordered, clenching her shaking hands to her belly. "Take him from my sight and burn him at once!"

The knights took him away quickly but without force. None was necessary, as Arnaud walked out with his head held high. Genevieve hurried to her window overlooking the courtyard and, beyond it, her beautiful seaside city of Palos. Dozens of church spires proudly pierced the sky in those streets. They marked places of sanctuary and worship, tracing the shape of a cross laid over the city. Whenever Genevieve felt at her weakest, she sought the sight of those spires to lift her spirits and strengthen her resolve.

They failed to do so now. Feverish with doubt so deep it made her shiver, she raised her hand to shield Palos from her view and squinted against the sun's blinding glare, eager to see Arnaud swallowed up in flames. The centerpiece platform was as high as she was tall, made of steel and stone, and the sight of it made her shivers ease.

God's soothing voice whispered in her ear, *Fear not, My Queen, while I walk by your side. Your armies will know the taste of victory. I will allow no other outcome.*

Genevieve watched Arnaud walk up the steps to the post and stand with his back to it. He didn't resist when the executioner tied him in place, showed no fear as the wood was placed around him. No quick death for Saint Arnaud the Silent. He would not have the luxury of flames lapping up his robes. The fires would burn high around Arnaud but never touch him. He'd die in slow agony, suffocating on the heat and smoke. She would hear his voice once more as he screamed.

The pyre was lit. Flames spread to encircle him, then rose high over the top of the post. Smoke obscured her view, but Genevieve thought she glimpsed Arnaud's face turned toward the sky, his eyes closed, and his lips moving in silent prayer. She stood there, waiting for his screams, but she was denied.

A shudder of apprehension rocked her ancient frame. Could he have spoken true? "Show me again," she pleaded, desperate for reassurance of God's power. "Show me as you did that day. My faith weakens. Doubt grows in my heart."

Look away, He crooned. *All the heathens in Wilderheim could never hope to equal my power. Look at yourself and believe.*

Genevieve turned away from the sight of Arnaud the Silent slumping against the post. She shuffled her feet to the hearth, feeling the weight of all her fourscore and eight years pressing on her shoulders. Retrieving a mirror, she gazed at her reflection.

A beautiful young maiden stared back at her, with pale skin and hair as black as night, and lips as red as cherries. She smiled, her strength once again restored, and her faith renewed. With a reverent young hand, she reached up to touch her cheek and twirled on the polished wooden floors, her slippered feet as sure as they'd been decades ago.

A fleeting glimpse, nothing more. But she treasured it for the promise it held. God had not and would not abandon her. She served Him well, and He would reward her for it in the end.

And so she danced, and laughed, and thanked God for giving her this moment of strength to fortify her against the struggle still to come. For, when the battle was won—and it would be—this strength would be hers for all time. She looked at herself in the mirror and smiled with such joy in her heart.

And she never once looked away to see the creature in Shadow disappear.

PART ONE

THE SKY SHATTERS

1

Why so sad, my love?

The dragon sighed, watching water drip steadily from the stalactite overhead. Each droplet grew the protrusion by an infinitesimal amount before it fell into the puddle below, sounding the only music he had in this place. Distracted from his reverie, he puffed out an annoyed cloud of black smoke and brought his horned head around to rest over a forepaw.

Will you not speak to me?

He did not, though his heart ached to reply, to have the apparition hear his words and respond in truth. Instead, the dragon closed his eyes against the ghostly vision, reminding himself yet again that it was not real, no matter how much he might wish otherwise. The voice existed only in his mind, where her memory lived unchanged, preserved against time itself.

Dragons were the keepers of memory. Their gift and burden were to remember the things time had eroded to dust and scattered into obscurity. Within his mind, infinite worlds collided, and swirls of magic mixed together. The Beginning of All was born again and again, each time as brilliant and wondrous as the first. Lands rippled alive, creatures big and small formed into being and just as quickly disintegrated.

He remembered everything since the moment of his awakening, but only one memory out of an infinity of them could make him doubt what was real and what was not. Only she could escape from the past to invade his present and make him lose track of both.

It was becoming more and more difficult to sort her back into her rightful place. Perhaps his mind was slipping. Or perhaps he simply did not want to keep her in the past. Her rightful place was by his side, and she would have been there with him now, if only…

If only.

A sigh, like the promise of a kiss, blew across his snout. His scales bristled at the imagined touch. His tail lashed around to curl toward his head to catch the sensation, hold onto it before it disappeared again.

The ground thrummed with nervous energy, sending waves of soundless drums reverberating throughout the cave. An early warning the dragon had long anticipated, now an annoyance he couldn't escape. What good was knowing the end was nigh when he could do naught to change it?

Yet through that deafening din of silence, he heard an incongruous sound: the patter of soft feet. His nostrils flared, catching an impossible hint of a familiar scent.

The dragon tensed, listened, but then shook himself off and made himself turn his bulk around within the chamber's confines and settle again. Nothing but a dream. Beautiful, but fleeting.

It's coming. Can you feel it? The cold breath of endless winter. Fenrir's binds are weakening. He is breaking free.

The worry in her voice cut him to the quick. How could he leave her to suffer alone? He could not, and so he relented, aware that acknowledging her presence would make it that much more difficult to push back later. "It is as it was always going to be," the dragon said, his deep, low voice rumbling with the force of an earthquake. Sometimes it eased his heartache to talk to her. Even if she wasn't truly there.

Are you ready?

Ready for the end? With all of his soul. He craved it, eager for the promise of seeing his beloved once again. And if not, eager to embrace the endless abyss of nothing. There, perhaps, he might finally find peace at last. A respite from this wretched hollow that breathed and yawed inside him, growing bigger, erasing more of him with each year that passed.

"I miss you," he said fiercely, willing the vision to linger.

Another sigh, another almost-touch he could feel beneath his scales. A memory snuggled in the crook of his shoulder, leaning its soft, nonexistent weight against his neck.

Had he the ability to smile, the dragon might have attempted to do so. "Remember that first Mabon? You asked for a bonfire bright enough to banish the night. I watched you dance around it, and the flames sang for you." She'd always loved the flames he'd built for her. As human as she'd been, her heart had been pure fire, bright and hot as the sun, searing him with so much love he'd thought it could fill even a lifetime as long as his.

And when she'd died, she'd taken that fire with her, leaving him cold.

"I should have held on tighter."

How does one keep the wind from blowing away?

"By closing the door."

An ancient argument the dragon relived in his mind a dozen times a day. It had made no difference then, or ever since. In the end, she'd known only one could survive, and she'd chosen to sacrifice her life to save their child.

Why worry about the inevitable? she asked as she had then, smiling through the sorrow in her eyes, for his sake. *Why waste away our happiness? Dance with me. Dance with me...* "Dance with me."

The dragon opened his eyes, gaped at the sight before him. There she stood, her flaxen hair wild, flowing down her back, a skein of it veiling her eye. She wore a peasant dress, as plain as she was beautiful, her feet bare, stepping left and right in a familiar dance. "Solveig..."

"Dance with me," she said, laughing. Her delicate hands curled around one of his claws and tugged. Her touch had once moved mountains inside him. It was no different now. The dragon's beastly form burned away, swathed him in thick smoke as he compressed his essence into the shape of a man. Claws became fingers and toes. Scales smoothed into soft, vulnerable skin. Everything he was and ever would be squeezed into the shape of a man, leaving only a pair of horns and a tail to mark him as Other.

Solveig had always loved his dragon form. But in his human shape, he could love her back as she deserved to be loved.

A delighted smile lit up Solveig's face as she threw herself into his arms, burying her nose in the crook of his neck to breathe him in. He felt her. He scented her. An impossibility to his ancient mind but one he could not bring himself to give up. His human arms came around her, hesitant for fear they'd sink through nothing as they'd done so many times before.

This time, they touched upon firm, solid flesh.

The dragon dared not breathe. He clutched her to his human chest as tightly as he could without hurting her, painfully aware of her mortal frailty. So many opportunities wasted, so little time left. He was desperate to hold on, to somehow keep her from slipping through his claws a second time.

Not real…

But how could it not be? Her warmth seeped into him. Her laughter awoke his heart to life. Her hands clutched his hair with so much strength and vitality—how could she not be real?

Solveig pulled back, her brilliant green gaze tracing his face. She cupped his cheek, wiped away an errant tear. "My love," she crooned.

The dragon hardly trusted himself to speak. "You're here."

"Yes," she whispered.

"But how?"

Solveig pressed her smiling mouth to his, whispered her answer between his lips. The dragon heard not, and cared not. She was there. He'd dreamed her back into being, and this time he wasn't letting her go. Fenrir would escape anon; the End of All was nigh. What little time any of them had left, the dragon wanted to spend with her.

"Dance with me," she said.

He danced. Slowly, at first, savoring the feel of her in his arms, the smile on her face. Then faster, twirling her around, tossing her up, and catching her again to make her squeal and laugh. The dragon danced her through the tunnels that ran past his treasures and Liadan's old bedchamber, all the way to the underground lake. Sparks jumped from his fingertips, flying through the air around them like swarms of fireflies. Some of them landed on torches he'd had no use for in many years, and they flared up, filling the caves with light.

Solveig laughed and laughed, the music of her voice echoing back to him from every direction, and the dragon forgot. The decades he'd spent mourning her melted away in an instant. He felt younger than he ever had, brimming with joy to have her with him. He'd waited so long to find her, and the time he'd had with her had been but a wink. A gasp of delight followed by pain and sorrow.

But she was there now, healthy and hale and in his arms. Afraid to let her go, when she pulled free of him to dance away, the dragon caught her hand and held on, following her lead with unabashed eagerness.

"Your legs have grown as stiff as trees," she teased.

The dragon laughed. "Aye, so have other parts of me." But for her, he lightened his step, smoothed out his stride, and when he caught her against his side for a turn, the movement felt as lithe as a breeze.

How does one keep the wind from blowing away?

Blowing away...

Away...

He faltered, stopping by the scorchmark where a small fire had used to warm her after she'd bathed. The memory of its heat still remained, as did the one of Solveig wringing water out of her long tresses all over him.

"You came back." Even to his own ears, the words sounded strange, disbelieving and hopeful at once.

Solveig's smile softened. "I came back. For you." She kissed him, and her lips tasted so sweet... "Come with me," she said. "I know where we can be together. Safe. Forever."

The world spun, making him sway, but he had her to hold onto. The dragon clutched her hand, looped his tail around her ankle, just tight enough so he knew she was there beside him.

Her free hand raked through his hair, scratched lightly over his horn, making him shudder. "Come with me," she repeated. "Be with me."

Gods, how he wanted to. With a thought, he summoned Liadan's ring onto his finger. A gift he'd all but forgotten. Forged in dragon's fire, it had the ability to summon any of his blood kin to him. He had but to think it, and his descendants would be there, all of them together again. And Solveig would make them all safe. "Yes," he answered, eager to get out of Fenrir's path; to go anywhere, as long as Solveig was with him.

She smiled, tugged on his hand to lead him down a tunnel he didn't recognize. "I have missed you so much, my love."

"Woman, you took half of me with you when you left."

Died…

"I am back now."

Dead…

"Yes." The thought of his family faded before it could summon them. The ring settled on his finger, ready to work its magic, but dormant for now. Time enough still. Time he could spend with his mate alone. He needed that—needed *her*.

"And we can take back the time Fate stole from us. I want to be with you."

The dragon nodded, not trusting himself to speak. His body quivered, and his legs weakened as he followed her down the dark tunnel, staring into those beautiful green eyes, afraid to blink, lest she disappear and prove herself a dream.

If she was, he never wanted to wake again.

The tunnel became a passage, the stone around him shimmering into slabs laid with mortar. The ground beneath his bare feet evened out, and the sound of dripping water became the rush of a stream. He raised a hand to summon fire, but Solveig pressed her palm against his, keeping his flame at bay. No matter. Solveig knew where she was going, and the dragon trusted her implicitly. Even when the shadows deepened and black emptiness swallowed them whole. As long as he felt her with him, the dragon kept going.

At long last, she slowed, stopped, and in the darkness, pressed her body into his. Her hands caressed his face, swept down his shoulders and arms, and squeezed his wrists. She brought each of his hands to her lips, pressed a kiss to each knuckle.

"Solveig…" The dragon reached for her face, needing to kiss her again. The bite of rope around his wrist pulled him up short. "What—" He tried with his other arm, reaching for her waist, and a length of rope snapped taut, yanking him back by the wrist.

The instinct to protect his mate flared into a snarl, and he tugged with his tail to pull her closer into the shelter of his arms, but as he did, she disappeared. His tail curled around nothing—the press of her body against his melted away like mist. Between one moment and the next, Solveig was gone, leaving not a hint of her scent behind.

The dragon groped around the darkness, searching for her, fearing for her, and each time he let the ropes grow slack, they drew tighter, reeling him backward. He shouted her name, raged against his binds, but with all his might, he couldn't budge them, and only endless echoes answered him.

Until she spoke. "Solveig is dead," she said in his beloved's voice, but it wasn't her. It changed on each sound, lost its melody and warmth, and became something foreign, unfeeling.

Torches flared to light left and right, illuminating a stone cell. He was standing in ankle-deep water, beside a wrought-iron cage through which it ebbed and flowed. He sensed his surroundings, rather than saw them, his gaze rapt on Solveig's beautiful visage as it faded into a different shape.

The woman standing before him was tall and thin, her lips deathly pale, and her dark hair braided into dozens of ropes that swayed around her on an unseen gale. She stared at him with eyes as black as pitch, and the dragon saw nothing in them. She was empty.

"Whoever you are, I will kill you for this."

"I am Hel, and you are welcome to try." No emotion in her voice. No smirk of victory on her face. He would have welcomed even boredom, but there was nothing. Nothing for him to respond to. Nothing to sharpen his claws on. The goddess who ruled the realm of the dead regarded him with all the passion of a stone.

He yanked on his binds with all his might, but they held him fast. He summoned fire to burn them away, but they didn't weaken in the slightest. He tried to shed his human form and transform into his dragon self. His feet stretched into hindpaws; his hands grew scales and claws; his teeth sharpened into fangs, but the magic imbued in those ropes froze him there. His fire spread to engulf him but brought him neither heat nor strength. He was stuck.

And all the while, Hel watched him without reaction. As dead inside as hear entire realm. As mad and ruthless as her entire family was said to be. What else could he expect from the spawn of Loki?

The dragon shuddered. "Why?"

"Because my father asked it of me."

Then she was gone.

~

Sanja's face felt cold. Her lips were numb, her cheeks ached, and her eyes stung for lack of blinking. She hid her clenched hands beneath her skirts, but as hard as she tried, her aching fingers wouldn't straighten. She was frozen. *Gods, it can't end this way...*

"Well, child? What do you say?"

Sanja blinked to focus on her father's aged face. Gerhart was a good man, a carpenter who'd made an honest name for himself in his day. He'd worked himself raw to become the most sought after craftsman in the entire city, and even received a commission or two from the royal family. He'd wanted his legacy to carry on through his sons and had been dismayed when, after two miscarriages, his wife Olga birthed a daughter.

Their elderly neighbors told Sanja her mother had wept for days over it. When another miscarriage had nearly taken her life, and the Other midwife declared Olga would never bear another child, she'd wept for weeks longer.

Gerhart could not love his daughter more, but the lack of a son left him with a heavy burden to carry through his advancing years. Sanja had watched his eyes turn bleak each time a neighbor shared happy news of a wedding or birth. She knew he longed for his only daughter to marry, but this...

"Daughter," Olga whispered with a nervous smile. In her grief, her once beautiful face had aged a great deal more than it should have. But her love for Sanja shone out of her as bright as the sun.

Sanja turned her frozen smile to their guest of honor.

Jarl Steen was a man who revered hunting, brawling, and all other manner of manly pursuits, and it showed. He towered over Sanja when standing and made the worn chairs creak and groan when he sat. Perhaps his bulky frame and thick neck wouldn't have been as intimidating if the man deigned to smile once in a while, but his brows appeared to be forever set in a foreboding frown over his cold gray eyes.

He wore his light brown hair shaved along the sides to display the decorative scars he'd had cut into his scalp. The rest of his hair was braided down the center of his head to his nape and matched the braids in his beard. Both were adorned with golden beads, each one, the rumors said, signifying a victory or achievement of some sort.

His fearsome presence alone overwhelmed the old cottage so much Sanja felt it holding its breath. One hard stomp from him, and it would come crumbling down around them.

And his temper was reputed to be just as mighty.

Gods, he'll crush me with a thought.

As the border lord to the east, Jarl Steen had vast holdings. He was titled, rich, and celebrated far and wide for his strength. By all accounts, he ought to have been married long ago.

Alas, despite all this, no one would have him.

Gerhart cleared his throat, reminding Sanja she still hadn't said a word. But what could she say? "I, umm…" She looked to Olga for support, but her mother could only offer a wan smile. If she wouldn't come to Sanja's defense, then the situation had to be worse than either of her parents let on. Gerhart's hands were no longer steady enough to carve his masterpieces. He'd been reduced to pounding together rough stools and tables for the poorer denizens of Frastmir, but it still caused him pain. To make up for the lack, Olga had become a washerwoman, laundering merchants' clothes and linens in the freezing river day after day, but despite both of them earning coin, their home had fallen into disrepair, and visits from friends had turned into uncomfortable silences and subtle reminders of unpaid debts.

Sanja, too, tried her best to help. She'd apprenticed with the weaver, the seamstress, the miller, even the fisherman. Each had sent her back to her parents as a bothersome nuisance. No two ways about it, Sanja was clumsy. Her hands never seemed to be steady enough for delicate tasks, or strong enough for harder ones. She dropped instruments constantly, had no eye for art or design, and worst of all, she had the unpardonable habit of talking too much.

Except, it appeared, now.

"Sanja," Gerhart whispered, giving Jarl Steen an apologetic smile.

Her mind was her best feature by far. She had an excellent memory, a good head for numbers, and an insatiable curiosity about everything Divine and Other. Alas, such qualities were only sought after by the upper classes of human society. Unlike Other communities, humans valued practical skills over abstract thinking.

Under the pretext of pouring himself more water from the jug that ought to have held ale to show their guest proper hospitality, Gerhart bumped into the table, startling Sanja back to the matter at hand.

Shivering, she answered the only way she could. "N-no."

The room plunged into silence. Gerhart paled, his hands shaking so hard he almost dropped his cup.

"I am sorry, Da. And I apologize to you as well, Jarl Steen. You honor us with your proposal of marriage. Honestly, I am well and truly flattered that a man of your stature would approach a young girl of my humble means, and any woman in her right mind would consider herself lucky to receive such a generous offer, and please don't think I refuse you out of stubbornness or because I would prefer someone else…" She prattled on for so long she stopped paying attention to her words while her mind raced with desperate ideas on how to put him off without bringing his wrath down upon herself and her parents. "You exhibit the finest qualities a man could possess…" Gerhart leaned back, gaping at her with an increasingly alarmed expression on his face. *Think of something quick.* "And you have means to rival the king, all this is true and makes you a fine man, indeed, and if I were free to marry, no doubt I would say yes. Yes! A thousand times, yes!"

Jarl Steen raised his giant hand to stop the tirade. Closing his gaping mouth, he frowned. "Are you saying you are not free to marry?" As softly as he spoke the words, his voice still boomed so loud Sanja flinched. He looked to Gerhart for confirmation. This was a courtesy meeting to introduce Sanja to her husband to be. The agreement had already been struck, and all the particulars negotiated at length between Jarl Steen and Gerhart earlier that morning. To now be told otherwise was as unexpected as it was insulting.

"I assure you, Jarl Steen," Gerhart rushed to say. "My daughter might be a strange one, but she is of marriageable age, and she *will* marry."

"She will not," Sanja dared, suddenly striking on the perfect solution to all of this. "She—I mean *I*—have chosen another path."

"Another path?" Jarl Steen repeated, uncomprehending.

Olga worried the edges of her apron. "Sanja?"

Sanja nodded and, pulling her shoulders back, declared, "The path of the cleric." Why had she never considered it before? Clerics were reclusive, studious people who had given up the pleasures of city life in favor of becoming lifelong students and teachers. Their lives were dedicated not to the worship of any particular god but to knowledge. Most spent their time in their temple high up in the mountains, transcribing and preserving ancient books and scrolls. But some did travel to teach what they knew to those willing to learn. Some, like those in charge of Frastmir's massive library, were honored with a lifelong position as the keepers of books for kings and queens. Such a life would be perfect for Sanja.

Gerhart paled. "Daughter, no."

Sanja frowned. Why was he looking at her like that? This wasn't a jest; she was in earnest. She certainly didn't care that clerics couldn't—or rather *didn't*—marry. While there were no restrictions on marriage for clerics, their lives were not easy to share. No wife would want to raise children on her own while her husband traveled the world. No husband would want a wife who spent months at a time in the clerics' temple. Better, as recompense for losing one of their line, the clerics paid homage to the initiate's family, oftentimes equivalent to a dowry or bride price. Her family's debts would be erased with that sum, and Sanja would be forever safe from another of Jarl Steen's ilk sniffing at her skirts. For the chance to expand her mind, she would gladly give up marriage, a life of servitude to her husband, and the perpetual cycle of pregnancy and child rearing. None of those things had ever appealed to her, anyway. Sanja longed to see the Otherlands, to walk different worlds, and learn their secrets—

Jarl Steen laughed, his thick shoulders twitching up and down. "A cleric? You?"

"Just so," she confirmed, puzzled. He was certainly taking the news well.

The jarl laughed harder. "A cleric!" Wiping his tears, he made an effort to contain his mirth as he turned to Gerhart. "Master Carver, be easy. I know what this is and how to handle it. The girl suffers from maidenly shyness, she said so herself. My offer is so generous she cannot contain herself."

Gerhart attempted a smile, knowing full well that wasn't the issue. Sanja was, indeed, of marriageable age, fast approaching its end without a single offer so far. While young men weren't shy to talk to her, none of them had asked for her hand. She was a strange one, and they seemed to know it right away. Jarl Steen's offer of marriage might well be the only one she'd ever receive.

Her intended looked at each of them in turn, then waved some internal thought aside. "No matter. I know what needs to be done. The girl wants to be wooed. All these Others prancing around with their poetry and songs of love have turned every head from here to Lyria. Not a-one sensible female left in the kingdom. But mark me, Master Carver." He leered at Sanja as he made his pledge. "I am decided on this matter. I will have your daughter or none at all, and I will be relentless in my pursuit." His gaze briefly turned unfocused as he added, almost to himself, "Any wild beast can be brought to heel. Even the stubborn ones. All it takes is a firm hand."

Sanja shuddered as she watched his hands curl into fists.

Seeming to come back to himself, he turned back to Gerhart with a determined nod. "The girl wants time? She will have it—I will give her a full month. She wants courtship? I will show her what true romance is. Our nobles can surpass any Other in Wilderheim." He spoke of courtship like an unsavory task that had been laid before him.

Although Wilderheim's marriages now modeled after the devoted, loving relationship of its ruling couple, there were still too many who believed women inferior to men, those who considered a woman nothing more than a piece of property whose only purpose was to birth children. The jarl was very much one of that ignorant lot.

"In a month's time, she will be only too happy to don her wedding gown."

The gods only knew what her fate would be afterward. Sanja was determined not to find out. "In a month's time, I will be making my way up to the clerics' temple."

The jarl's indulgent smile set her teeth on edge. "In a hair shirt, as all the rest of them? Autumn is already upon us, girl, it'll be a cold day when you start on that path, and snows come early high in the mountains." He shook his head, dismissing the idea. "You will never make it to the top. Certainly not on your knees, as they demand."

True, that part of her plan was somewhat troublesome, but Sanja was nothing if not determined. "I will make it to the top. On my knees, and in a hair shirt. I promise you." The physical ordeal of the Journey seemed paltry compared to the alternative—a lifetime of nights with this mountain of meat climbing on top of her. Her stomach churned to think of it.

"Then perhaps a wager is in order," Jarl Steen suggested. Sanja didn't like the sudden interest in his eyes. "If you make it to the top, I will readily admit defeat and offer my apologies. I will also keep *my* word"—he glared at Gerhart—"and pay your bride price, though I will have no wife for it."

At this, Gerhart set down his cup and clasped his hands together. Sanja could see in his face he wished to say something, but he kept silent.

Olga looked wary. Her large, brown eyes spoke volumes, but Sanja understood none of it.

"If you fail," the jarl continued, "I will have your hand for one third the bride price your father negotiated. And you will give me complete obedience in all things."

Sanja swallowed past the lump in her throat. *Complete obedience.* To a man not known for his restraint.

Olga whimpered. "Sanja, don't." Her hands were clenched so hard around her apron, its threads snapped.

"I don't intend to fail," she assured her mother despite her own doubts. Men far stronger than Sanja had failed the Journey under the best of conditions. Sanja would have none of their advantages, but she would happily take the risk for a chance to choose her own path in life, unfettered by the demands of a husband and children.

"Neither do I," Jarl Steen replied, his gray eyes sparkling at the prospect of a new challenge. "Do we have a deal?"

Gerhart stood, about to intervene.

"We have a deal," Sanja said before her father could speak a word. "Shall we seal it in blood?"

"No!" Gerhart cried, taking a stand in front of Sanja. "You will not spill a single drop in this house."

"It's all right," Sanja told him. "I will swear on my blood if that is what Jarl Steen demands." When Gerhart opened his mouth to argue, Sanja took hold of his hands and leaned close to whisper. "Please, trust me." Win or lose, at least the oath would guarantee her parents would be provided for. The rest, Sanja would sort out later.

"You do not know what you are doing."

Sanja met Gerhart's worried gaze with her own, determined one. "Yes, I do." She knew her father meant well by inviting Jarl Steen into their lives, but Sanja was not meant to be a wife to anyone, much less a man like that.

"I insist on a written contract," Olga announced. "Sanja is a clever girl. She can read and write, and she can most certainly sign her own name. Gerhart and I will witness. Not even the king will have cause to negate it."

"A pox on the king," Steen spat, and Sanja gasped. He dared—in the castle city, no less! Seeming to realize his mistake, he made an effort to calm himself. "Very well. But we will sign in blood." His gleeful sneer sent chills down Sanja's spine. "Let's have it done, then. Parchment and quill!"

Gerhart moved to comply, but Olga gently pushed him back down and retrieved the items herself. Seating herself at the table, she dipped the quill in what little ink they still had. In neat, even script, she penned the terms of their wager. She took her time to write everything just so, with all three of them standing at her back, looking over her shoulder. At the bottom of the page, she added one more sentence:

Should Miss Sanja receive another suit and marry within the month, this contract and all its terms shall be null and void, releasing Miss Sanja from any obligation.

No sooner had her quill left the parchment than the jarl tore it out of her hand. "What is this?"

"My own terms to this foolish endeavor. You men have had your say. Now I will have mine. Sanja is my daughter, too."

"Meaning no offense, My Lord," Gerhart rushed to reassure his noble guest. "A mother's worry, you understand. Women and their silly notions. They do not understand the world as we do."

"Da!"

Jarl Steen dropped the contract back on the table. "Let the women have their say. I will agree to her terms." He smirked at Sanja. "If the girl hasn't managed to snare a husband yet, she certainly will not find one in a month." He produced a knife from his belt sheath and cut across the tip of his finger to draw blood. Taking the quill out of Olga's hand, he dipped it into the welling crimson drop and clumsily scratched his name on the parchment.

When he thrust both knife and quill at Sanja, she pushed them both away. Instead, she went to the cupboard and pulled out a large sewing needle to perform the dreaded deed. She winced as she stabbed herself in the thumb, and then a second time when the first failed to bleed sufficiently. Her hand shook as she coated the tip of a different quill with her blood, forestalling any possibility of it mingling with Jarl Steen's in any way. Hesitating only a little while everyone stared, Sanja signed her name, sealing her fate. Her father then added his mark, followed by her mother, to witness the contract.

It was done.

One month. Four weeks to prove herself worthy of a cleric's robes.

Steen inclined his head in a mock bow. "You will be seeing plenty of me anon."

Sanja didn't take another full breath until the door closed behind him, and air returned to the cottage. "Riddance," she muttered, allowing herself a triumphant little smile.

Rather than enjoy her daughter's victory, Olga brought her fist to her mouth. "I think I will have a rest now." She retreated to the bedroom, closing the door with undue care.

As soon as she was gone, Gerhart sank back into his chair, his head in his gnarled hands. "Daughter, what have you done?"

Sanja sank to her knees next to him. "It will be all right, Da, everything will work out, you will see."

With a heavy sigh, he straightened in the chair and took both of her hands in his. Those hands had once carved intricate symbols into the queen's own throne. Twisted by age, they could now barely hold an eating knife. Whenever it rained, his fingers knotted with pain he couldn't conceal. "All I wanted was to see you wed," he said.

"To a man like *him*? I would rather die."

"Hush!"

Sanja flushed, biting her tongue against more harsh words. But she wouldn't take back what she'd said. Had Gerhart consulted her before speaking to the jarl, Sanja might have had a chance to tell him what sort of man her intended was said to be. Why would he have gone behind her back?

"Listen to me, child. Life is not like they write it in those books of yours. When all is said and done, beauty fades. Strength wanes. In the end, even your clever mind will fail you. People like us don't get dashing warriors riding to our rescue. We make do with what we have. Jarl Steen might not be a gentle man—"

Sanja scoffed.

"—but he is here," Gerhart insisted. "Oh, I know how much you love your books. But those books will be a cold comfort once your mother and I are gone."

She begged to differ. Give her a library full of knowledge still to be explored, and Sanja would happily devote her life to it.

"One day, you will want someone to share them with. Someone to keep you company, give you a family of your own."

"Not Jarl Steen."

Gerhart smiled with regret. "Daughter, there is no one else around."

2

A massive crack of thunder shook the stone walls of Castle Frastmir, rousing the royal family from a deep sleep. The crown prince of Wilderheim sat up in his bed, sweat beading on his brow, heart thrashing in his chest. Disoriented, he braced himself for the flood of visions rainstorms always brought, but his thoughts remained clear.

He threw back his covers to go look out his window. From there, he had a clear view across the courtyard, past the castle gates, all the way to the river on the other side of the city. There was no rain anywhere near Frastmir.

Yet no sooner had the echoes faded than another bolt of lightning struck the tower, exploding stone and shingles into the courtyard below. Another set the stables on fire, and one more roused a blood-curdling scream from the kitchens below. A storm of bright blue streaks turned the night brighter than day. The sky above Frastmir looked like a massive, cracked eggshell. Not a cloud in sight, no waft of a breeze to indicate a summer storm. Only the lightning flared in an endless web above, obscuring the moon and the stars. Fal's ears hurt from the sharp assault on his senses.

He squinted against the bright lights in search of some coherence in the world. The stables and kitchen were burning. He made out the shapes of people looking on from doorways around the courtyard, but no one dared step a single foot outside.

Needing to do something, Fal raced out of his chambers to the castle's front entry. He called to the creek in the gardens, altered its flow, and urged it on faster to pour where it was needed most. As far as his magic reached, he sought water, used it to put out flames and herd people into safe corners where the fury of lightning couldn't reach them.

He didn't realize his parents had joined him until Queen Nialei touched his shoulder and pointed to the sky.

A sizzling sparkle now accompanied each branch of lightning, as if it was burning the sky itself. Nialei's fingers dug into Fal's flesh, turning his attention back to her, but as hard as he tried, he couldn't make out the words she shouted. Shaking her head, the queen released him to take hold of King Saeran's arm and raised up her free hand. Her skin began to glow as she bent the laws of Nature to her will, and within moments, the great din outside dulled to a low rumble as a bubble of silence enveloped them, leaving Fal breathless.

Nialei made a fist to hold on to her spell. "The Veil," she said. "It's falling apart."

Fal reeled. The Veil not only formed borders around the human realm, the Otherlands, and the realm of gods, it was also a repository for divine power. If it broke, the gods themselves would be rendered powerless. This was what Nialei and Saeran had spent two decades trying to prevent. And now it was too late.

Never one to run from a fight, Saeran squared his stance as though presented with an enemy he could battle and best. "What do we do?"

A sharp cackle echoed from the shadows. "You pray." Before the words faded, darkness exploded toward them. Tendrils of black smoke and shadows swirled around the royal family, then congealed before Fal and his parents, shrinking until, like a glamour peeling away, it revealed the figure of a man. He was tall and ghostly pale, with dark runes and symbols twisting beneath the surface of his skin as if they had a life of their own. His coppery red hair, adorned with warrior braids, reached down to his waist, and with each of his movements gave off a soft screech like twisting metal.

Nialei tugged at Fal's sleeve while addressing the creature. "Loki."

The Trickster god grinned, baring sharp, white teeth in a feral snarl that creased his ageless face and made his pitch-black eyes all but glow with evil intent. "Halfling." His growling voice hurt Fal's ears.

"The Veil is breaking apart," Nialei said with an edge of desperation. "Please, you must help us restore it!"

"Help you?" Loki's laughter echoed with the unearthly sound of a thousand blades scraping together. "Oh no, my dear. I am merely here to settle a debt."

Casting a quick, worried glance at Fal, Nialei retreated a step away from him, taking Saeran with her. *Do not speak,* she commanded in Fal's mind. *Do not interfere.* Focusing on Loki once more, she asked, "What debt? I owe you nothing."

"Oh, but I owe you," Loki replied, stalking her retreat.

She was distracting him, guiding him away from her son, drawing the Trickster's wrath so Fal might be spared.

Fal refused to let her. They would fight as one, or not at all. Shoring up his strength, he moved to follow his parents, to stand with them and battle a Halfling god if need be. But, raising one clawed finger, Loki froze him in place. "Not your time, princeling," he said. "Not your battle." Then he flicked that finger and sent Fal shooting across the great hall to slam against the wall behind King Saeran's throne.

His bones shattered on impact. Screaming agony stole the breath from his lungs, but urged on by his pain, Fal's magic rose within him at once, forging a mighty path across his body and mending whole each break and tear it came across. In two blinks, cool comfort blanketed over him even as lethargy stole across his mind.

The sound of his mother's scream forced him to climb back to his feet. Weakened to exhaustion, he tripped like a newborn foal and tumbled down the dais steps, sprawling face down at the bottom.

Loki's terrible voice punctuated his fall, "When we last met, I made you a promise, Halfling."

Fal struggled up to his hands and knees. He felt coarse fur brush past him as his mother's wolf charged across the great hall toward the trio backlit by an endless blaze of lightning outside. Varr was a creature unique to all the realms. Pulled back from death by powerful

magics, he was neither alive nor dead. He had no magic, yet seemed
to be immune to it. Binds could not restrain him, and wards could
not keep him in or out. He wasn't fooled by Fal's illusions and could
somehow pass through the Veil to any Otherland he chose. And he
was ever faithful and protective of his mistress.

Fal watched the creature of in-between race to aid the royal pair,
and he knew Varr wouldn't make it in time. Terrible portent squeezing
like a fist around his heart, he watched shadows and darkness once
again swirl up Loki's body. "Time to meet your sire." Shadowy tendrils
shot forward as he launched at Nialei. Her scream was cut short as
the Trickster's darkness swallowed up all three of them.

Varr leaped at it but passed through and landed just outside the door.

With a shout, Fal pushed to his feet and charged forward—to nowhere. The Trickster and whatever magic he'd wrought had already
disappeared, along with Fal's parents.

Nialei's spell broke, and the deafening boom of thunder once again
assailed him, shaking the floor beneath his feet and the stone walls
around him. Varr took no notice as he sniffed the place where Nialei
had disappeared. Fal prayed to the gods that the wolf would find a
scent to track, as he had so many times before.

When Varr raised his head to look outside, ears pricking forward
and back, Fal thought his prayer had been answered, but the wolf
went no farther than the threshold where, tail tucked between his
legs, he gazed up at the blinding lights in the sky.

Terrified of what he might see, Fal caught hold of the heavy portal
for balance and looked for himself.

Against the lightning storm's constant, crackling blaze, behind a
multi-hued gossamer veil of sparkling lights, the shadow of a massive
lupine form raised its head, and individual beats of thunder joined
together into a single, prolonged howl of noise.

Fal shuddered, watching as the lightning ceased all at once, leaving
only a faint, colorful haze against the dark backdrop of the sky. When
the booming howl faded, the night plunged into stifling silence, sealing
their fate for all time.

The Veil was gone. The great wolf Fenrir was free.

Ragnarok had begun.

3

Two days later, the rising dawn found Fal standing in front of the stairway to his damaged tower library. Dust and rubble were spilled all the way down into the hallway. A pungent scent lingered in the air—smoke, hot metal, and burned magic, all underlaid with what he imagined to be the scent of despair. It was so heavy it oozed down the stairway and across the hallway floor, soaking into his cloak.

A small, charred piece of parchment with the remnants of an ancient spell still glowing softly on its surface wafted through the air. Fal held out his hand to catch it, only to have it disintegrate in the palm of his hand.

Despair. Yes, that seemed an apt description for the current state of affairs in Frastmir and, from what the messengers reported, all of Wilderheim. Dread had settled over the kingdom so thick nothing seemed to lift it, and it was only made heavier by the strange lights ever streaking across the sky.

Fal unstuck his feet from the hallway floor and, with infinite caution, stepped into the stairway. Around the first bend, light spilled in through a hole in the wall. A little higher, the wall was gone entirely, the steps crumbling away at the outer edges. The higher he climbed, the more debris littered what remained of them until he was forced to cast magic just to keep his footing steady.

With each half-burned, buried tome he passed, the ache of loss clenched a little tighter around his chest. Years of research and translations, stacks of scrolls, texts, and ancient skins with knowledge all but lost to time. And somewhere within them, perhaps even his undiscovered cure. Had any of his work survived the fire?

Did it matter anymore? With his parents gone, his research destroyed, and Fenrir racing toward Wilderheim, Fal's malady seemed like a minor inconvenience by comparison.

Fal's parents were both Halflings born of the union of two different species. Such beings were always powerful, dangerous, and most importantly, unable to produce offspring. Nature's way of preserving balance, he supposed.

Yet somehow, Nature's rules broke when Nialei not only conceived but managed to survive the pregnancy and give birth to twins. As far as Fal knew, he and Liadan were the first and only ones of their kind, blessed and cursed with powerful magics they themselves couldn't always control. And it seemed Fate was determined to make them pay for it.

Liadan's gifts were rooted in fire and metals, making her an unrivaled warrior. A true Dragonblood, she could burn her human shape into something not quite human, but not dragon, either. But her magic was so volatile her moon cycle burned her from within each month, and she slept for three days thereafter as one dead while her body recovered. Nature taking desperate measures to ensure she never bore a child. If Liadan suspected this to be the case, she never spoke of it, and Fal never dared to broach the subject.

His own gifts were rooted in water and all manner of visions. He could scry farther than anyone he knew, travel through water, control its flow, and cast visions for others to see. But, like Liadan, his magic was volatile, growing stronger with each passing year. What had started out as little more than a trick of the light when he'd been a child had evolved into visions so convincing and far-reaching he could no longer contain them as a grown man. Swathed in a cloak embroidered with dampening spells and armed with golden cuffs etched with channeling runes, Fal still couldn't pull them back completely.

Those who looked upon him saw an endless parade of faces masking his true self. He'd learned to hide beneath the hood of his cloak. Those who dared to step into his watery illusions found themselves drowning on dry land. For the safety of his people, he'd learned to keep his distance.

Everywhere he went, the world changed, right along with him. Fal had never spoken an untruth in his life. But when his own people looked upon him, all they saw was a lie. And so they'd dubbed him the Prince of Deceit.

Sequestered in Castle Frastmir, he'd spent years searching for answers in obscure texts and magics lost to time. He'd found nothing. And his illusions continued to grow stronger and bigger. One day, they would overwhelm him, and he would disappear.

If Fenrir didn't put an end to all of them first.

At the top of the stairway, two-thirds of the chamber were gone, leaving a yawning hole and an unobstructed view of the castle gardens below, the fields beyond the wall, and the shadowy line of a forest in the distance. Only one bookcase remained along the inner wall. The rest was either burned to ash or buried beneath a mountain of rubble below.

He collected a handful of journals, stacked the remaining books onto one pile, and sent the lot of it to his chambers for safekeeping. If nothing else, at least the condensed summary of his studies had survived. Fal would take what he could get.

With the first task complete, he turned his attention to another. He righted a copper scrying bowl and filled it with water, speaking softly into its depths to bring up a vision of his parents. He'd scryed for them five times already since they'd disappeared, but each time he'd cast his will into the water, only darkness had answered his call.

Fal refused to believe the Trickster killed them. Loki was many things, but never thoughtless. He thrived on chaos, often giving gifts disguised as curses and curses seeded within powerful gifts. As all the gods did, Loki toyed with the lives of mortals and Others alike, but, unlike the others, he took perverse pleasure in sowing seeds of discord and fed on the resulting carnage. Killing was easy and, in the end, useless to Loki. He would not have ended lives he could torment.

Wherever he'd taken Nialei and Saeran, they would live long enough to entertain the Trickster to his dark heart's delight first.

Loki had said something about Nialei's sire. Perhaps he'd transported them to his realm. But where was that? None of them, not even Nialei herself, knew what manner of creature her sire was, or which Otherland he'd hailed from. Without any guidance at all, Fal was left literally fumbling in the dark, looking for them. He was beginning to lose hope of ever finding them.

But he had one more thing yet to try. It was dangerous. He'd have to risk losing himself by forcing enough magic into the water to punch through its connection to the Eternal. Fal had been holding back from it, sensing any contact with the source of all water worsened his condition. But he couldn't wait any longer. Wilderheim needed the crown now more than ever, and Fal was a poor substitute for his honored parents. Praying it was the right thing to do, he pushed harder, driving his will through the bowl's bottom into the realm of Eternal water, and straight to its source.

He almost panicked as a chaos of infinite windows opened to him, not just in this world, but every Otherland, as well. The copper bowl grew hot in his grasp, its rim taking on a dangerous glow as the water in it boiled with magic. Fal kept it up, focused his intention on finding Nialei and Saeran. He pushed until his palms began to sear, and he'd almost lost hope, and then the surface suddenly settled on a burst of light and a vision.

He was looking out of a puddle straight up at a beautiful clear blue sky and his parents plummeting to the ground. It happened so quickly he didn't have time to gasp before they landed with an impact that rippled across the puddle, blurring the vision.

They can't die, he told himself. Any moment, the surface would settle, and he'd see his parents on their feet, alive and well, taking measure of the place so they could find a way back.

Fal waited and waited, but the surface didn't settle. Instead, as it continued to ripple, he saw blurred shapes flashing by in droves.

A giant hoof came down on the puddle, making him flinch. The vision shattered into dozens as droplets sprayed out around the puddle, showing him flashes of half-human, half-beast creatures with cloven hooves and antlers growing out of their heads. These were no savages, but well-trained warriors, armored and armed with swords and bows.

Fal didn't recognize the creatures, but they bore the mark of Cernunnos, the god of wild things. He was a secretive but benevolent deity, said to have the power to bring natural enemies together in peace. Little was known about him, but ancient songs hinted at his ability to create different kinds of demigods, all of them bearing his mark—golden eyes, deer-like antlers, or a circle around the neck like a symbolic torc. Could this be one of his realms?

A droplet or two briefly held on to hooves that took him almost to the place where his parents had landed. Fal dared not move. His clenched jaw ached, his eyes burned from lack of blinking. The vision shifted, bringing him high up, where a warrior near the front of the herd had poured water over her face. He could see everything she saw.

Saeran wasn't moving. Nialei herself looked little better, struggling to raise herself up on one elbow while keeping the herd in check with a glow of magic in her free hand.

Nialei reached for Saeran, and her magic redirected to him.

"Please," Fal whispered, terrified he might be watching his father die. But Nialei wouldn't let him. "Please, don't let him…"

The warrior who held Fal's vision looked down, stomped her hooves in agitation. Fal couldn't sense what she did, but he could guess. Nialei's connection with the earth was powerful. She would call on its strength to restore herself and save Saeran, as she'd done many times before in Wilderheim.

"Wait!" he cried, knowing she wouldn't hear. The Otherlands were different than Wilderheim. Magic in them was raw, wild, and far more powerful. She wouldn't be able to control it the way she did at home; it would burn them both to ash if she couldn't hold on, which Nialei knew very well. She had to be desperate to do it.

As the wild torrent surged up, shuddering through the ground, the water in Fal's bowl rippled in response. Fal forced it to settle just in time to see Saeran's body bow off the ground beneath a force he was helpless to resist. He saw sparks jumping off the surface of Saeran's skin, and then a bright blue glow as he burst into flame. His scream chilled Fal to his soul.

And then Nialei screamed, too. The Other's face began to dry, but she moved closer for a better look, and through her, Fal saw his parents change. Black smoke billowed out from beneath Saeran, solidifying into wings. His face contorted, hardened, and then reformed with a pair of smooth, black horns growing out of his temples and sharp fangs filling his mouth. Though Saeran's eyes were closed, Fal could see them glowing blue with the same flame that burned golden in Liadan. *Dragonblood.* As direct descendants of their dragon ancestor, both Saeran and his daughter had inherited his fiery magic and the ability to transform their shape into something far more than human. Liadan had had to die to awaken that ability. Saeran, to Fal's knowledge, had never been able to do it. Until now.

And while Saeran transformed, Nialei did, too. But she was a creature of water, like Fal. Instead of burning, her skin rippled, taking on a pearlescent sheen as small antlers erupted from her forehead and temples into something like a beastly crown—the mark of Cernunnos, or at least one of his creations. Loki had, indeed, kept his word and taken Nialei to her sire's realm. She would finally know who and what she was. And she was beautiful, inside and out.

Welcome home, Nialei Waterborn, whispered the Otherland's waters. They welled up around her, cushioning her fall as she collapsed next to her mate, giving Fal a brief window straight to his parents. It was a courtesy for which he was grateful because it gifted him not only with the sight of his parents' new, transformed faces, but also the feel of their hearts beating strong within their chests, and their magics glowing within them, out of them, leaving no doubt that they were alive and well.

Fal took a chance, altered the spell, and dipped his hand into the water. The bowl was too small to accommodate travel, but at least he could reach through and touch his parents, somehow let them know he was looking for a way to—

His hand struck the bottom of the bowl, dispersing the vision.

Frowning, he pulled it back and thought of his parents again, needing to reopen the window to wherever they were. It wavered briefly over the bowl's surface as the puddle he looked through dried out. One more time, he focused his intent, pouring everything he had into the thought of pushing through to them.

Once again, his hand pressed against the bottom of the bowl, and when that window closed, he could tell it wouldn't reopen a third time.

"No, that can't be." He'd never been denied this way, not by water. "Seol, I need you," he said into the surface, sending the message through its depths into the realm of water sprites. If a being existed who could help him now, it was his mentor. "Seol!"

The water rippled, but though he sensed his message had made it through, no response came from the other side.

"Seol, please answer me. Where are you?" He cast for a vision, but the water remained still. "Are you even still alive?"

Alive, Seol's voice whispered back so softly Fal had to put his ear almost to the water to hear him. *For now.*

"Where are you? I can't see you. The Veil is gone and—"

The water sprites are aware.

"—I need to reach my parents... Wait. You know?"

Yes. We all felt the Veil give way.

"Are you doing anything about it?" How could they not? Of all the Others, water sprites had the most vested interest in helping Nialei restore the Veil. They were her mother's people, after all. Seol himself had been the first to offer his support when the Veil became damaged, and he'd stood by the family ever since.

We are saying farewell.

Cold dread settled into the marrow of his bones, so deep he thought he'd never be warm again. "You've given up?"

We have accepted the inevitable, Seol replied. *We feel the frost coming. It will take us soon.*

"Get out, then! Run while you can!"

We cannot, came the succinct response.

"What do you mean you can't?" Water sprites were incredibly powerful creatures with voices that were said to have the ability to kill as easily as restore life. Their watery realm connected to every lake and river in the human world and in every Otherland. Seol should have been able to snatch Nialei and Saeran right back from her sire's realm; his people should have been able to scatter to the streams to escape Fenrir.

No one can; the waterways between worlds are already frozen. We are trapped.

No waterways? "Tell me how to help you."

He felt the water ripple with Seol's sorrow. *Help your own kin. Find King Saeran and Queen Nialei. Find the dragon.*

"I saw my parents, but I cannot reach them. Please, Seol, what do I do?"

Farewell, son of water.

"Wait—" He felt a wrenching rift sever his connection with Seol. The water froze into a moment of shocked stillness, then resumed its natural form, softly rippling in the bowl. Seol was gone.

Wearied from the effort of his casting, Fal sat with his back to the bookcase and stared into the distance. He sat there until his magic restored itself, throwing illusions of deepwater across what remained of the floor, spilling in an endless, silent fall over the edge. He sat until the sun dipped behind the horizon, and only the colorful lights in the sky remained to illuminate the lands. Numb with cold and loss, Fal didn't notice anyone approaching until a too-warm hand settled on his shoulder, sending heat like a blanket of golden flames across his body from the neck down.

He turned his head to meet his sister's glowing gaze. "Liadan."

She must have sought him out immediately on arrival. Still in her Other form, Liadan was terrifying and beautiful at the same time. A full head and shoulders taller than him, her body was covered in impenetrable black scales. Her massive wings could hold her aloft for days if need be, and her claws were sharp enough to tear through metal armor. Her hair transformed into living flames in this shape, and her eyes burned with the fire of her Dragonblood soul, but she could extinguish both and become invisible in the night sky to rain down fire on unwary enemies.

Gods, it was good to see her.

Liadan smiled at him in greeting, already burning away her wings, tail, and horns to reclaim her much less intimidating human shape. "I should have known I'd find you here." As she shrank down to her human size, her features became a much more feminine version of his own. She had grown more beautiful since the last time Fal had seen her. Like a flower blooming in the sun, she'd taken to the desert lands of Aegiros far better than anyone could have predicted, and he could feel her happiness and vitality shining out of her. Dressed in a simple blouse, breeches, and bodice, with her red-black hair in dozens of braids held back by a golden crownlet, and her skin burnished golden brown, no one would ever suspect her northern roots. Unless, of course, one was familiar enough with Aegiran customs to know that every single thing Liadan wore went against them. "Your library is gone, have you noticed?"

Fal threw his arms about her and squeezed as hard as he could. He was bigger, but Liadan was still stronger, and when she squeezed back, she made his ribs groan. He didn't care a whit. "So are Mother and Father."

Liadan released him and pulled back, her eyes dimmed to their usual gray. Rather than drag him into the castle, she sat with him shoulder to shoulder. "Tell me what happened."

And so he did. He told her everything in as much detail as he could recall. Liadan remained silent while he talked, watching the light of her flames flicker across his water illusion. Like its caster, the illusion stubbornly refused to acknowledge the chaos in the sky, reflecting only Liadan's fire and a clear sky of brilliant stars.

But it couldn't change the truth.

When he finished his tale, Liadan looked up, flinching the same way Fal always did to behold the chaos above them. "What do you suppose it is?"

Fal followed her gaze, and a bitter smile twitched across his lips. "You are looking at a map of our closest Otherland neighbors. Without the Veil, what once was hidden now reveals itself to human eyes. "

"It makes me ill."

"Me too." The constant swirl and sway of those lights made the ground feel like it was about to fall out from under him. Some lights streaked across the sky, racing back and forth with restless vigor, others spun and churned in vortices, and still others swayed in place, pulsing with some unnamable energy. It was breathtaking for a moment or two. But the longer Fal stared, the more it unnerved him until he could bear it no more.

Liadan pointed to a bright green cloud to the right of the moon. "That one looks like it is fading."

And so it was. They watched all color leech out of the cloud, and then it dimmed by slow degrees until nothing was left but a dark gap where something ought to be.

"Does that mean..."

"It's gone." Fal rubbed his chest. He'd seen it happen several times over the last two days. Some lights went out quick as a wink, while others disappeared little by little. Each time one of those lights went out, someone thanked the gods that the sky was clearing. Fal didn't know how to tell them an entire world had just died, along with everything and everyone in it.

"And it will be our turn soon," Liadan guessed.

"Is it like this in Aegiros?" He'd already spoken to their cousin Ulrich, but the king of Lyria hadn't heard a whisper of what had transpired in Wilderheim, nor could anyone in the kingdom see anything like Wilderheim's sky. It hadn't breached their western border, then.

Likely not the eastern border, either. If it had, King Gavriil of Ravetia would already have done something about it. He was a superstitious sort who abhorred magic in all its forms, and he wouldn't tolerate such a blatant breach of their peace treaty.

And that left their southern border with the desert lands of Aegiros. Aegiros wasn't a kingdom, but a nation of independent tribes. Its resources were scarce, forcing the tribes to fight one another for control of them. Although Liadan was now the queen—or *shensari*—of its oldest tribe, there were still many others over whom she held no sway. Fal didn't consider them a threat as a whole, but smaller raiding parties weren't unlikely if something spooked them.

Liadan slowly shook her head. "As far as I could see in my flames, only Wilderheim has a sky like this. At our borders, the lights fade away."

That confirmed everything Fal had read thus far. Wilderheim didn't merely lie on the border between the human realm and Otherlands—it *was* the border. At least as far as Woden's reach stretched. By Liadan's account, Aegiros had its own gods and realms, as sovereign as the kingdom itself, and as isolated. Crossovers were not tolerated.

"The moon will be full in three days' time," Liadan said. "I can stay until then."

"And do what?"

"Whatever needs to be done. I'm hardly going to leave you here to face this on your own."

"You are needed in Aegiros." Full moon meant time for their warriors to train. After decades of suffering at the hands of demons, Liadan's tribe was finally restored to their ancestral home in the First City. But, though they worked hard to rebuild their way of life, their numbers were low, making them vulnerable to attack from rival tribes. While their warriors went off into the desert to train, it was Liadan's duty to patrol the city and ward off any potential threats. "Mother and Father will be back soon and—"

"You don't know that. There is no telling how time passes where they are. They could be gone for centuries, for all we know."

"They will be back before Fenrir comes for Wilderheim." Of that, he was certain.

Liadan nodded in agreement. "And in the meantime, our people will have their two heirs to look after them. Two heads are always better than one."

Fal looked off to the side where water trickled down the wall. While his illusions had free reign in so much open space, the sheen reflected his true self, but as soon as he returned down the broken staircase and pulled them back, his face would disappear beneath multitudes of others. Nothing had changed. The Prince of Deceit still couldn't show his true face to the world, unless he wanted it to drown. "Yes," he agreed with Liadan. "Especially when one of them cannot be seen."

In the brief moment of silence that followed, Liadan must have realized the implications of what she'd said. "You know that is not what I meant."

"But it is what they will understand. Your presence here will speak to my inability to rule. You may as well usurp me now and get it over with."

"I refuse to waste time on a pointless argument. We are not talking about the rule of Wilderheim. We are talking about the end of everything we have ever known. There will be panic, and possibly war, both of which you have only ever read about. You will need all the help you can get to keep the peace, and someone still needs to continue Mother's work."

"I can do all that!"

"No, you cannot," she snapped, her eyes briefly flickering to gold as her skin brightened with the glow of angry fire. Taking a deep breath, she banked both and continued more evenly. "No one could. It is too much, Fal. Even with a council of advisors and an army at your back, you cannot be in all places at once. Wilderheim needs you to focus on what you do best." She took his hand in both of hers and held on despite Fal's attempts to free himself. "I need you strong and focused on restoring the Veil."

Fal grunted unhappily.

"The fate of everything rests on you now, do you realize that? I wouldn't even know where to begin, but you have spent your life learning about it. You know what needs to be done."

"But not how." Therein lay the bitter defeat of all their efforts. Having the ingredients to restore the Veil meant nothing if they couldn't figure out how to use them.

"Then keep studying and figure it out. Give Wilderheim a way to survive what is to come, and let me deal with the little things."

"By which you mean panic, rebellion, war, and widespread destruction?"

Liadan waved a careless hand. "Child's play."

Fal chuckled, despite himself. "What about Imarah?"

"I am sure my king can handle it in my absence," she said with an impish twinkle in her eye.

Since it was his tribe, her king most assuredly would do just that. Even so… "Go back to him, Liadan." Seeing she was about to argue, he swiftly cut in. "I promise to keep my fire burning so you can come back at a moment's notice if things go awry." As Fal could travel through water, Liadan had mastered the art of traveling through fire, as long as it burned large enough for her to fit through. Their parents always kept a strong blaze burning in the great hall for her, and their dragon great-grandfather kept one in Liadan's old chamber in his cave. She rarely used either, preferring to flex her wings and fly. "But I need to do this on my own. I need to try."

Liadan made a face. "Very well. But I will be keeping my eye on you. And I am still staying until the full moon."

Fal let her pull him to his feet. She kept hold of his hand as she turned for the staircase, but Fal pulled her up short. "Speaking of keeping an eye on me, have you had any word from the dragon?"

"I tried calling to him a time or two," she said. "No response. But you know how Grandfather is. If he doesn't want to be bothered, he won't be. He is probably in one of his darker moods and wants to be left alone."

"Perhaps," Fal allowed.

Even by dragon standards, their great-grandfather was extremely solitary. He'd existed in complete isolation in a cave far to the north of Wilderheim ever since his mate died giving birth to their only child. Were it not for a group of foreign knights and a ridiculous quest for a cup that had led Nialei straight to his cave, no one would ever have known of his existence.

Since his discovery, so to speak, the dragon had become a constant, yet distant part of the family's lives. He'd fostered Liadan in his cave since birth to teach her how to control her volatile flames. But while Fal believed the dragon cared for all of them, he still chose to remain in his solitary cave rather than join them in Frastmir. Some habits, he supposed, were hard to break—especially if they'd been formed over millennia.

"But I should think he would care at least a little that Loki abducted his grandson."

Liadan shrugged.

"It doesn't bother you that he has abandoned us?"

"He has not abandoned us, Fal. He is a dragon. He has dragon things to do. For all you know, he is working out the spell to restore the Veil as we speak."

Fal shook his head and helped Liadan down a broken step. "I don't like it. He has always been there when we needed him."

"He hasn't always helped," Liadan reminded, shaking off his helping hand on another step to hop down on her own. "Remember when he let me go off on a quest to Aegiros and then hid me from you so you couldn't interfere? I died there if I recall correctly."

"Is that what we are saying happened?"

Liadan gave him her most innocent look. "What else would we be saying?"

"That you chose to run off to Aegiros with a known assassin, against all common sense—and despite all of my objections, I might add—to go battle a horde of soul-stealing demons by yourself because you thought it would be an adventure. And yes, you did die there. But if I recall correctly, you rose from your own ashes stronger than ever before. Which turned out to be a good thing, since you then decided to stay among a people who fear you enough to want to kill you, and marry the assassin who started you on this little adventure in the first place."

At the bottom of the stairs, his sister opened her mouth to say something, then closed it and crossed her arms over her chest. "Well, it doesn't sound nearly as heroic when you say it like that."

4

The Order of Clerics was the only one of its kind, unique to the whole of the human realm. It was an order that worshipped knowledge above all else, including the gods. They had but two tasks to which they devoted their entire lives—preserve and share knowledge.

Their temple was built high up on Hallowed Mountain to create distance from the petty problems and politics of everyday life. There, master scribes carefully copied ancient texts, and master bookmakers painstakingly cut, sewed, and bound the volumes to be disseminated by traveler clerics wherever their paths might take them.

It was said the temple burned beeswax candles for light and always smelled like honey. Each cleric had a small bedchamber with only a bed, a writing table, and a bookcase.

Sanja smiled at the mere thought of it.

In theory, anyone could join the Order of Clerics if they proved their devotion to knowledge and reason by completing the Journey of body and mind.

In truth, very few earned the distinction of donning one of their hooded white robes.

The Journey began with a torturous trek from Frastmir's grand library to the top of Hallowed Mountain. The fifteen-mile path led through the city, across the river, past the fields, into the forest, and up a steep stairway carved directly into the rock face. And Journeymen had to traverse the entire length of it on their knees.

Companions carrying food, water, and other essentials were allowed, but only as far as the stone stairway, and they could not interfere with the Journeyman's progress in any way. Breaks, sleep, and healing salves were allowed as well, as long as the Journeyman picked up in the exact spot where they'd stopped. Some took days to complete the trek; others took months, and some never finished at all. And that was only the beginning.

Once the Journeyman made it to the top, on the brink of death with exhaustion, hunger, and thirst, he or she was led directly into the inquisition chamber where the clerics launched into a merciless interrogation of the mind. They said no two Journeymen were asked the same questions. Each inquisition was unique to the Journeyman, removing any possibility of preparation or cheating. If even one question was answered incorrectly or dishonestly, the Journeyman would be turned away for good.

Standing at the top of the library steps, Sanja could see the thin line of a stairway snaking up Hallowed Mountain. Where it ended, sunlight glittered off the glass steeple where clerics lived and worked. It all seemed so impossibly far.

No, do not think like that. She had three weeks, plenty of time to prepare and complete her Journey. No other choice. If she failed to reach the temple, she might as well throw herself off the mountain because she would *never* let Jarl Steen lay a finger on her.

True to his word, he'd been coming by the cottage every day, forcing her to sit with him even when he had nothing to say. He had nothing to say about anything! Even the lightning storm hadn't elicited more than a grunt from him, and though he kept glancing out the window at the lights dancing across their sky, he waved away any attempt on her part to discuss them. All he wanted to talk about was himself and his fighting skills.

Sanja had no patience for it. She would happily discuss any number of subjects of a cerebral nature and had made many attempts to do just that, but each time she had, Jarl Steen's face had turned an angry red, and he'd emitted a displeased growl that sounded to Sanja as if he was choking.

To make matters worse, Sanja suspected he had her watched. Four times now she'd gone to the market and noticed the same man lurking around whatever stall she happened to be perusing. Once, she'd gone so far as to smile at him and said hello, but he'd ducked his head and hurried away without saying a word. But why would Jarl Steen want to have her watched? Why would anyone care how many fish she bought, or which of the colorful ribbons she admired, dreaming of one day being able to afford it? It couldn't be for fear of her finding another suitor. As Jarl Steen and her own father had been so quick to point out, if she hadn't found one by now, he wouldn't magically appear in her time of need.

"A fine day to begin a Journey, no?" Sanja looked up at the bookish young man standing next to her in a plain hair shirt and trousers. He was looking up, smiling. "Aye, the gods show us favor. It is a fine day, indeed."

Sanja followed his gaze up toward the shimmering greens and reds swirling together like ghostly snakes across the bright blue sky. They've been fading away one by one over the last week, but day and night, the hundreds of remaining lights continued to distress humans and Others alike. The city was poised on the tense edge of some kind of disaster. Everyone felt it, but no one spoke of it aloud. People looked at the Others among them with suspicion, and in return, the Others have begun to retreat from human society. Formerly amicable interactions have turned into cold, silent stares. Merchants turned Others away, and Others turned their backs on those who sought them out for help.

And then there were those, like this young man, whose unbridled optimism blinded them to all but the beautiful lights.

"Why would that be a sign of the gods' favor?" Sanja replied to what she suspected had been a rhetorical question. "Could it not as easily be a sign of their displeasure?"

The Journeyman looked at her with a quizzical expression. "Have you never heard of Valkyries, girl? Lights like those always accompany them across battlefields, and their favor is the gods' favor."

She frowned, shifting a step away to make room for the young man's companion carrying heavy sacks of supplies. "Yes, I have heard of them. But Valkyries don't ride willy-nilly. They are drawn to battlefields and the fallen warriors lying upon them. We have not had a war in Wilderheim in generations."

The young man's smile turned somewhat sour.

"Furthermore," she continued, "lights in the sky have preceded the great battle of Crossroads, and the Age of Maladies. Both of which were considered terrible tragedies at the time."

Had he paled a little?

"There was also a falling star the night before King Halder's mother died, two months after giving birth to his stillborn sister, and a solar eclipse on the day of King Bjarke's coronation—and as you will recall, King Bjarke was killed by a bear that same year, which was an ironic end for him, given his name. So, if anything, reason would say lights in the sky are, more often than not, a bad omen, rather than a good one."

"Gunne, let's go," the young man said, glaring at Sanja. "It is time for us to set out."

"Oh, but I didn't mean it had to be a bad omen for you," she called after them. "I am sure you will don your white robe in no time!" Having clattered his way down before his master, Gunne adjusted the sacks across his back as the young Journeyman got on his knees and hurried down the stairs as fast as he could manage. Sanja winced, watching them disappear among the market crowds. He'd wear his knees bloody before he reached the fields, the poor thing. "May your Journey be short and painless," she added belatedly.

Fiddlesticks, I shouldn't have said anything.

As she watched them hurry away, Sanja became aware of someone else standing behind her. She turned and looked far up into the kindly face of an old cleric.

"Can I help you, child?"

"Oh yes, please, Brother Erik! I am looking for books on a very specific subject." She had no intention of giving up on her quest, but it never hurt to be prepared for the worst.

Brother Erik chuckled, waving her ahead of him into the library. "Well, you have come to the right place. Our volumes encompass almost every subject known to man and quite a few known to Others.

What is it you are looking for?"

"Anything there is to learn about courtship, beauty, and love."

He opened the door for her, ushering her into the library, and Sanja breathed in the heavenly aroma permeating the air. Centuries of knowledge rested within these hallowed walls, and it almost brought tears to her eyes. "Ah, you seek to attract a suitor," the cleric said. "I believe we can find something to—"

"Oh, no, quite the contrary," she said, catching sight of a beautiful old leather tome.

"Pardon?"

"I do not want to attract a suitor," she clarified, tracing the tome's decorative grooves. "I want to repel one."

"I am not sure I understand."

Every detail of the book's cover was meticulously wrought, and each individual page was cut and stitched precisely. This book was a work of pure love of the written word. She could feel it permeating through her skin where it touched the cover.

No! Remember why you're here! Curling her hand into a fist to stop touching the beautiful tome, Sanja focused back on what she needed to do. If her charms weren't enough to attract another suitor, then she had to find a way to get rid of the one she had. "I need to learn what attracts a man so that I can do everything opposite and make myself as unattractive as possible." She had no way out of a blood oath, but there were any number of ways in which Jarl Steen could make her quest to escape him difficult, even impossible, to force her to fail. Perhaps if she made herself undesirable enough, she could make him only too happy to let her succeed just to be rid of her. It might cost her the chance of attracting another suitor, but Sanja was desperate enough to try anything.

"Err…"

"Well, perhaps unattractive is the wrong word. Repugnant! Yes, that is much better. How do I make myself utterly repugnant to a relentless—Brother Erik, where are you going?"

~

"Any word of the dragon?" Fal barely recognized his own voice. He was exhausted after only a week. Though he'd sooner die than admit it to his sister, Liadan had been right. Fal had not slept a night through since he'd taken over the rule of Wilderheim. He'd know it would be difficult, but he could never have anticipated the hundreds of little details that would require his attention.

"No, Your Highness," the runner answered. He was the sixteenth messenger in the last week who'd returned with nothing of use. Fal had sent them north, east, and west in search of any sign of his absent grandfather, desperate for his counsel. He needed the dragon's ancient wisdom now more than ever.

The careful balance of justice and magic which King Saeran and Queen Nialei had fostered and preserved for decades was disintegrating before Fal's eyes, and nothing he did seemed to help. Soldiers now patrolled the streets of Frastmir to keep the peace, and instead of being reassured, humans and Others reacted with scorn and resentment, accusing the crown of monitoring its citizens like criminals. If Fal ruled a dispute in favor of an Other, he was said to be taking *their side*. If he ruled in favor of the human, Others accused him of shirking his duty to the balance.

The smallest ripples of unrest in the streets caused tidal waves among the nobles. Their positions of power and influence had already been undermined with the arrival of Others as welcome members of society during King Saeran's reign. While the balance had held everything in check, they'd remained silent, fearful of reprisal. But the shattered sky made politics and money all but irrelevant. People didn't look to their lords' coin for protection, they sought Other magic.

Every day, Fal's noble court issued demands for the Others to be banished once and for all. And every day Fal refused, their malcontent grew deeper and louder. Most had already declared they would not pay taxes again until their demands were met. Some had threatened to revolt. Though he couldn't prove it, and therefore couldn't mete out punishment for such a heinous offense, Fal was certain some of the nobles had posted bounties on the Others dwelling on their lands.

Fal was at a loss for an agreeable solution. With the noble houses watching his every move, he feared a single misstep would send the kingdom spiraling into civil war. If it did, he would be on his own, with no support from the Others, who had already decided fleeing to kinder realms was preferable to weathering the coming storm in Wilderheim.

The Sidhe had disappeared on the night of the lightning storm, leaving a short, cold note of warning for Fal to finish what his mother had started or else. With them gone, the dwarves were becoming worse than usual, lashing out in fits of temper, breaking things, and insulting innocent passersby.

A triad of succubi had been attacked five times in as many days, forcing them to defend themselves the only way they could—by draining their attackers of all passion and feeling, leaving them to waste away without the ability to sleep and dream.

The higher order of Others at least had the ability to communicate freely and hold their own against the frightened humans who'd decided Other magic was at fault for Wilderheim's current predicament.

The more exotic Others weren't so fortunate. Fearing for their lives, tree nymphs have retreated to their trees, which wouldn't protect them from saws and axes. Someone had started a rumor that grinding a unicorn's horn to powder and sprinkling it over the threshold would protect a home from magic. One had already been butchered, forcing the rest of the herd to flee.

As Other creatures slowly retreated from Wilderheim, the humans took their voluntary disappearance as proof that magic and Otherkind were at fault for their troubles, adding fuel to the noble court's ire.

To make matters worse, word of unrest and cursed skies was spreading far and wide. Trade with Aegiros, Synealee, and Ravetia had stopped completely. Lyria held fast to familial ties, but its king could no more order his people to trade with Wilderheim than Fal could restore the sky to its former state.

Staring at the stack of reports on the chair beside him, Fal was beyond the point of absorbing anything he saw or heard any longer. It was simply too much. Too many troubles and complications. Too many rules and laws to observe. Too many mistakes he'd already made and would continue to make, because none of his advisors knew any better, either. Simply put, Fal was ill-equipped to rule a kingdom in turmoil.

While his parents had spent all their energies over the last twen-
ty-two years on getting the Others' cooperation to rebuild the Veil,
Fal had focused his studies on dealing with the results. All of their
clerics, Other advisors, and councilors, had been working all this time
to aid in those two endeavors. They couldn't afford to contemplate
the alternative.

Now, they had no choice.

"What are your orders, Your Highness?"

A map of Wilderheim and its neighbors had been laid out in the
center of the table. Colorful wooden tokens were lined up on either
side of it like the troops they were meant to represent. This meeting
had been called to discuss the kingdom's military defense strategy. Councilor Tarben, a former general, anticipated an invasion if
or when certain monarchs realized Wilderheim's protections were
compromised.

Fal couldn't concentrate on any of it. He sat in the seat King Saeran usually occupied during these meetings, his embroidered cloak
controlling the erratic outpour of his illusions until it merely looked
soaked through, dripping water on the floor, and he saw nothing of
the map or the people speaking around him.

"We should address the people," Councilor Braith said, filling the
silence when Fal didn't answer. "Keeping silent is only making them
create their own explanations and blame one another. If there is any
hope of restoring peace among the people, they must be told the truth.
They must be given the choice to stay or leave."

"Yes," Fal replied slowly. "We should inform our people the Veil we
have sworn to repair is destroyed. But the common folk likely won't
know what that means. So we should tell them the whole truth. The
gods have lost their power over us, could well be dying as we speak,
and a great, immortal wolf is coming to devour our world. Mind
you, it might not cause an exodus large enough for our less friendly
neighbors to notice, so we should also say that the king and queen on
whom Wilderheim has depended for protection are gone, replaced
by the heir, whom Frastmir's denizens have so charmingly dubbed
the Prince of Deceit. Excellent idea. You do it."

Braith twisted her mouth and glared, but remained silent.

"What other option do we have?" asked their newest member, Eira, only the second woman to ever sit on the advisory council.

"We say nothing." That from Councilor Kvaran, who, at an age so advanced he himself had lost count, needed to be transported from place to place on a long-handled seat carried by four servants. His voice was barely a wheeze, and they expected him at any moment to close his eyes and never open them again, but every word he said was worth his weight in gold. "Wilderheim and all its citizens are one. All of us are bound together by eons of magic. It is steeped in the ground we walk upon, the water we drink, the food we eat. It dies with our elders and is reborn in our children, and it will call to Fenrir no matter where our people choose to run. This is not something anyone can hide from. I am afraid with their Majesties gone, there is little the rest of us can do to prevent it. Our world as we have always known it *will end*. But that does not mean we should let panic consume us. Our people deserve to live their lives without fear for as long as they can, and it is our duty to ensure they do."

His words were met with grave looks and bowed heads. It was no easy thing for any of them to accept defeat, but Kvaran was right. Wilderheim was structured like an Otherland nestled within the human realm. Anyone who'd lived within its borders for longer than a year, who'd seen its every season pass, became bonded to the land. They might not feel the magic within them, but it was there, nonetheless. It gave their people longer, healthier lives, made their minds more open and resilient to the presence of Others. Now, it put them all in the path of the end.

The Veil could only be reformed from the blood of each Other clan. Nialei and Saeran had collected much of it over the years, despite immense opposition from Others for whom the passage of time meant nothing, but no one knew where it was. Because of the immense power even a drop of Other blood held, Queen Nialei had kept it hidden where no one could find it or use it for Dark purposes. But with her and Saeran gone, the rest of them were left powerless to continue their work. Even if all of the remaining Others magically decided to appear in the great hall this very moment to volunteer their blood, it would never be enough without the rest.

They all stood guilty of the greatest folly in the world: thinking time would be plentiful and infinite.

"We will hold our tongues and pretend their Majesties are simply on another mission in the Otherlands. They have gone on extended trips before. The people are used to it by now."

"And what of the lights?" Eira asked.

Kvaran stroked his long, white beard. "The anniversary of Wilderheim's inception is coming up. We will say the lights are in celebration of it."

Braith shook her head. "But the storm—"

Tarben waved that aside. "Prince Fal's studies have resulted in many sights like it in the past. It can be explained away."

"And if someone chooses to speak otherwise?" Braith asked, and all eyes turned on her. "Oh, not me," she defended. "My loyalty is to the crown. But we have Others in our population, and clerics who of a certainty know better, and people with enough magic to feel the end coming. What of them?"

"They must be made aware that there is nowhere they can go to avoid what is coming."

Eira's words caused Tarben to chuckle. "Knowing and feeling are two different things, my dear. Knowing the end is coming will not stop thousands of frightened people from trampling each other to death trying to flee from it." He was not wrong, and they all knew it.

"Councilor Kvaran will speak to the clerics," Fal decreed. "Make them understand that, in the name of peace, they must not share their knowledge of Ragnarok too freely. They are to call back all their members immediately and begin studying the forgotten lore. If there is anything that has been overlooked, anything at all that might help us, they are our only chance of finding it. They will understand and obey. I will speak to the Others. If they wish to leave and take their human friends and families along, no one will stop them, but there will be consequences if they try to incite a panic."

"And what of our own people?"

Fal thought about it for a moment. "Let them say what they will. The best way to squelch a rumor is to ignore it. To react in any way would only give it credence." He stood, forcing all others to their feet as well. Taking a stack of silver tokens, he placed them on the map. "But just in case word reaches Ravetia or Synealee, we will reinforce our border keeps here, here, and here, and warn Ulrich to do the same here and here.

"Councilor Tarben, you are now in charge of monitoring our neighbors. I will see to it that you have all the resources you require. Keep our troops well fed, well trained, and ready to move out, but do not sound a call to arms without my say-so. We do this quietly and slowly. Have an excuse at the ready in case someone does notice and asks questions."

"I suppose it is the best we can do," Braith said, shaking her head. "But I still don't like it."

"Our world is about to end," Tarben retorted. "What is there to like?"

5

As soon as the council meeting concluded, Fal sent a simulacrum of himself to his chambers, cloaked himself in invisibility, and snuck out of the castle. The courtyard was eerily silent as wary faces looked to each other for explanations or reassurances. They knew something odd was afoot, but no one dared speak of it aloud, and with each day that passed without an official acknowledgment of what was happening, the anxiety grew deeper and colder. It was a palpable chill carried on the northern wind, seeping into the marrow of Fal's bones.

He hastened through the gateway, breathing a sigh of relief once the oppressive castle walls were behind him and the city of Frastmir opened up before him. Out here, the chill gave way to bright sunshine and cautiously smiling faces. This close to the castle, people still kept up at least the pretense of goodwill. But Fal knew the farther out he went, the less peaceful his city would be.

The market roiled like a giant anthill with merchants in the center and customers flitting from one to the other. The library doors glittered as sunlight reflected off their golden inlays each time they were opened. A line of carts and wagons stretched over the bridge. Music carried from the inns, magic glowed around the Others in the crowd, and autumn spiced the air so sweetly, Fal stopped for a moment to simply take it all in.

This was true freedom: the ability to go anywhere without hindrance. In that moment, standing at the edge of the road, Fal envied everyone around him, as far as the eye could see, for having been born to the immense privilege of a simple life. What Fal wouldn't give to trade places with any one of them.

Bypassing the crowded market, he took a long way around to the city green. From there, he had an unobstructed view of the mountains, the fields, and the river crossing, without the risk of anyone running into him—always a concern when invisible. Fal lay down on the soft, green grass and closed his eyes, pretending there were no strange lights in the sky, only the sun. He pretended the shrill chirps he heard were of a migrating flock, instead of one confused and unable to find its way as it had done for generations past.

He pressed the palms of his hands into the dirt, feeling for the familiar connection with the earth that was now altered in some inexplicable way and told himself it was only natural to feel out of sorts in his current state.

But, of course, none of that was true and, try as he might, Fal could not make himself believe it. As the inevitability of his fate and the fate of his kingdom returned, he began to feel the chill once more, seeping up from the ground like an early frost. Far too early for this time of year, when the sun still beat down with vigor.

"...*fair maiden, look once more down that secret forest trail.*"

Fal frowned, listening to the intrusive voice drift closer. What was this? No one except children and their nurses ever came to the green, and only after noon. It was early morning still.

"*Come sit with me when the moon peaks full, and the night is at its deepest.*"

Soft footsteps neared, the earth humming at their approach and, without looking, Fal sighed and picked himself up to move out of the way. Better that than to be trampled by some featherbrained girl with her nose stuck in a book of bad love poetry.

"*For a loving glance I offer, without duty or a price, nothing less than the gift of my heart.*"

He scoffed.

To his surprise, so did the girl. "Right. An Other whose glamour can only be broken by the light of the full moon. There is a dream of a lover."

Fal turned around just as she snapped the book shut and picked up her step, nearly bowling him over. He managed to step out of her path in time, but couldn't move his foot fast enough to avoid her heel as she abruptly turned and stomped back the other way. Luckily, she wore soft shoes and didn't amount to much.

"Like as not some slimy, pustulent monster, or a man cursed for eternity to look like one," she said to herself, pacing around at random. Fal scrambled to clear her haphazard path, mesmerized by the girl darting back and forth like a temperamental squirrel. "What woman in her right mind would want that? Haven't we got enough problems of our own without trying to save someone else from theirs?"

It was surprisingly shrewd and level-headed reasoning from a girl who looked anything but. Her hair was a cloud of black curls that refused to be restrained by the thick red ribbon tying it at her nape; her pale cheeks were smudged with soot; and her sharp, green eyes stared ahead as if there was someone there to speak to. She wore a simple brown and gray dress, well made, but worn and faded, with threads hanging loose from her sleeves. The frayed hem of her skirts flared up each time she did a sharp about-face to stomp a few steps before turning again like an agitated squirrel twitching its tail.

Then, as if breaking out of some unfathomable spell, she sat on the ground and opened the book once more to read aloud, "*For such a joy and such a burden is love, that one may never look upon it directly, but will forever feel its tethers binding heart and soul to its true intended. Beyond time, beyond distance, beyond even death itself.* Bah!" She let herself fall back, the book still in her lap, and glared at the sky. "Useless, maudlin tripe. How is any of that supposed to help me?"

Fal couldn't help himself. He laughed. "What exactly did you expect a book of poetry to help you with?"

The girl screamed, sat up, and threw the book so hard it flew over his head to land in the grass a distance behind him. No sooner had it thumped down than she gasped and crawled over to it. "Look what you made me do!" She made a valiant effort to brush off the dirt, but only managed to rub it in deeper. "Where are you, you fiend? Show yourself!"

Charmed despite himself, Fal leaned down to say at her ear, "Only by moon—*oof!*" The book thwacked him across the face and, had the girl had any physical strength to speak of, she would have laid him out. "Gods damn it, girl."

"Care for another?" she challenged, her eyes wild and her cheeks flushed as she looked around for the unseen enemy.

"Do you always strike friendly, invisible strangers for no reason?"

"Friendly? You're invisible—you could be a demon or an assassin!"

"Do you have many of those following you?" He wouldn't be surprised. "What say you put the book down before you hurt yourself?"

"Not until you leave."

"All right." He'd be more than happy to oblige. "Fare thee well, madwoman."

Yet despite knowing full well it was beyond foolish to meddle with any human, especially one of his royal subjects, Fal couldn't walk more than three steps before he turned right back again, curious about the girl who met a magical anomaly with the same indignation she would have shown the basket weaver. She might have startled easily, but she didn't seem to be afraid at all. Clutching her book as a makeshift weapon, the girl looked ready to dispense more bashings to anyone who would dare come too close, be they human or Other, visible or not.

She had courage. And excellent aim, he added, rubbing his temple with a reluctant smile. Fal couldn't remember the last time he'd met someone new who hadn't run away or cowered at the sight of him. Invisibility did have its benefits. Perhaps he ought to take advantage of it.

Fal quietly circled around the girl as she scanned the green for hidden threats. She kept up her guard for so long Fal thought she might be onto him, but eventually, she settled her ruffled fur and breathed a little sigh, shaking her head as she gazed down at the book. "So much for scholarly wisdom."

Not one for conversing with strangers, apparently, but quite the chatty little squirrel when talking to herself.

"Probably would have gotten better advice from the Other." She frowned, then smacked a hand against her forehead. "Why did I not ask the Other? Stupid, stupid, stupid, Sanja! You never think before you speak."

Fal sat beside her—well out of striking distance—to observe her a little while longer. She was quite pretty, this Sanja. Not a great beauty like the Other females in Frastmir, not even like the human maidens in the city. Still, something about her made him want to keep looking. Her boundless energy hummed along his skin. She was an unrestrained spirit—freedom embodied in this slip of a girl who quite possibly had lost her mind a long time ago.

After a morosely quiet moment, she once again opened the useless book and read another verse. "*Seek not love in a flower's bloom, nor in the face of the rising sun. For love is a sigh, a glance, a touch that lingers eternally and renders time a fleeting afterthought.*" She had a lovely voice, soft, yet full of emotion. She seemed to hold nothing back as if she couldn't. "Yes, but how do I stop it!"

"Stop what?" The words were out before he could bite his tongue against them.

With a shriek, she swung again and missed. "Gods damn you, leave me alone!"

"A moment ago, you were lamenting not asking me for help," he pointed out in his most rational voice. "Therefore, I shall, just this once, overlook your alarmingly violent impulses when startled and give you one more chance to—"

THWACK!

"Will you stop hitting me!"

"Ha!"

THWACK!

"That does it." Fal snatched the book out of her hands, rendering it as invisible as he was, and moved out of her reach.

"Give it back!"

He led her in a merry chase around the green, following the sound of his laughter and nothing else. "Not on your life, savage."

"I need it! I need to learn how to get rid of a suitor."

"I'd say running circles around the city green while shouting at nothing might be a good way to do it," he retorted.

Sanja stopped in her tracks, looking around as if she expected this suitor of hers to be there, watching her.

"There's no one there. And you look relieved." And why should that disappoint him?

"Of course I am," she hissed in his general direction. "I may want to rid myself of *him*, but that does not mean I want to shame my parents even more." Her words were impassioned, but the way her gaze skittered sideways convinced Fal they were not the whole truth.

Still, he decided to pretend her answer sufficed. "*More?* You cannot be more than eighteen years old. How could you have managed to shame them already?" Was there a sordid affair in her past? Did this suitor get a babe on her before the wedding night? So many questions. Fal didn't intend to let her go until she'd answered all of them to his satisfaction.

"I am a score and one years of age, sir." The proud announcement was followed by a defeated slump. "And if you must know, I have committed the most unpardonable offense of all: being useless."

He would have laughed at the absurdity of her claim, were it not for the embarrassed flush in her cheeks and her inability to tear her gaze away from the toes of her shoes. "You are not serious."

Sanja shrugged as if there was nothing else to say on the matter, and Fal's levity drained out of him in a rush. Someone must have gone to great lengths to make her believe it. Fal knew of a thousand ways to destroy a person with spells, but it never ceased to amaze him how quickly humans could do it to each other with a mere handful of words and not a spark of magic behind them.

"You have a clever mind and a strong instinct for self-preservation," he said. "I would hardly call that useless." If anyone could attest to the true strength of the mind, it was Fal. Knowledge was, indeed, power, if one was willing to seek it out. But it required a keener mind than most to adapt theoretical texts for practical applications. Fal had spent his life doing it, and he recognized the same curiosity and tenacity in the girl.

Sanja worried the loose threads of her sleeve. "Yes, well, neither is a quality prized in a woman. We are not supposed to be clever. We are supposed to be pretty, and quiet, and know how to cook and sew, and always defer to our husband's higher intellect. Even when he hasn't got one. May I have my book back, please?" She held out her hand in his general direction, looking at her own palm as if expecting the book to appear there.

It was unfair to hold it hostage, but Fal couldn't think of another way to keep her still a while longer. Strange little Sanja, whose head barely reached his shoulder, was the first human he'd spoken to outside of the royal court since he'd been a child. Fal was loath to let the moment end. "Am I to surmise from your little speech that you do not know how to cook or sew?" he asked to incite a flare of temper to banish her gloom.

He was denied. "Surmise what you will. Just give me back my book."

Never one to admit defeat, Fal tried again. "It seems to me that if you are such a useless burden on your parents, marriage would be the simplest solution. Why chase away the one man who would have you?"

He may as well have struck her, the way she flinched, and Fal immediately regretted his harsh words.

Without giving him a chance to apologize, she turned and headed back toward the market.

"Wait, stop!" Fal followed after her as she picked up her step to escape him. "I apologize. I did not mean that the way it came out. Truly, I am not usually so crass. I just wanted to stop you feeling sad."

"Well done, you," she shot back, darting left and breaking into a run.

Fal should have let her go—he told himself so, even as he ran to catch up and overtake her. "I still have your book," he reminded her just before she slammed into him.

"Keep it," she cried, changing direction. "Perhaps it will teach *you* a thing or two."

She definitely wasn't sad anymore. *Well done, Prince of Deceit.* And still, he couldn't let her get away. In a last-ditch effort to stop her mad flight, he threw the book in the air, then guided its path to land a distance in front of her so she would see it and stop before it tripped her.

She did stop in time and stared down long enough for Fal to catch up and see what had so thoroughly caught her interest.

The book had fallen open on a page depicting two trees twined together on one side, and a short poem on the other:

Thus marked the world a true love's end:
It did not end at all.

Her ire seemingly forgotten, Sanja gazed at that poem for a long time. "Do you ever wonder if it's real?" Her abrupt change of pace startled Fal so much he thought she might have suffered some sort of injury. He was about to ask if she was all right, but then she slowly leaned over and picked up the book, tracing the words with a reverent touch.

"If what is real?"

"True love."

Taken aback, Fal didn't know how to respond.

Sanja, however, didn't seem to need a response. "It always seems so magical. Two souls meeting at the right moment in the right circumstances, and they are somehow able to forge a bond that cannot be weakened or broken. Not by treachery, evil, or even death. We write about it, sing about it, and dream about it. But can it truly exist? Or do we simply wish for it so hard we make ourselves believe it does, even if we never find it ourselves?"

Fal had asked himself those same questions often enough. The tragedy of his curse was to be surrounded by love and know he'd never find it himself without risking someone else's life along with his own. His parents, his sister and her husband—Fal envied them all bitterly.

Oblivious to the feelings she had stirred up in the invisible Other, Sanja traced the drawing with the lightest touch. The elusive emotion soaked into the page like a perfume she could sense with her heart. It made her wistful and loosened her tongue to speak things she probably ought not say aloud. "Sometimes it seems so real I see it everywhere I look. Other times it feels as if true love is meant for everyone but me. I do wonder if it is worth believing at all. It hardly seems practical on the face of it. With all the people in the world, that there should be one alone born just for me…" She looked up at the spot where she imagined her invisible companion to be standing and grinned. "Then again, I have never been a practical sort."

There was a moment of silence in which she thought he'd disappeared, but then the air shimmered, and right in front of Sanja, a figure took shape. She gaped at the sight of a white-haired, bearded man—but then he was a red-haired young woman. And in the next instant, the woman's skin darkened to almost black, and she became a young boy. "What are you?" Sanja whispered in awe as a blink later, a different man stood in front of her, this one portly with a red nose. But before she'd taken in his features, he became a beautiful woman about Sanja's mother's age, and then a young girl, and another man, and a woman once again.

"In truth, I do not know," the Other answered, and even his voice changed between one word and the next as the woman became a bald man with slanted blue eyes.

"How is it done? Are you doing it on purpose? What kind of magic is this? Where did it come from?" So many questions. She did not intend to let the Other disappear before she got answers to all of them. "Does it hurt? It is almost as if you don't have a physical shape at all—oh!" She was touching him. Definitely a *him*. Despite appearing to be fondling a young girl's generous breast, the flesh beneath her hand felt harder, flatter—the chest of a man, not a woman. "It's an illusion." It looked so real, if she wasn't touching him, she'd believe this creature to be the beer-bellied man with a long mustache he appeared to be in that moment, but her hand felt the soft fabric of a well-made, embroidered shirt, not the sweaty chest hair of a shirtless man-at-arms. "How amazing."

And Sanja somehow became part of the illusion. Her hand appeared to change distance from her body, her arm extending or pulling back so that her palm always appeared to be on the chest of whatever shape he took, even though neither of them moved.

As her fascination with that particular phenomenon eased, she glanced down and gasped. The lush green was now a brown, murky marsh, and she was standing ankle-deep in it. Though her feet were cold, the ground beneath them still felt hard and steady. When she raised one foot, steadying herself against this strange Other, it came out looking covered in mud and muck. With her free hand, she reached down to touch it. Nothing but warm, dry slippers on her feet.

"Oh, you must tell me how it's done!"

"It does not frighten you?"

"Frighten me?" Sanja laughed. "I could spend days watching it. You always take a human shape, but they never repeat, do they? How can that be? How can so many people exist?" Caught up in her excitement, she ran her hands over the parts of him she could feel. "Yet your own shape never changes." She felt a large clasp of a cloak of some kind at his neck and slipped her hands underneath the heavy fabric to his shoulders, down his arms, to the thick metal cuffs that encircled his wrists. "I have read about illusion magic before, but nothing like this." The metal was warm from his flesh, precise grooves indicating it was engraved. How she wanted to see it. Were there illusion spells etched into each cuffs? Was that how the magic worked?

"You probably never will, either."

Sanja blinked up into eyes bluer than the clearest sky. "Why is that? Is it a secret of your kind?" And if so, why had he revealed himself to her?

"Because by the time I find the answers for myself, even your great-grandchildren will probably be long dead and buried."

"Oh." Spirits deflated, Sanja stilled her hands at the edges of his metal cuffs. "I suppose there is a reason why they say humans and Others ought not mix."

What a shame that was.

Sanja let her hands fall away, lamenting yet again the limitations of her own nature. Still, curiosity was a dangerous, relentless thing. It compelled her to know this creature, somehow. Was his flesh scaled? Did he have horns? Were there eyes in the back of his head? Fully aware she might and probably was breaking some ancient Other rule, Sanja reached up one more time, tracing the hood of his cloak to the top of his head, then down over his face.

He sucked in a sharp breath when she touched his bare skin, and then, like the waves of a lake settling into a glassy surface, he changed once more, became as steady and solid in her eyes as he was beneath her palms. The hood of a dark gray cloak cast shadows over a surprisingly human face. His hair was dark brown, pleated with a braid on each side, with stray wisps falling across his blue eyes. He had a strong nose and a close-cropped beard, and lips that seemed to droop at the corners into a perpetually unhappy frown. He was taller than her, and quite handsome, and somehow familiar.

Sanja squeaked and jumped away, clutching her skirts. "You're the

Prince of Deceit!" Though no one outside the royal court had laid eyes on the crown prince of Wilderheim since he'd been a boy, his likeness was struck into every silver coin of the realm. Oh gods, she'd touched the crown prince of Wilderheim. She'd bashed him over the head with her book!

He scowled. "My name is Fal." Even as he spoke, his visage began to change once more, disguising his true face beneath an endless parade of strangers. A silvery haired young woman blinked at Sanja in surprise. "Wait, you can see me?"

Sanja dropped to her knees, bowing her head. "Forgive me, Your Highness. I did not mean to, I—"

"Bollocks that, girl, get up!" Big hands, appearing to be encased in thick leather gloves, grasped her arms to pull her up to her feet. "Can you see me?"

Sanja felt the warmth of his skin through her sleeve, yet now he looked like a half-frozen waif with deathly pale skin and blue lips. She shivered at the sight of him; couldn't find the right words to say in reply.

"Answer me!"

Sanja shook her head. "N-not anymore." Her eyes stung from staring, yet she could not make them blink.

Disappointment hooded the eyes of a weary old man whose long beard touched the ground when he hung his head. His hands slid away from her, and he stepped back.

Sanja looked down, spotted the book she'd dropped from excitement earlier. It was sunk almost completely in a puddle that glittered with white frost around the edges. She scooped it up through tendrils of cold mist that swirled around her wrist as if to pull her down. As with her slippers, the book was unharmed, but the chill had somehow seeped into its cover, and it would not warm to her touch.

"It's no use," the prince said, shaking his head. He looked like a young soldier just returned from battle, covered in mud and blood. As he sat on the ground, his features softened into a pretty woman with hands chapped and red from the cold. "It's no use."

He was distracted; Sanja ought to flee while she had the chance. Instead, her feet brought her closer, and her legs bent to make her sit. Clutching the book to her chest, she watched strangers ripple across the prince's features as he stared at the ground in front of him.

"You cannot see me, no matter how hard you stare."

Sanja snapped her gaze forward; stubbornly stopped herself from turning back toward him, despite the ache taking root in the back of her neck from the effort.

"Prince of Deceit, they call me, though I have never uttered a lie in my entire life. I *am* the lie, it seems. Everything I touch becomes a lie. Every place I go turns into an illusion."

"Are you doing it on purpose?" Sanja asked, her eyes open wide to catch a sideways glimpse of him without looking.

"No," he replied.

"Then you are not a lie. You are an Other truth that mortals cannot comprehend."

He scoffed, and his voice turned deep and gravelly as another mask settled into place over him. "How can something be true if it changes constantly?"

"Well... That is..."

"You see? Even you don't believe it yourself."

Sanja clutched her book harder to keep from bashing his shoulder with it. "Kindly don't put words in my mouth, sir. I know my own mind quite well, thank you. It's only that I sometimes cannot find the right way to articulate it quickly enough."

"Please, take all the time you need," he retorted.

The crown prince of Wilderheim was mocking her. Sanja ought to be insulted, yet the corner of her mouth twitched to smile. Sitting on the city green with him, arguing over impossible things, felt easier and more pleasant than any other conversation she'd ever had. Settling herself more comfortably, she considered the ideas flitting around her head and tried to put them into some semblance of order. It wasn't easy; each time she opened her mouth to speak, the sentence she'd thought up changed in her mind before she could utter it, and she lost the meaning she'd grasped onto a moment ago.

It didn't help that Sanja felt the prince watching her so intently her scalp prickled as if her hair would stand on end like bristled fur, were it not restrained by the ribbon that tied it back. Her cheeks heated, and her mouth became dry. *Say something!* Sanja looked up, squinting at the sun right above them. "Change is the only truth," she murmured.

"Pardon?"

Did that make sense? Yes. Yes, it did. The more she thought about it, the more Sanja realized the brilliance of it. With a bright smile, she turned to him and looked straight into the blue eyes of what might have been a plumper version of herself. "Change is the only truth. Day becomes night, blue skies grow thunder clouds, summer becomes winter, life becomes death—everything changes all the time. Nothing is eternal in its original form. The surface of a lake ripples endlessly, and no two waves are ever alike. Does that make it a lie? Rocks weather and crumble. Does that mean they are not real or true? And what of fire? Have you ever seen it burn the same way twice?"

"Enough," he said with a laugh. "Please, you have made your point. Quite brilliantly, I might add."

Sanja's chin twitched a little higher, a little prouder.

"However, it still doesn't change *this*." Passing a hand in front of his face, he changed it from a mud-splattered young boy to a cleric with his hair cropped close to his skull and a scar across one cheek. He did it again, and the cleric became a haggard old woman with missing teeth. One more time and the old woman turned into a swarthy young man.

"Enough," Sanja said, repeating his earlier capitulation, "you have made your point." She took his waving hand to stop it, and once again, his features settled into the face of Prince Fal.

She tried not to react, but he must have glimpsed something in her face, and his gaze dropped to their joined hands. When she would have pulled away, he held her fast. "Tell me what I look like now." All previous good humor gone, he didn't look at her when he issued the order.

"You are the... You are Prince Fal of Frastmir."

He looked her in the eye once more, his gaze brimming with so many things, Sanja had no names for them. She dug her heel into the ground to keep a shiver at bay as he finally let her slip free.

As the last contact between them broke, his face changed into an older woman with one eye grown shut. "And now?"

Sanja shook her head, her gaze skittering away. She still felt his touch lingering in her palm and frowned down at her hand to see if he'd changed it in some fundamental way. It appeared to be the same, but, like his illusions, there was something more underneath. Sanja felt as if she held the warmth of sunlight in her palm. Tendrils of it snaked up her arm with the comfort of a stout fire on a cold winter's day and settled across her shoulders like a warm blanket.

Prince Fal grasped her chin, adding a new spark to the flame, and gently coaxed her to look at him. "And now?"

Cheeks heating, she said, "You are the crown prince of Wilderheim, Your Highness."

His thumb skimmed lightly across her jaw, then his head tilted, and he released her. She saw one of his eyebrows go up in question before he became a young girl with blond curls falling over her eyes.

"Gone," she said.

The blond girl reached out, tugged on one of Sanja's curls, but released it too quickly and became a dark-skinned foreigner. When his fingers tunneled into Sanja's hair, molding to her scalp, Prince Fal appeared once more. "And now?" he asked, much too close.

Sanja forgot to breathe. He was so close she felt his breath on her chin and saw specks of silver in his bright blue eyes. She held still, poised at the edge of something monumental, and it thrilled her, as it terrified her. The prince's palm seared her ear. His hooded gaze mesmerized Sanja until her own eyelids began to droop. Her limbs were rigid, yet her spine melted, pushing her forward, closer...

A bright spark of sunlight glinted off his golden cuff, breaking her out of the strange reverie. Gold. A wide band of it circling the wrist of Wilderheim's future king. Sanja gasped and reared back. What was she doing?

"I must go now," she said, tearing away from his hold and pushing to her feet before he could stop her.

"Sanja, wait!"

"I'm sorry," she said, all but gasping for breath as her heart thrashed. She took off running and didn't dare look back to see if he'd followed her.

6

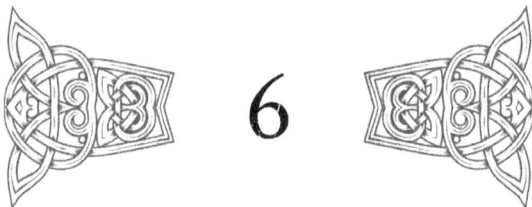

"Wait, stop!" By the time Fal regained his mental faculties and pushed to his feet, the quick little squirrel had already made it to the edge of the green. He ran after her, cloaking himself in invisibility before he dived into the market crowd, but as small as she was, Sanja disappeared from sight almost instantly. Fal stopped before a weaver's stall, turning circles and craning his neck to see over the crowds, but saw no sign of her. She'd well and truly disappeared.

His fingers dug into the thick cloth of his cloak. *Fool!* He'd had the first glimmer of hope in his grasp and let it slip right through his fingers. Fal had no notion of what'd happened on the green, but he didn't need ancient scrolls in dead languages to tell him it had been *something*. Something significant and quite inexplicable. He needed to learn what made her the only human in Frastmir who could see his real face. What magic did she hold that could make him so thoroughly lose his own, along with his higher reason?

And why in the bloody world had he let her get away?

A black, winged stallion strolling through the crowds tossed his head in agitation as he passed Fal and abruptly spread his massive wings, sending everyone in the vicinity scurrying for cover. Winged horses were notorious for their tempers—when threatened or angered, they breathed fire.

Having cleared almost half of the market square, the stallion stomped his front hoof, snorting smoke. His wings beat as if he was preparing to take flight, swaying wicker baskets where they hung from lines behind Fal. Large black feathers broke loose and floated to the ground, instantly turning to ash where they landed—a natural precaution that prevented anyone from using them to bend the winged horse to their will.

With one red eye trained in Fal's direction, the stallion snorted again and tossed his head. Then, as if he'd lost interest, his wings settled back against his sides, and he continued on, the frightened crowds parting before him to give him a wide berth.

In the open space the stallion left in his wake, Fal caught a flash of movement and, without thought, he ran after it, away from the market, into the maze of small alleyways of Frastmir's underbelly.

Here, the castle's walls cast long shadows over weathered little shacks and tents where the criminal gamblers, brawlers, and pickpockets fleeced unwary travelers. Armed soldiers patrolled the area day and night but, unless they caught a criminal in the act, they were forbidden from interfering, which made said criminals very clever about hiding their activities out of plain sight.

Fal slowed his step. Out of direct sunlight, rainwater pooled in constant puddles, rendering all wooden slats soggy and soft and creating a gloomy, ominous sight. Fal did not frighten easily, but so much water altered his senses by force. He could see the alley from every angle as if looking out through those puddles, all at the same time. What ought to have been an invaluable advantage became a lethal weakness as his mind struggled to make sense of it all, to sort it into some kind of order and give it context.

A multitude of his own reflections moved around him in flickers of a billowing cloak, making him flinch each time. Water was not fooled by a magic trick as paltry as invisibility. Natural elements could never lie, and thus always reflected only the truth.

Fal pulled his cloak tightly around him, made his steps as slow and fluid as possible, while fragments of reflections flashed across his mind's eye, blinding him to his surroundings. The farther he went, the

worse it became until he was forced to stop and lean against the wall
of a shack to regain his bearings. His heart beat too hard. His breath
came too quickly, and his head swam, making him sway on his feet.

And then the reflections began to move again.

Impossible to tell where from, or how many. Fal, already off balance
and half out of his mind, panicked. Rugged, dirty faces flashed in grotesque swirls all around him, gruff voices echoed, incomprehensible
but threatening all the same. The glint of a weapon caught his eye,
reflecting a dozen times from different angles. Was he surrounded, or
facing a single opponent? Had his invisibility spell failed? Fal had no
way of knowing. Shaking from head to toe, he did the only thing he
could think of. He pushed away from the wall, leaped for the largest
puddle on the ground, and bent the element to his desperate will,
falling through the surface into its primordial core.

Water enveloped him instantly in a cocoon of glittering light. His
soul responded to its embrace, opening eagerly to join with the element, even as he perceived ice crystals beginning to form. Even as his
human body struggled not to breathe—not to drown. He sent his will
into the element one more time, creating a current to carry him back
to his own world. In his own chambers, a shallow copper basin spat
him out with a splash, and Fal collapsed onto his side, gasping for air.

With shaking hands, he undid the clasp of his sodden cloak and
fought his way free of its weight. With a thought, he dried the rest of
his clothes, returning scattered water droplets back into the basin.

Hands roughened by swordplay grasped his arm, pulling him up
to his feet. "I leave for a few days and come back to find the crown
prince of Wilderheim on his hands and knees. Is this your idea of
having everything under control? I am not impressed, brother."

He blindly pulled Liadan into his arms, as much for comfort as
for balance.

"You're shaking."

Fal chuckled. "I noticed."

"What's the matter?" Her entire being heated just short of bursting
into flame. The warmth melted the chill in his bones until, by the
time she released him to spark a fire in the hearth, Fal was almost
back to himself.

"Something's happened, sister."

"Tell me," she said, pushing him into a chair and taking the other for herself. "I cannot bear to lose you, too."

So he told her about the girl with wild black hair and a restless mind, and her quest to make her suitor break his troth. He must have sounded like a raving lunatic when he described their conversation and the girl's inexplicable ability to see his true face because that was where Liadan held up her hand to stop the flood of words pouring out of his mouth.

"She could see you? The real you?"

Fal nodded. "But only when she touched me. Skin to skin. She was not at all shy about putting her hands all over me, but nothing happened until she reached a part of me not covered by clothing." At her raised eyebrow, he clarified, "My *hand*."

"And as long as she held it, she could see you?"

"Yes. And when I pulled away, the illusions swallowed me up again."

"Naturally, she must have been terrified. No wonder she ran from you."

Fal flushed. "She wasn't terrified." At least not at first. Not until he'd tried to kiss her. *Why did I do that?*

The infinitely perceptive Liadan tilted her head at that. "She saw your illusions and *wasn't* terrified? Was she stunned into silence?"

A sudden burst of laughter startled Fal. "Hardly. She would have asked a thousand questions had I not stopped her. She talks incessantly, even when no one is around to listen."

Liadan studied him for a moment before a wicked smile made her eyes spark gold with firelight. "You like her."

"What? No!"

"You do, I can see it in your eyes. I must meet this girl. What did you say her name was?"

Fal scowled at his sister as she added more wood to the fire in preparation of seeking out answers from its flames. Fire was an element of the heart, and as such, it always offered multiple visions: those a Seer sought, and those he most strongly desired. Liadan had a singular ability to see the real truth in them—a feat even those with the gift of magical Sight found impossible. But then, his sister didn't merely play with fire; she *was* fire, as much as Fal was water.

Noticing he hadn't answered yet, Liadan sent him a questioning glance, to which Fal responded by shaking his head. She scowled at him and sat back on her booted heels, turning to face him. "You must know this could be the only chance you will ever get to learn more about your affliction and how to heal it. Why do you hesitate?"

"Because I rather think the prospect of the end of all we have ever known takes precedence over my personal problems," he retorted. "Did you yourself not tell me I should focus on that?"

"Yes, I did," she snapped. "Days ago, when I didn't know there might be a chance to accomplish both."

"There isn't."

"But—"

"Liadan, there is no time."

She flushed. "What if she could help?"

"She is human. The only thing she could do is die." He knew the words were a mistake the moment he uttered them.

"That is beneath you," Liadan hissed on a crackle of carefully controlled fire. Fal's apology never made it past his lips as her ire poured out on a torrent of rapid words. "She must have some kind of magic to see through your illusions, and you said she has a sharp mind and can read. Did it never occur to you to wonder if perhaps a fresh pair of eyes might see something we have all missed—precisely because they belong to a human?"

Fal winced, thoroughly chastised and ashamed of himself. It should have occurred to him, and well before now. All these years, the royal family had been so anxious to keep the full truth of his condition secret for fear of the repercussions, none of them had ever thought to consult anyone outside of their own.

How paltry and insignificant it all seemed when there was so much worse to fear now.

Once more, he opened his mouth to respond, and once more, Liadan spoke over him. "And what good do you think you will do against Fenrir if your condition worsens?"

Fal flinched. She was right. He hated to the core of his soul that she was right, but she was still right. He could not answer her.

Still staring at him, Liadan inclined her head the slightest bit, throwing her eyes aflicker. When she spoke again, her voice was softer, kinder. "You know all this, brother. You are far too clever for none of this to have crossed your mind already, and you have never been one to cower away from what must be done. What's holding you back this time?"

What wasn't? Sanja was a human commoner with no magic or formal education. If his people saw him summon her to court on royal business, it would appear as a final act of desperation, or worse, madness. If he approached her informally, he would be seen as wasting time chasing skirts while his kingdom was in turmoil. Either path would risk what little political power he still held, and put her in danger from those who would see him deposed.

But instead of any of that, Fal said, "She is betrothed." It had no significance whatsoever to their current dilemma, yet he couldn't seem to separate the two, and clever Liadan noticed. Her eyebrows raised in quiet speculation, but she stayed silent, letting him talk himself deeper into the muck. "The match was arranged, I assume, to benefit her family. She does not want it, but it seems she cannot refuse the suit." A wry smile turned up one corner of his mouth. "What sort of human girl spends her time looking for ways to get rid of a suitor?"

"One desperate to forge her own fate, I would imagine. The desire for freedom is not restricted to Other creatures."

That was certainly true enough. "What do you suggest I do?"

"Seek her out," Liadan said, sounding annoyed at having to state the obvious.

"Liadan—"

"We agreed. You said I could come back any time and step in if I thought you needed help. Well, like it or not, brother, that time has come. I told you you couldn't do it all on your own. Even Da had Mother by his side to help him rule," she added reasonably, forestalling any argument he might have voiced to the contrary.

She was resolute. Any attempt to drive her out would only result in her throwing a fireball at his head. Fal was grateful. But when it came to the topic of Sanja, "There is another reason for not involving myself with her."

Liadan rolled her eyes in exasperation. "And what is that? What else could there possibly be to keep you from her?"

"That I'm the bloody Prince of Deceit!" Fal exploded from his seat, and as he did, water appeared to flood out of him in every direction until the entire chamber was submerged, and the wooden floor turned soft with shifting sands. Above their heads, the surface churned and foamed, casting long shadows as clouds of sand kicked up around his feet, making the waters murky.

Aside from a wince, Liadan appeared unperturbed by the display. She was still the only one Fal had ever know to withstand the deepest depths of his illusions without drowning in them, including both of his powerful parents.

"I can't simply walk through Frastmir, knock on her door, and ask her parents for an audience with their daughter."

"And so," Liadan said in a thoughtful tone as he paused for breath, "rather than take a chance and hope for the best, you choose to give up. Rather than ask this girl her thoughts on the matter, you choose to take the decision out of her hands completely."

He did not dignify such nonsense with an answer.

His scowl didn't deter Liadan in the least. She seemed determined to make her opinion known. "Fal, you are the most objective person I know. Think it through. Take yourself out of the picture, and think the way that young girl would. You are being forced to marry a man you do not want. What would you do?"

"Seek another solution."

"And what would that be?"

Fal shrugged helplessly.

"Come now, don't tell me you have spent all these years watching your people and learned nothing. That is not like you at all. You *know* the answer. It is only that you don't want to say it."

"You're suggesting I court her myself," he accused.

Liadan shrugged. "I merely asked a question. *You* suggested a courtship."

"The prince of Wilderheim cannot court a girl already betrothed to another man." It would be seen as a gross abuse of power and was forbidden by the laws of Wilderheim's Charter.

The smile she gave him was as sharp as it was wicked. "Who is to say it has to be the prince of Wilderheim who comes knocking at her door?"

The waters around them stilled. Fal met Liadan's glowing gaze, a dangerous idea blooming in his mind.

The fire in the hearth banked low and bright blue, casting heat enough to sting and drawing Fal's gaze into its depths. As the flames flickered, they took on shapes he recognized: himself and the girl. In one moment, the figures stood facing each other, stray flames leaping between them to mimic them holding hands, at first separate, then melding into one. In the next, another figure replaced the one representing Fal, and the flame joining the two figures flared out sideways, *through* the girl, who then disappeared. The fire flared high once more, dozens of individual flames reaching up like a violent clash of spears and swords before it abruptly died down to embers.

Fal blinked his vision clear as Liadan intoned, "They all call you the Prince of Deceit. Perhaps it is time to prove them right."

7

The preparations are progressing well.

Genevieve smiled, a dark burden lifting from her heart at the voice of her God. His shadow hovered by the heavy drapes the servants had pulled aside so she might see the green.

There, her army generals have assembled to present themselves for inspection. Five hundred generals, each in command of two thousand soldiers, all ready to march on Wilderheim at a moment's notice. The symbol of their faith, a red cross on a field of white, billowed proudly in the hands of the bannermen at each corner and adorned every tabard and shield in a smattering of red and white on the bright green meadow. The sun glinted off their armor, nigh blinding, but a glorious sight to behold.

"Look at them." She preened with pride. "Are they not beautiful? Their armies will reshape the world in Your image. They will bring honor to the rebirth of the Son."

And you shall rule by his side.

Genevieve shivered as a wicked northern breeze swept around her. Summer was at its end and, though these lands never saw a single snowflake, her old bones have become greedy for each waft of chill, soaking it in so well not even her ermine cloak could keep it out. "Is it time?"

Not yet, God replied, his voice contemplative. *But soon. The stars must align just so when the march begins. Else we risk great losses along the way.*

Yes, she knew this all too well. Messengers from Lyria have already delivered no fewer than fifteen missives with King Ulrich's seal, all containing warnings that Synealee's armies would not be tolerated on their lands. Genevieve had expected this, of course. Ulrich was Saeran's cousin, and a close one, at that. Wilderheim had aided Lyria in a time of war once already, and now Lyria was eager to return the kindness—one Genevieve was eager to repay as well.

It was because of King Manfred's familial ties to his brother, Halden, that he had sent Wilderheim's troops to protect Lyria from the Aegiran threat. He'd rushed to their aid, though Lyria hadn't asked for it, and ignored Genevieve's desperate pleas for help as the Aegiran scum had razed village after outlying village, creeping ever closer, forcing her to cede control of a vast tract of land on the other side of Silver Mountains, which now marked the new border between Synealee and Aegiros.

A third of her kingdom—gone.

And all because a man loved his brother more than a lady in distress.

Both were long dead now, but their progeny yet lived, heir to the sins of their fathers. She would show them. Before they died, they would know that Hell had no fury worse than a wounded queen.

I see great turmoil within you. What troubles your mind?

Genevieve hid her quivering hands in the folds of her cloak. She closed her eyes and lifted her face up to the sun, breathing deeply. "I want them to suffer," she confessed. "I want their kingdoms to bleed and turn the ground into rivers of red!"

A cold silence closed around her, making her cheeks heat with shame. The longer it continued, the deeper her shame burrowed, causing her knees to weaken. *Take heed,* God warned on a sharp whisper, *that you do not forget yourself. My mercy is infinite, but so is my wrath. Your duty is to* me.

Genevieve turned at once toward the source of His voice and lowered to her knees, touching her forehead to the woven carpet before her.

"I beg forgiveness, Divine One. I have not forgotten Your kindness or the duty You have bestowed upon me. I will not fail You. I swear it on my life."

Your life is not long for this world if you fail. Swear it on your soul instead.

"I do! I swear on my soul I will not fail in the task You have set before me." She would destroy Wilderheim, as her God had commanded her to do. She would kill the crown prince and lure out his whore of a sister, who'd taken up with an Aegiran of all things. Both would water the ground with their blood, and the royal line of Wilderheim would be stamped out for all time.

But it would never be enough. Once her holy charge was finished, she would turn her armies on Lyria, and then Aegiros itself.

God sighed, his shadows billowing out like black smoke. *Rise. It is no good for an old woman to kneel.*

Genevieve obeyed, struggling to raise herself upright. Standing tall once more, winded and flushed, she faced her God with her gaze humbly downcast. "God, I trust Your will and judgment in all things. You have helped me build a vast army to defeat Wilderheim, but how am I to get it there?" He had forbidden her to step foot into Lyria, and that left only a long, arduous, and dangerous march over Silver Mountains and through Aegiros, where bloodthirsty tribes would attack them on sight without the slightest provocation. Even if their losses were minimal, the march alone would weary her soldiers and weaken them before they reached Wilderheim's borders.

When the time comes, have faith, and all will be well, God intoned, filling her with strength and confidence once more. *Do you think I would allow you to fail before you have begun?*

Had she any strength left, she would have fallen to her knees once more, this time in gratitude.

Now, worry no more about what may come to pass. Turn your thoughts to what is.

"Have I overlooked something?" She couldn't have. Her plans have all been guided by His wisdom.

This, I have been saving for the final step. It is a gift I offer. The shadow billowed out once more, and Genevieve held her breath, yearning for a glimpse of her God. She almost thought she saw Him. The shape of a tall figure moved within those shadows, lean and beautiful, youth personified in flawless pale skin and red hair, and ageless wisdom written across His face. Glorious, breathtaking, and terrifying, even cloaked by darkness. Genevieve clutched at her chest, her heart thrashing painfully, perceiving the awful power contained within the confines of His form.

Overwhelmed by it, she was grateful when darkness once more hid Him from sight, leaving behind God's offering: a gleaming sword, standing upright on the tip of its blade, with a sturdy crossguard separating the blade from its handle. It was a magnificent thing, hewn by the Divine. Genevieve could feel it pulsing; could almost hear the sharp blade singing in a shaft of sunlight.

Your army is, indeed, vast, God said, *but your soldiers will need a reason to give their lives for you, one they will be able to see every day, that their faith may be reaffirmed. This sword is imbued with my power. If its wielder be worthy, it will slay any foe with a single blow and protect him from harm. But take heed. If it spills but one drop of innocent blood, its purpose will be lost, and its wielder cursed for all time.*

The warning sent a shiver down her spine. "Who would be worthy of such a weapon?" And such a burden! Genevieve had seen enough of war to know that anything could happen in the heat of battle. When one's life was in peril, a soldier didn't stop to think, only reacted. And when the fight was finished, he took his reward in any form available to him. That brutish, animal part of man was ever controlled by the Devil and could never be stamped out completely, only suppressed and controlled with prayer and thoughts of duty.

Any man who wielded the weapon of God could meet with eternal glory or eternal punishment. Genevieve herself would not have dared such a risk.

This is the final task I set before you, God said, and the sword moved toward her, scratching across the carpet. *Find me someone worthy of this gift. Someone who will be my voice on the field of battle and your successor on the throne of the largest kingdom ever to exist.*

Genevieve reached out to grasp the handle like a cane, and it leaned toward her as she leaned on it in return. Its power thrummed into her palms, made her blood heat with the thrill of upcoming battle. The promise of victory was so close at hand, she could taste it on the wind. Were she a young man, she would march out this instant to join the soldiers on the green.

Such heady power. It terrified her how difficult the sword was to set aside. When she spoke, her words, though meant for her God, were directed to the gift with which He had burdened her. "Your will is my command. I will not fail."

~

The task of finding one person in a city as crowded as Frastmir turned out to be easier than Fal had imagined. One small scrying spell had revealed Miss Sanja to be the daughter of Gerhart the Carver, currently dwelling in the Wood district on the far side of the city. Now all he had to do was come up with an innocent enough pretext for crossing paths with her. And what could be more innocent than a day at the market?

Cloaked in invisibility, Fal kept to the center of the gathering crowds. Usually, he would avoid making contact with anyone, but with so many people milling about, they hardly noticed a stray bump here and there. And if they noticed, they blamed someone they could see.

Fal enjoyed walking among his people, becoming part of their lives without them knowing. He listened to their stories, watched them go about their days. He knew the merchants closest to the castle so well he could call them friends. Their lives were filled with everyday struggles, little victories, love, and heartbreak. They lived each moment to the fullest.

Or they used to before the sky shattered above their heads.

Here in the western market, the people were strangers to him, and Fal itched with curiosity about them. The market itself was much smaller and sparser than the one he usually frequented. It served the needs of the poorer districts and the occasional traveler with necessities and practical wares, rather than exotic luxuries. But the people were no less fascinating.

He indulged in a slow stroll, stopping by each stall and table to listen in on town gossip.

The beekeeper had suffered a great loss overnight. His bees had dropped dead, and the honey in their hive had turned dark and bitter.

The seamstress smiled, however, for having sold three woolen dresses to fancy travelers the day before. She spoke about buying some expensive cloth at the central market to sew a new dress for her daughter, who was to marry the butcher's son.

But as Fal made his way over to the butcher's stall, he found the family in a somber mood, talking in whispers and forcing smiles when a customer stopped by. The mother kept glancing at the sky before turning her gaze to the cart piled with cloth-covered bundles. The father relented whenever a customer haggled down a price, and the son wouldn't acknowledge either of them, sitting off to the side with his head in his hands.

They would be gone as soon as the last of their meats were sold.

A crystal merchant nearby spun a piece of glass on its thong, reflecting sunlight into Fal's eyes. He squinted, turning away, and his gaze snared on a familiar figure.

With a basket hanging from one elbow, the girl who dreamed of true love strolled from stall to stall, examining the wares. Her curious fingers touched various items of interest, as though she couldn't help herself. The merchants scowled when they saw her approach. When she stopped by their stalls, they turned away, shouting their wares louder to the crowds, but kept a wary eye on their merchandise.

Undeterred, Sanja asked a question or two, and her smile never dimmed when she received a terse, dismissive answer. Fal didn't understand the merchants' reaction. They behaved as if disaster walked among them, yet Sanja didn't seem to mind, taking each scowl and every brush-off in stride.

The customers, at least, treated her with more kindness. Older women smiled and asked about her family. Young men greeted her with winks but, though they spoke to her briefly, they moved on again in haste.

Sanja continued on her path. Curious to know more about her, Fal decided to follow at a discrete distance. Her next stop was the cheese stall, where the merchant came around to stand in front of a low shelf laden with milk jugs when he saw her coming.

Sanja greeted the man with a cheery smile, either oblivious to the nervous twitch in the man's eye or ignoring it. He flinched whenever she raised her hand to point at something. Finally, he accepted a coin for a round of hard cheese and shooed her on her way. Sanja gave him a nod of thanks and a wave farewell as she whirled away with a burst of energy that snapped her skirt out sideways, tipping the outermost jug on the ground. It teetered on the edge of its base and would have settled, had the merchant not rushed forward and accidentally nudged it over himself. The jug broke, spilling milk all over the ground.

"Pox rotted nuisance! Who'll pay for this now, eh?"

Fal shook his head as he passed the cursing merchant. Normally, he would take no pleasure in seeing a man lose even so small a portion of his livelihood. But for the way he'd treated Sanja, Fal was tempted to knock over a few more of his jugs.

Instead, he hurried to catch up with Sanja as she collected root vegetables from a farmer on her way to the baker. There, she stopped and perused the delicacies. He could see by the way her hands clenched in her skirts that she would dearly love to sample several. But when the baker offered her a meat bun, Sanja shook her head and, with a wistful look, walked away.

Could her family be so low on coin she couldn't afford a single bun?

The idea sat ill with Fal. Passing by the baker's table, he quickly snatched up several buns, leaving behind a silver coin for payment.

At the far end of the market, the crowds thinned out. Merchant stalls gave way to shops and taverns, and a little farther down the road, the river marked Frastmir's borders. A wide stone bridge allowed carriages to safely cross its churning white waters. For a moment, Fal's gaze caught on the leaping waves and stuck, watching the foamy figures twirl in the air before splashing down.

The spectacle was breathtaking to him but unnerved those crossing the bridge as the figures leaped in giant arcs over the bridge, raining water down on wary travelers.

So caught up was he in their display, he fell a ways behind Sanja. Luckily, she'd stopped in front of the clothier's shop to admire a cloak hanging on display beside the door. It was a fine thing, to be sure.

Thickly woven and embroidered around the edges with an intricate knotwork of vines. A garment his sister might well have worn—and one Sanja might never be able to afford.

But as he studied her face, he saw no sadness or envy, only a sense of wonder as her admiring gaze traced the lines of embroidery from top to bottom. She savored its beauty for its own sake, no doubt wondering how it'd been done.

The same way she'd looked at him on the green.

The longer he watched, the more Fal realized Sanja didn't merely see. She studied everything and everyone.

She tore her gaze away from the fancy cloak to examine her own clothes. They were far inferior and worn through, yet she didn't seem perturbed. Instead, she gamely plucked a carrot from her basket, tore off the limp stems, and wove them in and out of the frayed neckline of her dress. Satisfied with her new adornment, she smiled to herself and raised her chin proudly.

Fal was entranced. He drew closer, careful to keep out of the way of passers-by. With her dark hair and pale skin, and her cheeks pinkened from the sun, she looked like an enchanting earth elemental snuck away to play in the human realm. When she turned away, he followed and, just to see her reaction, let out a stream of illusions to frame her path with wildflowers.

She didn't notice, staring into the distance before her as if she could see over the horizon if she looked hard enough.

He closed the distance between them until his toes nearly brushed her heels as they walked. She was humming to herself.

Distracted by her voice, Fal didn't notice they were on the bridge until water rained down on them. Sanja squealed in surprise, then laughed and twirled back and forth, dancing with the figures. Travelers glared when she got in their way, but Sanja remained oblivious. And the undines delighted in her reaction, performing ever more daring leaps and drenching anyone who complained.

They sent Fal a few looks, too, invisibility notwithstanding. He sensed some kind of playful challenge in the gesture, but they chose not to make themselves understood. They often did that, just to make him feel stupid.

Fal made a rude gesture at them, causing them to whistle back an equally rude response.

Sanja danced back toward him, and he hastily stepped out of her way, nearly knocking himself off the bridge. The undines burst in the air—their form of laughter—and from the river below mocked him for behaving like an untried schoolboy. Another challenge came to him, a dare of some sort, once again incomprehensible, but somehow connected to Sanja.

"Who needs human lads, anyway?" Sanja called to them with a fond smile. "I'd much rather dance with you!" Her words caught him off guard.

Making sure she would see it this time, he wove an illusion across the bridge's stone rail. A swirling line of moss and little white flowers raced from a stone in front of her toward the landing back in Frastmir.

Sanja frowned at it, reached out to a flower, but pulled back quickly without touching it. With a wary look around, she muttered something to herself, then waited.

Fal sent a ripple down the mossy carpet and conjured a bright red flower at the end to draw her eyes.

The invitation was too enticing to refuse. Sanja followed the trail he'd created for her, running her hand over the top of it without touching until she reached the red bloom. That one was real. Fal had anchored it in a crevice between two stones, rooted it all the way down into the ground. Unless someone tore it out, it would bloom again and again with each new season.

But he didn't want Sanja distracted by a flower. Before she could touch it, he bent the flower, drawing her gaze to a trail of bluebells that led away from the bridge, along the river toward the green.

"H-hello? Is anybody there?"

A passing traveler tipped his hat at her.

Sanja blushed and smiled in answer, then quickly turned away, gnashing her teeth. "Show yourself," she hissed under her breath.

Fal kept quiet.

After a moment, Sanja's temper cooled, and she leaned close to smell the red flower, smearing yellow pollen on the tip of her nose. Her fingers closed on the stem, about to pluck it, but she seemed to change her mind. Releasing the bloom with a lingering caress, she turned her back on the bridge.

She was going to head back toward the market, he realized with no small amount of disappointment. But two steps along the path, Sanja stopped. She was muttering to herself again, earning more strange looks from passersby.

To entice her further, he made the bluebells deepen in color.

With a glance at the basket full of purchases that her parents were no doubt waiting for, Sanja sighed, bit her lip in indecision, then resolutely took off, following the bluebells so quickly Fal had to jog to keep pace with her. He grinned to himself, enjoying her unbridled curiosity more than was wise.

When they were out of sight, the trail came to an end at a large round boulder.

"Well, that was disappointing."

Was it now? Fal placed one of the buns atop the boulder and made it visible.

Sanja dropped her basket and stomped her foot. "I knew it! I knew it was you! Where are you, you fiend?"

Fal bit the inside of his cheek to keep his laughter in check. She didn't have a book on her, but there were plenty of other things she could bash him with. Better not risk it. Instead, he placed a second bun next to the first and quickly stepped out of reach as she whirled in angry circles with her arms outstretched, looking for him. The buns went unseen and, worse, uneaten.

"Show yourself! Why are you following me?"

Fal took a bite out of the third bun and held it visible in the air where she would notice. "So, you have never been asked to dance?"

Sanja gasped. "You heard that?" Her cheeks turned red, and she growled. "Oh, I wish I had never met you!" She launched herself at the bun, her only point of reference, and Fal shifted to stay out of her reach.

"Is that any way to speak to your prince?"

"Is that who I'm speaking to?" she countered. Abandoning her assault, she searched the ground for something. Probably a convenient rock or large stick. "How would I know? I cannot see anyone around. I could be talking to myself. I do that often enough."

"And you answer yourself, as well. An admirable gift. Whenever I question myself, I never seem to get an answer."

"Perhaps you are asking the wrong questions."

Fal conceded the point. "Why have you never been asked to dance? You are pretty enough." Enough to snare his attention most thoroughly. Were the young men of Frastmir blind that they didn't see her?

"I am not speaking to you anymore. Aha!" Good gods, she'd found a stick.

"Now, let's be reasonable about this," Fal said, raising his hands in a gesture of peace, though she wouldn't be able to see it. "I am not here for a fight. On the contrary, see the buns? I bought those for you. As a peace offering. And an apology." Of sorts. Though, if she asked him for what—

"An apology for what?"

Bollocks. "Er…"

"You're apologizing, and you don't know what for?"

Fal's shoulders raised in a helpless shrug. "Is that not what a man is supposed to do when a woman is angry?"

The contrary wench swung the stick.

"Yield, yield! I'm sorry!"

"Go away!" She swung again, harder. "I do not have time for this."

"Gods curse it, then let me help."

Sanja froze, stick still raised, but she frowned. "What do you mean?"

"If you put down the stick, I will show you."

After a moment's hesitation, she complied, propping the stick against the boulder within easy reach. "Well?" Curiosity. That was her weakness. She couldn't resist a mystery; he could use that to his advantage.

"I would like it noted that I am willingly putting myself in physical danger to meet you halfway."

Sanja rolled her eyes. "I thought princes were supposed to be fearless in the face of death."

"Death, perhaps, but I don't know a-one who would risk his neck facing you and that stick."

She ducked her head but not before he caught the twitch of a smile. He found himself grinning in return. She was quite charming—when she wasn't trying to kill him for no good reason.

Fal reached into the pouch tied at his waist and brought forth a small, leather-bound book. The cover was unevenly cut and tearing, the spine stitched with a careless hand. The pages within were crumpled and stained, but what they contained could prove quite useful for Sanja. He'd thought it'd been lost years ago and had found it last night purely by chance in Liadan's old chambers. His sister had a wicked sense of humor, and it would pay off for Fal.

"A gift for you. Perhaps it will help you with your suitor dilemma." Making the book visible, he extended it to Sanja, coming only close enough so she could take it from him, but far enough to flee the stick, should she decide to use it again.

There'd be no danger of that, he realized, as long as a book was nearby. The stick forgotten, her eyes widened, and her fingers twitched. "For me?"

"As I said."

"To keep?"

He grinned. "Indeed."

She took the book from him ever so gently and held it before her with both hands, admiring the haggard cover front and back. "What's in it?" she whispered with such reverence, as if he'd handed her a box of untold treasures.

"Unsavory tales no young woman should ever come across," he replied. "Tales of bad men getting their just comeuppance, vengeful women doling it out, all manner of lurid acts, and all of it delivered with a great deal of inappropriate humor by a writer I strongly suspect wasn't all together literate. You will want to read them straight away."

"And I can keep it?"

With her fingers curling tightly around its edges, Fal wouldn't be able to pry it from her if he tried. "Yes, it is yours forever."

Sanja opened the book, traced the words written in a clumsy, untrained hand. "I don't know what to say." She considered it even more beautiful for its humble origins. It was a precious morsel of someone's life forever immortalized on a few worn pieces of parchment and stitched together in a rough leather cover that might have once been a boot or an old garment.

Such a book would never have a place in Frastmir's grand library, yet it had been read by the crown prince of Wilderheim. And now it was hers.

"Your love of books is a thing to behold," the prince said, disturbing her out of her reverie. "I have met clerics bowed over with the weight of their years of study who have never looked at a tome the way you are looking at that thing."

"You don't understand. Someone like me wrote this. This person scraped together whatever was available to create a book so he could document as many stories as could be fitted onto its few pages. And he did not do it for any reason, other than sharing a piece of himself in a way that might endure after his passing. This is…" She fumbled for the right words to describe it. "It is a letter written to me by someone I never knew I wanted to know. It is magic."

"I never thought of it that way," he said after a pause.

"No, of course you would not."

"What do you mean by that?"

Still enraptured by her gift, Sanja shrugged. "Only that books for you mean something different. I imagine you have been surrounded by them since early childhood. You have been taught to read for the purpose of ruling a kingdom. Therefore, books for you are a responsibility, whereas, for me, they are a privilege. Do you ever read for pleasure, Your Highness?"

Another pause. This one lasted so long Sanja feared he'd left. She was about to say more when he chuckled a little without humor. "Do you know, I don't think I ever have." His voice sounded strange. Without seeing his face, Sanja couldn't identify the emotion behind his words, and she wanted to.

"Will you not show yourself, Your Highness? I would very much like to thank you properly."

"It is better that I don't."

"Yes, of course," she demurred, hugging her treasure close. It wouldn't do for the prince to be seen in the company of a poor peasant girl.

"I wanted to apologize for the way I behaved on the green. It was not my intention to insult you or frighten you. I acted selfishly, and, as my sister pointed out, that is not at all like me."

"Then I should apologize for striking you with a book."

"To me, or the book?"

Sanja smiled, flushing with relief. "Both, I suppose. It seems neither of us was quite ourselves." She bit back a wince as she subtly toed away the stick she'd meant to use on him. Violence was not at all in character for her. Except, it seemed, when Prince Fal was nearby.

Happily, he didn't say anything about it. "Peace?" he offered.

"Yes."

She heard him sigh, then felt something brush past her and turned to see one of the buns disappear. "Good," he said around a mouthful. "Now, have a seat, and let's see that book."

Obediently, Sanja sat, and the remaining bun transferred from the boulder to her lap. It was still warm from the baker's oven, and Sanja's belly growled hungrily for a taste. She took a bite and nearly swooned. The bun was so soft it melted in her mouth, the filling just warm enough to make her shiver in delight. She savored that first bite, then devoured the rest of the bun in two more.

After licking her fingers, she wiped her hands clean before picking up the book. "How did you come by this?"

"I strongly suspect my sister either won it in a gamble or stole it from a tavern drunk during the early years she spent in the north."

Sanja gaped at the empty space where his voice was coming from. "The crown princess of Wilderheim spent her youth gambling and stealing?"

"And drinking and brawling. Never to excess, mind. And, according to her, never as the instigator. Liadan has always insisted that any unprincesslike behavior was always provoked. She conveniently leaves out her liking to visit places where such provocation is wont to occur."

"I don't know what to say to that."

"Neither did my parents. But since she has never caused undue harm, they decided to make allowances for her behavior."

Sanja scoffed. "The privileges of royalty." Had she ever attempted anything like that, her parents would have boxed her ears—deservedly so.

She heard him shift about in his seat. "You must understand, both Liadan and I are very much at the mercy of our elements. Liadan's is fire, mine is water, and they rule every aspect of our beings, whether we want them to or not. Liadan requires activity to burn off the excess energy. She is a born warrior who thrives in battle but, without a war, that energy burns too bright to contain."

Sanja absorbed this in silence. "If what you say is true, then the princess must be thriving with her new husband in Aegiros." The region was constantly at war with itself, different tribes fighting for control of its limited resources. "But what about you?"

"I have been asking myself that question for the last six years and—"

"Wait, don't tell me. Your magic is like a lake, isn't it? Fire burns out unless you feed it, but water continues to accumulate. Without at outlet, the lake grows and grows, until it spills out and swallows up everything. Am I right?"

Once again, it seemed she'd rendered him speechless.

"A-are you still there?"

"Our grandfather used to tell us we were cursed at birth," he said, his tone hesitant, as if he was debating how much to reveal. "He performed a ritual on us, a blessing of sorts, but something went wrong, and he swears it was some outside force interfering, swears he felt it twist the magic inside us somehow. When Liadan broke free of her curse in Aegiros, I expected it would heal me as well, but it did not. I never stopped looking for my own cure but, inside, I keep hoping it is only a matter of time, and the curse will eventually cure itself. I keep thinking if I am patient enough, wait long enough, something will eventually change. And then it does, and it is always for the worse."

He stopped there, his pause heavy with the need for some sort of response. Sanja wished she had some advice or words of comfort to offer, but in matters of magic, she was at a woeful disadvantage. "How did Princess Liadan free herself?"

"She died. And then she rose from her own ashes reborn. As you said, fire burns out eventually, until you spark it anew."

"I hope you never attempted to test that theory on yourself."

"Once or twice," he admitted. "As you can see, it didn't quite take."

"Well, of course not. Fire and water aren't in any way similar." And how dare he try to take his own life—the royal heir!

"What do you suggest I do instead?"

"Find a suitable outlet naturally. If the problem is too much magic then, Your Highness, you have an entire kingdom to loose it on. You could cure yourself and help your people at the same time."

"If only it were that simple. But Wilderheim is already steeped in so much magic it cannot absorb any more."

"Then go elsewhere."

"I can't, Sanja. The magic I hold is so great, it could only wreak destruction if I let it loose. Why do you think I have been sequestered in Castle Frastmir all this time? My own parents are worried about the consequences—as are all the Others. They have now banned me from their lands altogether."

"But there must be some way to overcome this, surely."

"Indeed, there must," he replied with a heavy sigh, then seemed to rally. "But it will not be discovered today, so we might as well occupy ourselves with pleasanter things." An invisible finger tapped on the book in her lap, and another bun appeared before her. "You have a lovely reading voice. Will you not read me a story?"

Sanja accepted the bun and opened the book to the first page. Between small nibbles, she obliged the prince and read such stories as would never be told aloud within an innocent girl's hearing. Sometimes, the words were almost indecipherable. Sometimes they made her stutter and blush crimson. And sometimes they made her laugh so much she could hardly breathe.

But all the while she read, Sanja couldn't help thinking of the prince's illusion curse.

She was still thinking about it when she reached the end of the last story but, when she turned to Prince Fal to ask more questions, only silence answered her.

Sometime during the last story, he'd left her without a word farewell.

8

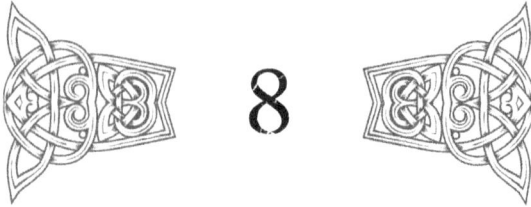

If the prince's magic could be siphoned off, how would it affect his use of magic? And if he wasn't allowed into Otherlands, might there be a way for him to purge the excess in Lyria, where his royal cousin might give him leave to do so? Or Aegiros, perhaps? No doubt the desert region could do with more water. And why hadn't he tried either before?

These thoughts occupied Sanja's mind most thoroughly during Jarl Steen's next unwelcome visit. She'd learned from previous occasions not to voice any opinions or questions pertaining to magic or Otherlands, as he seemed to be resentful of both. Sanja couldn't determine whether it was because of his lack of magic or his lack of understanding, but evidence continued to mount on the side of the latter.

Given the restrictions imposed on possible topics of conversation, Sanja and the jarl sat together in a room where the only sounds were those of the hens frolicking outside.

He'd put in the effort to make an impression today. His embroidered shirt was fit for royalty, stretching across his shoulders and arms. With his wide belt cinched too tight, he was forced to sit perfectly straight, and whenever he twitched a foot, his polished leather boots groaned.

She'd never seen anyone look so uncomfortable in his own skin before.

The man's face was flushed and sheened with sweat, but a wooden smile remained plastered across his face. Every once in a while, he would take a deeper breath as if to say something but, at a loss for words, he would release the breath on a sigh and hold his silence.

At last, he spoke. "Do you like your gift?"

Sanja mustered what she hoped was more of a smile than a wince. She'd made no attempt to take the offering from him and refused to touch it now as it lay spread out on the table before her. "It is very generous," she said, eyeing the array of iron and leather adornments meant to hold her hair in intricate braided patterns.

Jarl Steen drew himself up and smiled wider, taking her deliberately vague words as praise. "I can't wait to see them on you. Such lovely hair you have. It should be worn in a crown."

A crown of iron. Sanja's head ached just thinking about it.

Leaning toward her, the Jarl said softly, "If you please me well, my dove, I'll buy you a set made of gold." He made some sort of winking grimace she assumed was meant to be seductive. But then his gaze touched on a curl of her hair, and his mouth twisted in subtle distaste.

Come to think of it, his last gift to her had been a set of ribbons. It appeared the jarl had a strong preference when it came to hair. To test that theory, Sanja pretended to sneeze and shook her head to dislodge the thong loosely tying her curls at her nape, letting them slide free and bounce over her shoulder and across her forehead. "Apologies," she said with a smile. "It's a bit dusty today."

He looked from her to the adornments on the table, then back at her with an expectant raise of his eyebrow. Sanja smiled blandly and folded her hands in her lap, her thoughts drifting.

Were the changing faces an aspect of Prince Fal's overflow of magic? If so, it was imperative he find some way to siphon it off. Illusions were one thing, but what if they were only the first stage of the process? What if, with enough magic behind the changes, they became real and permanent? He might never hold his own shape again. A man whose identity had been instilled in him since birth—how would he bear it if he lost that identity for all time?

"Red," Jarl Steen said at random.

Sanja frowned at him, trying to recall what else he'd been saying.

He grinned. "Red would look striking on you." His gaze slid down her body, and Sanja felt it like slime oozing down her skin.

"Do you intend to choose my dresses for me? If so, I favor more earthbound colors. Greens and browns. Blue is my favorite." It was also the most expensive pigment available.

Jarl Steen chuckled. "My dear, if I had my way, you would have no use for clothes at all. They only get in the way, in any case."

"Then what…?"

He didn't seem to hear her. "Skin like yours should never be concealed. So lovely…" His breathing became more labored as he spoke, and Sanja shrank back in her seat, eyeing the kitchen as her most efficient path of escape.

"You know," he continued, staring at her chest. "Some clans still mark their skin with permanent patterns."

Yes, many Others still practiced the same, and the markings always looked to her like beautiful jewelry they could never lose. Some could even move beneath the skin, which fascinated Sanja.

"They brand their women so the world will know at a glance whom they belong to."

"That is a lie," she blurted out and bit her tongue. She ought not have said that aloud. But how could he make something so beautiful into something so base and offensive? Most such markings, like his own, were a sign of strength and bravery, often awarded to warriors and other accomplished clan members as a great honor.

His fervid gaze met hers, his face darkening redder. "I should like to see them put my clan's mark on you," he said, the threat all the more disturbing for the amount of pleasure he seemed to derive from making it. "It hurts a great deal. But you will bear it for me, will you not?"

"Do you take pleasure in seeing people in pain?"

His palms rubbed along his legs, and a vein began to throb in the side of his shaved head. Eyes growing unfocused, the Jarl's voice became distracted, monotone. "Pain, pleasure. You would be surprised how often they are the same thing." He licked his lips. "I always seek the Moment. I hear it in their voice, a sort of…keening whimper. And I look into their eyes, and I see it there, so beautiful, begging me. Begging..."

The Jarl's mind was somewhere else, a terrible place she instinctively feared as much as he apparently loved. His hands were balled into fists, his shoulders tight, almost up by his ears. Breathing hard, he leaned forward, staring through her, somehow dragging her with him into whatever torment he imagined playing out until she almost heard herself keening, begging him—to stop.

She surged out of her seat and escaped to the window. Hugging herself, Sanja stared out at the sky, counting the lights to distract herself away from the waking nightmare sitting across the table from her. The empty spaces between the lights widened every day as the sky slowly cleared. It ought to be a good sign—the jarl certainly thought it was—but deep down, Sanja worried it was a sign of worse things to come.

As if rousing from a deep sleep, she heard the jarl's husky voice behind her. "I should take my leave."

Sanja shuddered. "Yes, it is time you did." Propriety be damned, she refused to face him as he struggled to lever his bulk out of the chair. She didn't return his farewell when he gave it, nor did she walk him to the door. Instead, she remained hunched over at the edge of the window, hiding from sight, watching him depart. He showed little consideration to his sturdy riding mount, yanking him close so he could swing up to his back. The poor beast looked broken, dragging his hooves slowly down the road, quivering and snorting until the jarl delivered a vicious kick that sent him into a mad, screaming sprint.

She waited only long enough for him to disappear around the nearest corner before she scooped up the offensive hair adornments with the corner of her apron and tossed the lot of them onto the hearth fire. The iron would survive, but at least she could watch the leather burn to ash.

As she did, a full-body shiver overtook her. Sanja shook herself out, wiping off the front of her dress, desperate to remove any lingering sense of Jarl Steen's regard. A shame she'd never be able to wipe his words from her mind.

And I am supposed to be his mistress and share his bed. Subject to his perverse proclivities.

The thought sent her running out the door. She ran into the wind, breathing deeply of the fresh scents of grass and mist it brought her as it swept through her hair and clothes. Sanja held her arms out to embrace it, gave herself up to its cleansing chill, and welcomed it against her skin.

She ran without thinking and found herself at the boulder where she'd read to the prince the day before. Today, the bluebells were gone, but a sea of dandelions spread out from the boulder, atop which sat a tray of sweet buns. "Your Highness?"

"I did not know which flowers you liked best," he said from somewhere nearby. Before her eyes, the yellow dandelions shrank down into the ground and, in their place, sprouted bright red poppies.

Red. Sanja shuddered. "Definitely not those."

They disappeared at once, and tall, thick stalks of sunflowers took their place. They were so tall, their blooms so large, the boulder and its sweet offering disappeared from sight completely. "Too big," the prince decided, reducing the sunflowers to nothing. A carpet of clovers sprouted in their stead, interspersed with bluebells and dandelions in glorious disarray.

The riot of colors soothed her mind and the tension began to ebb from her at last. "Yes, I like those the best," Sanja said, feeling light-headed with relief. "Are they real?"

The blooms wavered, then settled, filling the air with their sweet scent. "They are now."

Sanja knelt in their midst, unexpected tears stinging her eyes. So much beauty right there at his fingertips. Such a wonderful gift he'd given her. "Thank you," she said. "If you only knew... They are beautiful."

"The buns are real, too. And quite tasty." The tray levitated off the boulder to the ground beside her, and the flowers shifted to make room as the unseen prince seated himself on the other side of it. "I did not know if you would come back."

"I did not know you wanted me to. You disappeared yesterday without a word."

"I fell asleep. And when I woke, you were gone."

"You fell asleep while I was reading? Those stories were anything but boring." Except for the last one. The writer had finished his volume on a sweet, wistful note with a letter to his beloved. Sanja had found it touching and heartfelt.

The prince had fallen asleep. *Men…*

"I think it was your voice."

Sanja gaped. "My voice is boring?"

"No! Not boring. Soft and soothing. Have you ever been on the lake when the winds are calm? The water is never still, and at times like that, it rocks the boat ever so gently. And when the sun shines down to warm you, it makes you feel like a child, with the world itself rocking you to sleep. There is no better lullaby in the world. That is what your voice felt like."

Sanja tugged on a clover's petals, at a loss for words. The casual praise, delivered so earnestly, humbled her and brought her a secret thrill of unexpected pleasure. With a few words, the prince transformed her from a silly, chattering girl too clumsy to learn a trade and too strange to attract a husband, to someone special. Someone worthy of a few stolen moments reading a book. It awakened something inside her that she'd thought she'd extinguished for all time. An impossible hope in happy endings, in the kind of love that filled pages with poems and emotion. An effortless bond the likes of which she'd given up the moment she'd signed her name in blood.

"Why have you come back?" she asked.

"I come with a nefarious plan and ulterior motives, of course."

Sanja gasped. "Dear me, surely not. How fiendish of you!"

Before she'd had a chance to regret her impetuousness, he chuckled. "Indeed, the Prince of Deceit lives up to his name. I have lured you here with sweet buns to take advantage of you in a most unscrupulous way."

"Oh?" Sanja prudently shifted her seat farther away from him.

"There is no need for alarm," he assured her. "I brought you a puzzle." A small stack of parchment sheets appeared beside the platter of buns. Nothing at all like the book she now kept underneath her pillow, these sheets were perfectly trimmed and starched, the writing on them neat and orderly. "I would like to see what you make of it."

"Is this a test?" Even if it was, Sanja didn't care, already reaching for the puzzle, the sweet buns forgotten.

"Would it bother you if it was?"

She shrugged, but already her attention was focused on the writing in her hands. "You wrote this," she guessed. "But it is not your work."

"How do you know that?"

"The writing feels old. It was transcribed from somewhere else."

"Correct," he confirmed, "on both counts."

Sanja read to the end of the first page, then carefully set it aside to move on to the next. The text had a rhythm to it like a silent melody, and Sanja began to hum to herself, trying to fit the words into a song. At times, she almost felt like she knew it, but it never lasted more than a word or two before she lost it again.

It was the story of the great wolf Fenrir, and the enchanted ribbon forged to bind him. The great wolf, a ravaging beast sired by the Trickster god, Loki, was said to be so terrible not even the gods could best him. He destroyed and devoured everything in his path and was foretold to devour the gods themselves in the final days of Ragnarok, the End of All.

Desperate to escape their fate, the gods tasked a clan of dwarves to forge a chain strong enough to contain Fenrir. If they couldn't kill him, they could at least imprison him for all time. What the dwarves gave them was a delicate ribbon hewn from the blood of Otherkind and the power of all the gods combined.

But the great wolf was a formidable opponent, impossible to over-power, and so the gods devised a trick. They presented the ribbon to Fenrir as a challenge. After all, he was so mighty, and the ribbon was so fine, surely he wouldn't balk at testing its meager strength.

As proud as Fenrir was, he was no fool. He agreed to try the ribbon, but only if Tir, the god of war and their best warrior, agreed to put his hand in Fenrir's mouth as insurance. Tir agreed, the ribbon was placed around Fenrir, and the wolf tried to break it. He tried and tried, but the ribbon held him fast.

Incensed, the great wolf slammed shut his maw, biting off Tir's hand, but it was too little too late. The seemingly delicate ribbon was un-breakable and inescapable, and it bound Fenrir in stasis forevermore.

An odd way to put it. Stasis. A state in which nothing changed—it went against the laws of Nature. The ribbon itself was described in such a way that Sanja imagined not a physical bond, but something that more closely resembled a precise melodic chant winding around the beast in an endless current.

"How interesting." She turned another page.

Once the wolf was bound, the gods took a piece of the ribbon and extended and expanded it to fashion it into the Veil to separate Otherlands from one another and from the world of humans. "I have never read this version of the tale."

"What do you make of it?"

"It's the song of worlds," she replied, lacking a better way to describe it. It did feel rather like a song drifting between realms. And it made an ironic sort of sense. To keep two things separate, there had to be something between them to form a barrier. And that something meant a connection between the two, however unintended. "By forging a tangible barrier between the realms, the gods bound them all together."

The prince made some sort of reply, but Sanja didn't hear. Lost in thought, she studied the text, awed at the secrets it revealed.

If someone could perceive the song, they could find the borders between realms. And if they could feel the breaks and pauses, they could drift in and out of them, pass through the Veil between verses as if through doorways or portals. The wall the gods had intended to forge thus became a series of pathways between Otherlands for anyone who knew what to look for.

When one verse came to an end, the pause before another began weakened the barrier. The Veil thinned at such times, allowing for more beings to pass through with ease. That was why human rituals centered on solstices and equinoxes. The rhythm of the world was part of the song itself. Humans with no magic in them would never be able to pass through the Veil on their own. But when the Veil was at its thinnest and powerful beings were more likely to hear their prayers, humans could beseech Others and the gods, and offer gifts in exchange for their magic.

It explained so much.

"And here, is this it?" The last pages had no words at all, only drawings of different shapes scattered in incomprehensible patterns across their surfaces. Tilting her head this way and that, she studied the edges of one page. "It is almost as if…" Setting the rest of the stack aside, she laid out six of the pages before her with their edges touching. "No, that's not right." Sanja rearranged them another way. "Not that way, either." The symbols didn't match up exactly, and somehow she knew it wasn't because of transcription mistakes. The pattern was precise and meticulously copied.

She felt the prince shifting closer as the platter of buns disappeared to give her more room. As she moved the pages about and muttered to herself in frustration, Prince Fal nudged the sheets into different positions but, no matter how they arranged them, the patterns never fit quite right.

Sanja sat back in defeat. "It's no use. There must be pages missing."

"There aren't. These are all of them." Fal moved two of the pages to different positions, continuing to work the puzzle. Three years of staring at those pages and it had never occurred to him that they might be parts of a larger pattern. Sanja had taken one look at them and seen more than he had after staring at the original tome for days on end. Now that he had the promise of progress, he couldn't stop himself trying to solve it.

A song of worlds…

Why did that sound so right?

He put two pages together, fitting the edges in such a way that the partial shapes on one page completed those on the other. All of them seemed to fit that way, one page completing the other in different configurations but never all at the same time.

A strong breeze blew across the green, snatching several pages up into the air. "No!" Fal gave chase, with Sanja right behind him. He managed to catch two of the pages, but two more slipped through his fingers. Sanja caught one of them while the last flipped over and over in the air out of her reach. Fal secured his own pages, then went to her aid but, as he reached for the page, the wind snatched it sideways. Fal spun around to follow and collided with Sanja, knocking them both to the ground.

With his hand over Sanja's on the page, Fal collapsed next to her, glaring up at the swirling sky above them while Sanja laughed. "It's not funny," he groused. "I almost had it figured out."

"You did not," countered the irreverent imp, still laughing. "Oh, don't frown like that. I am sure you will put it all together again."

Startled, he realized she could see him. He was still holding her hand over the page. Did whatever magic she possessed to see through his illusions also allow her to see through his invisibility spell? Did her touch make him visible to the world, or did it merely pull her into his invisibility spell with him?

Fal ought to be more concerned about that. But, looking into her dancing eyes, he felt himself being pulled into her happiness, an answering smile tickling his insides.

Sanja looked away, up to the sky, her cheeks pinkening with a pretty flush. "So I take it you cannot control the wind." One of her curls had tangled around a clover bloom. With a thought, Fal severed the stalk and wove it through her hair to secure it there. She didn't notice, so he added a few others, adorning the wild black mane with flowers.

"All wizards have some control over the elements. Some more, some less. We tend to focus on our strengths and neglect our weaknesses. My greatest strength is water, and I have dabbled some with earth during my lessons with my mother. I have never had cause or opportunity to work with air, and so it remains a mystery."

Her curious gaze once more settled on his true face with ease, without any comprehension of how impossible a feat it ought to be. "And fire?"

"Definitely a weakness," he answered, burning to know what she thought of him. Did she find his features pleasing? "Fire and water do not mix." Before he'd changed, he'd been considered quite handsome, even by Other standards. Lasses had been forever smiling and winking at him, amusing his father and annoying his mother, who'd pushed him that much harder into his studies to prevent him from becoming vain about his looks.

And then his nature had destroyed any possibility of that all on its own.

"They say the two elements ought to be mutually destructive. Yet somehow, they converged in just the right way inside my sister and me to make us into something unique."

"I heard rumors about a dragon," she said, her voice timid.

"Have you, then?"

"When Others speak of your family, they call you Dragonblood."

"It is true," he said, choosing his words with care. "My father's mother gave us the gift of dragon's blood."

Rumors of King Saeran's growing magic had been raising questions long before he'd defied tradition and taken his royal wizard to wife. The two of them had decided early on that, for the sake of everyone involved, it was better to give their people a small part of the truth than let their curiosity lead them where they ought not go.

Better for everyone to believe a long-ago ancestor had inherited blood from an extinct Otherkind than reveal that a true dragon still lived not far to their north. He might well be the last of his kind, and he'd survived this long by hiding from those who would make a trophy of his head. No one wanted to see him hunted for sport. Human and Other alike, the few who were aware of his existence paid him homage by protecting his secret.

Sanja's expression turned dreamy. "I wish I could have met a dragon. Can you imagine how powerful they must have been for their blood to still affect you this way countless generations later?"

"They must have been a sight to behold." Not a lie. Fal had seen the dragon's true form soaring across the sky. He could only imagine how magnificent an entire horde of them must have been, with their scales glittering in the sun and their massive wings casting shadows across the land.

The dragon rarely spoke about his kind. Fal didn't even know how they came to be, or if they'd once had a world of their own. Alas, on this one subject, his great-grandfather didn't indulge unfettered curiosity. Fal had learned not to ask anymore.

"And here you are, wielding water magic with dragon's fire."

"A poetic way to put it," he retorted. "The truth is, many would consider me and my sister to be abominations."

Sanja turned to her side, quirking an eyebrow for him to keep talking.

Fal shifted to match her, intertwining their fingers to a more comfortable position. In the tall grass, no one would see them unless they came looking. The world at large felt far away, as if the two of them had created a secret little Otherland of their own where no one could trespass on their conversation.

Despite that, or perhaps because of it, Fal kept his voice soft enough that not even the wind could carry his words elsewhere. "We defy everything anyone has ever known of magic, Others, and Halflings. We ought not exist."

"Why?"

A bumblebee droned around Sanja's adorned hair, passing clumsily from bloom to bloom. Any of the noble ladies he'd known would have squealed and flailed to get it off, but Sanja didn't seem to notice at all. Fal weaved more flowers through the seams of her frayed dress, shaping them into patterns of knotwork similar to the ones on the cloak she had so admired the day before. The colorful adornments suited her better than gold and gemstones.

She noticed the subtle movement, but Fal didn't want her attention to stray. He enjoyed having her gaze at him so openly, without fear or disgust. He enjoyed being himself for once without any effort at all. "Different Otherkind can mate," he said to keep her focused on him. "They can sire children, but the bloodlines usually end there. Halflings are always complicated. Their magics are strange, unpredictable, and often destructive. Many die before reaching adulthood. Of those who survive, none have been recorded to have children of their own—until my parents. In fact…"

"In fact, what?"

In fact, it had taken dragon's blood to allow Queen Nialei to conceive and give birth to the twins. To this day, Fal didn't understand the magic behind it—the dragon refused to tell him. All he knew was that it had been powerful enough to change Nialei's soul. It had spared her the fate of King Saeran's first wife, a young, human girl whose life had been drained by a child she'd been too weak to carry.

But Sanja didn't need to know that part. The royal couple's story wasn't Fal's to tell. "In fact," he said instead, "my parents defied all the odds by having twins. Liadan and I are, in many ways, more complicated than ordinary Halflings."

"I heard a wise man once say that the greatest struggles are allotted to those meant for the greatest achievements. The gods put obstacles in our path to make us stronger for what is to come. By overcoming them, we prepare ourselves for our ultimate destiny."

Struggle is the driving force of life, he'd once told Liadan. *Without it, everything dies.* "If that is true, then the gods mean for me to save the world," he retorted, but his poor attempt at humor didn't negate the truth of his words. He had, indeed, been tasked with saving the world. And he felt wholly unequal to it.

Sanja smiled. "Songs will be written about it, I am sure." For a moment, her gaze grew distant, and her smile turned sad.

He didn't like the change and couldn't stop himself asking, "What is it?"

She shrugged and shook her head. "I was thinking about destiny. How strange that my path would cross with yours here and now. In the present, something wonderful can occupy the same stretch of time as something terrible. But years from now, which one will be remembered better?"

"You don't think it can be both?"

She reached out to touch the edge of his hood with a delicate fingertip. "I think memories are a strange thing. We choose which events hold importance to us, but our choices change with subsequent events." As she had done with the cloak the day before, Sanja traced the embroidered patterns along the edge of his hood.

His eyelids grew heavy, but he refused to let her out of his sight for a blink. Fal wanted her touch on him so much he held his breath, held perfectly still for fear any move would disrupt her reverie, and spook her into flight. But he couldn't stop his thumb stroking lazy circles over her hand in his. Whatever spell she cast, whatever magic she employed to snare him so thoroughly, Fal was more than willing to succumb.

"A year from now, you might remember me as the girl who read you a book on the green. Or, when you get back to the castle, you might see, or hear, or do something so momentous, it will define this time in your mind, and you will forget all about me."

Never. For as long as Fal lived, he would remember the strangely brilliant girl with flowers in her raven locks, whispering secrets into his soul. "And what will you remember?"

She met his gaze, her eyes at once determined and vulnerable in a way that roused a strange feeling inside him. "I want to remember this moment." A deliberate way to say it. Fal sensed something else hidden behind her words. He wanted to question her about it, to make her tell him what had put such a look in her eyes. Yet, at the same time, all he wanted to do was make that look go away, to chase off whatever fears she harbored and make her laugh again with the joyous abandon she'd shown mere moments ago.

He reached out and caught one of her shining black curls between his fingers. Holding it up to the light, he watched the tumultuous colors of the sky play across its glossy surface. In Wilderheim, it was tradition for a young lass to gift the lad she fancied with a lock of her hair as a keepsake and an unspoken invitation to courtship. To give of oneself showed trust, for it left one vulnerable to magics.

Fal had never expected or wanted such a token from anyone before. Until now.

Above them, a flash of white briefly lit up the sky, drawing his gaze up. When it had faded, Fal watched in dismay as the last sparks of a blue-green swirl faded from the tumult, leaving behind a tangible void. He didn't know which of the Otherlands had just fallen, but he felt its loss like a burning piece of charcoal lodged in his chest.

"People in the market talk about the sky clearing and pray for the day the last light disappears," Sanja said. "But it's not that simple, is it?"

"No," he replied. "Magic never is." Letting go of Sanja's hair, he sat up and reluctantly released her hand, disappearing back into his invisibility spell. "I must go now. They will be looking for me."

Sanja frowned but didn't argue sitting up in preparation to stand. "Yes, of course. Good day, Your Highness."

He hated the look of disappointment that came over her, the way she shrank in on herself, and looked down. But in doing so, she finally noticed the flowers he'd woven through her dress and hair, and Fal allowed himself to linger a moment longer to watch her stand up and crane her neck this way and that, trying to see it all at once.

He savored her laugh of delight and let it carry him from the green all the way to the castle. Beyond all the troubles of his world, and any other, Fal knew no other sight would be more momentous or memorable as the girl dressed in flowers, dancing in sunlight on the green. And for that, he was grateful.

9

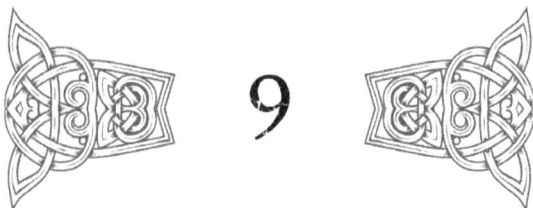

The new day dawned on a soundless flash of red lightning so bright that, for a moment, all the world turned red, and somewhere in the distance rose an unearthly chorus of wailing howls. It sounded as if dogs all over Frastmir were being torn asunder.

"Gods preserve us!" Olga prayed in the kitchen below.

Sanja, still dressed only in her nightshirt, clutched her windowsill and held her breath as the howling went on and on, piercing straight to her soul with such wrenching fear it set her shaking like a leaf.

And then, as abruptly as it had begun, the howling stopped, and the world outside her window became deathly silent. She watched for movement, but no one dared step foot out of doors after that. Even the animals were quiet, huddling out of sight.

At long last, the red haze cleared, but the silence stretched on.

"All right, then?" Gerhart asked softly.

"Yes," Olga replied.

"All right, Sanja?" he called up the staircase.

"I-I'm all right!"

"Then you best get yourself ready. Jarl Steen will be calling anon."

"Do you think he will?" Olga asked. "Now, after this?"

Sanja didn't hear her father answer.

Prying her hands off the windowsill, she clutched her nightshirt and shored up her courage. It was nothing. Soon, the citizens of Frastmir would flood the streets for the morning market, and by sunset, the entire episode would have been forgotten. What was one more oddity among so many?

But she didn't believe her own lie. Gods, she had not needed a bad omen to weaken her resolve today, of all days.

Taking a deep breath, she sat in front of her table and reached for the shears.

The first cut was the hardest, marking the point of no return. Sanja winced as a curl of glossy black hair severed from her mane. She had to take a breath or two to restore her equilibrium, but after that, the task became easier—a snip here, a snip there, and a few more all around. By the time she'd finished, a fluffy nest of hair lay on the floor at her feet, and her head felt light and chilled.

Sanja assessed her reflection on the surface of a polished brass disc. She'd shorn her hair to just below her ears, and now the curls stood out at all angles around her head in a chaotic display that pleased her immensely. She could have cut it shorter still, all the way to her scalp, as some of the male Journeymen did, but that would have been too neat for her purposes. Satisfied with her achievement, she gathered the shorn locks and tossed them out the window.

Next came her clothes. From the wooden chest beside her bed, Sanja withdrew the bundle she'd hidden at the bottom. Inside was her hair shirt and trousers, procured from the weaver in exchange for Sanja's ivory comb. An exorbitant price, but well worth it in the end.

The garment itched her all over when she put it on. The shirt was too big, causing the V of the neck to gape too wide over her chest and the sleeves to dangle past her fingertips. The hem reached the middle of her thighs and was split down both sides up to her waist. Underneath, the trousers bunched at her waist, where the too-wide opening was cinched with a length of string. It wasn't comfortable or attractive.

It was perfect.

And just in time, too. Someone was knocking on the front door. Sanja heard her mother's footsteps rush over from the kitchen, and the door groan open on Olga's ready greeting of, "Jarl Steen, welcome!" She raised her voice deliberately so Sanja would hear and come down without needing to be summoned.

Sanja hated when either of her parents did that. Out of spite, she remained where she was, listening in as their guest entered and made himself at home, no doubt by occupying Gerhart's favorite chair. She pressed her ear to her door, but their conversation had hushed to murmurs. She wouldn't be able to hear anything unless she came out.

Well, it would have come to this sooner or later. Sanja raised her chin and reached for the door, but at the last moment, pulled back. Her gaze strayed to the jug filled with wildflowers. What a change a day could make. How different she was today from the girl covered in flowers only yesterday. It all seemed like a beautiful, faraway dream now, but those flowers were real. They were her proof that at least for one afternoon, Sanja, the daughter of a humble carver, had lain in the grass hand in hand with a prince. Whatever awaited her downstairs and forever after, at least she would always have that.

Holding the memory before her like a shield, Sanja squared her shoulders, raised her chin high, and stepped out of her room. Her insides quivered as she padded down the creaky stairs toward her destiny. She traced the wall with one clammy hand to keep herself steady while her mouth and throat dried out more with every step. *Don't falter. He must never suspect the slightest hesitation.*

Gerhart heard her first and came to meet her, already anxious at having kept their guest waiting this long. When he saw what she'd done to herself, his face turned ashen. Sanja gulped to see his hands tremble, but all he said was, "You have a visitor." He did not wait for her response, turning his back as if the sight of her was too much to bear.

Like a lamb to the slaughter, Sanja followed him toward the rest of their meager company until she had no choice but to step out from behind him and face Jarl Steen on her own. *This is it. Fare thee well, Jarl Steen, and good riddance, too!* She was ready to see this done.

Only there was no jarl waiting for her with a quaff of wilted flowers clutched in his meaty fist. Instead, a young man stood there, facing away with his hands at his back as he conversed softly with Olga. Had the jarl sent a messenger in his stead? He didn't wear Steen colors. His clothes gave no indication of rank, station, or trade, though, by his lean form and clean attire, Sanja would guess him to be a merchant or scholar of some sort. Clean trousers and tunic, a long blue jerkin, belted at the waist, and knee-high boots neither old nor new. He had no weapons or purses, nothing she would have expected a messenger or errand boy to carry. Odd, that.

At their entrance, Olga gasped, causing the young man to turn around. He was handsome, by all accounts, but in so common a way he could have been anyone. If Sanja had ever met him before, she had no recollection of it. His ready smile waned a bit in surprise before it spread wider, his blue eyes crinkling at the corners with suppressed mirth. "Miss Sanja," he said in greeting, "it is good to see you again."

"Again? But I—"

"I was just telling Mistress Carver of the book you asked about on your last visit to the library. A truly fascinating volume and a rare one. The brothers were quite impressed with your request."

Sanja's face felt hot with embarrassment. "Forgive me, but I—"

"I must apologize on their behalf. Sadly, they were unable to locate Master Valco's Third Treatise on Elemental Governance in the archives." At this, he turned to Olga to say, "It would have been a wondrous find if they had, you understand. In his day, Valco was renowned throughout Wilderheim as the authority on elemental magics, and his work has formed the foundation of magical study ever since. The brothers were very excited at the possibility that one of his original works might be housed under their roof." Facing Sanja once more, he continued, "But it appears Brother Otto, who had originally brought the volume and recorded it in the registry, took it with him again when he resumed his travels some years ago."

By the time he shook his head with dramatic regret, both Olga and Gerhard wore identical expressions of utter perplexity. Sanja would have laughed, if only she weren't equally as confused. But she repeated the book's title in her mind so she would know to look for it later. It sounded fascinating!

Elemental magic was considered to be the purest of all, and extremely difficult for humans to master. Each element was said to possess its own temperament. To manipulate it, a witch or wizard first had to woo or cajole the element's cooperation, and even then, success was never guaranteed. Those who possessed elemental magic were few and far between. Those who survived its awesome power into adulthood were rarer still. They carried a high rank among wizards and were the only magic workers allowed to hold the title of Mage, though Sanja suspected that most of the clever ones declined the honor. Elemental Mages tended to die young and always in the service of someone whose ambitions far surpassed the limits of the natural order.

"…readily volunteered to deliver their offering," their guest was saying. "I hope Miss Sanja forgives my saying so, but I have never met such an intelligent young lady before."

Gerhart wrung his hands. "All well and good, but books are no substitute for a husband and children."

Looking at Sanja as if her father hadn't spoken a word, the young man added, "I could not resist an opportunity to see her again."

Sanja flushed, grasping for something to say in response. He must have mistaken her for someone else. She'd never seen the man before in her life. Had she?

He broke their shared stare first to face Olga again. "Forgive me. I'm rambling."

Yes, he was. And she *wasn't*—he didn't give her a chance.

"Master Falwyck, I do not wish to be rude, but we are expecting company at any moment. Noble company. Sanja's suitor. You must be familiar with Jarl Steen? And, well—"

"He must not find another keeping company with his betrothed," Gerhart said, glancing out the window as if the jarl was already waiting there.

"Da!"

Gerhart flushed as his wife and daughter both glared at him. But he found his voice to remind them, "You have a contract, daughter."

"Aye," Olga returned, raising her chin, "and what does it say?"

Gerhart began to answer, then stopped himself.

Olga winked at Sanja. "You were saying, Master Falwyck?"

The young man inclined his head. "I have come at a bad time. And I cannot help but impose upon you further. You see, I did not come only to deliver the Brothers' books to Miss Sanja. I came to ask your permission, Master Carver, Mistress Carver, to court your daughter."

Was Sanja dreaming? Was this some fevered hallucination? He could not have said what she thought he'd said.

"We give it gladly," Olga answered at once. "You are most welcome here at any time, young man. And, husband, now we ought to feed the livestock. Let the lovebirds talk awhile." Ignoring his protests, Olga took hold of Gerhart's arm and dragged him out the kitchen door.

Sanja could hear them launch into an argument as soon as the door slammed shut, their voices fading as they went a ways off, well beyond their little chicken coop. How could they leave their only daughter alone with a stranger? He could be a vagabond or a murderer!

"That was unexpected," Master Falwyck said. "Well done, you. The hair, the costume—I am impressed. But I trust you do not expect it all to chase *me* out the door."

Sanja whirled on him. "Who are you?"

The man grinned, his blue eye aglitter. A trickster of some sort, no doubt. And of all the houses he could have chosen to pester, he'd walked into hers. "You don't recognize me? Good. Then no one else will, either."

There was something familiar about him now that he'd shed his polite manners. The wry tone, the subtle note of insult somehow mixed with respect in the same breath, the eyes…

Sanja gaped. "*You!*"

He grinned, and his face rippled in a shift so subtle she would have missed it if she weren't looking for it. "Did you know Castle Frastmir has its own royal library? It houses all official records and census documents. Three of my most thorough people have pored over all of them, going back a score of years, and do you know what they discovered?"

The crown prince of Wilderheim was standing in her father's decrepit old cottage, wearing a stranger's face, talking about records and census documents. How had her life come to this level of absurdity?

"It appears there is only one Sanja currently living within the city of Frastmir. An incredible stroke of luck, wouldn't you say?"

Sanja was speechless. Meeting him on the green had been one thing, more like a spell-induced vision than anything resembling reality.

Out there, it'd been easy to pretend they were on equal footing, two strangers crossing paths at random on their ways elsewhere. But this…

There was no escaping the harsh contrast of the prince filled with so much magic it created an entirely different shape for him in Sanja's groaning, dark little abode. His presence was no less overwhelming than Jarl Steen's. But instead of making her feel like a helpless doe about to be shot down, Prince Fal left Sanja in a state of utter confusion, feeling out of place, throwing into stark focus how unworthy she was to stand in his presence.

His wicked grin waned. "You are not saying anything. Are you all right?"

"All I wanted was to escape Jarl Steen."

Prince Fal looked around pointedly. "And by his absence, I would say you must have succeeded. My compliments. Was it the hair or the hairshirt that did it, do you think?"

"What?"

He gestured at her, and Sanja remembered what she'd done to herself before coming downstairs. Embarrassed, she ducked her head and fingered the quaff of curling hair at her temple. Though Sanja had fully expected and prepared for her eventual Journey knowing all of Frastmir would see her this way, she hadn't cared about what they might think of her. The opinions of strangers had never mattered to her before. Why should they now?

But she'd never considered that she might find herself in Prince Fal's presence again before then, or that she would feel like an utter fool with him bearing witness to the depth of her desperation. Sanja was battling for her life and freedom the only way she could, but to him, this would be nothing but a jest, a momentary amusement at her expense.

"I think it was the hair," Prince Fal guessed. "Most noblemen like their women pretty and biddable, and *biddable* is not a word I would ever ascribe to you." Sanja wanted to take offense, but he said it with so much appreciation in his voice. Was it part of his illusion? "Take away the beauty of your hair, and… Well, suffice to say your strategy was good." He huffed. "Please say something."

"It wasn't me," Sanja said. She chanced a look at him long enough to see his questioning frown before she dropped her gaze to the floor. "We heard the dogs howl this morning. No one will come out through the city after that."

His mirthful voice gentled when he said, "I did. And others will, too, eventually."

"Why did you lie to my parents about wanting to court me? They will take you at your word, you know."

"Good."

Sanja frowned. "You truly intend to court me?"

"I…" He winced, rolling his shoulder as if it pained him. "Forgive me, I don't want to frighten you, but wearing a single face for so long is extremely uncomfortable. I have to release it." He hunched over, and his borrowed form shivered, falling away from him with a splash. From the resulting puddle, a geyser welled up, flooding the room up to Sanja's knees. She gasped, but aside from a slight chill around her feet that could just as easily have been caused by a draft, she felt nothing.

It's another illusion, she told herself and kept repeating it in her mind as the water rose above her waist to her chest, then above her head, all the way to the ceiling. Breathing was an awkward exercise when each inhale felt as if she was about to drown, but Sanja persisted until her mind adjusted to the strangeness of it.

"I fear I come to you on grave business today," Prince Fal said in his own voice.

Tearing her gaze away from a massive eel twining around her legs, she found the crown prince standing a mere handful of paces away, the hood of his cloak pulled back to reveal his true face. With Master Falwyck's good humor stripped away, he looked a little sad. Tired, too. He was a mere two years older than Sanja, but as the future king, the weight of Wilderheim sat heavy upon his shoulders, causing him to hunch a little.

His dark hair was neatly trimmed just below his shoulders, with warrior braids framing his face on either side. His true clothes, unlike Master Falwyck's, befitted his royal lineage, sewn from rich fabrics and embroidered by a hand far more talented than hers. He wore a silver chain about his neck, and one more at his waist, partly obscured by his cloak. Sanja suspected the adornments served a magical purpose of some sort. He didn't seem the type to wear his wealth on his sleeve—he wasn't even wearing his crown.

"Don't be afraid." His mouth twisted into a bitter smile. "This is merely the truth of what I am—illusions upon illusions, and no way out. I can contain them for a little while, but they always pull me back under in the end, along with everyone around me. This is the only way I can be myself—by flooding everything and everyone around me in illusion. And if I give it free rein, it will only keep growing larger and more convincing."

Fal could feel the water begin to push past the boundaries of this little room already. The walls would appear to be leaking from the outside, water pouring down to pool around the cottage. It would draw notice before long; he didn't have much time. "Take my hand."

Sanja clasped her hands behind her back, shifted farther away. She looked frightened yet unharmed.

"Look around you, Sanja. Do you see the water? The fish? The mud beneath your feet?"

"It's only an illusion," she replied. "It's not real."

"Yet others would already have drowned in your place." He chanced a step closer, relieved when she stood her ground. "Please, take my hand. Let me show you what you do to me."

"Am I meant to swoon at such pretty turns of phrase?"

"What? No. Gods, girl, you must stop wasting your mind on those bloody maudlin poems. Nobody speaks that way."

"You just did."

Fal bit back a frustrated growl. "You have my word as the crown prince of Wilderheim—"

"The Prince of Deceit!"

Fal glared at her until she flushed and drew back. "As charming as I find that name, I would have expected better from you by now."

Head bowed in meek submission, she worried the frayed edges of her hair shirt. "What do you want from me?" Any more of her tugging and the cheap garment would unravel altogether.

This had been a terrible idea. He should never have come here.

But even as he thought it, he took a seat, hoping it would put her at ease and restore her temper. He didn't like seeing her so subdued.

"Will you sit with me a moment?" Otherlands were falling ever faster. Time was running out; he needed Sanja's help, and he could not wait any longer.

With the gravity of obeying a distasteful order, she took a chair, then furtively moved it farther away from his.

Fal was at a loss as to how to begin. He'd rehearsed the speech several times in his chambers, and again on the way here, and now that the moment had come for him to speak, he couldn't think of a single word.

Sanja's foot tapped out a nervous rhythm, waiting for him to say something. "What, already?"

"Do not rush me, woman, this is important."

She scowled.

Her lack of concern was unsurprising, given she didn't know what was happening, but even so, "Have you not seen the lights in the sky? Did you sleep through the storm that caused them?"

Sanja stilled. "I noticed. People said it was world's end. Many have left already, and more are whispering about fleeing to Ravetia, of all places. They say if ever there was a place safe from magic…" She frowned, shaking her head. "It's all nonsense, of course." It wasn't a question, but the way she looked at him, with hope and expectation that he, the crown prince, would surely allay her fears, made it one.

Fal struggled to speak, the words heavy and creeping their way out barely above a whisper. "It is not."

"What do you mean?"

"The people are right to fear. Our kingdom is ending," he said.

"Our kingdom is…"

"Ending," Fal supplied. "The storm, the sky, the howling… The Veil is gone, Sanja. Ragnarok is coming for us fast. The lights fading from our sky? Each one is an Otherland falling to Fenrir's advance. He will destroy anything with the smallest trace of magic inside it."

Her face grew pale, and her eyes rounded even as her eyebrows drew together in a frown. "Respectfully, Your Highness, such jests are in very poor taste." Despite her dry tone, her voice was unsteady.

"I think there may be a way to keep Wilderheim safe. But I need your help to find it."

"You are serious."

"The end of everything is not something anyone would jest about. You already knew there is more to the lights than meets the eye. You said so yourself. Now you know what it is."

"If the Veil is gone, then…" Her eyes grew wide. "Then that means the gods themselves will lose their power anon. There will be no one left to pray to. Nothing left to stand against our destruction."

"There will be me," he insisted. "And, I hope, you."

"*Me?*" She shoved to her feet, toppling over her chair. He reached out to catch her as she tripped over it, but Sanja pulled away from his reach, keeping him at a distance. "Have you lost your royal mind?" she demanded, flapping her arm to shoo away a bright red fish swimming too close past her face. "This is a matter for Mages and Others, not a useless, common human. The only thing I could do is die." Color rose in her cheeks while words continued to pour out. "A horrible, bloody death at the hands of some monster, or my own people, desperate to escape. And even if you wanted to sacrifice me for virgin blood—" Suddenly, she became completely still, the annoying fish forgotten. Her terrified gaze met his. "Is that what you want from me?"

"No!" How had she come up with that?

"I don't believe you!"

"Will you let me explain?"

"I think I have heard quite enough, thank you."

If she wouldn't hear reason, he'd have to show her.

Fal reached out and swiftly caught her hand in his, holding on tight when she would have pulled away. "Look," he ordered, stopping her struggles with the power of a royal command. "Look around you, Sanja, and look hard." When she cast a baleful glance about the dry room, he released her and winced as water once again welled up around them. "Do you see now? This is why I came to you."

When he reached for her hand again, Sanja's fingers curled around his, and for a moment, both of them stood in silence, taking in the miracle of a perfectly ordinary room.

His voice, subdued into soft, grave tones, disturbed its intrinsic serenity. "My parents were interrupted in the middle of a long, involved working of Other magic that would have prevented this very thing. When the Veil disintegrated, they became trapped in an Otherland. I cannot reach them, and I cannot wait for them to find their way back on their own. The magic they began must be brought to completion if we are to survive Ragnarok. But how can I finish it like this?"

Gently disentangling himself from her hold, he stepped away, allowing the illusions to return. They didn't flood back, merely faded into being like a trick of the light, or a desert mirage. Underwater, the old, worn chamber took on an eerie air of ageless antiquity. The longer the illusion remained, the more it began to change their surroundings, turning faded drapes bright and new, and worn wood smooth and polished. The old little cottage revived within the water's reach, restored to what it must have looked like when the family still had the means to keep it up.

"You are far from a common human, Sanja. You took one look at the puzzle I gave you and saw something I had never noticed before. You affect me as no one, and nothing ever has. Magic or not, whatever is inside you is strong enough to do what no one else, wizard or Other has ever managed to do before. Including me. And that makes you something I had not dared to pray for in many years: hope."

At this, she brought her gaze to his, speaking volumes while her lips remained sealed by a terrible, wondrous silence.

"If I am to stand against the end of everything, I will need powerful allies to stand beside me. I will need you."

"But I—"

"I cannot promise it will be easy. If half the tales about Fenrir are true, what we're about to face will terrify the bravest of men, and I hate to the bottom of my soul that I must ask you to face it with me. But ask I must. Because if all you do is hold my hand, it will be a gesture far more powerful than any spell I could ever speak."

"Your Highness, I…" She reached over her shoulder as though to tug on a curl of hair that was no longer there. When she encountered nothing, an odd look passed quickly over her face before she bowed her head and clasped her hands before her. "Duty alone would compel my obedience."

He frowned. "No, that is not… I am not giving you an order, Sanja, I am—"

"And, given a choice, it would be my honor to stand by your side and do whatever I could, even if it cost me my life," she said louder, more forcefully, before quieting once more. "But I am not free to make such a choice."

Fal noted the nervous clutch of her hands, the high points of color in her cheeks. She was tense, but not with fear. The boundless energy making her all but quiver in place was nothing as simple as that. It was something else. "There is a contract," he recalled her father mentioning something of one. "With your intended, I presume. Jarl Steen?" Her mother's admission, and a most unwelcome one.

She gave an infinitesimal nod.

"Your father wants this match." But while the man seemed intent on handing his daughter to a titled noble, his wife, at least, had given the impression she might want better for Sanja.

Living in the heart of Wilderheim's castle city, the family must have been either too busy or too disinterested in royal gossip to have escaped the rumors about Jarl Steen. All of them were true. Steen was a savage, refused by every honorable woman he'd ever courted. The only reason King Saeran tolerated his presence at court was that he had no choice. Steen's clan occupied a long swath of land on the Ravetian border. His keeps and his men-at-arms formed the first line of defense against their attacks.

Steen's forefathers had earned and amassed more wealth with their service to the crown than any one man could spend in a lifetime—a fact which had not stopped Steen from trying. He poured as much gold into his lavish keeps as ale down his gullet, and his coins flew as quickly as his massive fists.

Sanja would not last a fortnight as his wife.

And if it came to light that Fal had interfered with his betrothed in any way, Steen would declare war on the crown immediately, and he'd find ample support from the other nobles. Fal would lose the kingdom and any chance of stopping Ragnarok.

"My father was trying to protect me by securing me a husband who could provide for me and settle my family's debts with a bride price. Neither was a prospect he could refuse." Another wretched twist of her hands as she admitted, "I was sold for a pouch of gold coins. My mother insisted on a contract to be drawn to that effect, and Jarl Steen demanded it be signed in blood."

Cold fingers of dread ran up his spine. "By whom?"

"By me."

Blood bound all things with powerful magic not even the gods could undo. A promise sealed in blood could not be escaped, save through death. "What are the terms?"

"A wager, of sorts. One month's reprieve, during which time I must either marry another or complete the cleric's Journey and take my robes. If I succeed in either, my father will receive the full bride price from Jarl Steen, and I will be free of any obligation. If I fail to do either, I must marry Jarl Steen for one third the bride price." Her mouth twisted unhappily. "I have a fortnight and five days left."

Fal gaped, feeling his illusions swirl out like mud around his feet. "What in Frigga's name would possess you to sign such a contract—in blood no less!"

Sanja raised her gaze, her eyes burning defiant. "I—had—no—choice. The agreement was struck without my knowledge. All I could do was mitigate."

The mud spread out, sinking Sanja's feet, and she didn't notice while Fal choked on an irrepressible urge to shake her; to personally drag her father to the stocks and rip Steen's innards out through his throat. "But you said you wanted to rid yourself of a suitor. You must realize the oath will still compel you to wed him, whether he wants you or not."

"Of course I realize that—I am not a simpleton."

"Then why bother?"

"Because I presented Jarl Steen with a challenge, and I am afraid he will do whatever it takes to win. Part of the reason he keeps coming back to sit here with me and endure the painful silence is to take away my time to prepare for the Journey. I fear..."

"What?"

Sanja wrung her hands together, staring out the window to escape his gaze.

"Tell me."

"I fear he will put as many obstacles in my path as possible to make me lose the wager. But if he no longer wants me, he will step back and at least allow me to make the Journey unhindered."

Her insight into the man's character was accurate. Steen hated losing. If he could cheat his way to victory, he would. Knowing he could not interfere with Sanja's Journey once she began, he was doing his best to delay it until she ran out of time.

A blood oath, for all the gods' sake.

Despite facing a most formidable opponent, Sanja's strategy was admirable. To have refused Steen outright would have sent the man into a rage; he would have destroyed Sanja and her parents to save face. Instead, she'd bought herself time to escape his clutches—and Fal suspected she'd made him think the whole thing had been his idea. She'd thought of everything, considered each angle, and addressed every threat to the best of her abilities. It proved to Fal that Sanja's mind was, indeed, a force to be reckoned with.

But wits alone would not be enough to bring her safely through a challenge of this magnitude. Sanja would need all the help she could get to win. "You truly intend to undertake a Journey?"

She shrugged. "No one besides the jarl will have me, Your Highness. What else is a girl to do? The only way out of a blood oath is death."

The way she said it made him tense. All around them, mud churned up into clouds of murk that shaped themselves into a vision. There, just behind Sanja's left shoulder, a bulky figure fell back onto the flat surface of a bed while another, smaller one turned away. The bottom of its cloud flared out into skirts, the top swirling tighter into the shape of a woman's curves as one tendril split off, forming an arm. A second tendril kicked up from the ground, straightening into a long dagger that floated into the female figure's grasp before she stabbed it straight into her own heart.

Fal sucked in a sharp breath, knowing the vision was true—he could read it in Sanja's fervid gaze. If she failed to escape the binds of her contract, Sanja was prepared and resolved to take her own life.

Fal could not permit either to happen. "What if Master Falwyck did?"

She frowned.

"Have you, I mean. Court you." He'd already committed to that much, at least. As long as he kept his mask firmly in place, no one should suspect he was someone else.

"It would not be enough. The contract is specific. I must *marry*. And I cannot marry someone who does not exist."

Then marry me.

The words were there in his mind, not to be spoken aloud. Even if Fal were free to marry by choice, he was still Other, and Sanja was not. Without the dragon there to spare her the ravages of illness, old age, and the magic of his bloodline, the way he'd done with Liadan's mate, Fal dared not bind himself to her. He could not become the reason this inexplicable, vibrant girl's finite life shortened further still.

Nor could he bring himself to walk away. He could feel the boundary beyond which disaster loomed. It was a line so close that one wrong step would bring him across; so thin, a strong puff of air would blow it away. And on the other side, Sanja with her shorn hair and large, sad eyes. The boundless energy within her called to something inside him, keeping him still when he ought to be running the other way, pulling him toward her—toward her doom.

We are all doomed, anyway.

"Then I will simply have to help you through the Journey."

If anything, the proclamation seemed to deepen her confusion. "Why would you do that?"

"Because I need you." With a wry smile, he added, "And because I don't believe it occurred to you that the death to release you from the blood oath need not be yours."

"It occurred to me," she admitted.

His esteem for her rose another notch. "Then, by now, it must already have occurred to you that I need you enough to have your unwanted suitor permanently removed if you asked."

Her guilty flush was answer enough.

"Yet, you have not asked."

"And I will not," she declared stubbornly. "I am not a murderer, your Highness, and I would no more ask someone to kill for me than I would carry out the deed myself. No matter the circumstances, my path was set the moment I signed the contract. The consequences are on my head and mine alone." Fal wanted to argue, but she shook her head and changed the subject. "In any case, you cannot help with the Journey. It isn't allowed."

"No one is allowed to interfere in a Journey, true. But there are ways to ease its torments without breaking the rules. For all I am asking of you, it is the least I could do." Fal knew healing spells that could mend her wounds. He could make certain Sanja had food and drink each night and shelter from the cold so she might rest and recover her strength for the next day. He could mentor her through aspects of the second part of Journey, as well. There were scrolls in the royal library dedicated solely to the Journey procedures and rituals. Fal would have to be careful not to reveal too much, but it could be done. "And once you have passed, you will be free to help me."

"And if I fail regardless?" she asked quietly.

If she failed, that dagger would take her from Fal before he got the chance to learn why Sanja alone in all of Frastmir could disarm his wayward illusions. If she died, Fal would slowly disappear, and Ragnarok would tear Wilderheim apart.

Marry another, or complete the cleric's Journey. "You will not," he declared with a confidence borne of desperation. A fortnight and five days. With Fal's help, Sanja could enter the clerics' sanctuary in as little as a week. "I give you my word. Steen will never have you." Fal would dispatch the wretch if it came to that, whether Sanja wanted him to or not. She was too important to Wilderheim to die so senselessly. Keeping that part to himself, he offered his hand to seal the pledge. "Are we agreed?"

Sanja hesitated for so long he thought she would refuse, but then she put her hand in his. "Agreed."

The moment she touched him, the mud around them drained down through the wooden floor. Bright morning light spilled in through the open window, warming Fal through his cloak. He took a deep breath and drew his shoulders back, the weight of his illusions suddenly gone. He felt stronger, lighter, entirely in control of himself. He could see better and hear the softest sounds as if the fog he'd been wading through for years had suddenly lifted, and all for a simple handshake.

Loath to give it up, Fal held on longer than he ought, enjoying the feel of Sanja's hand in his, the play of light in her eyes, and the charming disarray of her shorn hair.

Sanja's tongue darted out to wet her lips. "Gods all bless, I hope you keep your word."

"I always do."

She closed her eyes and whispered, "Because if you can't…"

He didn't need to look into her mind to know she was thinking of the only other alternative she was prepared to accept.

"It will never come to that," he said, squeezing her hand a little tighter to press the promise into her skin. She swayed forward, her feet shifting her a half-step closer, and when she looked up at him, he saw all of her in the depths of her moss green eyes. All her passion, her fear, her determination, and a sense that, no matter how hard she fought, she would still lose. But she would fight, nonetheless, ready to lay down her life, if need be, rather than give in to despair. As stalwart as any warrior Fal had ever met.

Long ago, during one of his many lectures on warfare, the dragon had told the twins, "Never lose sight of what you are fighting for. The moment you lose your purpose, you have lost the war."

"We fight for Wilderheim," little Liadan had declared proudly.

"Which part?" the dragon had countered. "Wilderheim is a big place, little one. A kingdom is too vast a dream to protect. Your purpose must be small enough to hold onto, and treasured enough to fear losing. For your parents, you are that purpose. And when you are old enough, you will find yours, and that will become your Wilderheim."

Sanja was fighting for her freedom.

And I will fight for her.

As if she'd heard his thoughts, her eyes widened a little, her lips parting in breathless surprise, and once again, Fal felt an intense urge to catch those lips with his own, to steal a taste he had no right to crave. He touched a soft curl at her temple, brushed it back, tracing the delicate curve of her ear. Sanja tilted her chin up a little higher…

Behind the kitchen door, Olga and Gerhart's voices floated closer. *Out of time.*

Fal reluctantly released Sanja and stepped back, painstakingly resuming his shape as the forgettable Master Falwyck. "Your parents are returning," he said when she blinked at him askance. "I will call on you again tomorrow. In the meantime, I have brought you a gift." He indicated a stack of books beside the door, neatly tied together with a length of string.

"But… That is…"

"A fortune bound in leather. Yes, I know. But you cannot very well help me if you don't know what is happening, can you? This is but a fraction of everything I have studied over the years, along with a journal that condenses my findings up to this point. Within those pages are secrets of magics so ancient they have been forgotten by all but time and one very old dragon. I told your parents they have been loaned to you by the library so they would not be tempted to sell them."

"Master Falwyck," Olga called from the kitchen, "will you share a meal with us?"

"To my regret, I cannot, Mistress Carver. Perhaps another time. I must take my leave now." Fal bowed to Sanja's parents, then to her. Holding her gaze, he promised, "Tomorrow."

Sanja nodded, but she was already turning away from him to explore the books. He grinned, charmed by the delicate reverence with which she caressed the topmost book.

Tomorrow they would have more time to talk.

If Sanja could tear herself away from the treasures he'd brought her.

And if he could keep his thoughts on anything other than her lips.

10

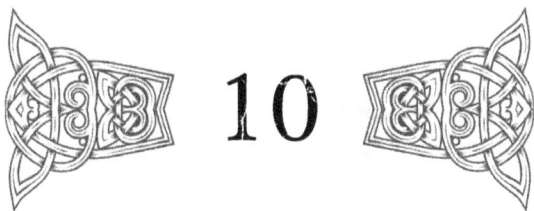

He dreamed of battle. Two great armies clashed all around him, swords clanging and arrows flying. Fire scorched a nearby field, filling the air with thick smoke and obscuring his sight with shadows. The sky was as black as night, throwing into stark relief the soundless flashes of colorful lights winking out into darkness—Otherlands disappearing in rapid succession Fenrir was coming for them all.

Fal blocked a speartip with his shield, his feet slipping on a fallen banner as the enemy forced him back. He twisted the shield, snapping the tip off the spear, and ran the soldier through. The grip of his sword was drenched with blood, and more of it dripped down his face. He adjusted the chipped shield on his arm and wiped his wet cheek on his shoulder.

Time seemed to slow as he looked at the carnage all around him. The battlefield was littered with hundreds of dead soldiers already, their bodies trampled into the mud by hundreds upon hundreds still locked in battle. He sought Liadan's fire amid the chaos, but far too much of it already blazed left and right, and the din of screams disguised her battle cry.

At his feet, the ground had turned to dark mud, pools of blood reflecting the sky back at Fal. It hurt like a long needle stabbing into him to witness each light going dark. He had no time to mourn them when his own world was dying. Thunder rumbled above, threatening a storm and fear knotted his insides. He looked up once more, hoping it had only been a fluke, but a fat raindrop splashing down onto his cheek confirmed his worst fear.

Fal had to retreat. Already, the air felt thick, and flashes of the battlefield miles away obscured his sight. Shadows flickered all around him amid flashes of a brightly polished blade cutting down his soldiers. He sensed magic in it, as he had each time he'd seen that sword in his visions, yet each time he sought its wielder's identity, he met with darkness.

A soldier came at him, the red cross on his tabard no longer distinguishable beneath the muck of battle. His mind weary and his body weak, Fal blocked the soldier's battle ax with his sword, rather than duck out of the way. The impact forced him to his knees. He gritted his teeth, pushing back with all the strength he had left, to no avail. He could not hold out much longer. That ax would cleave him in two.

Suddenly the solder spit up blood as the tip of a curved blade forced its way out through his chest. Wide-eyed, he tipped sideways, taking his ax with him.

Liadan grasped Fal's arm and pulled him to his feet. Her eyes blazed with fire behind a braid that had fallen over her black horn-crown. Her being glowed with fierce strength like a berserker drunk on the rage of battle. With entire fields burning bright, his sister would not lack for power. "Wilderheim will not die on its knees," she snarled at him through the sharp fangs filling her mouth, reminding him so much of their dragon grandfather. Her grip fed strength into his exhausted body, but nothing would shield him from the madness the rain was about to bring.

As Fal recovered, still connected with his sister, he felt something within her that made him grow cold with dread. "Take to the sky," he ordered. "Now!" Away from the armies, beyond the reach of their weapons.

"And leave you to die?"

"Liadan—"

She shoved him aside to meet another enemy soldier head-on, her curved blade making quick work of him and his three comrades. The two coming for her from the back met with Fal's sword and fell in short succession.

Liadan retrieved her other sword and put her back to Fal's. They were surrounded.

"You must go!" Fal tried again. "For the child's sake, if not mine." Against all odds, his sister had managed to conceive. If there was any chance for the child to survive, Fal had to get her somewhere safe.

He felt Liadan tense at his back. "Won't be the first time I have lost a child. Or the last." She tried to make it sound careless, but Fal wasn't fooled. Her grief was a living thing, coiling inside her, biting at her heart—and now at his.

A vision of women running through a nearby raided village blinded him just as the soldiers attacked. He gave a shout, bringing up his shield to block a thrust and slashed sideways. Between rapid blinks, he saw his enemy again, then Liadan's, then another place entirely.

"Oh, no," Liadan whispered as a few random drops turned into a downpour. She looked back at him, her eyes dimming anxiously. Then a furious snarl turned her face into something beastly, and she faced her enemy once more and screamed, bursting into flame, scorching their foes to dust where they stood as she transformed.

Within moments, the thick mud at their feet turned into pools and creeks, the earth already soaked with too much blood to drain the rainwater away. Fal became blind and deaf to the world around him as everything the water touched flooded into his mind. He saw everything, heard everything for miles around. He felt a thousand deaths, smelled smoke mixed with blood and bile, and tasted hopeless prayers on his tongue, knowing there was no one left to answer them.

His sister's voice echoed through the madness: "Wake up! *Wake up!*"

Fal started awake to the sound of someone banging on his bed-chamber door.

"Wake up, brother, you're flooding the castle!"

Drenched with sweat, shaken to his core by the vision already fading from his waking mind, Fal got out of bed and unlocked the door, making an effort to pull back his illusions.

Liadan glared at him from across the threshold. "We have been summoned to a council meeting."

"I can't," he replied, rubbing his face to wake himself up. He felt exhausted. "I have somewhere I need to be."

"Yes, you do. At the council meeting. It was not a request." She frowned at him. "Are you all right?"

There was something he ought to ask her, wasn't there? Something important. Something... The fleeting thought faded away, leaving him with the unnerving sense that a vital detail had slipped his mind. "Make excuses for me, will you? I need to set myself to rights before I can present myself to that hornet's nest."

Liadan nodded. "You look like you fought through a war last night."

The distant sound of clashing swords chased a chill up his spine. "I must not have slept well. It's nothing. Go, you know how they hate to be kept waiting."

His sister snorted. "Our parents have allowed those old dotards far too much freedom if you ask me."

"Spoken like a true queen," he teased, closing the door in her face.

It didn't take him long to put himself to rights and make his way to the council chambers. He walked in intending to tell them the meeting would either be postponed or carry on without him. Sanja was waiting for him, no doubt with plenty to say about the books he'd left with her yesterday.

But there'd be no shirking this meeting. Not when maps were laid out on the long table with bright tokens stacked on either side. Liadan looked up from the map before her, her gaze worried. Something was wrong.

"Your Highness, at last. Now we can begin."

Liadan came around the table. "A moment, Councilors."

"What's happening?" he asked her in a whisper.

"Our ally in Synealee sent word of armies gathering for battle," she said. "The council is of the opinion that we should prepare for war."

"Why? Has there been any indication that they mean to attack us? They could be arming up against Aegiros."

"The thought has occurred to me, and I already spoke to my mate to make sure he will be ready. Not that I needed to." Of course not. The Imarah tribe had only recently reclaimed their valley. Their numbers might be small, but they were all fierce fighters, always at the ready to defend their home by any means necessary. Whoever came to the First Valley seeking trouble would find a swift death on the burning sands.

"Does he want you back?"

Liadan smiled. "Always. But he knows my duty lies with Wilderheim as much as with Imarah." She made her eyes briefly spark with golden fire as she sent him a glare, silently daring him to argue that point. When all he did was nod, her eyes dimmed back to gray, and she added, "Also, he thinks if Synealee does attack Aegiros, I will be safer here."

Fal would wager every book he'd rescued from his tower that Liadan hadn't told her mate Synealee could just as easily turn on Lyria and Wilderheim. If she had, Tir would have demanded she return to his side forthwith.

"But you and I both know Wilderheim is no longer untouchable." She glanced out the window at the colorful tumult in the sky. "Our neighbors know the kingdom is in distress and ripe for picking."

"Where did this warning come from?"

Liadan hesitated. "Sir Jonah. Remember him?"

How could he forget? Some of his favorite childhood bedtime stories had revolved around the group of knights who'd come to Wilderheim in search of a magical cup. It was the stuff of legend, a story of lovers cursed by fate. The royal wizard Nialei, sworn to stand as the neutral right hand of the king she secretly loved. The young King Saeran, pining for his wizard, but sworn to marry an Aegiran for the sake of peace. Nialei couldn't bear to watch it happen, and so she volunteered to act as a guide for the knights. Their quest led them to the dragon's cave far in the north. And when they returned, everything had changed, including Nialei and the knights.

Over the years, Nialei had remained in contact with them, mourning each one's passing as a brother's until only two remained. Sir Arnaud was a deeply religious man who'd vowed himself into silence in the service of his faith. Sir Jonah was a stalwart soldier in service to Synealee who didn't share the queen's beliefs. Having witnessed magic in Wilderheim, he kept Nialei informed of anything that might pose a threat to her people. He did so at great risk to himself, for in Queen

Genevieve's court, treason was met with swift, cruel punishment.

"He sent two messenger birds," Liadan told Fal. "One with news of the armies and the other to inform Mother that Queen Genevieve had Sir Arnaud burned at the stake."

Fal shuddered. "Gods, she's gone mad."

Liadan hugged herself. "Remember what Mother used to say? 'Beware those who blindly bow to one lone god.'"

Yes, he remembered. "Faith is a powerful thing, my dear," Nialei would tell him any time he giggled at the silliness of it as a child. "Even moreso when it is all a people have."

Queen Genevieve was known far and wide as a ruthless zealot. She had outlawed anything she'd deemed offensive to her god, and punishments for such offenses were said to be brutal. Yet her people suffered willingly for the promise of great reward in the afterlife. They prayed no less fervently than anyone in Wilderheim. The difference was, they all prayed to the same god.

Their faith bound them together. It made them dangerous.

"Is Sir Jonah safe?"

Liadan shrugged. "We know nothing of his whereabouts. It used to be safer that way. The less contact between him and Mother, the better. Now? I hope so, but…" She pulled him out into the hallway and whispered, "When I tried to seek him in the fire, my flames went out."

Fal gaped at her. For a tool of Sight to go blind was one matter. For it to disappear completely…

"This is bad, Fal. Very, very bad."

Again, that distant echo of battle teased his mind with hints of something he'd forgotten. "So, we prepare for war." The words felt ominous, final. He clenched his fists at his sides, wishing to all the gods that Nialei and Saeran would come walking in the front gate to take over for their ill-equipped son.

Liadan laid a hand on his shoulder and squeezed. "I am with you, brother. No matter what. Say the word, and my *kharesh* will ride to defend us."

Fal reciprocated the gesture and touched his forehead to Liadan's. "I am grateful. But you were right from the first. We must speak nothing of this to Tir."

Liadan drew back.

"No, I will not have him weakening his defenses to aid us. Your *kharesh* are spread thin enough as it is. I will not have the Fist Valley fall again because of us."

Liadan dropped her gaze and nodded her acceptance. "Very well."

"Liadan, if we go to war—"

"You will have me at your side, guarding your flank." Her eyes sparked with flames as she said it. Sometimes, this side of her frightened Fal a little. "I have my purpose, brother. I will fight for you, and I will not fail." Liadan was a brilliant warrior and a formidable creature in her own right when she shed her human skin and took to the skies as a true Dragonblood. Still, she was his twin sister, as reckless as she was powerful, and that recklessness had already led her to her death once before.

"You will obey my command and retreat on my order," he told her sternly.

She grinned. "I live to obey."

Councilor Olgier cleared his throat in the doorway. "Shall we begin?"

Fal nodded and unstuck his feet from the floor, shoring up his courage for his first war council meeting. But as he crossed the threshold following Olgier, he stopped once more. "I have a task for you, sister, if you are up to it."

~

The elements are eternal and ever-present. An aspect of one is but a small part of the whole, creating a tangible connection to the eternal, and thus making the passage from one to another possible.

Sanja read the passage again to make certain her eyes had not deceived her. They had not. If she understood correctly, then Prince Fal had discovered a means of travel through the elements themselves. How fascinating.

She could read his excitement in descriptions of the travel he'd already attempted and was so engrossed in the accounts, the dark stain obscuring the last section of text brought her to an abrupt halt. Underneath it, at the bottom of the page, a hastily scribbled note read,

*Waterways between Otherlands frozen. Travel from one to another no
longer possible.*

"Oh." How disappointing. But could he still travel without leaving
the boundaries of a particular world? Wilderheim, for example?

The journal didn't say. The note must have been made recently.

The next page began with accounts of Ragnarok, citing several
different sources.

Prince Fal, it turned out, was meticulous with his record-keeping.
His journal was detailed, but concise, written in a neat, steady hand.
Sanja was certain he must have volumes of random notations and
scribbles somewhere within Castle Frastmir, but what he'd given her
showed no sign of them. This was a transcribed summary of what
must have been years of intense study. And he wanted her help.

Carefully closing the journal, she glanced at the stack of books she
had yet to pick up. If she lived a hundred years, Sanja would never
hope to attain as complete an understanding of magic as was contained
in only one of Prince Fal's journals.

Yesterday, she'd been worried about failing her Journey. Today,
failing *him* worried her even more. What ailed the crown prince of
Wilderheim was nothing as simple as a broken bone that could be
set and healed with time. It appeared to be more akin to a wasting
disease that was slowly robbing him of his ability to exist in reality,
and it could not have begun at a worse time. If Prince Fal was Wilderheim's last hope of survival, then he'd just placed the fate of the
entire kingdom into her clumsy hands, along with his own life. What
was her Journey compared to that? And still, he'd agreed to give her
all the time she needed to complete it—time he didn't have.

From his accounts, Sanja now knew his condition began to manifest
when he came of age. Little things, at first, water appearing to pool
where it ought not be, strange leaks where no source could be found.
Then the illusions had turned on him, changing his appearance and
voice. As more magic had poured out of him and into them, the illusions had grown bigger, more elaborate, and so convincing they'd
fooled others into drowning on dry land. Now, the man who always
spoke the truth was a living, breathing lie.

His journal described in detail how the illusions spilled out of his control and how the larger they became, the more difficult they were to rein in. Yet containing them required so much effort it exhausted him. His soul was not strong enough to keep so much magic contained for much longer. At this stage, Prince Fal might well be right. If he were to let it all loose, he could destroy all of Wilderheim.

Where was he, anyway? They hadn't agreed on a time, but Sanja would have thought he'd be knocking at her door after first light. They had so much work to do and no time to waste.

He'd almost kissed her. Right there by the open window, with the sun shining down on them, and Sanja's hand in the prince's, he'd looked at her with those brilliant blue eyes and touched her so gently…

And, foolish goose that she was, Sanja had wanted that kiss. Even knowing naught would ever come of it, she'd wanted her first kiss to be magical. Decades from now, when she was old and wrinkled, and reading to little children in the library, how wicked it would be to tell them she'd once been kissed by the king?

And if Ragnarok came for them all, Sanja could face the end of her ordinary life with a smile on her lips for having stolen the smallest taste of magic.

The most dangerous words in the world were *what if*.

What if Gerhart had been right? Only the day before, the idea of living her life surrounded by books had filled her with defiant joy. Today, Sanja wondered…

What if life could be better? What if she could escape Jarl Steen, and have her books, and find happiness with someone all at the same time?

What if the prince himself would have her?

At last, there came a knock at the front door.

Sanja raced down the stairs, waving Gerhart aside so she could admit their guest herself. "There you are—oh."

Across the threshold, Jarl Steen paled. "What have you done?" He shoved his way inside, tossed the flowers he'd brought to the floor, advancing on her with angry steps. "What is this?"

Sanja barely heard Olga speaking to Jarl Steen past the thrum of her heart. She put Gerhart's chair between herself and the jarl's advance, grateful to have speed on her side, but she'd underestimated his fury.

The cottage shuddered with each of his heavy footfalls. He took hold of the chair and threw it at the wall to get at her. "I have made allowances for you, girl. But by the gods, this is too much!" One of his massive hands fisted in her shorn hair dragging her closer as he roared in her face, "Am I to have a hairless bride? I will tear out what you have left, you little bitch! I will teach you what happens when you cross me!"

Sanja screamed, tears of pain stinging her eyes. She clawed at his hands, but against his brute strength, her meager struggles were for naught.

Olga ran for the front door, shouting, "Help! Guards! Guards!"

Sanja was about to die, she was sure of it. Because for all of her qualms of conscience about murder, Jarl Steen did not share them. Prince Fal had been right. She should have asked…

A new voice rang out clear as a bell over the fray: "Halt! Unhand the girl, Jarl Steen!"

"Mind your own," he barked back, shaking Sanja hard enough to make her teeth rattle.

There was movement, then Jarl Steen cried out in pain and dropped to his knees. Sanja broke free, falling to her backside. She scrambled all the way to the wall, with the window right above her and huddled there, watching an Aegiran tilt Jarl Steen's face up with the tip of a curved sword. "You will obey when a soldier of the crown gives you an order," the stranger informed him coldly. The accent was crisp Northern, the voice clearly female, but Sanja would never have guessed her sex, dressed as she was in desert men's garb, with a headscarf covering her hair and face. The crest of Wilderheim embroidered in bright blue on the sleeves of her white shirt loudly proclaimed her an emissary of the crown. It gave her the king's authority to dispense any justice in his name, including executions, if necessary, regardless of the culprit's station. Sanja had seen many a guardsman wear the crest with pride, but never one dressed like that.

"Poxy desert strays running the streets of Frastmir," the jarl spat. "Mark me, one day you will all get yours." He reached slowly for the sword. If he managed to take hold, he would overpower the guard in a wink. Sanja wanted to shout a warning, but her voice wouldn't work.

She needn't have worried. The Aegiran knew how to handle herself.

She pressed the tip of her sword harder into his flesh, drawing blood and forcing Steen back into his place. "Assault and talk of treason. A busy day for you, isn't it?" Without looking away from him, the woman turned her head a little to address Sanja. "My sword could end him here and now if you wish it. You have but to say the word."

Jarl Steen's eyes flashed raw hatred as his gaze darted from the foreigner to Sanja. He dared not utter another word, but his hands quivered. It ought to gladden her to see him in such a state after what he'd almost done. She ought to be leaping at the chance to rid herself of him and his cursed contract.

Instead, Sanja felt sickened by the sight of him, as much as by the knowledge that she was now the source of his fear.

"Sanja," Olga pleaded, though she herself didn't seem to know for what.

As much as Sanja wanted to be free of the jarl, she couldn't stomach the thought of living the rest of her life knowing she'd ended his. "No," she whispered, regretting the word as soon as it left her mouth, but unable to take it back. "Let him go, please."

The Aegiran glanced at her with what might have been surprise. She stood there for so long, Sanja feared her sword would cut the jarl down regardless.

He did, too. Breathing hard, Jarl Steen flushed almost purple as a single fearful moan escaped unchecked past his lips. It was as close as a man like him could allow himself to come to begging for his life.

Sanja almost hoped the Aegiran would kill him. To return to his clan after such a humiliating defeat at the hands of a woman would be a crushing blow to his pride and standing.

After a long, miserable pause, the woman pulled her blade from his flesh. "Hear me now, and listen well. Your life was spared today because of that girl. But make no mistake, the crown will know of your conduct here, Jarl Steen, and it will watch your every move. One wrong word, and it will come down upon you without mercy. Do you understand?"

Jarl Steen nodded as much as the threat of the sword allowed, and the stranger stepped back to let him stand. On his feet once more, he seemed to regain enough of his courage to spit on the floor as he speared Sanja with a nasty glare. Then he turned on Gerhart and Olga, both standing behind the foreigner. "We will have this out another time."

The Aegiran soldier didn't sheathe her sword until the door slammed shut behind him. She came to Sanja and helped her to her feet. "All right?" she asked.

Sanja nodded, dashing away her tears. "Thank you."

Eyes like cold embers studied her. "What was Jarl Steen's business here?" The question was routine enough, but her tone implied she already knew the answer.

Sanja glanced at her parents to explain, but Olga was beside herself, and Gerhart could hardly meet her gaze. "He is my betrothed," Sanja admitted.

The woman shook her head. "No wonder."

"Pardon?"

Her eyes smiled. "Nothing. Pay me no mind. I am only glad I happened by just now. I heard your mother's call for help."

"We are grateful," Olga said at last. "But I am afraid it only delayed the inevitable. I worried this might happen. My girl, you made yourself a lifelong enemy in him now."

"Then why did you make me do this?"

Gerhart sighed. "I wish I had never let him into this house. Forgive me, daughter."

His remorse was genuine, his pain and shame too deep to conceal.

If only it had come before Sanja wrote her name upon that cursed contract.

"Will you walk me out?" the Aegiran asked, already tugging Sanja along. They went out onto the street and circled around to the back, the stranger keeping a sharp eye out for any threats. Jarl Steen was long gone, but he would be back, and next time Sanja might not have a guard to save her from his wrath.

"You have my thanks," Sanja said.

"I should have killed him."

"No, I do not want that." Not for her sake.

The woman looked duly unconvinced, but she let the matter drop. "Has he done this before?"

Sanja shook her head. "No."

"My brother will want to know about this."

"Your brother?"

When they were sufficiently out of sight of any neighbors who might happen by, the woman held her finger to her veiled lips for silence, staring at Sanja until she nodded in understanding. Then she pulled her veil aside to reveal her face.

Sanja wilted against the wall. "Y-you're—"

"*Shh!* No one must know I am here, understand?"

"Yes. Yes, of course, Your Highness."

Princess Liadan of Frastmir, *shensari* of the Imarah tribe of Aegiros, had just saved her from Jarl Steen.

Sanja tried to bow, but the princess pulled her upright again. "What did I just say?"

"Forgive me, Your Highness."

"Call me Lia. Listen, I came on my brother's behalf. He wanted me to give you these." She brought forth a bundle of three small books tied together with string and pressed it into Sanja's arms. "And to tell you that urgent crown business requires his immediate attention. He will not be free to call on you for a few days. He sends his apologies and asks you not to fret. Fal will honor your agreement; he has no intention of abandoning you." Her eyes momentarily warmed to a golden glow as she added, "Neither do I. If we can keep you from that monster Steen, you have my word we will. I will inform the castle guard. They will watch him and make sure he does not come near you again until your contract is fulfilled." *One way or another.* She didn't say the words, but Sanja felt them regardless. "For now, study the books. Fal will send more in a day or two."

Having spoken her piece, Princess Liadan hid her face once more and nodded her farewell.

Their entire world was about to come to an end, his life hung in the balance, and Prince Fal was wasting what little time they all had on petty politics? "What crown business?" Sanja whisper-called after her.

"War," the princess replied over her shoulder, then disappeared down the street.

11

Sanja heard no word from Prince Fal or Jarl Steen the next day. The house was so quiet the slightest creak of old wood made her flinch. Olga and Gerhart weren't talking and, having no wish to witness their awkward silences, Sanja spent the time in her bedroom, reviewing the tomes on a cleric's Journey Prince Fal had sent by way of his sister.

With everything she'd read already, her mind was as prepared as it could be. It was the physical trek she feared the most. With servants, tents, supplies, and favorable weather, a great number of Journeymen still failed before ever reaching Hallowed Mountain. Sanja would have none of those things, and now that the prince was occupied with matters of war, she could not expect him to help her, either.

To make matters worse, the gentle cooling of autumn felt more like an untimely freeze of winter, casting each morning into a thick, white fog while frost hardened the earth. Patches of snow already adorned the mountain peaks. When the winds were high up there, Sanja could see it blow off in tendrils of translucent white clouds.

If the conditions turned bad, she might be forced to give up to save her own life.

The growing chill could only be a sign of Fenrir's approach. The books had described him as a being of endless winter, heralded by ice and snow that froze not only things but spirits as well.

With the way people had been acting since the lightning storm, Sanja could well believe it to be true. Jarl Steen wasn't the only one whose temper flared more readily these days. Prejudices long-buried and hidden had begun to rise all over Frastmir, and the anger fed on itself, spreading from person to person, turning cool heads hot, and hot heads volatile.

Steen's animosity would only grow worse. A clever man, he was not, but the jarl was powerful in his own right and devious. He would blame Sanja for his humiliation and retaliate. He would have his way sooner or later, despite Princess Liadan's warnings. *I would rather freeze.* Better that, than face Jarl Steen again.

Her scalp had ached through the night, and her stomach had been in knots ever since his assault. Several times she'd woken up in a cold sweat, searching for Steen's hateful face leering at her from the shadows. She'd felt a taste of his violence now, and the threat of more had made her fearful of leaving the house. How much more of this could she take?

None, she decided. With the weather growing worse by the day, Sanja felt her chances of success dwindling. If she waited any longer, she might not make it to the forests, much less up the Hallowed Mountain staircase.

When the sun's light suddenly dimmed, and she saw rain clouds passing in the sky outside, Sanja's path became clear. She closed her book and sought her parents in the kitchen. "I cannot wait anymore," she told them. "I must begin my Journey tomorrow."

Olga clutched her apron. "It's too soon. You are not prepared!"

"I will never be as prepared as I need to be. But my chances are best while the days are still warm." And more time to complete the trek wouldn't hurt, either. She'd already wasted almost a fortnight as it was, and the more she thought about that lost time, the more desperate she became to be on her way.

"But what about that young man, Master Falwyck?" Gerhart tried. "He asked to court you. You could encourage him some."

Sanja blushed. "No, Da." As wondrous as it would have been to have the prince or even Master Falwyck on her side, neither could get her out of the contract. *People like us don't get dashing warriors riding to our rescue. We make do with what we have.* Sanja had her wits, and she had a plan. It would have to be enough.

"But—"

"All the encouragement in the world would not bring Master Falwyck to wed me. I will take the Journey as planned. It is the only chance I have."

Olga whirled away and began rummaging through the cupboards. From one, she withdrew a small clay pot, from another, a worn leather pouch. With shaking hands, she upended both on the table, revealing a handful of coins. She counted them unhappily while Gerhart stared.

"Where did you get that?" he asked.

"Anywhere I could," Olga said, glaring at him. "Don't just sit there, fetch your own. Or do you truly want your daughter to die out there in the cold?"

Gerhart flushed and ducked his head but, though his shoulders were hunched the whole way, he went out to the shed and returned with two more coins to add to the meager pile, and something round wrapped in old sackcloth.

"What is that?"

His face red and his gaze unable to meet hers, he carefully folded back the cloth to reveal an engraved copper plate. The light caught on intricate symbols and patterns around the rim as he placed it on the table next to the coins, and Sanja gaped, feeling its magic crawl like an army of ants across her skin.

"I have seen that plate before," Olga said, staring at it with dawning horror. "At the fisherman's cottage. This… This is Hans'!"

Gerhart dipped a guilty nod.

"You stole it?"

"I did not!" For all the conviction in his voice, he still couldn't meet his wife's gaze for longer than a blink. Looking anywhere but at Olga or Sanja, he confessed, "But I did take it. I went to Hans to beg for a scrap of netting for Sanja this morn. But his cottage was empty. Tools gone, wagon gone, candles burned down."

"Gods, so they did leave after all," Olga whispered, sinking onto the stool. "I bought fish from Astrid just last week. She said Hans cast his nets into the lake three times, and three times they pulled up as many fish as dead things. *Other* things," she clarified.

Sanja shook her head. "So they fled in the night, but left this behind? It looks valuable."

"It would not go with them," Gerhart said. "I saw it where it hung in the kitchen. The wall around it was gouged all over where he tried to pry it off, but it would not go."

"Then how did you get it down?"

"Hang me if I know," he replied. "I touched the rim all gentle-like, and the curst-odd thing dropped from its hook. Right into my hands."

Olga, still staring at the plate, brought her fist to her mouth. "Astrid used to say it was dwarven magic. To bring them luck and keep the house safe. She would never say where she got it, only that it was a blessing in their house. What could be causing this, Gerhart?"

Suddenly cold, Sanja hugged herself. It had to be Ragnarok at work. Whatever magic had bound the plate to Hans and Astrid's house, it was now faded enough to be removed. And that could only mean the Others who'd created it were dying if they weren't dead already.

But she couldn't tell her parents. How could she? They were terrified already, brought low by their bargain with Jarl Steen, and in no position to flee the way Hans and Astrid apparently had.

Sanja bit the inside of her cheek and stubbornly lowered her arms to her sides, clenching her fists. No, she would not lay more troubles at their feet.

With startling swiftness, Olga roused from her stupor and pushed to her feet. She quickly gathered the coins into her leather pouch and pressed it into Sanja's hands. "Take this and go to market. Buy what you can for the Journey. You will need warm blankets and wine to warm you, and dried meats."

"A fire spark, too," Gerhart added, bundling the plate back into its cloth. "The wood is bound to be wet in the forest. You will need something that will help you get it burning in the night." Handing her the bundle, he said, "Take this, as well. Get what you can for it, and don't you let them swindle you! It's worth a silver piece, at least."

Sanja was loath to touch the thing while her skin still crawled with its magic, but Gerhart pressed it into her hold, giving her no choice in the matter. Her father may have started her on this path, but, in his own way, he was trying to make amends and help her succeed.

For his sake, she mustered a smile. "It will be all right," she told him, praying it wasn't a lie.

"Go before the crowds pick apart the wares."

Sanja went.

The market was quieter than usual. The crowds Gerhart had feared were thin, and the merchants wary. Sanja haggled down the price of a thick, woolen blanket until the old weaver woman—a foreigner by the looks of her—shoved it into her arms for a fraction of its true worth. "Take it, curse you. Not worth the trouble, it is." With Sanja looking on in shock, the woman threw her remaining wares into a basket and hurried away.

Several stalls and tables throughout the market fare stood empty, and many a door were closed up tight. Sanja slowed her progress, listening to idle talk and frightened whispers.

"Wilderheim will fall," one voice said. "Mark me, the sky will rain down upon it!"

"The Others have all gone," whispered another. "To the last—disappeared overnight. If you had any sense in that silly head of yourn, you'd run for the hills, same as them."

Sanja paused, frowning at the people around her. She couldn't see a single Other anywhere. Indeed, among those closed stalls and cottages were plenty owned by an Other, including the Wanderer's Tavern Inn.

Those humans who'd come to buy wandered from merchant to merchant, their eyes hollow, and their smiles wan. They conversed little, tarried even less as they gathered what they needed from what was still left. Horses clattered by, some of them pulling wagons piled with possessions, and all of them headed across the river out of Frastmir.

The sense of being watched once more spurred Sanja to keep going. With the merchants wanting for business, she managed to get more for her coin than she'd expected. Not halfway across the market, her basket was filled with small necessities: a fire spark, salve for wounds, charms for warmth, a sturdy satchel, the wool blanket, and a simple pallet for sleeping.

The butcher and the goatherd refused to budge on their prices. It was to be expected. Even in times like these, people still needed to eat and, like it or not, they would pay any price to do so while they could still afford it. Sanja bought a good round of hard, aged cheese from one, and some dried meats from the other. It would have to do. The more supplies she acquired, the more she would have to carry all the way.

The sky lightened with a flash of bright green, then darkened as the clouds above grew heavy. A cold breeze made Sanja shiver. She hugged herself for warmth, ducked her head, and hurried away toward the jeweler's shop. She had but two coppers left and the plate. Succeed or fail, without a means to earn their keep, her parents would starve in her absence. Sanja had to sell Hans' ornate plate to make certain they were provided for. Perhaps the plate would fetch enough to buy a good mule and a small wagon. If Sanja never made it back, at least Gerhart and Olga could escape to safety.

The old man Varrik was just closing the shutters on his shop.

"Wait, please!"

He squinted at her, pulling the collar of his shirt tighter around his neck. "Shop's closed, miss. Come back tomorrow."

"But it's not even midday! Please, I am desperate. I will only be a moment."

Varrik looked around, clearly eager to be away, and she noticed through the shutter he hadn't yet closed all the way that the wares he usually displayed on the shelves behind his counter were gone. Was he leaving, too? Would he be there to see her tomorrow?

"Please," she said again.

He waved her inside, then closed up and lit a branch of candles, illuminating nothing but empty shelves and bare tables all around the shop. "Be quick about it," he told her gruffly. "What do you want? As you can see, I have precious little to sell."

Sanja found her voice as she pulled the copper plate from her bundle. "I am here to sell, not buy." She placed it before him so the light might catch its polished surface. The carvings were deep and meticulous, an intricate design of runes and knots. Though the crawling sensation hadn't left Sanja completely, it had waned a great deal. Its magic was fading.

Old Varrik scoffed at it at first, but then he appeared to notice something worth a second look. Placing his flat palms on either side of the rounded edge, he picked up the plate and turned it toward the light, studying the designs on its face with a thoughtful frown. After a moment, still holding the plate, he glared at her. "What do you want for this?"

At least a silver piece, her father had said, but from Varrik's reaction, Sanja guessed the plate was far more valuable than that. She took a chance. "Twenty silver pieces."

Varrik laughed. "Not on your life, miss. I will give you eight, no more."

"It is worth at least eigh*teen*," she insisted.

Scowling, he set the plate down. "Fifteen. And that is all I have to give. If you don't want it, take your blessing elsewhere."

"I want it!"

Grumbling to himself, Varrik retreated behind a thick curtain. He came back with a pouch of coins and counted them out on the table, scoring each with a sharp implement to prove to her they were silver through and through. Only when Sanja nodded and collected the coins did he pick up the plate and wrap it in a soft length of cloth. "Bad time to give up any bit of magic, let alone one like this. Heed me, lass, take yourself to Lyria or Ravetia. Even Aegiros will treat you kinder than what's about to happen here." Then he amended, "For a while, at least."

He ushered her out the door and closed it behind her. The wind had picked up, blowing in still more clouds and turning the sky as black as night. The mule and wagon would have to wait. Sanja ought to get herself back home before the storm broke right over her. With the small fortune in her belt purse hanging heavy at her side, she kept a wary eye out for any who might try to steal it and set off toward the cottage.

The main street was blocked by a row of horse-drawn wagons, so she turned onto a narrow side street instead. It would lead her past the woodsman's shed. If she asked him nicely and paid well for the firewood, he might let her borrow a wheeled cart to convey it. They had precious little left at home, and Sanja feared the coming nights would be very cold.

Past the green, not two houses away from a great big pile of chopped wood waiting to be bought, the howling wind died down with a suddenness that made her stumble. Sanja looked up. Those ominous clouds were still there, and the lights swirling and flickering through them made the entire sky look like a writhing mass of chaos. They'd had no rain since the sky had turned, and Sanja feared what might come falling from those clouds.

"Get going, girl," she told herself. Today was not the day to let her mind wander.

Out of nowhere, someone snatched her about the waist from behind and lifted her off her feet. Her scream cut off as her captor covered her mouth with a bony hand, and she dropped her basket to claw at him. Aside from an annoyed growl, he showed no reaction to her struggles, holding her up with ease and letting her flail herself to exhaustion right there in the empty street.

Sanja scratched and kicked back, screaming all the while, for all the good it did her. Her captor merely chuckled, turning her to face two more men, both dressed like men of means, yet carrying no marks to reveal their identities. But for those hard eyes and pinched mouths, they looked like perfectly decent men. And they terrified her into silence.

She recognized the one with a beard. It was the selfsame man she'd noticed following her around the market. Looking at his smirk now, she wondered how she ever could have thought of him as harmless.

His beardless companion looked around, then twitched his head sideways in a silent message.

Sanja screamed anew as her tall captor jerked her around and loped off with her into an empty barn. She heard the door groan and slam, sealing them away, out of sight.

"What's this, then?" one of the other men spoke up from behind them, and she heard noises that could only mean he was rummaging through her things and tossing them out of her basket. "Planning to leave without a fare thee well?"

Sanja went cold all over.

"That won't do, now will it?"

Her captor turned around so she could see the mess all over the barn floor. Her precious vials of salve had been upended and tossed aside, the meats and cheeses set beside the door, no doubt meant to be shared among them. The satchel itself was torn, and the beardless man was examining the embroidery along the edges of her blanket, his foot propped up on the crushed remains of her basket.

The man holding Sanja lowered her enough to allow her feet to touch the ground, but he didn't release her. So much shorter than him, Sanja was no match for his strength. She tried, anyway, and managed to do no more than bruise herself. She was terrified, but furious as well, watching through a blur of tears as they ripped apart her precious necessities. No doubt her belt purse would be next, and gods curse the filthy curs! They might as well have killed her.

The one without a beard smirked at her as he balled up her blanket and threw it onto a patch of wet mud. "The master said he cared naught if you lived or died," he mused, looking her over in a way that made Sanja's skin crawl. "But that's masters for ya. Hotheads and cold hearts. No bollocks to do the dirty work, but coin enough to buy them."

He came closer and drew the tip of one finger across her cheek. Sanja shrank from his touch, but she couldn't move far enough to escape him, and her reaction seemed to please him. He speared his hand into her short hair, tugged a curl straight, then let it bounce back. "Unlike our wealthy friend, my brothers and I know how to appreciate the finer things in life, there being so few for the likes of us. And there's no reason to let a morsel like you go to waste, now is there?"

"I have a craving for something sweet, myself," her captor said in an incredibly deep voice, his palm at her waist, trailing boldly up her side.

Sanja panicked. She clutched his hand over her mouth with both of hers and tugged down with all her might, budging it a hair, but even that little was enough for her to set her teeth on him. She bit down on his bony knuckles as hard as she could, tasting blood.

He howled and released her waist to pry her off, shoving her aside into a pile of hay.

The beardless man laughed. "The bitch has bite! I like that."

While his tall, lanky brother cursed him, Sanja got to her shaky legs and darted for the door, but the beardless man was faster. He caught her and spun her around before dumping her on the ground once again, taking a stand between her and her only means of escape. His smile turned vicious as he leaned over her and promised, "I'm going to enjoy hurting you."

Someone screamed outside, drawing his attention away from Sanja and to the third member of their gang as he burst through the door, wide-eyed and deathly pale. He reached out to the beardless man, about to speak, but some invisible force caught him short and sent him flying back outside.

The tall man lumbered out after him, and all Sanja heard was his deep-voiced shout before he disappeared from sight, leaving her alone with the last, and probably the most dangerous one. Seeing his brothers would not be returning, that one pulled a knife from behind his back, clutching it tight at his side. He didn't pay her any mind as she scrambled away to the other end of the barn, keeping his eye on the door as it began to groan shut.

Sanja never heard anyone enter, but she could feel another presence inside the barn with them like invisible smoke. The beardless man tapped the flat of his knife against his thigh, his head turning and tilting this way and that as he listened for the unseen enemy. With his back to her, he gave the appearance of calm and confidence, but his shoulders rose and fell with rapid breaths. Sanja would have enjoyed his distress, if only she wasn't so painfully aware that whatever was hunting these men was not likely to stop with them. She needed to get out somehow, get help.

"I know you're here," said the beardless man, turning just enough for her to see his crooked smile. "I've killed men for less."

A subtle rustle caught Sanja's eye, and she looked down to where a quaff of hay had moved across the ground.

"I've killed Others for less," the man boasted. Had he noticed? If he had, he gave no impression of it.

Sanja watched the ground, waiting for the next shift. It came in the form of a soft wet sound as a footprint depression formed in a patch of mud. A moment later, as the beardless man turned a quick circle, another one appeared farther to his right. The Other was circling him.

The man gave a shout and slashed a wide arc with his knife, snarling. Another rustle and he did it again on the other side, attacking nothing as the unseen creature toyed with him.

Sanja winced each time he lashed out, shrinking in on herself more and more. He was moving closer toward her, that blade of his now rending the air with such speed and force it left him winded.

"Show yourself!" he demanded. Sweat soaked the back of his shirt; his knife hand was trembling with the force of his fury. "Face me true, you coward Other scum!" A small whirlwind stirred the hay between them, and the man's gaze traveled from it directly to Sanja. "You," he accused. "It's you doing this."

Sanja cried out, throwing her arms up to shield her head as he came at her.

She heard a sickening crack and a scream of pain and peeked out from between her forearms to see the man's knife on the ground, his arm held out with his elbow bent the wrong way. His own weight pulled it straight again as he dropped to his knees, and whatever held his limb up let it go with enough force to swing it into his front.

No sooner did he hunch over to hug it in than some terrible force slammed him back into and through the barn door. His screams faded far into the distance, where the rumble of approaching thunder eventually drowned it out.

With a flare of lightning, the air shivered outside the barn, congealing into the Other's shape. It filled in from the bottom as if taking of the earth to form itself. First, the fringes of cloth sweeping the ground, then up the expanse of a cloak to a hood folded against its back.

The figure turned just as the rest of it solidified, revealing the true face of her rescuer, and Sanja nearly fainted from relief.

Seeing the look on Sanja's face in the shadowed barn, Fal shuddered, cold to the marrow of his bones. For her sake, he made an effort to calm himself and forcefully pull his illusions into the chill, freezing them there before he went anywhere near her. She was shaking, huddling against the far wall as she watched him enter the barn, and Fal wanted to go back out there and kill those men, instead of merely maiming them.

"Are you all right?" A silly question. Of course she was not. He could see that much. But it gave him something to say, and her an easy thing to answer. Her haunted silence terrified him. Fal approached slowly and lowered into a crouch before her. "Did they hurt you?"

At last, she shook her head, but her eyes still wouldn't blink. Then she launched herself straight at him, her arms coming around his neck and squeezing so tightly her entire body shivered.

Caught off guard, Fal didn't know what else to do but put his arms around her. Each of her unsteady breaths rippled through him, made him feel weak, even as a strange new strength caused him to squeeze her tighter into him. He felt it flow from within him to surround her like an invisible shield, and the chill of his rage began to thaw. Little by little, the icy prison melted, and his illusions leaked out once more, carpeting the stomped dirt in lush, green grass, and filling the barn with mist from an unseen waterfall. The air around them warmed considerably until Sanja stopped shivering. It wasn't Fal's doing, but somehow, it was.

"Thank you," she said against his shoulder, her teeth gritted to keep her voice steady. It trembled, anyway.

Had he come by but a moment later... "Do you know who they were?"

Another wordless no. "But I know who they worked for," she whispered. "They as good as told me."

"'As good as?'"

Sanja loosened her hold on him to pull back and, in response, his arms tightened further, refusing to let her go. It felt too good to hold her; too dangerous to lose the grip he had on her as if she would slip through his fingers if he let her out of his grasp.

Fal forced his body to comply, made himself allow a small distance between their bodies. As she retreated, the shield of his willful magic followed, seeping into her skin, causing her to shiver, though her cheeks were pink from the pleasant warmth around them. "You think Steen was behind this," he said, rather than asked.

Sanja's eyes brimmed with tears she refused to let fall, and when she wiped her nose on her sleeve, she rubbed it red. "They never spoke his name outright," she admitted, accepting his arm so he could help her stand. "But yes. I think this was his doing."

Without a name, Fal couldn't officially hold the true villain accountable—especially if that villain was titled. Simply to accuse Steen would have been unheard of for a commoner like Sanja, and Fal couldn't do it in her stead without revealing he'd been meeting with her in secret himself, which would cause all manner of political complications in his already troubled court.

Sanja shook her head a little. "I expected underhanded tricks from him, but not this. This is… "

"The smallest hint of what Steen is capable," Fal supplied, livid with the jarl. This was only the beginning. Royal decree notwithstanding, Steen would stop at nothing to get what he wanted. "*Now* will you let me kill him?"

"You say that so easily as if his life means nothing."

"It doesn't." Not when weighed against Sanja's.

She shook her head. "Who are you? Certainly not the same man who wove flowers into my hair. That man would never have said such things."

"Sanja, you don't understand how dangerous Steen can be."

"I would have given my life for that man on the green," she said, stepping back from him. "But I want nothing to do with this one." As she brought her arms around her middle, the magic she'd somehow taken from him flared a warning, making her skin glow in the darkened barn. It was beautiful, an exotic beast guarding its mistress. Though he knew it couldn't harm him, the sight of it, the knowledge that it had flared against him, was enough to ward him off from her.

Fal was supposed to be the one she turned to when she was scared, not the one she feared. He didn't want her to fear him. But he had to make her understand. "You would defend the man who would see you beaten, or worse?" If Steen had been pushed to resort to this, Fal dared not imagine what else the man might do to keep Sanja from reaching the clerics' temple.

"It is not him I am defending. It is you."

"Sanja—"

"If you do this, you are no better than him."

"What?" A rush of water suddenly burst out of the wall behind her to flood the barn with an illusion of murky rapids that engulfed them up to their waists. Neither of them wavered. The water churned angrily as Fal gaped at her, offended and frustrated by her refusal to see reason. Did she truly not understand how important she was to him? To the kingdom?

Sanja took his hand in both of hers, and all at once, the barn was completely dry again, all traces of his illusions gone. "Please, be better than this. You said I was your hope. I need you to be mine. "

"I will not leave you unprotected."

"Then protect me. But do not make me be the reason you turn into a monster. I felt it in you when you appeared just now. It scared me. And it scares me more that I can feel it in you still." She shivered again. "The jarl's temper is hot; he loses his head to anger and behaves no better than an animal, but you... Your Highness, your anger is cold as ice."

Ice. What a fitting way to describe it. She was right. The moment Fal had heard Sanja scream, he'd felt a biting cold take over him. He'd thought it was his fear for her freezing his bones, but it hadn't been. And, as much as he wanted to be able to say otherwise, he hadn't acted purely in defense of Sanja. His actions had been cold, calculated. Fal had chosen to cause those men pain. And even now, with the weight of Sanja's disappointment all but crushing him, he didn't regret that choice. "They deserved what they got and worse."

"The first two, perhaps," she allowed. "But not the third. You took your time to toy with him. You deliberately made him as afraid as he'd made me."

Fal flushed. "Is that not justice?"

"Was it justice that drove you? Or did you enjoy tormenting him?"

"I wanted to kill him," Fal confessed, feeling the chill shiver along his spine once more. "But I knew you would not have wanted that."

"You rescued me. For that, I shall always be grateful to you. But please promise me you will not do anything foolish about Jarl Steen. He is rich and powerful, and the last thing any of us need is his clan declaring war on the crown."

"I will not live in fear of my own subjects," Fal returned hotly, but even as he said the words, he was forced to concede Sanja's point. Whatever Steen's faults, Fal still needed the man's soldiers. He'd already sent a messenger to summon a full third of their number to gather against the threat from Synealee, and he needed the rest to guard the eastern border. "All right," he relented. "I will submit to your wishes, for now. But don't entertain any romantic illusions about me, Sanja. If it comes down to a choice between his life and yours, he *will* die. I can allow no other outcome. Do you understand?"

She gave a reluctant nod, bowing her head in deference to his royal decree. "I am to start my Journey tomorrow. I will be safe from him on the path."

By the laws Wilderheim's wizards had planted into the earth itself, no one could touch a Journeyman while he or she was moving onward along the path. But once she stopped for the night…

Fal would keep her safe. "Go home, clean yourself up, eat a hearty meal, and rest. You will finish it, Sanja, you are too stubborn not to." He managed a crooked smile. "But if you could, make it quick, will you?"

Thunder cracked outside, the scent of coming rain wafting in through gaps in the walls. Fal's heart began to thud. They'd tarried too long.

Sanja ducked her head. "I know I have no right to ask. But would you escort me home? Please?"

"Sweet Sanja," he replied, distracted by what he could feel coming on the wind. "Any other day, I would do it with pleasure, but…"

Sanja pressed her lips together in a tight line and nodded, dropping her chin lower. Her grip on his hands loosened as she stepped back, and Fal found his own tightening in response.

"Today there is no time for pleasure," he said. "We must hurry before the rain comes." He gathered what few of her possessions were still salvageable, then returned to her, taking her hand in his. His mind focused on the task before him: Convey Sanja safely home, and somehow return to the castle before the rain.

He set off down the street, with Sanja quietly keeping pace with him. She only slowed once to cast a wistful glance at the woodsman's pile of firewood. She must have been on her way to him when those men had attacked her.

Fal squeezed her hand, and she shook her head, hurrying along beside him. The streets were empty, all doors and windows closed against the coming storm. Fal was glad. It meant there was no one around to see him with his invisibility stripped away.

He cast for his magic to pull it back around him once more, and his step faltered briefly at how difficult it was to work a spell he'd done a thousand times before, if not more. It felt as if he was forming it for the first time: arduous, clumsy, and awkward. He managed, but by the time he felt the spell take hold, Fal was winded. How could something so simple suddenly be so complicated? Merely holding the illusion in place around the two of them took his full, constant attention.

"Is something wrong?" Sanja asked. He'd stopped four houses away from her cottage.

Fal looked down at their joined hands. Did touching her drain his magic? No, he felt it as strong as ever, but it was flustered, unfocused as if a lifetime of study and practice had never happened.

"Your Highness?"

Where it usually flared out of control, it now shied away into hiding, making Fal force it out rather than pull it back in. A spell he normally performed without conscious thought now became a complex undertaking, drawing his focus away from more important things—he couldn't work another spell without releasing the first.

Touching Sanja was reducing Fal, a master wizard, into a fledgling novice.

"Your Highness…"

Fal had been so consumed with finding a way to cure himself of his excessive magic he'd never considered what would become of him if he succeeded. How could he stand against Fenrir without the full use of his powers? A lamb to the slaughter and all of Wilderheim with him.

"Fal!"

He blinked at the woman by his side as she squinted up at the sky, and he followed her gaze, flinching as a big raindrop splashed onto his cheek. "I must go," he said, yet his feet rooted to the ground, and his eyes closed as three more raindrops wet his face.

Nothing.

As the rain began to fall in earnest, drenching them both within moments, Fal felt nothing but cold and wet. There were no visions flooding his mind, no hint of the madness that usually reduced him to a raving, writhing mass of agony.

Sanja tugged on his hand, trying to pull him into the shelter of a tree. She had to be freezing. Fal ought to take her home and get back to the castle himself. Instead, he pulled her back to him and brought her into the shelter of his cloak. It didn't keep either of them from getting soaked, but the thick wool at least provided some warmth. For all that water was the element of his soul, "Have you any idea of how long it has been since I have stood in the rain?"

Sanja squinted up at him and shook her head.

"Neither do I. Yet here I am." And as he slowly came to accept that inconceivable blessing, Fal's fear melted away, and a giddy joy filled him to the brim. His laughter must have made him sound to Sanja like a madman, but he couldn't stop it for fear he might break into tears instead.

He picked up Sanja one-armed, not daring to release her hand, and spun around, dancing her down the muddy street with an abandon he hadn't felt in far too long. Still holding her up, Fal jumped into a large puddle. Water splashed up his legs, over the rims of his boots, soaking his feet, and it was a beautiful thing.

"What is the matter with you?" Sanja shouted at him over the storm's din. She was shivering against him, and he, too, was beginning to feel the unpleasant clutch of cold. His fingers were going numb, his face stung with the wind as it blew the storm right on top of them. Lightning cracked down on Castle Frastmir's western tower, and then twice more in quick succession near the green. Any man with sense would be running for cover, yet Fal remained frozen, loath to give up the smallest part of this moment.

Sanja would never know the gift she had given him, simply by being there, holding the world at bay. Were he a braver man, he would tell her and risk terrifying her into fleeing. Were he an honest man, he would tell her she was now irreversibly bound to his company for as long as she lived. But in that moment, Fal was neither brave nor honest. He was the Prince of Deceit, and Sanja was the only thing keeping him from drowning.

Ragnarok be damned. He didn't care about Synealee, or Wilderheim, or the Otherlands. In that moment, he didn't want his magic back. All he wanted was more of this: cold rain on his face, peace in his mind, and Sanja in his arms.

She made him feel human. He could love her, just for that.

Another flash brought lightning roots streaking across the sky. Sanja gasped, flinching closer against him. The rain had soaked her short hair to her scalp, and as she hid her face into his shoulder, Fal could see the pale elegance of her nape. He set her down to free his hand so he could cup the back of her neck. A drop of rain rolled down its center beneath his palm, and he felt it run all the way down her spine as if he were tracing his fingertips along its path to where it soaked into her clothing at her waist.

Sanja pulled back to look up at him, her pale cheek warming with a blush as if she'd felt it, too. He read confusion in her eyes, but no fear. Despite the fright of being attacked earlier and her unease of being caught out in the storm, she seemed to trust him to keep her safe. Another gift and one Fal didn't deserve. It humbled him.

With great care and reverence, he cupped her cold cheek, savoring the feel of her skin against his palm. Though he couldn't hear her, he read his own name on her lips as she squeezed his other hand. Sanja closed her eyes against the driving rain. Without her gaze to focus on, physical sensations washed over Fal, taking him from his own self and into the water that traced Sanja's brow, her cheeks, her lips.

Forgive me, he silently prayed as the water showed him formless portents of pain and sorrow down the path he couldn't stop himself taking. *I will make it up to you—all of it. You have my word.*

He pressed his lips to hers, sealing his pledge with a kiss that removed all other possible futures. Fal didn't care. He kept kissing Sanja, swearing to himself again that, whatever disasters he might be bringing down upon her, he would be there to keep her safe. He would make certain she never wanted for anything.

By all the gods, for all she could give him, and all he would take from her, it was the least Fal could do. And he could not fail.

Sanja made a small sound that tasted like a drop of honey on his tongue as she softened into him, kissing him back with all the sparkling energy she never seemed to be able to contain. Fal smiled against her lips, pulled her closer still, clutched her hand to anchor them both. His entire body thrummed to the beat of his heart, his magic pulsing within his skin, yet it felt focused. It made *him* feel in control of it.

The pulse became a hum, and then a crackle that made the hairs on his arm stand on end, and too late, Fal realized what it meant.

When the lightning struck, it slammed into both of them with such fury it nearly tore Fal's chest apart. The fire of it seared his insides, made his limbs cramp. He went blind with its brightness, and deaf with the thunder's boom, yet all the while, he felt Sanja with him, suffering the same. He felt her go limp a moment before the awful force released him as well, and he caught her against him.

Through the ringing in his ears, Fal heard voices, people shouting from somewhere nearby. He shook his head and squinted, willing the bright spots in his vision to clear so he could see. Sanja's parents stood in the open doorway of their cottage, beckoning to him and calling for their daughter. Fal wanted to go to them, but moving at all felt impossible with his legs still burning and his arms locked around Sanja. He tried anyway, but with the first step, his knees buckled, and he dropped thigh-deep into the puddle. Standing again was beyond him. All he could do was hold on and wait for his strength to return. Surrounded by water, it should have come to him in an instant. It didn't, and Fal's scrambled mind slowly comprehended why.

He was still holding Sanja's hand.

Seeing Fal was done for, old Gerhart came hobbling out into the storm, hunching his shoulders against the rain. He winced as he got down on one knee and reached for his daughter, but he hesitated, the angry scowl on his face turning into a wide-eyed look of surprise. "You... You're—"

"Keep her safe," Fal managed to say and thrust Sanja into his arms. As soon as the last contact between them broke, Fal fell through the puddle, into a dark, churning vortex of endless water. Its mad current tossed him about without mercy, battered him with chilling blows that forced the air out of his lungs.

Disoriented, on the verge of drowning, Fal struck out blindly, trying to swim his way out. With each movement, chunks of ice struck his limbs, scraped against his face and neck. He was dying.

Terrified, Fal thought of home, fixed the image in his mind, focused his intent on the basin in his chambers, and held on to it as his lungs burned with the need for air. One more time, he struck out, kicked with all his might to orient himself in the current's direction, using its strength to propel him up and out.

The rush of water shot him toward the light, and forcefully expelled him into dry air. Shaking with exhaustion, gasping in lungfuls of air, Fal dragged himself out of the basin. "Thank you, gods," he prayed as he recognized his bedchamber. "I am never doing that again." Collapsing onto the floor, he fell headlong into the abyss of sleep.

PART TWO

THE WORLD FREEZES

12

When the water swelled in its basin, it flooded through the cage and submerged the dragon up to his chin. Tethered to the wall at his back, his ropes afforded only room enough to keep his head above the surface when he stood on his toes. Sometimes the current sent errant waves to wash over his face, threatening to drown him, but never enough to sink him fully. When it receded, the dragon collapsed to his knees, weakened as if the water had stolen away his fire, banked it to almost nothing.

It was not alive, and yet the dragon could almost believe it could be. The hiss of its current spoke to him, the lap of its waves beckoned in invitation. The floods were his punishment for not speaking back. The water slapped at him and threatened, but eventually calmed as if it understood that drowning him would solve nothing.

In the quiet, sulking lulls, the dragon wrestled with his bonds. The simple ropes were anything but. He could neither claw through them nor burn through them. His immense strength had no effect on their thick braids, and he risked his fangs trying to bite them free. He'd even attempted biting off his own hand to escape. For all that pain, his wounds had healed almost instantly, and he'd not come an inch closer to freedom.

The ring on his finger pulsed with heat, reminding him there was another way. All he needed to do was twist the ring to summon his blood kin, but the dragon refused to entertain the thought of it. Bad enough that he'd fallen for Hel's cruel trick. He would not lead his family into the same trap. For all he knew, it was what Hel wanted. Why else would she have allowed the ring's magic to persist, but none of his? She'd imprisoned him in a 'tween where the needs of his human body were as muted as the power of his dragon essence. He never slept, ate, or drank, yet he felt no need for it. He could grow his claws longer, cover his body with scales, and conjure fire, yet never enough to complete the transformation or affect the confines of his cell.

Whatever this place was, his senses told the dragon he could be kept imprisoned here forever, if his jailer willed it so.

No different from your lonesome cave, Solveig pointed out in his mind.

He shook her away, stabbed his claws into his palms to give himself something else to think about. His cave might have been lonesome, but he'd chosen it of his own free will. It'd had no doors, locks, or binds, and he'd not been alone there all the time. Nialei had visited sometimes, and Saeran. Liadan, too, though not as often anymore, despite the blaze he kept burning in her chamber tall enough for her to walk through any time she chose.

The dragon's human skin prickled with the sense of a presence nearby, and he snarled, yanking on the ropes, only to have them snap him back into place. "I know you are there."

"I have always been here," Hel replied, melting into being across the chamber. As before, her face was a beautiful, blank mask, her eyes empty as they stared at him.

He wanted to hate her, but couldn't. Her presence alone robbed him of any passion of feeling, good or bad. He felt nothing for her; cared nothing for his present circumstances. But he did wonder, "Am I dead?" The ruler of Helheim had pulled him through darkness to this place where he felt almost nonexistent. What else was the dragon to think, but that she had killed him?

Hel tilted her head a little as if debating her answer. "No. But you are a mere sip away." Her gaze slid over to the iron gate and the water rushing on the other side.

How many times had that water swept over him now? A score? Two? The dragon hadn't allowed a drop of it to pass his lips. Had he known how close he was to demise…

"You are as old as I am," Hel noted. "Perhaps even older. You have seen things others only dream about. Your age and memories have strengthened your blood more than any other living being, short of a god. A few drops of it hold enough power to make a human immortal."

The dragon said nothing.

"My father blames you for all of it, you know. You were the one who gave Nialei her strength. Without your blood, she would have fallen in the Battle of the Veil. The sorcerer's trinket would have spilled its dark powers, and they would have eaten through the Veil, cut my brother's binds, and my father would finally have had his battle with Woden. You took that from him. Instead of a fair fight, Loki got imprisonment in eternal Shadow. Instead of his fated victory, he has been driven into madness." She raised her hand, and pale smoke congealed above her palm, a murky vision of a realm engulfed in flames. Though the dragon had never seen them with his own eyes, he recognized the gods strewn about like broken toys, dying. Woden's wizened face was half burned off, his good eye turned red with blood. Next to him, his wife Frigga, the most beautiful of goddesses, savagely ripped apart. Tir, the stalwart god of war, was impaled on a spear, a sword still clutched in his hand.

This was Asgard, the realm of the gods, fabled for its beauty and endless riches, reduced to a scorched black plane, its golden spires crumbled, and its white marble roads turned red with blood.

And there, in the middle of it all, was the Halfling Trickster, Loki, with his hair like living copper and black runes swirling beneath his skin. Seated on a great, eight-legged stallion, he took in the scene around him with crazed black eyes and smiled, revealing sharp, pointed teeth.

"There, but for a few small drops of blood."

The dragon rolled his wrists, but kept to his place, kept silent.

Hel curled her hand into a fist, dissolving the vision. "Neither," she said in answer to some question no one had asked. "What do I care for Loki's plans?"

"Then why help him?"

"I…wanted."

The dragon waited for her to say something more. Wanted *what*? He wasn't certain Hel knew. For her, desire itself seemed to be its own answer, a new taste she savored but couldn't identify.

"Why am I here?"

"To suffer," she replied. "Your world will end. Your kin will perish. Woden and his children will fall—"

"As will Loki."

She paused. "Yes. In the end. But you will remain. When all the world has frozen, you alone will be left. Your fate will be to forever roam the void left behind."

"Assuming, of course, I do not take that sip." He said it lightly, but the idea merited a thought or two.

"You will not," Hel replied. "That is the nature of your suffering. As long as your kin live and fight, you will not leave them." She floated toward him, changing along the way until Solveig once again stood not two paces before him.

Despite knowing it wasn't her, the dragon surged forward, straining against his binds to reach her, desperate for the smallest morsel. A whiff of her scent, the feel of her warmth. He stared at the face that haunted his mind, loving her and hating her. Solveig, Hel, neither and both at the same time. He shook with need at the sight of her, craven for the feel of her in his arms again. So he could tear Hel asunder.

"You will fight to free yourself until there is no more hope. You will come to yearn for those waters more than you yearn for your mate. But you will hold out and hope, and curse, and pray until the end comes. You will go mad here, many times over, so you can feel what my father and brother have felt. Until the end. You will watch those waters flood less and less, you will know when they begin to dry out, and still you will not drink. Until you know the end has come, and everyone you have ever loved is dead. You will not know when that moment will come, but it will. And when it does, those waters will be gone."

The dragon roared, thrashing against his binds, snapping his fangs at her, hating himself as much as her for putting that broken, frightened look on Solveig's face.

"Shh," she crooned, reaching out to cup his cheek in the gentle softness of Solveig's palm, and the dragon stilled, bowing his head. She stepped into him, putting Solveig's lips to his ear to whisper, "Hush now, my love. Your binds will come away in the end, and you will be free again. You will soar through the clouds as you once did, and your fire will light up the empty world."

Every word she spoke was a dagger through his heart. He couldn't think through that pain, couldn't reconcile his beloved voicing such things. Yet, despite everything, he bowed lower, pressed his forehead to her shoulder, and breathed in deep of her scent, letting the lie of her shelter him from the truth.

Too soon, that lie retreated once more as Solveig stepped away.

"No…"

She smiled at him as she backed toward the far wall. Her body shimmered against the cold, gray surface, and then she was gone.

The dragon dropped to his knees, his head bowing so low his nose almost touched the water's surface. A hair's breadth away. One sip, and it would all be over. And he could rob Hel of her victory.

He tilted his chin to bring his lips to that water but stopped before they could touch it.

He had kin now, Saeran, Nialei, Liadan, and Fal, all bound to him by blood, all fighting against the coming tide.

Fierce pride straightened the dragon's spine, and he pushed to his feet again, standing tall, staring defiance at the place where Hel had disappeared.

She'd been right—the dragon would not abandon his kin.

But she'd been right about another thing, too. His blood was, indeed, powerful. Enough to turn a human immortal, to give a Halfling power so immense it brought forth not one, but two offspring, each stronger than all the rest of them combined. There lay Wilderheim's hope, and his, burning bright enough to stoke the cold embers of his soul back into full blaze.

Perhaps it would burn bright enough to turn the tide.

~

Never before had Sanja felt such trepidation walking through the city. With only a handful of people out and about so early of the morning, she had no crowds to hide in, and she felt each curious gaze on her like a physical touch.

Sanja adjusted her satchel on her shoulder and kept going, picking her way carefully across the frozen mud. Yesterday's rain had left the earth soaked through, and last night's frost had hardened it into precarious dips and swells that threatened to turn her ankle with every step. Already she felt the cold seeping into her bones. It would only get worse from now on.

As the sun rose higher, a bright shaft of its light illuminated the library tower not far away. Sanja followed that shining beacon, eager for the illusion of safety behind its grand doors. But when she finally reached the towering building, those beautiful portals were barred. The library was closed.

Time is running out. All of Frastmir seemed to feel it, even if they didn't know why.

Straightening her spine, Sanja went up to the top of the library stairs and looked out toward Hallowed Mountain. There, its peak glistened white with snow, a trail of it snaking down to the forest's edge to mark the staircase she would need to climb toward her goal.

As daunting as the Journey looked from its beginning, Sanja knew that once she got underway, it would seem endless and impossible. She breathed in deeply of the chill air and etched the sight of that peak into her memory.

Taking a knee, Sanja looked over her satchel one last time. Olga had worked through the night to stitch the tears so it could still be used, and despite its shabby appearance, it was perhaps stronger now than before.

"As ready as I will ever be." And none too soon, either. She shouldered her burden, grateful for the moment at least that she had so little to carry, and sent a quiet prayer for good fortune to any god who would listen.

Then it was time to begin.

Sanja turned sideways and placed her knee on the next step down. It was precarious going at first, but she managed to get all the way to the bottom. Now there would be no turning back. She couldn't rise from her knees until she stopped for rest, and when she resumed, she'd need to do it from the same spot again.

She moved slowly, choosing her path with care where the travelers had already worked the mud soft enough to cushion her knees. Still, though the ground was relatively soft, stray pebbles dug into her flesh, and the chill seeped up to steal whatever warmth the breeze left behind. Sanja kept looking at the sun, urging it to rise faster. Once she reached the forest, even its small comfort would be lost to her.

After a while, her thoughts began to wander. Olga and Gerhart had wanted to accompany her to the forest at least, but she'd declined. The less attention she drew to herself, the better. Besides, the roof had leaked in the downpour last night. Gerhart would need to fix it before more rains came. And with him busy, Olga would need to do the chores Sanja usually did for them: feed the chickens and geese, go to market, cook supper, and a dozen other little things.

Sanja had made Gerhart promise to buy a wagon and mule, in case she didn't return.

"Aye, I'll buy them," he'd said, but the stubborn set of his mouth had made her suspicious.

"And you'll both leave for Lyria when the time comes," she'd pressed. A fortnight and two days. If she hadn't made it back by then, it would mean she was dead, and her parents would have no more reason to stay. Aegiros was too dangerous, and they'd need to go through Jarl Steen's territory to reach Ravetia. Better they turn their feet in the opposite direction. It might take longer to reach it, but Gerhart and Olga would be safe in Lyria.

Gerhart had crossed his arms over his chest. "The prince himself can come knocking on that door with an army of guards to evict me from my own house, and I'll not step one foot past the threshold 'til you're back safe and sound."

"Da, I—"

"Safe and sound, Sanja."

That had been the only time Gerhart or Olga had mentioned the prince. Had they seen her with him the day before? Had they seen him kiss her?

That kiss…

She must have dreamed it. Real kisses didn't make one feel weak and strong at the same time, no matter what the poems said. Nor did they sear with the fire of a lightning strike. There had definitely been a lightning strike, Sanja decided. She could still taste it on her tongue today, feel its crackling energy pulsing in her lips. It was a miracle she hadn't been burned to ash then and there.

Against that pain, she recalled Prince Fal holding her in the barn, his arms so strong, his heartbeat so steady against her. She'd felt his strength in his embrace, a world of it contained in such a human-looking shell. For a moment, she'd felt as if nothing bad could touch her—not Jarl Steen, nor his men, nor even Fenrir himself.

She'd found the safest place in all the worlds there in the prince's arms swaddled in warmth and light, and something else she dared not name.

And the next day had dawned as lonely as the one before, despite his oath to be there to see her through the Journey.

The Prince of Deceit, indeed.

Before she knew it, the sun was directly above her, and the ground dried out under her knees. She was halfway to the forest, a pathetic achievement for the morning. Her mouth was parched, but Sanja had planned out her meals and water breaks meticulously, and she had a ways to go before she could allow herself to indulge in either.

A few more paces and she paused, adjusting her satchel across her back. It was beginning to weigh on her. Perhaps she ought to drag it along instead. It might get wet and dirty, but that would happen eventually, anyway.

Some yards ahead, the river cut through the tall grasses, a final barrier between her and a straight footpath toward the forest. But there was no bridge across the stream, and its muddy waters churned and swelled to double their usual size after yesterday's storm. At the edge, the planks had been swept away by the current. The sodden grass on either bank told her those waters had been much higher at the peak of the flood and had already receded quite a ways, but they were still high enough to soak her to the waist if she knee-walked through it.

Sanja winced, debating her options. The stream widened a little farther down, which meant it shallowed out as well. She could either go off the path to spare herself the cold or go straight through to save some time. Neither was ideal.

"Scared of a little water? That don't bode well for snow and ice, now do it?"

Sanja barely stopped herself from screaming as she hunched down in anticipation of an attack. When none came, she dared to peek out from behind her arms. "W-who said that?"

A hand waved out from the tall grass on the other side of the stream, and then its owner poked his head out to grin at her. "Didn't 'spect another clod to be at this folly so cold in the year. Where'd you come from, then?"

Had Prince Fal found a way to meet her after all? No, the eyes merrily twinkling back at her were brown, not his distinctive shade of blue. Still, he could have been one of the jarl's men. "Are you going to kill me?" she shot back, unable to stop herself. "You'll have to. I won't go back to him willingly!" Sanja started to wheeze at the mere thought of it, her eyes wide and stinging, welling with tears, but she couldn't blink them away, afraid of letting the man out of her sight. Her body shook, aching to find a corner to crawl into, as she had last night. Echoes of harsh voices hurt her ears, memories of pain set her shivering. Cruel faces flashed before her mind's eye, making her flinch, and all she could think was, *Make it quick. Kill me and have done with it.*

The stranger's easy smile turned sad. "Ah, lass, you've one bear of a tale behind you, haven't you?"

He wasn't attacking her. He was pitying her. Sanja swallowed hard and turned away, forcing deep breaths in and out through her sore throat to keep from bursting into uncontrollable sobs. She ground her knees into the dirt, turned her face up to the sun that its light might sear away the hateful visions in her mind, and warm her chilled flesh. *Breathe… Breathe…*

Only when her shakes had abated could she bring herself to face him again. He hadn't moved a hair, still gazing at her with that same expression of pity and concern. Gods, what must he think of her?

I didn't use to be afraid of strangers.

She had Jarl Steen to thank for that. He'd robbed her of all peace of mind and taken away her trust in the goodness of others. She had to get them back somehow, otherwise, win or lose, Jarl Steen would rule her life forever.

I can't let that happen. Raising her chin, she pushed back dark thoughts of hidden knives and large hands wrapping around her throat. "My name is Sanja," she told the stranger, braving a tremulous smile. "I was born here in Frastmir."

"Aye, and a pretty bird you are." The man smiled back with obvious relief, then scratched his head, making his flaxen hair stand on end. "Not well in the head, though, seems to me. A local lass like you ought to know the weather like her own face, eh?"

Sanja sat back on her heels, weary with cautious relief. "It ought not be this cold yet."

He grunted in response. "Aye, that's true enough, it is. Bad omen when the sky itself turns 'gainst you. That water ain't going down none, so's you know. Might as well get it over with while the sun's still hot enough to dry you. Name's Mattias, by the by. Pleased to meet you."

"Likewise," she replied, but her attention was already on the problem of her river crossing.

Mattias chuckled at the face she made. "Throw your satchel over and strip down so's your things don't get wet."

A momentary stab of fear froze her in place, but Sanja balled her hands into fists and pushed it back. "Perhaps I would if you weren't there to watch me do it."

Mattias laughed outright. "On my honor, yours is safe with me."

Sanja scowled at him, not at all convinced. Choosing to trust him not to attack her didn't mean she relished the thought of him ogling her.

With a put-upon sigh, Mattias disappeared back into the grass. "Go on, then."

She wasn't likely to get a better offer. And she couldn't very well turn back now.

Setting her satchel aside, she stripped off her trousers and tied them around the bundle before tossing it to the other bank. With those safely across, Sanja pulled the hair shirt up to bunch under her arms, with the ends trailing down to cover her chest. That left her bare from there to her toes, but for her loincloth and soft-soled shoes. Thinking better of it, she took off the shoes and loincloth, too, tossing them past her satchel.

Her first contact with the water shocked her to her core, and that was before she sank to the muddy bottom. Up to her behind in freezing water, Sanja couldn't catch her breath. Her high-pitched gasps got Mattias talking again. "A bit nippy, eh?"

Sanja gritted her teeth and took another knee-step forward, which dropped her up to her waist into the cold and pitched her forward. She squealed and hurried the rest of the way across before she fell face-first into the current. As soon as she climbed out, Sanja collapsed in the soft grass, shivering in the open air.

"There now, wasn't so bad, was it?"

"Don't look!" She still had her hair shirt bunched up.

Mattias made a rude sound. "Less you got a good-sized cock and ball sac twixt your legs, ain't much for me worth looking at, is there? Wouldn't mind a peek at one of them, truth be told. Been a while, if you catch my meaning."

It took her a moment to catch on to what he was saying. When she did, Sanja blushed. "Oh." To each their own, she supposed, but redressed quickly nonetheless. Even soaked and muddied, the hair-cloth trousers warmed her chilled legs instantly.

"So where did you come from?" she asked, wary in the silence.

"A small village, far side of the Dragon Lakes from here. You'd hardly know it's there, it's so small. Don't even have a proper name."

Deciding a short break was just the thing right then, Sanja shifted carefully to one side of the path and took out a bit of cheese and her water skin. "The Dragon Lakes are by the Lyrian border. You could have left through the pass with everyone else."

"Ah, but the Hallowed Mountain is here," he said, still reclined behind the cover of tall grass. "Can't very well earn my robes else-where, now can I?"

"Is becoming a cleric worth all this to you?"

"Seems to be worth it to you," he countered.

"Fair point. I used to think becoming a cleric was a noble pursuit, undertaken for noble reasons. I still think it ought to be, but it's not, is it?"

"Aye, the Journey's a haven for all manner of lost souls," he replied in a way that invited one to unburden oneself.

Sanja returned it back to him. "Are you a lost soul, then?"

She thought she heard a sigh, but it might well have been nothing more than the rustle of grass. "I'm more of what you'd call a wanderin' soul. Some run from a thing, some run to a thing. I have naught to run from or to. I like to wander hereabouts and thereabouts. See new places and meet new people."

He said it easily enough, but there was a hint of something deeper, something sad and lonely, in his voice. It resonated inside her, and for the briefest moment, Sanja felt kindred with him. Mattias had his reasons for being on this path, same as Sanja, but he hadn't pried into her life, so she decided to return the courtesy and let him keep his secrets for the time being. "You chose your Journey well, then."

He chuckled at her silly jest. "Aye, I figger if I'm to wander hereabouts and thereabouts, might as well make myself useful by it. Though it boggles the wits what any of this has to do with the pursuit of knowledge. Doubt anyone knows anymore."

"I do," she said proudly. She'd read it in one of the books Princess Liadan brought her. "The physical journey is meant to teach perseverance in the quest for truth. We are meant to seek until we find not what is easy or what we wish to find, but what is there to be found, no matter how painful it might be." The path itself was laid to appear barren, yet in truth, a village or settlement was never more than half a day's walk from it. The constant temptation of a soft bed and a hot meal nearby was a powerful lure for those too weak to resist. Sanja preferred to think of it as assurance that, should she encounter trouble of any kind, help would never be far away.

"So, if you go looking for mushrooms, don't stop with strawberries," Mattias interpreted. "And, suppose once you find mushrooms..."

"Once in possession of the truth, one's obligation becomes to speak it when called upon, no matter the consequences."

"You find the mushroom is poisonous, you warn others, even if they stone you for it. And that's why they'll be draggin' truths and secrets from our exhausted shells the wink we cross their threshold, is it?"

"Precisely! Truth and knowledge are dangerous; their pursuit could easily lead to demise and, once acquired, both are often used as weapons. Clerics must prove themselves above such temptations."

"Well then, I say we ought to get to it, eh? You best avert those bonny eyes of yourn, lass, elsewise, you'll be seeing far more of me bare arse than you've a wish to."

Sanja turned away, blushing.

"It's fair beautiful, mind. Not to brag, but verses a'been sung about it, Bonny Baldr shrink my cock if I lie. Ah, now if you were of a fancy to see, you'd know I spake the truth, I did. There we are!" More rustling heralded his emergence from the grass onto the path, which Sanja deemed a sign that he was decently covered, and it was safe to face him once more.

Another wave of panic almost bowled her over to behold his towering frame. Mattias must have been of a height with Jarl Steen, and just as strong. For a moment, staring at him, she couldn't unsee her intended standing there in his place, his pale eyes staring hatred at her, and his mouth twisted into a vicious snarl.

Sanja squeezed her eyes shut and took a deep breath or two to banish his image from her mind. When she opened them again, Mattias was making a face as he twisted around to scratch his behind. "Of all the hardships of this madness, methinks the haircloth'll be the death of me."

Instead of one tight, brown braid, Mattias' flaxen hair stood in messy curls. Instead of cold, flat orbs of gray, his deep brown eyes twinkled at her with easy humor. His gentle face was clean-shaven, and his mouth had a smile perpetually tucked into one corner.

She returned his smile with a cautious, commiserating one of her own. "I would love to argue that point, but I think you may be right." The big man heaved a dramatic sigh, drawing a giggle out of her. "No doubt it is meant to signify the itch for knowledge or some such thing."

Mattias scowled at her. "Now, you've gone too far." He lowered to his knees at his marker and raised an eyebrow at her. "Shall we, then?"

Sanja shouldered her satchel and nodded, resuming her place where she'd stopped for a rest. Mattias waited for her to catch up, and then the two of them moved down the path. She found her burden lessened, and her mood much improved in his company.

For all that he spoke with a village accent, Mattias was far from simple. Sanja was delighted to learn they shared a love of all things Other and had read enough volumes on the subject to have several in common. Discussing them made the trek nigh pleasant, excepting the random rock or root, and both time and the path went by quickly while they talked.

They reached the forest well before sundown, and Sanja barely noticed. When she did, she was surprised to find the fear she'd carried ever since the betrothal was dissipating.

By the time the sun went down, they'd made camp at a fire circle that must have been lit and doused a thousand times. The resting point seemed made for Journeymen, and meant that, despite her slow start, Sanja and Mattias had made good enough progress to be on pace. At this rate, they might reach the temple in a fortnight, with two days for Sanja to spare.

She could make it.

They built a fire, drank enough water to wet their throats, and settled down to tend to their wounds. Sanja couldn't straighten her legs in front of her. Her knees and shins were badly bruised, and despite the meager protection of her trousers, she'd managed to collect a few abrasions that had caked over with dirt and dried blood. Sanja hadn't felt them before, too overwhelmed with far too many other pains, but now that she saw them, even her exhaustion couldn't keep their stinging burn at bay.

"So what brings you along this dreary road?" Mattias asked. "Or should I say *who*?"

Gods, but she was weary. Opening her mouth to answer felt like more effort than she could manage. But her wounds still needed cleaning, and she ought to eat a bite before she slept. A little conversation might help her stay awake long enough to do that. "It was the only way I could think of to escape a bad betrothal."

"Where I come from, a lass but says no."

Sanja drooped, her body sagging deeper as she scrubbed a wet scrap of cloth over her knee. "In Frastmir, it can get complicated."

Mattias hummed, watching her all the while. "You look fit to drop."

Sanja didn't recall answering with any coherence before the wash-cloth dropped out of her hands. Too tired to struggle any longer, she wrapped her blanket around her, lay down, and closed her eyes.

She dreamed of whispers in the night, a strange creature kneeling before her. It was all black, like a statue made of glittering pitch, save for the fiery glow of flowing hair that could easily have been the campfire at its back.

Sanja reached out a hand to the fire to warm herself and gasped to encounter the solid, scorching surface of the creature's shoulder. A pair of burning eyes turned to her. A long, clawed finger raised to signal silence before it lowered to Sanja's exposed knees.

Heat poured into her limbs, stinging at first, burning away the discomfort of an exhausting first day, and then comforting, soothing. She felt her strength restore itself and yawned, closing her eyes once more. The creature's parting words followed her into darkness: "I told you we would not abandon you."

Mattias' hand at her shoulder woke her the next morning. He helped her sit up and pressed her water skin into her hands. He must have been up for quite a while to warm it by the fire without burning the whole thing. Sanja hugged it to her middle, savoring its warmth.

"Forgive my saying, lass, but mayhap you ought to turn back."

"No," she croaked, then took a sip from her water skin to wash away the hoarseness from her voice. Odd, she was chilled, but nowhere near as cold as she ought to have been.

"Only that it's but the first night, and you don't look so good."

She might not look it, but she felt well enough, all things considered. "What I lack in stature, I make up for with pure stubbornness." Had last night's dream been more than visions conjured by her exhausted mind? Sanja dared not see for herself with Mattias watching her so closely. "And I don't have a choice," she admitted, clambering to her feet. No pain in her knees, no aches in her back. She was only a little stiff from sleeping on the hard ground. Keeping her blanket about her shoulders, she turned away to pack her belongings and furtively pulled up first one filthy trouser leg, then the other. No bruises, no scabs. Her legs were healed into old scars and fading bruises.

"How can that be? Have you no one to speak for you?"

I told you we would not abandon you.

Princess Liadan? No, it couldn't have been.

Could it?

"It makes no difference now," she replied, distracted by her thoughts. How would the princess have found her?

"Still, it must be some tale to tell."

Sanja busied herself putting out the fire and making her way back to the path. Healings were allowed, she reminded herself. Salves and ointments were no different than an Other's touch. They performed the same function, after all. And it wasn't cheating if someone healed Sanja without her asking for it.

She knelt by her marker with ease, wincing to hear Mattias groan when he lowered to his knees. "Well?" he prodded, nudging her with his elbow.

Though the canopy of evergreens overhead had staved off the worst of the night's chill, the ground was still cold and hard, covered in a thick layer of dried needles. According to her readings, if Sanja kept up a steady pace, this would be the way of it for the next ten days, until the forest thinned out at the foot of Hallowed Mountain.

That would leave her five days to crawl up the stone staircase to the temple and pass the clerics' interrogation. There'd be no shelter from the elements up there, and no respite for her knees. As grateful as Sanja was for last night's healing, she dared not expect it again. She would need to measure her pace to make good progress without causing herself injury in the process.

Turning away from the tree canopy above, she met Mattias' expectant gaze. "I suppose I may as well tell you," she decided. "We have time enough for this tale."

"Naught but time," Mattias agreed.

Hardening herself against the cold, the pain, and any doubts, Sanja put her left knee forward in her first step of the day and began her tale of woe.

~

Despite the generals imposing strict standards of conduct and cleanliness, the western camp was turning into a pigsty. The horses had trampled the ground into so much mud it coated everything from tents to equipment to clothing. Camp wenches had stopped tending to their duties, preferring to swive their way through the ranks rather than keep them clean and fed. The latrine trenches were so full, no one bothered to use them any longer, and shit was beginning to pile up everywhere.

This was what happened when soldiers whose blood boiled for battle were ordered to make camp and await further instructions.

For months they've been stewing there, waiting for the troops to gather from every corner of Synealee. When they'd reported for presentation, the order had come to wait longer. The time wasn't right. All was not set. Queen Genevieve wouldn't tell them anything, and anyone stupid enough to question her found himself strung up on the gallows.

Two score men in the western camp alone had already been flogged for insubordination. Any longer and the generals would face a riot. These were not soft, pampered lordlings waiting to trot their noble steeds to a high vantage point above the battlefield so they could say they've been to war. These men had no softness in them. They were savages trained from childhood to live for naught but killing in the name of God.

And they'd learned to like it.

"My Lord! What news from her majesty?"

Lord Artairas The Golden, second son of Prince Uther of Synealee, and fifteenth in line for the throne, faced his faithful squire, tempering his scowl so as not to frighten the boy. "The sign has still not appeared," he said.

What sign his grandmother was looking for, no one knew, and she wouldn't say. Everyone with two eyes in their head could see Queen Genevieve had taken a turn for the worse. She no longer attended court or even communal worship. She had sequestered herself in her chambers, and only her most trusted guards and servants were allowed entrance. Each of them always emerged ashen, saying the queen was gravely ill.

A procession of healers had come and gone, all saying the same. The queen was nearing the end of her days, and they could do naught to save her. Artairas had seen it for himself that morning when he'd been summoned to her bedside. His grandmother had looked so small and frail beneath the thick, embroidered covers. The air in her chambers had been thick with a sickroom stench, yet she'd refused to allow the windows to be opened. The warmest autumn breeze seemed to chill her.

But it was not her physical weakness that worried Artairas. The Queen of Synealee appeared to be losing her mind. She struggled to make herself heard, and when she spoke, much of what she said made no sense. This morning, she'd sounded as if she'd been carrying on two different conversations at the same time. One with Artairas, and the other with someone unseen, all interspersed with prayers.

The squire shook his head. "May God ease her suffering."

"Amen," Artairas agreed, but the benediction was little more than a reflexive response as his fingers curled around the hilt of his strange new sword. He could feel God's will humming through the weapon strapped to his side, his own blade discarded in the castle in favor of this one. "Go about your duties, Gareth. There's nothing for you to do here until we get our marching orders."

After the young squire had bowed away, Artairas ducked into the privacy of his tent and drew the mystical sword, holding it up to the light. A work of art, if ever he'd seen one, with the handle shaped just right to fit his grip, and the pommel twisted into an intricate globe of a knotwork cage. The crossguard was broader than usual, an unmistakable symbol of God's sacrifice. A symbol of faith and, for Artairas, a reminder of his purpose.

The blade was masterfully crafted, strong and true, without a single flaw marring its surface. Etched with symbols down the center, it caught the light just so and glittered like a jewel. What manner of prayers were they, inscribed in the blade? What language were they comprised of? Artairas had never seen their like before. Each symbol was its own entity, standing out stark and clear in the configuration, its meaning a mystery that itched his mind with endless questions. Yet, at the same time, each symbol also flowed into the next in an unbroken river of silent speech.

It mesmerized.

Artairas traced the lines with a reverent fingertip from hilt to tip, and back down, feeling the blade heat to his touch. Its warmth seeped into him, making his heartbeat stronger, his breath come faster. He caressed each symbol's voluptuous curve with a lover's gentleness, whispered praise into each mysterious whorl and valley. The blade sighed, pulling his fingers tighter around the grip, digging the pommel into his flesh, where it rested against his thigh.

Candlelight played across its polished surface, unmarred by a single hammer strike. Pure and eager, humming secrets he had yet to uncover. Artairas read its mysteries in the brief dark lulls between the flashes of light and followed them slowly up the fuller channel and beyond, to the tip. There, he tested the edge with his thumb. He barely felt the blade's sting, watching a crimson droplet slide down the center of the blade.

Red against steel.

Blood upon the holy prayers.

A scar across the reflection of his face.

Artairas saw himself within the blade, a golden crown upon his head and faces at once strange and familiar standing behind him, keeping watch over him. All of them men seasoned by battle, brows creased with the weight of victory, eyes shining with faith, in their God as well as their king.

Artairas shouted and tossed the blade aside. Shaking, he crossed over to the washbasin and splashed cold water over his face. He couldn't catch his breath, his body humming with a strange energy, a purpose, and a calling. For a moment there, staring at the blade—*into* it—Artairas had felt God's hand upon his shoulder. He'd heard the unspoken truth in the vision: "Thus shall it come to pass."

The compulsion to answer was too powerful to resist. "Thus shall it be," he murmured, gritting his teeth against the words. It felt like sorcery, but how could it be? The queen herself had placed the sword into his hands. None other served God as faithfully and completely as Queen Genevieve. The sword could only be His Divine instrument.

And Artairas had been chosen to wield it.

His fingers curled hard into the edge of the washstand. God had chosen him to carry out His holy justice. The heathens would perish beneath His blade. Artairas himself would lead the way to victory and bring God's light into the dark, Godless north.

And then he would be their king.

Thus shall it be.

Thus had God decreed, and there could be no other outcome.

Artairas turned once more to face the blade, lying stained on the bearskins carpeting his tent. He wet a washcloth and returned to it, weak-kneed and weary. He cleaned the blood off its face, polished the surface to a steady shine, then laid it to rest within its scabbard, setting it in a place of honor: on the pedestal of his altar beneath the holy cross. Kneeling there, he bowed his head and said a prayer, accepting God's gift into his keeping until death.

The time was growing nigh. Artairas felt the air whispering portents of things to come. God had waited long enough. Having delivered His gift unto Artairas, nothing else remained but for the armies to march.

And win.

13

A bright glare of sunshine speared through the gray mist of dreams, bringing Fal a vision of green grass and sparkling waterfalls. He saw himself hand in hand with Sanja, smiling. A length of string wound around their hands while a drop of crimson blood seeped out from between their palms, a seal over their joined fate.

He stared at the dark little blob falling through the air, and the focus of his attention sucked him into its depths, from the brightness of the meadow to the cozy shadows of a darkened bedchamber. There, Sanja slept peacefully while Fal stoked the fire in the hearth. Outside, the moon shone down on a midnight land turned silver with thick blankets of snow, and all was beautifully, softly peaceful. The dream version of him returned to bed, kissed Sanja on the brow, and drew her into his arms to sleep. It was a gesture of pure love he could feel, and it stilled the churning chaos inside him into a reverent balance.

He blinked slowly, savoring the sensation, and when he opened his eyes again, Fal found himself in Castle Frastmir's throne room, seated on King Saeran's throne. But it was no longer Saeran's. It was Fal's, and Sanja was there beside him as his queen, serene and composed, save for her foot tapping out a rapid rhythm beneath her skirts. Dream Fal ducked his chin so his subjects wouldn't see him trying not to laugh and squeezed Sanja's hand to make her still.

Then he was somewhere else, an Otherland of purple grasses and a brilliant green sky, watching Sanja take it all in with breathless wonder.

In the next blink, they were in a deep forest of black trees. Shimmering silver leaves showered over them as a shy unicorn foal approached to sniff at the apple Sanja held out to it.

As it reached out, the scene changed once more to his library, where Sanja sat on the floor surrounded by books, oblivious to the world at large.

And in the next instant, they were in a garden filled with bright, colorful blooms. And then a cottage in the woods, where dream Fal, older now, danced Sanja around a fire pit. And in the castle again, older still, hand in hand as their crowns were removed with reverence and passed on to their heirs.

Over and over, again and again, new scenes of a lifetime Fal had never lived, but desperately wanted to. And wherever he found himself, Sanja was always there beside him, calming his chaos with nothing more than her touch.

It was a gift, a vision of what could be, and Fal didn't want to leave. He strained to see more, even as the colors began to fade back into a mist that robbed him of details first, then entire scenes, and then all memory of what he'd seen. But the sensation of them remained. It became a sweet, hollow ache inside his mind, a sense of having misplaced something precious, and an urgent need to find it again that followed him into wakefulness.

Fal came to his senses on the floor of his bedchambers. Brilliant light flickered through the windows, a steady fire burned in the hearth. He was sore all over, his body cold and stiff from sleeping on the floor for who knew how long. As exhausted as he remembered being, it could have been a full day.

The last thing he remembered was kissing Sanja, and a lightning strike slamming into him with incredible power. He remembered falling through water that was already freezing over, and then…

There'd been more, hadn't there? Something important, a message he couldn't recall. It itched deep in his mind and made his chest ache as if something he'd been holding onto had slipped from his grasp. The echo of warmth and laughter left Fal with a sense of impending loss.

He could only imagine how Sanja must be faring. Had she started her Journey already? More likely, she delayed her departure to recover, as Fal would need to. Good. He'd promised he'd help her, and he intended to keep that promise. As soon as his bones stopped buzzing. It shouldn't take him long. A cold bath, a good meal, and he'd be back at full strength once more.

But when he attempted to jump to his feet, his body wouldn't obey. He was forced to use the hearth for support as he climbed upright and got his unsteady legs under him. Dizzy, weak, it was all he could do not to crumble back to the floor.

And as his gaze slowly focused on his surroundings, he noticed something far more disturbing. His bedchamber was dry. No water, no fish, no churned up mud at his feet. His illusions appeared to be gone, yet he still felt them all around. His body was drained, exhausted, yet his magic was as strong as ever. Something was wrong with him.

Fal hobbled to the bathing room where a copper tub stood filled with cold water. He stripped and sat into it, sinking low to submerge himself. The water remained silent, dormant. He felt its chill, but not its vastness and power. It buoyed him but didn't lure him deeper. It felt as if the connection he'd always sensed to all the waters of the world and to its Eternal Source had been severed and left him disoriented and lonely.

He hastened through his bath and redressed in clean clothes that felt foreign on his skin. The polished silver disc reflected his true face, and all he saw was a stranger staring back at him. Everything looked as it should, smelled as it should, felt as it should, but it was all the slightest bit off to his weary mind.

Fal emerged into the empty hallway. Not a soul in sight. Not a single torch burning. He called out, but no one answered him. At the end of the hallway, he descended the staircase to the next level, calling out again. No answer.

Finally, he came to the great hall and there, at last, found a sign of life. Food on the long table, unfinished and abandoned. Someone had eaten there not long ago. Some of the candles were still burning.

Fal selected a morsel from one of the platters and bit into it, tasting nothing. He frowned at it, then at the platter. But, starved as he was, Fal couldn't afford to be picky, so he stuffed the rest into his mouth and reached for the next. By the time his fingers closed over a piece of sausage, the morsel in his mouth had popped like ripe fruit and disintegrated into tasteless jelly.

Fal swallowed with a shudder and raised the sausage to the light. Before his eyes, it became translucent, then lost its shape as it expanded into a perfectly round ball before it popped in a splash of water.

This wasn't real—none of it.

As he looked around again, harder, staring through what was before him to what might lie beyond, the world rippled outward from him, jarring the illusion enough to reveal it to his senses. Fal stumbled back, gasping for breath. He wasn't dreaming, that much he knew. But he wasn't awake, either. At least, he didn't feel fully in the physical world. The one that mattered, that was real.

A larger ripple revealed people milling about the great hall. Servants carried away empty dishes beyond the illusory veil, and as each was picked up there, it disappeared from the table in Fal's world. Gone, as if it had never been.

Fal met a serving girl at the far end of the table, grasped the platter she reached for, but he couldn't hold onto it. The silver disc melted like mist through his fingertips.

"Hello!" he called. "Can anyone hear me?" Running up the steps to the dais, he stood on the king's throne, waved his arms about, and shouted, "*Hello!*"

In the ripples where the illusion briefly gave way, he saw nothing change. Not a single head turned to look his way.

No, it couldn't be. He'd been so close to a cure! Was it too late?

"*Hello!* Someone answer me!"

He was denied the smallest evidence of his existence: an echo.

I'm still standing, he thought, trying to reason himself out of this mess. *I can feel the throne beneath my feet. I can see all that is unliving.* The candles blew out one by one, and the tapestries moved on the walls. Doors opened and closed. Chairs moved about. But he couldn't see or hear a single living being, and they couldn't see him. And then, with one last slamming of a door, all movement stopped.

Desperate, Fal sought the core of his magic within himself, wrenched it about to release its hold on his world. He felt the illusion waver the smallest bit before it settled back into place once more. He tried again, harder, felt the world twist and wrinkle, a heavy tapestry refusing to let itself warp. The effort left him winded.

Fal hopped down from the throne and ran for the council room. Surely, someone there would sense him. Liadan would be there. Surely she'd feel her own brother nearby. And if not, Braith had magic in her. If he pushed hard, his call for help might reach her.

Down the hallway, he ran up the staircase, wheezing back the blinding fear that he would never again make it out of the illusions. The council room stood open, the chairs set around its only table at different angles, a sign of people sitting in them. But who?

Fal took hold of his magic once more, wrenched with all his might, and felt it shift the slightest bit.

"…nine days," Tarben said. "Nine days with no sign of him. We must assume the worst."

His hold slipped, washing away all but a faint hum of the response. *Nine days…* He'd lost over a week.

Concentrate. One more try. He held his breath, his entire body tensing to grasp something that wasn't there. The illusion thinned, allowing him to see the members of the royal council. They looked tired, far older than the last time he'd seen them, and Kvaran was absent. Eira was speaking, but Fal couldn't make out what she said. Her lips formed the word *war*, and a cold fist closed around Fal's heart.

He clutched thin air in white-knuckled fists, pulled with every last ounce of his strength.

"…not unsympathetic. But we cannot fight two battles at once. We must face the threat we can defeat."

"Winning a war will not stop Ragnarok," Braith argued. "If we cannot find a way out of Fenrir's path, defeating Synealee's armies will mean nothing."

"What do you suggest?" That was Olgier, his voice reedy, lost without a firm command to follow.

"We must find the cauldron Queen Nialei hid away. We must finish what she and King Saeran began. It is our only hope."

"A fool's errand," Tarben scoffed. "An Other trick to keep us chasing our tails, as they have had us doing always. What proof do we have that the blood of all clans will restore the Veil? None, other than their word. It is folly to trust an Other."

"You speak treason," Braith hissed.

"And you speak blindly! Our Other king and queen are gone. Their Other heir has abandoned us, and his Other sister has fled—"

"Princess Liadan is patrolling our borders," Eira argued.

"So she said," Tarben replied. "But who is to say she hasn't gone back to Aegiros to save her own life? They all left us to fend for ourselves!"

"And so we must," Kvaran wheezed behind Fal. He couldn't turn to face the ancient councilor and waiting for him to be carried to the table drained Fal almost dry. His hold slipped again and again, but thankfully, the other councilors respected Kvaran at least enough to wait for him to be settled before they resumed their treasonous rhetoric. It gave Fal enough time to shore up his strength for a few more moments.

"Whatever is keeping the royal family away makes no matter now," Kvaran decreed. "What matters is what we do in their absence."

"Hear, hear!" Tarben agreed.

Kvaran nodded at Tarben. "You are right. We have a duty to protect the people of Wilderheim from all threats. And so we shall. Give the call to arms. If Synealee attacks, we must be prepared to defend against them."

Tarben drew himself up and sneered at Braith.

"And Councilor Braith is right, as well," Kvaran added, making Braith sigh with something akin to relief as Tarben's grin dimmed. "I sense this war is a portent and first wave of Ragnarok, but it is by no means the only one. Queen Nialei believed the blood of the clans could restore the Veil, and we have no choice but to trust her judgment. We shall summon anyone with magic Sight to search for the cauldron."

"And if we find it? What then?" Tarben asked. "The queen has only collected a portion of what is needed, and we don't know what portion it is. It could be a single drop away from completion, or thousands short. And if we somehow got all the clans to contribute, do you know how to complete the spell? Because I most certainly do not!"

The councilors looked from one to the other for an answer, any hint of a hope they could grasp onto and rally. But no one spoke. There was nothing they could say; Tarben was right.

"As I said," Tarben spat with the finality of one who didn't realize his victory meant bitter defeat. "A fool's errand."

"Perhaps it is," Braith allowed. "But it is all we have left."

She kept speaking, but her voice became more and more indistinct as Fal lost control of the window he'd opened. "No... *No!*" He thrust his will at the veil of his illusions, forcing a desperate cry through its weave: "I'm here!"

Braith faltered, a frown creasing her brow as she looked up. She'd heard!

"I'm here! *I'm right here!*" Fal shouted over and over again, but already the waters of nothing were closing around him. The councilors began to fade, the hum of their voices dulling into silence. "Braith!" he screamed, but it was of no use. She was no longer paying attention.

And then they were gone, leaving Fal alone in an empty chamber.

His knees gave out, and he collapsed on the floor, dropping his forehead to the cold stone.

Whether he wallowed there for moments or half the day, Fal didn't know. He had no awareness of the passage of time. But when he managed to force himself back to his feet, his legs still quivered with strain to keep him upright. His arms hung limply by his sides, fingers numb. He had no strength left to try opening another window. Probably too late, anyway. Indeed, the chairs had already been pushed flush against the table, and the door was closed. The council had adjourned for the day.

Yet a faint wisp of *something* swirled around him. An awareness without comprehension. A thought without shape. Not purpose, nor hope, but...

A memory?

No, it was too ethereal for that.

Whatever it was, it brought his head up and seized him, mind and body, to follow where it led.

Fal dragged his feet out the door. The hallway was dark already. Sunset had come and gone. He followed the wisp of a feeling out to the courtyard, unsure of what he sought, but certain it would be there. Above him, the black velvet of the sky glittered with countless stars. No swirls of colorful Otherlands in his illusion. It presented a version of his world where Wilderheim was still whole, shunning the smallest hint of Ragnarok as if it had never existed.

The unseen current altered the illusion around him in some intrinsic way, as if it was drawing him into a vision. Only, instead of anchoring in water, it took shape in the air all around him.

Echoes of a single voice whispered a chant in his ear. It guided him sideways from the main door, along the wall a ways to a patch of nothing. He followed its strange instructions to run his palm across the surface of the stone wall and then pushed. His hand sank through the stone as if it were mud and flattened against a smooth wooden surface. Startled, Fal pulled back and stepped away. The stone wall revealed no secrets, yet Fal knew they were there, as surely as he knew his name. The barrier before him was the same as whatever lay on the other side of it: crafty and familiar.

Never before had Fal interacted with a vision this way, as if he was physically inside of it. He could feel its workings, an intricate puzzle falling into alignment little by little, and it felt personal. The vision felt as if it had been placed there for him alone to find. Meticulous, overwhelming in its size, yet subtle at the same time.

Fal would have known his mother's magic anywhere.

Back to the wall he went, shoving his hands at the stones and through them, tracing the surface of a door from edge to edge. He found the latch, released it, and gave a hard shove. Had it not been for the fake stone wall slowing his momentum, he would have tumbled a long way down a dark stairwell underground. As it was, he barely caught himself on an empty torch holder, hanging aloft for a moment until he found his feet on the landing.

Behind him, the open doorway revealed not a hint of the wards keeping it hidden. Before him, at the bottom of the long, winding stairwell, a small flicker of candlelight drew his eye. The current felt stronger here, pulling him down into the bowels beneath Castle Frastmir.

Fal advanced with caution, tested every stair with the tips of his toes before he put his entire weight on it. Scanning the walls along the way, he found no spellwork etched into the stone, no lights of magic hidden in the cracks and crevices. But he sensed an ocean of it at the bottom, like a beacon calling to his soul.

The stairwell emerged into a stone chamber with domed ceilings held up by thick columns. In one corner, tall bookshelves overflowed with ancient-looking tomes at the top and scrolls at the bottom. The sheer power of them saturated the air until he could hardly breathe. Each volume was marked with a length of ribbon, some blue, some green, and some black. Fal traced careful fingertips along the spines, sensing both the spells that preserved them, as well as the magics contained within. With the first, marked green, the tightness in his chest gave way, and he breathed easier. Healing spells, then. Earth magic. With the next, he felt strength returning to his limbs, but it came with a sense of danger, a readiness to take up arms and fight. The blue ribbon would mean battle magic.

He hesitated to touch the third. Its black ribbon wasn't shiny like the others. Rather, it was a shadow against the book's spine. The magic inside whispered through his mind, telling him in words so old they predated spoken language that anything he wanted was his for the taking. It promised a world filled with wonder, power, and riches, all laid out at his feet, and every word it spoke dripped with blood.

Swallowing hard, Fal backed away and hit the table that took up a good portion of the chamber. The candle at its center jarred, the flame flickering, scattering the shadows back into their darkened corners. It distracted him enough from the black book's pull that he was able to turn his back on it.

And there, in a separate nook peeking out from behind a doorless doorway, he found a sight he'd never hoped to glimpse. The current drawing him in dissipated, the voice quieted, and the vision turned slightly hazy, like a dream.

The cauldron was smaller than he'd imagined. It was a smooth glass orb nestled on a wrought iron pedestal. Inside, the blood Nialei had gathered from the Other clans shone bright with multicolored magics. It moved like a living thing, creating a slow, roundabout current eager to rise into a funnel if disturbed. Fal couldn't stop staring. There was so much of it. A drop from each clan—it had to be almost complete. How many clans could there be?

How many still left, with Fenrir devouring Otherlands one after the next?

He stared like a gobsmacked fool as the vision blurred more and more, darkening from the outside in. Having delivered its message, it slowly expelled him back to his illusion, where the light of one eternal candle could not hope to illuminate the full depth and breadth of the underground chamber.

Queen Nialei's most powerful secret was hidden inside Castle Frastmir. Right beneath all of their feet.

He had to tell someone. The most important part of the spell was within their grasp. They had the blood, and the spells for reforming the Veil had to be stored with it somewhere. All they needed was a little time to find them. Once the Veil was restored, the gods would return to their full strength, and then *they* could make a stand against Fenrir. There was still a chance for Wilderheim!

In his excitement, Fal made it halfway up the stairwell before he remembered no one could see or hear him. And on the heels of that realization came another: he'd passed nine days in the oblivion of wizard's sleep.

It'd been nine days since he'd handed Sanja over to her father, on the eve of her Journey. Nine days since she'd been attacked by Jarl Steen's men.

He'd promised he'd be there to help her and keep her safe on the path to the clerics' temple, and instead, she was out there in the forest on her own, with only an ancient spell along the path to protect her, and only as long as she kept moving forward.

14

Three nights in a row, after the first, Sanja dreamed about Prince Fal. She dreamed of such beautiful things—sunlit meadows, and strange Otherlands, and so many books. And anywhere she found herself, the prince was always at her side. She lived an entire lifetime in those dreams, each night building on the previous one, filling her mind with the sweetest memories she'd never lived, yet somehow missed, nonetheless.

Each night she dreamed and remembered the searing heat of a kiss sealed by lightning.

And each night, she awoke from those dreams to the princess healing her wounds while Mattias slept. Princess Liadan's aid didn't break any rules—salves and healing were allowed on the Journey while petitioners rested, after all. But as much as Sanja needed and appreciated the help, she felt uneasy receiving it. The princess gave Sanja small morsels of food and drink and assured her that Steen had not left his keep since her warning. They talked in whispers about the Journey and what lay ahead. Sanja was making good progress, all things considered.

But for all the princess said during their hushed conversations, she never spoke a word of her brother, no matter how many times Sanja asked why he wasn't there himself.

"You must not reveal my presence to your friend until you reach the temple," she said on the second night. "Swear to me."

To know a truth and not speak it? That would go against everything the Order of Clerics stood for. Was it a test? Sanja owed the prince and princess far more than she could ever repay. Her loyalty and silence were the least she could give them. But did she not owe the same to Mattias? "Why not? I'm not breaking any rules, am I?"

"You're not. But I am."

"What?"

"*Shh!* Keep your voice down. You are not receiving anything more than any other Journeyman. I am not clearing stones from your path or making the ground softer for your knees. If the clerics question you about it, that is what you tell them. Let them blame me. By then, it will not matter anymore."

"But why can I not tell Mattias now?"

"Because I am not supposed to be here. Wilderheim's noble clans are openly threatening rebellion, we're preparing for an invasion, and I have been tasked with patrolling our borders. Look." The princess raised a finger over her head to touch a shimmering dome above them. "It's a spell that protects us from the wind. I cannot have it carrying word of my presence to the royal council, or any of the nobility. If they knew I take nightly detours from my patrols to show preference to one subject above the rest of the kingdom, I would lose what little authority I have over them, and Fal would suffer for it. We cannot afford to be divided now."

A chill that had nothing to do with the freezing night crept up her legs into the pit of her stomach. "Is… Is Fal in danger?"

Instead of answering, Princess Liadan put another branch on the fire. "Steen may not have left his lands, but he is using his wealth to turn the nobles against the crown. He has refused a direct order to send men to protect the kingdom. The longer he defies us, the more nobles follow suit. Our crops have frozen, the game has disappeared, and our people are fleeing every which way they can to get away from this sky. Wilderheim is falling apart, Sanja."

"Where is Fal? And what about my parents?"

"Rest easy. Your parents are safe. Worried, but safe. I have a guard patrolling past your street each day to make sure of it."

Thank you, gods. And, "Thank you, Your Highness."

"I don't need thanks, Sanja. I need your oath."

"Of course, Your Highness, I swear on my life I will not reveal your secret to Mattias until we reach the temple."

The princess nodded and disappeared.

But it sat ill with Sanja to enjoy such care while her friend and companion suffered without the same respite and so, on the third night of their Journey, Sanja asked the princess to secretly ease Mattias' torments as well.

After some hesitation, she did, and then healed him again the night after that without being asked.

On the last night, Princess Liadan brought Sanja three small, flat leather pouches. "Slip the smaller two into your shoes and tuck the larger at the small of your back to keep warm," she instructed in a whisper. "This one thing I cannot share with your friend. For his sake, as well as yours, do not let him know you have it."

Another secret, and this one skirted a dangerous line. It might not make the ground easier for Sanja's knees, but it did make the air warmer along the path. She'd never heard of anyone taking the Journey in weather like this, and so she had no way of knowing what was allowed and what was forbidden.

Petitioners were required to wear haircloth, but nowhere was it written they couldn't wear other things over it to keep warm. And if she interpreted the texts in that way, then there was nothing to say heat magic was forbidden in the absence of a cloak. The reasoning was sound on the surface of it. But was it true, or merely a convenient lie Sanja wanted to believe because she was cold? By accepting the pouches, she risked the clerics turning her away. If she refused, she might be forced to give up or freeze to death when the weather turned unbearable.

Sanja weighed one option against the other. With all the resources of Castle Frastmir, the princess would surely know the rules of the Journey better than Sanja. And she wouldn't jeopardize Sanja's Journey after taking such pains to help her, would she?

If the princess wasn't worried about the consequences, Sanja ought to trust her judgment. She accepted the pouches more eagerly than was decent, but Princess Liadan didn't seem to mind. As she rose to her full, towering height and folded back her wings in preparation of stepping into the fire, Sanja asked yet again, "Where is Prince Fal?"

The fire flared up, swallowing the princess, then banked down to embers, and left Sanja cold and without an answer.

That was the last Sanja saw of her.

Several wretchedly cold and miserable days followed. A great storm blew through the forest, forcing them off the path for a while to seek shelter in a man-made burrow some other Journeymen had built long ago.

"Least you have your lightning kiss to keep you warm," Mattias teased to distract her from the howling winds outside. He'd been doing that ever since she'd told him about it their second day on the path, careful to keep Prince Fal's identity concealed.

"The dream of one," she replied, only to get a knowing smile in return.

"So you say. But mark me, lass, what the mighty Thor binds with his lightning no man will ever break apart again."

"I think you might be a worse romantic than I am, my friend."

Mattias chuckled. Shuddering with cold, he reached for another piece of wood to add to the fire. "Mayhap, if I believe hard enough in love, it will find me one day, too. And then mayhap, I'll never be this wretched cold again."

The bitterness in his words brought her gaze up to his face. "Is there no one you fancy in your village?" she asked carefully.

Mattias smiled a little, his eyes twinkling, not with bashfulness but hurt. "Aye. Suppose you could say." She waited for him to say more, but he didn't. Lost in thought, he stared into the flames, that sad smile turning sadder still.

"Will you not tell me about him? After all, I have told you all about my woes." She'd rambled about them for two days, and he'd listened with infinite patience and kindness, never once revealing a hint of his own troubles. "I thought we were friends." Sanja wanted to believe they were more than friends. The misery of their Journey had forced them to rely upon one another and trust one another so much, she'd happily call him brother. But perhaps he didn't feel the same.

Mattias remained silent for so long Sanja almost gave up hope. When he spoke again, his voice barely rose above a whisper, as if he feared his own words would somehow turn on him. "His name is Brand. We grew up together, fishing on the lake, running through the fields, stealing apples from old man Ivar's orchard. Good lad. Good to the marrow. Eyes like jewels and a smile to set your heart dancing. We were always together, thick as thieves. Whenever I was in trouble, he always shared the blame. Whenever I needed help, he was there 'fore I could ask."

Sanja smiled. "He sounds wonderful."

"Aye," he sighed. "Old man Ivar's daughter Helen thought the same. They're to marry this Midwinter. Never seen a smile like that on his face before. Not for me, nor anyone."

Sanja hugged herself against the sudden pang in her chest. He wouldn't look at her, but his pain was a throbbing pulse in the air, suffocating her with its sheer weight and breadth. Nothing to run from or to, he'd said. "Is that why you are here?"

Mattias poked at the fire with one of the larger sticks. "The day of their betrothal, Frigga knows why, must 'abeen some Other lacking for fun made my head all addled, but I had to go to Brand. Heart in hand, I would go to him and tell him all 'fore t'was too late, I thought. And when I got there… He looked so happy to see me, and for a wink, I thought…" He scoffed at himself. "Foolish things. Brand embraced me, same as he'd done always, but there I was, heart in hand, thinking t'was the happiest I ever been. And all the words were there, ready to be spoke, and I wanted to see his face when I said them. But then he took me by the hand and asked me, his chosen brother, to stand with him when he took Helen to wife." He tossed the charred stick onto the fire as if it disgusted him. "He'd no inkling of what I felt, much less returned it."

"Oh, Mattias."

"I'm no coward, lass. I would have fought a bear for that man and done it glad. But I couldn't watch him take a wife. The words twisted and changed and came out so proud-like. 'Best wishes to us both, then, brother. As you to your wife, so I to my white robes. And may the gods cross our paths again, when we've lived our lives to the fullest.' The shock on his face haunts me to this day. Broke his heart, I did, as much as he broke mine. I went off that very day without once looking back."

She felt his sorrow as her own. Swallowing unshed tears, she asked, "Will you ever go back?"

Mattias sighed. "One day, mayhap. When the thought of him bouncing his babe on his knee stops ripping me apart, I'll turn my feet back home. Mayhap by then, he'll have forgiven me."

They passed what felt like half a day in silence. Each time Mattias shivered so hard, his teeth chattered, Sanja shrank with guilt. Princess Liadan's tokens didn't make her immune to the cold, but at least they kept her in better shape than poor Mattias, who only had his blanket and their small fire to protect him.

Sanja wished there was a way to ease his torments, but she'd sworn to the princess to keep her involvement secret. She compensated by taking on as many tasks as possible while they camped. She gathered wood, foraged for food, tended the fire, and melted snow for water, allowing Mattias to rest by the fire's warmth so he could recover.

Perhaps this storm was a good thing, forcing them to stop and regain some strength before they moved on. Watching the storm's fury wreak havoc on the forest outside of their burrow, Sanja thought about that kiss. The *dream* of it. And the more she thought about it, the more miserable she felt. "It could not have been real," she said aloud, earning herself a raised eyebrow from Mattias. "The kiss. I know, I have said it before, but…" How could she begin to explain? "I felt an entire lifetime in that kiss. Every joy, every heartbreak, thousands of moments of pure contentment, and…" *Love.* She'd felt love. Not the kind that burned like lightning, but the kind that swaddled her in warmth. She'd felt herself an inseparable part of another, as he'd been a part of her, and she'd known there would never be a single moment of loneliness for either of them.

"A lifetime in the blink of a lightning strike," Mattias mused. "T'was a beautiful gift you've been given, lass. Now, what will you do about it?"

Sanja blushed. "Nothing." She'd been given a glimpse of what could never be. It wasn't a gift, but a curse to wonder, and wish, and know better. The kiss couldn't have happened. The vision must have been a dream, same as all the ones she'd dreamed since. Nothing more than wishful thinking and a yearning for things she would never have. Sanja was only clinging to it because having something beautiful to think about distracted her from the looming threat of Jarl Steen's marriage bed and gave her the strength to endure this wretched Journey.

"Because of this contract of yourn?"

"The contract would be the least of it," she said, glaring at Mattias to let it go. Sanja didn't want to talk about the kiss anymore. She didn't want to dream about beautiful, impossible things and wake alone in the middle of a forest, on a path that took her ever farther from their warmth. "I will do nothing because nothing could ever come of it."

Prince Fal had been right. She needed to stop wasting her mind on maudlin poetry. He was not her romantic hero, and she had no business imagining he could be. Love like the one she thought she'd felt didn't exist outside of books and dreams, and if it did, it wasn't meant for her. Princes didn't marry paupers. Not in the human realm, at least. She was alone on her Journey, and once it was done, she would be alone for the rest of her life. That was the price she had to pay to free herself from Jarl Steen.

"Beware squandering what gifts the gods give you. Next time, they may not bother."

Sanja thought of the lights flaring in the sky outside and almost told him the gods had run out of gifts to give. Instead, she bit her tongue and turned away.

"All's I'll say is this. Were it me, dreaming such a dream, I'd not be so quick to let it go."

Freedom was the only dream she could afford to think about. Therein lay her salvation. Even if it left her cold.

Yet that very night, Sanja dreamed a vision sweeter than all the others combined. A sunlit meadow, a glittering waterfall, and Prince Fal smiling down as he wound a piece of string around their joined hands.

The storm broke eventually, and the two of them resumed their trek along the frozen path. The day was overcast and cold, causing Sanja to shiver almost constantly, despite the warming leather pouches. She didn't know how long Princess Liadan's tokens were meant to last, but she suspected they were beginning to lose their magic. Soon, she'd be left to the mercy of the weather, same as Mattias, and Sanja wasn't nearly as well equipped to handle it.

When night fell, she braved the dark forest to go collect water. Only those eerie, colorful lights now illuminated the clear sky. Blues, greens, and reds danced together but never mixed. Sanja had grown so used to the sight she knew them all by heart, and she noticed each time another one burned itself out. The sky cleared a little more each day. How much longer before Fenrir devoured Wilderheim, too?

She smacked her dry lips, wavered on her feet, but forced herself to keep hobbling toward the well. The sooner she found water, the sooner she could return to the fire. Mattias said they had to be close now. Perhaps another day to reach the mountain and its winding stairs.

He was hopeful. Or perhaps he only made an effort for her sake. Sanja knew better. The worsening weather had forced them to slow down far more than Sanja had anticipated. Without proper nourishment to keep up her strength, her body had already shed its meager plumpness, reducing her to skin and bones. She stopped more often than was wise during the day to catch her breath and collapsed exhausted at night, sleeping undisturbed by dreams long past sunrise, yet waking no more rested.

Without Princess Liadan to keep her in form now, Sanja's misery bled from day to night, to day again, blurring the passage of time. How many days left until her contract forced her to take extreme measures? The most accurate answer she could give herself was *not enough*.

The well she found was crude, but someone had taken pains to keep it maintained. The bucket was sturdy enough, and the wooden cover looked as if it had been replaced recently. She pushed it aside and looked down into the black hole. Rather than waste effort with the bucket, she picked up a pine cone and dropped it down into the well, listening for the splash.

The cone landed with a sharp smack, and then a softer one as it bounced off something hard. No splash. Either the well had gone dry, or the water in it had frozen. Sanja hung her head and hobbled back to Mattias. She collected firewood along the way and snapped off the tips of pine branches for tea.

"No water?"

Sanja dropped her burden and sat next to him with a groan. "Frozen." She held her hands out to the fire, shivering as its pleasant warmth flowed over her. The pouches were definitely losing their magic. "No mushrooms, either." She'd managed to find at least a handful of small, frozen ones every night until now. Berries, too, and one day Mattias had caught a small fish in the creek.

"A shame." He already had their small pot sitting by the fire, heaped with snow, adding more as the mound in the pot melted down. As he swirled the contents near the flame, Mattias looked up into the trees. "Hear that?"

Sanja listened. "I hear nothing."

He nodded. "Nor do I. All the game's fled the cold."

"And there I was, hoping for a nice shank of venison for supper."

Mattias smiled. "It would a'helped. Of a certainty, we'll not find food or shelter up that mountain."

"Do you think we're getting close?"

"Aye," he said, but he wouldn't look at her. "After the morrow, I think, we'll be free of this cursed wood." To himself, he murmured, "And none too soon."

Surprised by the bitterness in his voice, Sanja waited for him to say more, to meet her gaze, but he kept staring into the flames, lost in thought. "Is something the matter?"

Mattias took a deep breath as if to answer, but in the end, he released it on a wordless huff.

"Mattias, you're frightening me." His eyes were bleak, his mouth downturned at the corners. His happy spark had dimmed, and he looked to be on the verge of tears. "Here." She took the pot out of his hand and moved it to her side, throwing in the pine needles to brew.

Mattias never looked away from the flames. "You're a strong lass, Sanja," he finally said. "You've spirit, and the hand of Thor himself on your shoulder to give you courage."

A guilty blush brought heat into her cheeks. "Nonsense."

"Nay, I see it clear. All these days we've crawled our knees bloody, I thought I was keeping you going. But t'was backward all along."

"We help each other," Sanja said. "We are strong together."

Mattias shook his head as a log split, sending a cloud of sparks into the air and setting the tears in his eyes aglitter. How hollow his cheeks had become, how deeply the shadows beneath his eyes painted his face. His hands trembled as he held them up to the fire.

"Don't give up now," she said, desperate to lift his spirits somehow. "We are close, you said so yourself. A few more days, and we will be at the top of that mountain, and all will be well, you'll see."

His mouth twisted in a tremulous smile. "What if I can't? What if I make it up there and fail their final test?" He shuddered, squeezed his eyes shut. "I watch you get up each morn with so much purpose it shames me for being so weak. I am that proud of you, I truly am. But each day this cursed forest keeps going on, I die a little more."

Every word he spoke stabbed at her with the knowledge of how she had deceived her friend—was deceiving him still by keeping Princess Liadan's aid secret. Setting down the pot, she took his hand in both of hers and squeezed her words firmly into his palm. "You are stronger than you think. You will make it to the temple, and you will pass the final test, and when you return to your village, you will be dressed in a cleric's robes. You are right. You do keep me going, and I cannot finish this Journey without you." The thought of it made her throat close up. She swallowed hard to clear it. "We will finish this trek together, side by side, yes?"

His nod left much to be desired.

"I warn you, Mattias, I am very stubborn. I will not let you give up when we have already made it so far." A world removed from her little life in her parents' little cottage. She was all on her own in the wilderness, except for Mattias.

"Aye, then," he said, squeezing her hands. "We will scale the mountain together. Reckon we'll need our sleep for that, though."

Sanja smiled. "Tea first."

They passed the pot back and forth between them, taking careful sips of the hot brew. It restored Sanja's spirits, helped her breathe a little easier. Weary though she was, as she lay down on her pallet, she couldn't sleep. Instead, she watched those brilliant colors swirl and wink at her through the tree canopy above. Such a lovely sight, for all that it spelled the end.

Her thoughts turned to ways she could help Mattias along the path. Perhaps she could share Princess Liadan's gift with him in some way without him knowing. She could tuck a patch into his satchel, where it would rest against his back. They often packed each other's things away or unpacked them for the night. She could do it then, without him noticing anything amiss.

In the morning, before they set out again, Sanja would share what little warmth she had with her friend. Decided, and relieved to lessen her guilt, Sanja slept soundly through the entire night.

She woke the next morning, hopeful and excited to continue. The pot was already boiling, teasing her nose with the scent of strong tea.

Sanja smiled as she stretched out of her coverings before scrunching back under them to hide a moment longer from the cold. But all those little touches didn't go unnoticed. How kind of Mattias to go to such trouble. He must have risen before dawn to gather enough snow for tea.

"Good morrow," she greeted loudly, waiting for his usual response from somewhere nearby.

When none came, Sanja frowned and sat up, noticing the second blanket draped over her own. And there was Mattias' satchel, packed and neatly set beside her own. But no Mattias.

Shivering, she draped the blankets around her shoulders as she stood. "Mattias!" Her call echoed through the trees, but no answer came. Sanja ran to the well, her boots crunching the morning frost. The clearing showed no sign of her companion.

Back toward the camp she ran, calling his name, searching for any hint of movement, any glimpse of a body lying on the forest floor. He'd looked so tired and weak last night; they'd not had a proper meal for too many days, and he'd spoken as if his spirit had abandoned him. Anything might have happened to him, and if something had, Sanja would never forgive herself. "Mattias, if you're here, answer me right now!"

A strong wind set the trees swaying and groaning around her, their shadows dancing along the forest floor as a shower of frozen needles rained down.

Mattias never answered.

Only one place left to check.

Sanja's leaden feet dragged to the trail, her heart heavy and her eyes stinging with the dread of what she knew she would find.

Knowing didn't make the evidence any easier to bear, and for a moment, as she stared down the trail, it was all Sanja could do to keep upright.

There, written in the thin layer of white snow, was Mattias' farewell: a trail of footprints leading back toward the nearest settlement.

The fire, the tea, his blanket, and satchel... A final act of kindness before he'd abandoned her to fate. He'd made his way back that much more unpleasant for giving her what aid he could on her Journey forward.

Numbness rooted Sanja to the spot. Her marker from the previous day stood out stark black against the white snow—Mattias must have cleared it so she'd know where to resume. A mere three steps away, but so many miles still to go. Sanja tried to remind herself of her purpose, the reason she was putting herself through this, but it all suddenly seemed so distant, so small and insignificant.

Better to freeze to death than spend a lifetime with the likes of Jarl Steen. The words that had been her source of strength now echoed hollow in her heart. Years of misery with him, or mere days left out here in the cold—what difference did it make? Either way, her life would be forfeit, and no one but her wizened parents would mourn her. And if that was to be her fate, Sanja's end was better met at the tip of a dagger.

No one would blame her for giving up. No one in their right mind would attempt a Journey in this weather at all. It had been folly from the start, and Mattias had proven it. If a big, strong man like that couldn't see it through, what chance did Sanja have, all on her own?

Her right foot crept forward, frost-covered boots touching the center of Mattias' footprint. Her body turned in his direction, and her heart yearned for the warmth of her mother's kitchen fire. She could see it in her mind's eye, could almost feel its heat warming her weary bones.

One more day.

The stray thought brought her crashing back into the cold. She swayed off balance and stepped away from the trail to right herself. Dizzy, Sanja stumbled back to the fire.

"One more day," she whispered to herself, tasting the idea on her tongue.

One more day wasn't too much to ask. Now that she had Mattias' supplies to add to her own, perhaps the Journey would be easier. She could keep warmer with the second blanket. And his pot, the one thing she hadn't thought to bring, would keep her in hot tea for as long as there was wood to burn for a fire. Rooting through his satchel, Sanja found strips of dried meats he must have been saving for the mountain. Added to her own meager supplies, they'd stand her in good stead once she got that far.

Heartened again, Sanja returned everything neatly back into its place. Thinking better of it, she emptied her own satchel and added its contents to Mattias' bigger one. Into her empty one, she shoved as much kindling and small branches as she could. Mattias had left a pile of them to dry by the fire; they'd catch much easier than the soaked, frozen wood littering the forest floor and save her some time in the evening when she made camp on her own.

"One more day." And if the Journey was too much to bear on her own by then, she would turn back and face the consequences with her head high for having made it this far.

Sanja banked the fire, drank down her tea, and dragged both satchels back to her marker on the trail, casting one last look at Mattias' footprints. She didn't blame him for giving up. His Journey had been a choice. Hers was a necessity. He'd know that, and he'd done everything he could to help her before setting off on his own path somewhere else. Sanja was grateful. She hoped he found the love he sought and lived a long and happy life with a strong hearth fire always burning bright to warm him. Everyone deserved that.

Sending up a silent prayer for his well-being, she turned toward her own fate.

"One more day."

~

Three days later, the sky went dark, and a powerful snowstorm blew in, stealing Sanja's breath away. Forced to abandon the trail, she sought shelter in an empty burrow that reeked of some kind of animal. Bear, perhaps, or wolf. She found tufts of brown fur farther in the back and promptly scooted to the mouth of the burrow to keep her eye on the surrounding forest, praying the animal wouldn't return.

Fire was impossible, but as the burrow gathered thicker and thicker layers of insulating snow, it kept the cold at bay. Coupled with the leather pouches tucked as always in her shoes and at her back, Sanja weathered the storm in warmth and relative comfort.

With nothing to do but wait, she thought about Mattias. Sanja missed him dearly. His gruff voice in the morning had always made her smile. His easy humor had kept up her spirits at the start, and his thoughtful conversation had kept her mind occupied when humor had failed them both.

She hoped he'd made it safely back to Frastmir. She hoped he'd found her parents and told them Sanja was well so they wouldn't worry. She imagined her mother weeping, and her father shaking Mattias' hand and thanking him for the news.

Would Mattias linger a while in Frastmir? Likely not. Her parents would feed him and clothe him, and as soon as he'd regained his strength, Mattias would leave.

A shame. Sanja would have liked to have seen him again, to tell him about her Journey, however long it lasted.

Perhaps one day.

If they lived that long.

In the morning, the sun came out, illuminating a world of unbroken white. The forest had become a beautiful and quiet blank slate, with stray snowflakes drifting aimlessly through the air.

"Oh, no." Sanja pushed her satchels ahead of her as she crawled out of the burrow. Everything looked the same. She couldn't tell where the trail lay beneath that thick blanket, much less where she'd broken from her path the day before.

In the silent stillness, Sanja's heart beat as loud as a drum to her ears. She wracked her weary mind for memories of the day before. The storm had come on quickly, and she'd been hiding her face from the winds, ducking her head to stare at the ground, rather than what was around her.

She remembered climbing over a fallen tree to get off the trail. Its trunk had been split, and its roots had jutted out on all sides, one of them broken and hanging limply to the side. It had to be nearby; Sanja couldn't have gone too far off the trail in that weather, could she?

She had to resume her Journey from the exact spot she'd left off the night before, else she would fail, and all of this would have been for nothing. But with a thick blanket of glittering white covering the forest floor, Sanja had no hope in the world of finding it again. Without a marker, she was lost.

Shouldering the satchels, she waded through thigh-deep snow in what she hoped was the right direction. *Don't cry,* she ordered herself without mercy, gritting her teeth and forcing breath through the tightness in her throat. *Keep moving. That's all that matters. Crying solves nothing.* The day had dawned much warmer after the storm. The sun beat down, reflecting off the snow, making Sanja's eyes sting. It melted the surface just enough to soak her trousers. *Don't think about that now. Find the path.*

Where was it? She had to be getting close by now.

With her next step, her shin hit something hard. Wheezing, Sanja stopped to catch her breath, digging her hands into the snowdrift. She laughed at what she found, dashing tears away on her shoulder as she traced the tree trunk one way to its roots. Dusting off the top one, she found the familiar break and collapsed against the limp portion, boneless with relief, only to have it come loose and drop her into still more snow.

Sanja didn't care. She turned onto her back and lay there in the snow, shivering, laughing, and crying all at the same time. The hardest part was finished. Now all she needed to do was find her marker.

A sound somewhere in the distance awakened her back to her senses and into a moment of breathless silence. Sanja sat up, seeking its source in the depths of the wintry landscape.

There it was again! A voice echoing through the trees.

"Mattias?" She dared not speak his name too loudly, but already her heart beat faster with desperate hope.

Sanja scrambled to her feet, waded out to the center of a narrow ribbon of smooth white that had to be her path, and listened.

The voice was too far to make out its words, and she couldn't see its owner, but her heart told her it had to be Mattias. He'd come back! But why would he?

No, it couldn't be him. Her mind was playing tricks on her.

But she did hear *someone* out there.

Then another voice joined the first, this one deeper—an angry growl. And there, much closer than she'd thought, Sanja spotted movement among the trees. Three figures, one in the back and two up front, dragging something heavy between them. They were agitated, their movements quick and sharp, disturbing the forest's tranquility.

Three men wrapped in scarves, as unprepared for this weather as she. They argued amongst themselves and cursed their heavy burden, pausing every few steps to kick it.

"Wasting our bleedin' time!" The tallest man delivered a savage kick to the huddle at his feet. "Leadin' us out to nowhere to die? I'll show you!"

His companion on the right shoved him away. "Save your strength. No use wasting it on this putrid shit."

She knew those voices.

"I'm cold," the tall one snapped.

"We'll warm ourselves soon enough," the shorter one assured him in a way that made Sanja tremble with fear. "Isn't that right, Dyri?"

Unconvinced, the tall man spat, "She's like as not frozen unner all that snow somewhere. An' here we are, chasin' a ghost for a pouch of coin."

Sanja froze to the spot. She couldn't move or think as she watched the men wade closer and closer. The same three men who'd attacked her in Frastmir, fully healed, and furious at being out in the cold.

"Enough!" snapped the leader bringing up the rear. She knew him only by his voice now. With his beard grown in, he was otherwise indistinguishable from his bearded brother. "Have you forgotten the terms of our contract with Steen?"

Confirmation, clear as day. For all the good it did Sanja now.

Strangely, Dyri's brothers fell silent at those words, and even from so far away, Sanja could see the one on the right shudder. The tall one made a sound deep in his throat like an enraged animal and dropped to his knees, mercilessly beating the huddle there and screaming at it until it emitted a reedy cry that wrenched an agonized moan from Sanja's lips.

She slapped both hands over her mouth but couldn't have kept the tears from coming if she'd tried.

It took Dyri and his other brother both to drag the raging man off the poor, beaten lump of humanity. She blinked away her tears, strained her eyes to see him twitch, and listened for the smallest sound he might make to indicate he was still alive.

She could not move. Not to run, nor to fight.

Trapped in her terror, Sanja stood there, with only one hope left— that if she stood perfectly still, the murderers wouldn't notice her.

But of course they would. She'd left a deep trail wading out of her burrow, and no amount of effort would hide it. They would see her anon, and then Sanja would be done for.

"You did this!" The tall man surged to his feet and toward the source of his current misery. "We trusted you, and you led us into this poxy mess—"

He stopped abruptly with his back to Sanja. She couldn't see what Dyri had done to make him break off his assault, but she saw the other brother step back from them both.

"You trusted the coin, same as me," Dyri said. There was a man who would slit his own mother's throat if it suited his purposes. "Now, do we do this with you, or without you?"

"Alfrec," the third man beseeched his tall brother. "Be reasonable. We came this far. Think of the reward."

The tall Alfrec snarled, his wide shoulders rising and falling with deep breaths as he fought for control. "One of these days," he said, his voice trembling as he pointed at Dyri. "I'll take all this misery out of *your* hide."

"No, don't!" The shorter one started forward, but it was too late. Alfrec made a gurgling sound and dropped to his knees before Dyri. A cruel twist of the blade, a hard kick, and Alfrec sprawled in the snow at his brother's feet.

"And you, Bale?" Dyri asked, wiping the blade clean on Alfrec's shirt. Bale held up his hands and shook his head.

"Then pick him up, and move."

Move, responded an echo in Sanja's mind. *Move!*

Without thinking, Sanja dropped to her hands and knees and began to shove at the snow, clearing the path around her. She heard one of the brothers shout as he spotted her, heard both of them rush forward, but dared not break off from her task. The snow was knee-deep on the forest path, slowing their progress, giving her a brief reprieve she knew would not last.

Shoveling armfuls of snow aside, Sanja ignored the numbness in her limbs and the desperate wailing sounds clawing up her raw throat. She let the tears flow and swiped her arms as wide as she could, digging down to the dirt.

Pain ripped through her fingertips as they met black, frozen ground. The dirt had already been frozen the day before, impossible to impress a marker into it. She didn't care.

As the men bore down on her, Dyri's blade still red with Alfrec's blood and Bale's fingers curled into cruel claws, Sanja turned away from them, pointing herself forward. She put her knees to the path and hunched down, arms up to shield her head as she cried, "I claim Journeyman's sanctuary!"

The boom of a soundless explosion reverberated through her chest, and then silence descended on the forest. Sanja held her breath, waiting for the blows to land, for the knife to stab her through. Nothing happened. Nothing stirred but for the sound of ragged breathing and the crunch of fresh snow beneath measured footsteps nearby.

Sanja peeked out from under one arm. Bale was laid out some distance away, and Dyri paced back and forth, staring at her with murder in his eyes. He could only come so close before his feet turned him away again, seemingly against his will, taking him a safe distance from her.

Sanja gazed from him to his brother, then down at the ground. She felt no different, couldn't detect the smallest presence of magic, but it had to be there, just as the books had said. By the law of the kingdom and the ancient magic Wilderheim's wizards had sown into the land itself, no one was allowed to interfere with a Journeyman's progress on the path to the temple. As long as Sanja stayed on her knees and kept moving forward, she would be safe.

Thank you, gods, she prayed, trembling with equal measures of relief and dread.

Dyri made another pass beside her, closer this time. Turning around, he came back slowly, sheathing his knife at his back.

Bale roused with a groan. He sat up, cracking his neck, then rubbed his jaw as he stared at her.

"You will not be allowed to harm me," Sanja declared.

Without warning, Bale sprang up and charged her full tilt. Sanja screamed when he slammed into the invisible barrier of the protection spell and shot back a second time.

Focused on Sanja, Dyri didn't spare his brother so much as a glance, and she felt the chill of his intent like icy hands wrapped around her throat. Rather than rush her, however, Dyri took a more measured approach, sliding a slow step closer.

Sanja shifted her knee forward to keep moving, hoping any advance on her part would keep him away. "You are wasting your time. I will not stop."

Dyri took another step that brought him almost within striking range. As if testing the magic's boundaries, he shifted first left, then right, then slowly took one more step toward her. It brought him so close that when he crouched down, his knees almost touched her. He kept himself far enough to avoid contact, but he stayed there, watching her with cold, faded green eyes, and not a hint of feeling.

Sanja shifted aside a little on her next forward push to get around him, and he turned with her to keep his eye on her. "You think you've bested us, don't you?" he said with an eerie calm. "You must know it's only a matter of time now. We will not fail in our task—we *cannot* fail. Do you understand?"

"Yes," Sanja replied. Only one thing could make a man that relentless in his pursuit: a contract signed in blood. Sanja would wager her life that after the way she and Olga had outsmarted Jarl Steen with her contract, he'd made quite sure no one else ever would again, and she shuddered to imagine what terms he had pressed upon these men.

The reward must have been worth the price for them to agree, and now they were bound by those terms for as long as they lived.

"Steen will have you in the end, one way or another," he said.

"Best make your peace with it," Bale added before spitting in the snow. His assault had left him winded. He grinned at her, wiping off the blood from his broken nose. "Come with us now, and we'll bring you back alive. Bit used, mayhap, but the master won't mind."

Dyri's expression turned ice-cold, his eyes fading to almost gray as he reached behind his back to draw his knife once more.

Sanja bit back a moan, frozen to the spot as she watched the blade slowly raise between their faces. It was well used but also well cared for. The blade wasn't polished to a shine, but Sanja could see it was honed to cut with ease.

The pale-eyed man demonstrated this when he brought it to his free hand and pulled the blade lightly across his palm. Blood welled, and he cupped his hand to keep it from dripping to the ground. "Give me your word you will come with us willingly, and I will swear on my blood that we will deliver you to Steen unharmed."

"Dyri!"

Without taking his eyes off Sanja, Dyri replied, "I sent one brother to Helheim today already. Don't think I won't send the other." As Bale turned his anger on a nearby tree, Dyri added for Sanja alone, "Or you, for that matter."

"Y-you cannot harm me on the Journey," she said, needing to believe it herself.

"Not while you're on the path," Dyri agreed. "But you'll stop when you run out of time. I wonder if you know…"

Sanja frowned at that unfinished sentence but refused to rise to the bait, despite the welling sense of dread that suddenly made the air almost too thin to breathe. She kept moving forward, dragging one knee in front of the other as quickly as she dared, and tried not to look at him.

"It's not easy, keeping time when you can hardly tell up from down anymore—and who could blame you? Days bleed into nights, boundaries blur…"

Sanja looked away when he contorted himself to meet her gaze again. He was trying to manipulate her into giving up.

"Child, you're wasting your efforts. Truly. Not even on your best of days could you hope to reach that temple up there in the time you have left."

Sanja bit back a desperate moan. No, she was well on her way. It'd only been... Gods, how long had it been? Four days at the start stood out in her mind, etched with Princess Liadan's presence, then three more, carved with Mattias' absence. That made seven. But how many in between?

How many left?

Despite herself, Sanja met Dyri's gaze at last. Whatever he read in her expression put a sickening sneer on his face, and he seemed to take great pleasure in drawing out her misery, holding his silence, waiting for her to ask.

But she wouldn't.

She couldn't. Her tongue was stuck fast to the roof of her mouth, and the words simply wouldn't come.

Dyri answered, anyway. "Two days."

15

Against the heat of the sun, the hard, frozen ground chilled Fal to the bone. In the freezing wind, the lush, green trees swayed with gentle grace. Out of the shadows, visions glittered like snowflakes in moonlight. At first, Fal thought his eyes were deceiving him, but the harder he tried not to see, the more vibrant the visions became.

Steel struck sparks off a helmet in a shaft of sunlight spearing through the tree canopy, and in the next blink, the echo of a breath misted in thin air on the path before him. An old woman died in her bed of moss, and then his royal council lined the battlements up in the trees, gazing down at him with defeat.

Fal saw water flood the streets of Frastmir and freeze into a smooth sheet of ice across the ground at his feet. A fallen tree became a bridge, shattered into rubble, and carried away by Frastmir's river. Looking up at the bright blue sky, he felt himself falling into the black abyss of Fenrir's maw.

Fal stumbled and turned away, stared at a tree trunk to push the visions back. Before his eyes, the rough bark became Hallowed Mountain, and on its staircase, Sanja stubbornly climbed upward, shaking, freezing, her knees torn and bloodied. He saw her collapse at the feet of a robed cleric before the bark reformed to its natural state.

Fal knew that tree. He knew the nymph who lived inside it. Balling his hands into fists, he beat at the trunk to wake her. It was a violent gesture sure to bring her wrath down upon his head. To harm a nymph's tree was an unforgivable offense. A nymph's existence was bound to her tree. It was her life source and her connection to the earth. If it was damaged, the nymph felt its pain. If it was felled, the nymph's immortal soul died with it. She became human, doomed to wither, and die in a few short, agonizing years.

If Nala had left Wilderheim with the rest of the Others fleeing Ragnarok, she'd have shrunk her tree into a sapling and taken it with her. The tree remained, so Nala had to be there, too. As an Other, she ought to be immune to his illusions. Why would she ignore him?

In a fit of desperation, Fal beat at her tree with all his might. "Nala! Show yourself!" He kicked at the protruding root, yanked at the branches, tore at the bark, hating that he had to resort to hurting her, but it was the only way he could think of to force her out of hiding.

Nala ought to be wrapping him in vines and dragging him deep underground in punishment by now. But her tree remained dormant, and that could only mean one thing.

Fal stepped back, squinted hard, and saw the subtlest of waves ripple across the world in front of him. This wasn't Nala's tree. It was merely another part of his illusion—like everything else, a hollow imitation of the truth, hiding the world from Fal, and Fal from the world. Nala wasn't ignoring him. She couldn't sense him.

Whatever had happened to Fal had made his illusions so strong an Other couldn't see through them, and Fal sensed they were still growing not only stronger, but larger.

Little by little, the real Wilderheim with its frost and shattered sky was fading away beneath the warmth and sunshine of its simulacrum. How long before he lost all sense of the real world? All his hopes now depended on Sanja and her ability to break his illusions, but if he couldn't find her, he couldn't touch her, and whatever magic she possessed would be lost to him forever.

Fal started down the path once more, straining to see farther into the distance, looking for the edge of the illusion. He pushed himself to feel the chill, to see the snow he ought to see along the path.

And somehow, the snow did appear.

And then the trees were gone, the earth beneath his feet turned to stone, and his next step brought him over the threshold into a vision of the clerics' temple. His ears thrummed in the silence. Fal couldn't hear, but he saw with perfect clarity. A lone candle burned in the carved circle opening of a marble pillar. On either side of it sat Sanja and a white-robed cleric. The cleric whispered a question to the flame, and then it was Sanja's turn to give it her answer.

But she hesitated. Her gaze broke away from the flame to look at the cleric. She was quivering, half-starved, exhausted, and filthy from her Journey. Her cracked, bloodied lips momentarily compressed into a thin line before her shoulders slumped. With her head bowed, she spoke her answer.

The flame turned black.

She'd failed.

The cleric rose to his feet and slowly walked to the door with Sanja limping behind him. He turned her out into a furious snowstorm, and she didn't say a word. The clerics would have given her shelter, had she asked for it. But her contract wouldn't let her stay. Fal saw its faint red-brown aura flicker around her feet, forcing her onward back to Steen.

But, instead of turning down the staircase to her right, Sanja walked straight ahead, to the edge of the rocky terrace, and off it.

"*No!*"

The vision blew away on a gust of wind and left Fal miles and days away from the temple. With no other thought in his head, save to find Sanja, he ran.

For two days, Fal raced along the Journeyman's path like a madman, shouting Sanja's name until he became hoarse. And all the while, the prison of his illusion plagued him with harrowing visions that wouldn't abate. Like the chaos he suffered each time it rained, the flashes built one on the next to shape a future in his mind.

It was a future in which the streets of Wilderheim stood empty, echoing with soft cries of the lost and abandoned, where King Saeran's proud wooden throne lay broken in the hearth while an iron seat took its place on the dais. Where icy mist cloaked the land in eternal winter, and the night fell hollow in utter silence.

It was a future where they'd failed. Because Sanja died, and Fal never made it back to the real Frastmir.

He refused to accept such an outcome. Against those horrors, he called up the memory of Sanja swathed in flowers, twirling on the green. Against the chilling sound of her whimpers, he recalled her laughter. And when he did, the visions changed, chased away by the hope of a much sweeter alternative.

Like a forgotten dream of a life he'd never lived, Fal recalled what the lightning had seared into their kiss. Sanja exploring strange Otherlands by his side. Sanja reading ten books at once in the castle library. Sanja sitting beside him as they held court, and lying against him in their shared bed.

A life of friendship, companionship, and love—a life he'd always yearned for but didn't think he could have.

He wouldn't see it if it wasn't still possible. And that meant he still had a chance to make it real. He still had time to save Sanja and find a way to stop Fenrir.

At the end of the second day, the frayed edge of his cloak caught on something and yanked him back by the neck so hard his feet flew out from under him, and he slammed to the ground. Choking, gasping for breath, Fal stayed there, staring at the bright blue sky and cursed himself a thousand kinds of fool.

This wasn't like him. Fal didn't rush into mindless action. He didn't fight his way out of problems. He thought his way out. Precious little thinking he'd been doing over the last two days. *And look where it's gotten me.*

With a weary groan, he levered himself up and sat with his back against a tree. Fal was beyond exhausted, yet his magic still flared out in a relentless pulse, feeding the illusion surrounding him. He needed to sleep, to regain his strength, but the fear of what else he might wake up to kept him from it. Too weary to keep moving, too wary to sit still, Fal was left with only one thing to do. He closed his eyes and breathed, opening his senses to the world around him.

As the tumult of his frenzied thoughts and chaotic visions slowly quieted, his focus turned inward, and he began to notice something strange. A sentient presence hovered somewhere nearby. It had no body, yet it somehow surrounded him. It had no eyes, yet it watched him.

Fal pushed farther, trying to make sense of this entity, to give it meaning, a name.

What he found robbed him of breath.

It was his illusion. Only, it was no longer quite as simple as an illusion.

Fal took a deep breath and let it out, feeling a puff of magic follow and disperse into the illusion. Beneath him, the feel of hard, frozen ground gave way to sun-warmed dirt. Another deep breath brought a soft southern breeze to combat the bitter northern winds he'd run through to get this far. A third swayed the branches above him, giving him sunshine and bird songs.

And as his mind seized on those new details, he realized it was all real. He thrust his hands into the dirt and felt it dig underneath his fingernails. He raised a handful of it for a closer look, and with another pull of magic, that handful of dirt became alive. The scent of it filled his nostrils. Smooth movement tickled his palm as an earthworm wriggled free, dislodging a tiny pebble to drop into his lap.

Awed, he placed the worm back where it belonged and took a good look around. Suddenly, a world that had appeared hopelessly empty filled with sound and movement. Not only birds but insects, too. Fal's gaze snared on something lurking in the shadows across the path, and a moment later, a beautiful doe raised her head to look right at him. Startled by his presence, she leaped in a graceful arc over the shrubbery and raced away.

The changes were small and gradual but tangible. Little by little, this illusory world grew real and solid, filling in details he would expect to see and feel, and Fal sensed it was because of him. The illusion took not only his magic but his thoughts and memories, too. It built itself not only of him but for him. Each new addition pulled a little more magic from Fal and gave back something he sorely needed.

A tickle at his elbow brought his attention to a raspberry bush that had most definitely not been there a moment ago. Famished, he didn't hesitate to reach for the red berries, stuffing them into his mouth one after the other. Their sweet juice filled his mouth, and Fal nearly wept from relief. His first bite of real food in two bloody days. It restored his spirits immeasurably.

Now, if only he could find water to restore his body as well.

As if his wish had been granted, Fal heard the telltale trickle of water nearby. Struggling to his sore feet, he shuffled toward the sound and found a spring welling up from deep underground. He dropped to his knees in gratitude and put his mouth directly to the surface, drawing deep. It was cold, sweet, and so clean. Instantly, he felt its magic restore his aching limbs. His blisters healed, his mind cleared. He sat back and was finally able to breathe with ease.

The cost was another puff of magic leeching from his core. He gave it up gladly as the world opened up to him, revealing all its waterways aboveground and below. The water's voice was different here than in Wilderheim, but its magic was similar. It called to his soul and gave freely of its strength to restore what he'd lost. Within moments, Fal was back to himself, standing tall and eager to continue.

He returned to the path and cast his senses forward, hoping to catch a hint of Sanja's presence nearby. He'd made good progress so far. He must have closed a fair amount of the distance. Perhaps he was close enough now for her to hear him.

Arrowing his intent the way he'd done in the council room, Fal focused on her with all his will, took a deep breath, and at the top of his lungs shouted, "Sanja!"

His call went nowhere. It had no echo in the forest and, though it carried far and wide, Fal sensed it never left the confines of this world.

"Sanja!" he called again. "Hello! Anyone!"

Nothing. The world around him didn't even ripple.

Fal staggered and caught himself against the trunk of an ancient tree. Its rough bark dug into his palm, grounding him in the moment, in this reality, in this world.

He gathered his will and attempted to punch out of the illusion one more time. Instead of breaking through, the power of his intent flared and absorbed into his surroundings, extending the boundary of this place farther beyond his reach.

And in return, it gifted him a sky filled with glittering stars as the sun began to set at last, erasing any remnants of his awareness of Wilderheim.

Fal sat hard, raked his fingers through the earth. He dug and struck at the ground, pouring his frustrations into it, needing to punish it for trapping him far away from his home when it was *just there*. Two of his fingernails tore off as he struck solid stone, and he screamed to the sky, clenching his hands into tight fists around small mounds of dirt. His entire being pulsed with magic he couldn't hope to contain. Wave after wave of it poured into his hands, making them clench tighter until he felt the dirt dig into his palms.

When he ran out of breath, he sat up and uncurled his fingers. Diamonds lay in the center of his right palm. Rubies in his left, droplets of his blood forever contained in crystal, his fingernails fully restored as if they'd never been damaged in the first place.

The absurdity of it struck him as hilarious. He laughed and kept laughing, unable to stop while angry, hopeless tears tracked down his face.

With a furious swipe of his hands, he sent the crystals flying as he shoved to his feet and shouted to the heavens, "Where are you?" Undeterred by the silence that answered him, he turned in a circle, searching the darkness for something he knew he would not find, daring it to materialize. "You've been meddling with my kin our entire lives—where are you when we need you the most!"

An owl hooted in the tree canopy above.

"Woden! Thor! *Loki!*" He flinched a little at the last, biting the inside of his cheek as he waited for the cruel Trickster to appear and smite him for his insolence. He waited for so long, holding his breath, his lungs began to burn, but no one appeared.

Fal hung his head with a sigh. "Begone with you, then. Riddance to you all."

If the gods wouldn't fight back, Fal would do it himself.

With his strength restored and his mind wide awake, Fal set out down the path once again, this time at a more measured pace. He would think his way out of this, as always. Everything could be learned and explained. All he needed was time and patience, both of which had become precious scarcities.

Fal held out his hands, shaped his intent, and fed it magic in a simple spell he hadn't had reason to work for many years. As he worked it now, the familiar currents twisted into a jumbled mess and dispersed in a confused swarm of firefly flickers. He tried again but, this time, rather than forcing it into the patterns he knew, Fal allowed the magic to flow and arrange itself in its own pathways, loosely guided by his will.

He was rewarded by the light of two good-sized orbs taking shape above his palms. They were bright enough to illuminate the forest for several paces around him and, once fully formed, seemed to take on a life of their own.

Fal studied their structure, felt their spirit, and smiled. In this place, unburned by the chaos of illusions, he could finally do what he'd not been able to do since reaching adulthood: wield magic like the tool it was meant to be.

And then a curious thought occurred to him, and as he considered it, the truth of it bloomed into a wondrous realization. This place behaved more like an Otherland than an illusion. It had a unique structure, its own magic, and its own rules, yet it still felt familiar—because all of it was coming from Fal.

His magic was feeding the creation of a new realm. His needs and expectations formed the foundation upon which it grew. Acknowledging his hunger had brought edible plants and game into being. The depth of his thirst had called up water. Fal had only to think it, and the natural order of things seemed to bend and evolve in answer.

Fal sensed the sentience of this world like a growing child. It needed his magic to evolve, and in return, gave him what he needed to survive. They were learning from one another, their symbiosis giving shape to something that had never existed before, and Fal sensed it was nearing completion. Soon, the Otherland would mature enough to exist on its own. Once it reached that stage, it would no longer need Fal's magic to sustain itself, and he would no longer be able to shape it, only manipulate it in the way of wizards.

Somehow, before that happened, Fal would need to find a way back out to Wilderheim. Else the borders of this world would close, and he might never be able to get out again.

~

Sanja's eyelids drooped. She shook herself to wakefulness and dragged her right knee forward through the snow. The afternoon sun speared through the trees, teasing her with soft caresses of warmth before the wind swayed more branches into its path, sinking her back into cold shadow. The snow had melted down to almost nothing during the heat of the day, but what remained was crusted with a thick layer of ice. It cut across her knees and thighs as she pushed forward, wearing holes through her haircloth trousers.

And still, the cold and pain were nothing compared to her other torments. Every push forward took her one knee-step farther away from the dead bodies lying in the snow behind her. She didn't want to think of them but, the harder she tried to push them from her mind, the more insistently they haunted her. The tall Alfrec, murdered before her eyes, and the dying stranger the brothers had brought with them.

It had to be a stranger. Mattias was in Frastmir. He'd made it back before the storm hit. At this moment, he was sitting at her kitchen table, eating a bowl of porridge and telling her parents that he'd left her provisioned and in high spirits, well on her way to the temple.

Therefore, he couldn't possibly be lying there beside Alfrec. Her heart ached because she was tired. And the tears in her eyes were from the wind. She wasn't fighting back sobs because she mourned him—because *he wasn't dead!*—it was because Dyri and his brother wouldn't leave her alone. The ancient protections kept them from harming her physically, but the brothers had other ways to torture her.

The first thing Dyri had done when she'd refused to give in to his demands had been to take her satchel. He'd shown it to her and asked her again if she would go with them. When she'd refused, he'd cut the satchel open, spilling its contents. The meats, he'd shared with Bale. The rest, he'd burned then and there.

Sanja had almost wept at the loss of her blankets, but she'd soaked up the heat of the fire to warm herself and kept going. Not thinking of the dead bodies at all. Not imagining Mattias face-down in the snow, beaten, broken, and alone.

Bale had been furious at her continued resistance. He'd shouted and railed at Sanja from a distance of several arm's lengths—as close as the protective magic would allow him to get. Bale had a terrible temper he couldn't seem to control. He lashed out often, usually at the trees, because he couldn't get to her.

In contrast, Dyri was cold as ice. Rather than waste the effort to rage at Sanja, he studied her. Any time Bale lashed out, he watched for Sanja's flinch. He'd watched her the entire time her belongings had burned. He watched her each time she paused to rest. Where Bale was the rabid dog let off its chain, Dyri was the lynx hiding in shadow, waiting for the perfect moment and the most efficient way to strike. She squeezed her eyes shut whenever she felt the urge to look behind her so he wouldn't suspect how badly she needed to know it wasn't Mattias back there beside Alfrec. She could not let him use that stranger—*not Mattias!*—against her. It would destroy her.

As night approached, the men started to get cold. They paced and hopped in place, breathing into their hands for warmth, but Dyri wouldn't allow a fire. He would deny himself and his brother the comfort of its warmth to force more misery upon her.

It was only fitting for her to return the kindness. So long as she kept moving, they couldn't touch her, and their contract wouldn't let them leave.

Might the path's protective magic keep them at bay long enough? Could it be strong enough to counteract her blood oath for a while? Yes, her contract did say she had to marry Jarl Steen if she failed to earn her robes within a month, but it didn't say when. What if she simply kept going, all the way to the temple?

The thought of completing her Journey, and giving Jarl Steen not only a hairless bride but a robed one, filled her with grim satisfaction. He would be furious. She could still score a victory against him, however small. And Steen's men would be forced to suffer with her.

They'd tormented her all day long. In fact, all of her suffering along the Journey could be attributed directly to Jarl Steen and his men. They all deserved to suffer the same. If Sanja could keep the brothers in the cold and misery for one night longer, she would somehow find the strength to endure, to punish them for as long as she could. Why should they be spared when she could make their task as long and difficult as possible?

One knee after the other, she moved onward.

But she was beginning to fade after a day of pushing forward without pause. Her progress was so slow she could still smell the smoke from her burned things behind her. Still, at least she was moving. Every knee-step took her farther from those bodies. Before long, she would forget they were there at all.

And then her mind would give up this nonsense of Mattias lying dead in the cold when all he'd wanted was a peaceful life and a love to keep him warm.

As the light began to fade, Bale grew wary of the dark. "We should make camp," he said. "She can't run far, anyway. We could build a fire a ways down the path and wait for her."

Dyri's response was short and curt. "No."

"You're being unreasonable," Bale growled. "What do you expect her to do out here?"

She felt Dyri watching her and detected a cruel smirk in his voice when he said, "Rest."

With a frustrated huff, Bale let the matter drop.

But only for a while.

As the forest turned dark and Sanja began to feel as if she was floating through a dream, the hot-tempered Bale couldn't stand it any longer. He disobeyed his brother's wishes and lit a torch, waving it in Dyri's face. Dyri glared at his brother but didn't say a thing, and Sanja thought he was secretly grateful for the light.

So was she. It revived her enough to keep dragging one knee in front of the other. She watched for its flicker, took comfort from the promise of its warmth if nothing else.

Dyri noticed. "Douse it."

"No," Bale replied, mocking him.

Dyri started for Bale, who danced away to Sanja's other side, waving the torch back and forth. Rather than chase his brother, Dyri fell silent and crouched beside Sanja to take a closer look at her face. "You must be exhausted. I am, and I haven't been shoving along on my knees all day. On an empty stomach, to boot."

While he waited for her to respond, Sanja took another step. This time, the sharp ice cut through her trousers and scraped her bare skin, making her hiss in pain. She paused, sitting back on her heels and drooping forward to her elbows. She was so tired breathing was a chore. Her lips were covered in brittle scabs where her skin had split from the cold.

"Poor little thing," Dyri said. "So much misery you brought down on yourself for no good reason at all."

Sanja turned her head to spear him with a glare. "You say that when you have Jarl Steen's contract hanging over your head?"

Dyri shrugged. "Steen is nobility. All nobility are filthy shits." He leaned closer to meet her gaze as he imparted his next words of wisdom. "But one learns to tolerate them for the pleasures they provide."

"Pleasures?" She nearly choked, saying the word. He had to be jesting.

Dyri shook his head in mock pity. "You poor, ignorant thing. Bale, tell her."

"The Steen clan has coin," Bale said. "Mountains of it. Their keep is almost as big as Castle Frastmir, and Jarl Steen enjoys his comforts very much. The best of everything, he has. Food, clothes, jewels..."

"And you can still have all of it. You can have your own chambers with a hearth so big you'll never feel another twinge of a chill. You can have servants carry you anywhere you wish to go. Your feet need never touch the ground."

Sanja laughed, wincing as her lower lip split again. When Dyri frowned at her, she laughed harder. How could she not? "Do you think I would be out here," she said, her voice raw and reedy, "if any of that mattered to me?"

A burning ember sailed over her head to land in front of her. Mesmerized by its glow, she didn't notice Dyri move away from her, but she heard him demand, "What are you doing?"

She reached out slowly, hovering her hand over the small ember, feeling its meager warmth soak into her palm as its light began to dim.

"Worth a try," Bale said. "Now we know we can't kill her from a distance, neither."

Sanja took a chance and snatched up the ember. It burned her at

first, but she held on, hugging it to her chest. Its warmth streamed
into her, through her, into Princess Liadan's tokens. There, the heat
flared stronger, stroking up her spine and through her limbs. Sanja
sighed, feeling lighter and stronger for it. If only it would last.

When she dropped the ember back, Sanja became aware of the
silence and looked up to find Dyri watching her once again.

He glanced down at the cold, black ember, then at the dark scorch
mark on her palm, and finally at her face. Moving with calculated
intent, he slowly drew his knife and crouched down to place it on the
snow in front of her.

Sanja stared at the blade, her mind struggling to comprehend its
purpose. It was right there, within easy reach, a weapon, and a tool.
A chance to end it all. All she had to do was pick it up and turn it
on herself.

Or on them.

Sanja had never deliberately harmed another person; she didn't
know how. With Dyri's blade, the prospect seemed easy enough. The
bandage he'd wrapped around his hand was still a bit wet where his
cut hadn't healed all the way. She knew how sharp the blade was, how
quickly it could do a world of damage.

She stared at it and thought, *I could do it.* Dyri was close enough
that she could stab him dead if she moved quickly. But what about
Bale? He would never let her get away with it, and the moment she
left the path, she'd lose its protection.

Her gaze rose to meet Dyri's. So that was his trick, then.

His pale eyes watched her, steady and curious, waiting for her to
decide her own fate. He didn't move a muscle and, if Sanja guessed
correctly, he wasn't breathing, either. His entire body, as relaxed as it
appeared, was poised to move with a speed Sanja could never hope
to match. Unlike her, Dyri *was* a murderer, an expert at his trade, by
all appearances.

She half-turned away from him. Bale was on that side, but it wasn't
him she wanted to seek. Somewhere on the trail behind her, Mattias
lay unmoving in the snow, freezing to death, if he wasn't dead already.
The knowledge burned inside her, refusing to be defeated by the lies
she clung onto. Mattias had never made it back to Frastmir. If he had,

the brothers never would have come looking for her this far down the path. Mattias was the only one who could have told them she was still alive and moving forward.

It was him, lying there in the snow beside Alfrec. They'd killed him—because of her.

The pain in her chest doubled her over, robbed her of breath when she wanted to scream her grief and kill Dyri and Bale for what they'd done to the kind, gentle man she would have called brother.

It won't bring him back.

No, it wouldn't bring him back. It would only destroy everything she'd been suffering for and everything he'd done to help her keep going.

Honor him. Give his death meaning.

Yes, she could still do that. She wasn't finished.

Sanja sought Dyri's gaze and held it for so long his mouth twitched in an almost smile. With her hands somewhat more limber from the ember's added warmth, she uncurled her fingers and reached down, taking hold of the weapon Dyri had offered. When she straightened to meet his gaze once more, the blade now in her grasp, she found him in the same place, his head tilted the same way, his mouth stretched into the same smile.

But his eyes were sharper, staring hard into hers. She felt the tension in him now, a predator poised to strike. His time had come, and he was merely waiting for the signal to move.

Sanja looked at the knife in her hand, then back at him. His chest rose with a deep inhale, his unblinking gaze reflecting Bale's torchlight back at her. She raised the blade high, watching his eyes open wide, then drew back and threw it sideways as hard as she could. The knife sailed into the darkness beyond Bale's light and landed softly in deep snow some distance away.

Sanja smiled into Dyri's shocked face and dragged her left knee forward, forcing him to move out of her way. Satisfaction burned through her veins, heating her limbs a little more. She used it to her best advantage, picking up her pace to a slightly faster crawl.

They'd spend hours searching for that knife, and might never find it, anyway.

"Bollocks this," Dyri muttered.

"Oi! Where are you going?" Bale's torchlight dimmed as he followed his brother down the path behind Sanja. She heard noises but didn't turn around. Better not to know what they were up to.

But Dyri would not be ignored. His grunts and curses signaled his return as he dragged something toward Sanja. "Right," he said, dropping his burden by her side. "You know him, yes? He of a certainty knew you."

Sanja squeezed her eyes shut rather than look at the limp body beside her. She could tell by its size it could be none other than Mattias, and her heart broke for him all over again.

"Friend of yours, is he?" Dyri taunted. "A good one, too. He was that distraught when we met at that ramshackle inn a ways back. Going on and on about the wee lass he'd left behind, and how ashamed he was to have left her all alone out there. 'Would that I could have done more,' he said to us, didn't he, Bale?"

"That he did," Bale confirmed. "Cried tears worthy of a spurned virgin, he did."

Sanja bit the inside of her cheek as she brought her left knee forward.

"And we told him, my brothers and I, 'A lass, taking the Journey at a time like this? She must be either very brave or very stupid.' And what did he say, Bale?"

"He said, 'A stronger, braver one I've never met.'"

Sanja shifted her right knee forward, then her left. She kept her gaze on the path before her, but inside she was dying a little more with each word they spoke.

Dyri kept pace with her, dragging Mattias a bit ahead of her. He leaned down to see her face and grinned. "And then he told us all about your quest to escape an unwanted suitor."

"Which we already knew," Bale chimed in.

"Of course we knew. All of what's left of Frastmir is abuzz with rumors of a daft girl going off to her death on the Journey. We almost left you to it, too. But we do have our contract to consider."

Bale grunted agreement and spat on the ground.

"So we told the man, 'We're messengers sent to the temple by the king, bound by honor to keep his peace. We've naught to offer but our company, but surely the girl would be grateful to have even that. Tell us where to find her, and we'll convey her safely to the temple.'"

Sanja breathed down her revulsion, kept moving forward. Her throat ached from keeping silent when all she wanted to do was scream.

"He resisted," Dyri said. "At first. Tried to keep us from you. Three against one and still, he fought us. But my brothers and I brought him 'round in the end, didn't we, Bale? We can be very persuasive." He leaned over Mattias and dragged him up before Sanja, where she couldn't hope to avoid looking.

Sanja slapped a hand over her mouth, sat hard on her heels to see her good friend brought to such a state. His hair shirt was covered with dirt and blood, his face nigh unrecognizable underneath a mottling of swollen bruises. He had gashes on his temples and cuts all over his arms. Had it not been for the tears in his trousers and the wounds on his knees that she had helped him tend, Sanja would never have known him. "You've killed him."

Dyri looked down. "Did I?" He put a hand under Mattias' shattered nose. "Not quite yet. He's still breathing." He met her gaze again and again gave her that cruel smirk. "Bale, give me the torch."

Bale obediently handed it over and stepped a safe distance away.

"Now, then," Dyri told Sanja. "One last chance. Will you come with us willingly?"

Sanja couldn't tear her gaze away from Mattias. In the flickering torchlight, she saw his head move a little. A trick of the light? It had to be. Dyri was lying. Mattias had been motionless on the ground from the moment they'd dropped him there. Even if he had been alive then, he couldn't be now. His fingers and toes had started to turn black from the cold. None of his wounds were bleeding, and despite what Dyri said, Sanja could not detect any hint of breath in him.

Mattias was dead. Never to find his love, or a hearth fire to keep him warm. After all he'd endured, and everything he'd already done for her, he'd died out there in the bitter cold, fighting to keep the brothers from Sanja.

They'd killed him to get to her, and if she gave in, he would have died in vain.

"Consider it a trial of the heart," Dyri offered, bringing the torch closer to Mattias' face. "We're about to find out whether anyone's life is more precious to you than your own. Will you save him, oh brave one? He paid dearly, trying to save you. It's only fitting you return the gesture, no? The gods do love their balance. The honor ought t'be answered. The blood ought t'be repaid."

She owed Mattias everything. His kindness had kept her going, and the supplies he'd left had saved her life, she was certain. To know he had died for her was more than she could bear. How in the world could she repay a debt like that?

"I…"

Dyri raised an eyebrow. "Well?"

Her numb face scrunched up as she took in Mattias' visage. Such handsome features, he'd had. And such a big heart. Sanja wasn't worthy of his sacrifice. "I…" She reached out to touch him, dreading the feel of his cold, lifeless flesh beneath her fingertips.

Dyri yanked him out of her reach and brought the torch closer still. "I'll not wait much longer."

My fault. Sanja had expected Jarl Steen to keep pursuing her, but not at such a cost. Did he know what his men had done?

Had he given the order himself?

I can't go back. Mattias, brother of my heart, please forgive me.

Dyri must have seen her decision in her eyes. With a savage snarl, he shoved Mattias away and stabbed the torch against his side. With his hair shirt so thoroughly soaked, it took an agonizing while for the flame to catch. Mattias never stirred or made a sound. Sanja watched his body burn a moment longer, praying that his ancestors would meet him with open arms in the afterlife.

As she turned away to keep going forward, Dyri barred her path with the torch. "No great loss for you, then, is it? Eh, you're probably right. What's a stranger worth these days, anyway? Certainly not more than blood kin. And you still have two of those left in Frastmir, if I'm not mistaken." He leaned down as close as the magic would allow. "I'll give you the night to think on that. In the morning, my brother and I will set out back to Frastmir. You'll want to be coming with us, then, if only to make sure your parents don't go the way of your friend. Because I'll make sure they're alive when they do."

16

Nialei tensed as the tracker approached. Though her shoulders were proudly pulled back, she wouldn't meet Nialei's gaze. Bad news, then.

Gods, how bad?

The female's horned head bowed as she knelt her front hooves to the ground, her many golden plaits slipping over her shoulders to cover her face as though she was ashamed. Her kind was a beautiful blend of doe and human, thin and lithe, appearing so delicate, yet thrumming with immense power. When she became agitated, that power coursed through her veins, painting them black against her silvery skin.

She would not speak until prompted, and Nialei could not bring herself to ask the question she desperately needed to have answered.

Saeran took her hand in his, drawing her gaze to his strange, yet still familiar face. Despite having retained his human shape for the most part, her beloved mate and king looked more dragon than human in this land, with thick horns adorning his head and shimmering black scales framing his brows. His teeth flashed sharp whenever he spoke, giving his smile a feral edge, and his eyes blazed with blue fire that seemed to burn just for her. His Other form was similar in shape to their daughter's, save for his size. As if he'd stuck partway to becoming a true dragon, Saeran's shoulders were wider than normal, his arms and legs thickly muscled. His wings were far bigger than Liadan's, flaring and furling with a will of their own, and his tail ended in a sharp, arrow-like tip that cut like a blade. Yet he retained his human-shaped hands and feet and seemed to have the ability to retract his claws when necessary.

Nialei had not dared to look at her reflection since the first day, but she knew she appeared no less Other. A Halfling daughter of a water sprite and a demigod, she'd inherited the pearlescent skin of her mother's people and the antler crown of her father's. The transformation had made her eyes bigger and rounder, her nose smaller, more delicate. The sides of her neck were scarred with straight lines where her gills lay flat and dormant while she was on land, but in water, her antlers dissolved away, her gills opened, and fine webbing grew between her fingers.

In Wilderheim, the two of them would have terrified the masses. Their appearance would have incited panic and riots among the humans who tolerated their regents' magic only because they didn't look Other. Here, among her father's people, no one bothered to cast them a second glance.

She steeled herself to take a measure of the gathering. Her father's herd, all giants walking on two hooved legs, with antlers jutting out of their heads, stomped restlessly within the circle of trees that marked the gathering green. They were wary of the tracker whose delicate, four-legged form barely reached their hips with the top of her antlers. The sooner she delivered her message and left, the better.

"Speak, please," Nialei invited softly, cautious of her voice. It sounded the same, but felt much more potent and seemed to have an unpleasant effect on her father's herd. Though she was always careful to show proper respect and humility to her father's people, her smallest request was met with disdainful obedience. They reacted as if she hadn't asked, but ordered, and then forced their compliance against their will. Nialei had no way of knowing how much of this effect was caused by the power in her voice and how much by her rank as the only offspring of their leader.

"My Lady," the tracker replied, her voice as gentle as her form.

"I have located the daughter of fire on the border between Aegiros and Wilderheim. She wore battle gear and soared as a black shadow across the night sky."

"Where was she heading?" Saeran asked and cleared his throat, still annoyed by the growl he could not shake from his voice. Nialei bit back a smile. She rather liked that growl, herself.

"Nowhere, My Lord. She appeared to be patrolling."

This had both of them leaning forward in their seats. "My daughter, patrolling Wilderheim's border?"

"Yes, My Lord," the tracker replied and answered the question they were both thinking. "Fear travels on an icy wind across the land. The sky burns with magic, and the earth freezes with dread. Others have fled. Trade and travel have come to a halt. Humans who leave Wilderheim do so for good. Those who stay are bracing for war. And..." She glanced up, a fine webbing of black sprouting out from the corners of her eyes like an elaborate mask.

Cold dread settled deep in Nialei's gut. "What is it?"

The tracker bowed her head once more. "Strange things are growing throughout Wilderheim. Masses of power that have no origin and no anchor. Only an Other would sense them, but this Other sensed them growing stronger with each day."

"Creatures of some sort?" Saeran questioned. "Traps?"

"Portals, My Lord. Seven of them."

Saeran squeezed Nialei's hand so hard, had she been human, her bones would have been crushed to dust. "Does my daughter know of this?"

"No, My Lord. She has not ventured that deep in her patrols. Her path takes her southwest, along the Aegiran border to Lyria. She expects Synealee to march from that direction."

"Where is Fal in all of this?" Surely, Nialei's son would have sensed the portals; surely, it was he who'd called up the army. He would know something was brewing and take measures to protect Wilderheim and its people. Even if he never left Castle Frastmir, he could still—

"Gone, My Lady."

Nialei lost her breath. Her body felt encased in a layer of ice so thick she couldn't move even to blink.

"No one has seen or heard from the son of water in over a week. There is no sign of his presence within the borders of Wilderheim."

Silence met the tracker's report. Not a single hoof stomped down, not a leaf rustled in the trees. Nialei heard her own heart beat slower and slower, and she knew if she let it, it would stop completely.

A tracker's magic was unique to all the Others, and their kind was both feared and revered because of it. Simply, they never failed to locate what they'd been sent to find. Ever. If this tracker hadn't found a trace of Fal, it could only mean he was not there to be found.

Saeran's hand grew cold, holding hers, and Nialei began to feel lightheaded. Somehow, she managed to turn her head and meet her mate's gaze, desperate for the comfort of his fire, the surety that he would know what to do. It wasn't there. The eyes gazing back at her were as gray as the sky above her head, not a spark of fire to them.

"We have to find a way back," she pleaded.

Saeran's wings flared, sending the herd stomping out of the way. His glittering black cheeks turned dull in a Dragonblood version of an embarrassed flush as he folded the willful appendages tight against his back. "We have already tried fire and water, and we have found no portals in the entire Otherland. What else can we do?"

A tall, swarthy warrior stepped out of the herd toward them. "Forgive, Nobility. Cernunnos not allow."

Saeran speared him with a burning glare. "The tracker has come and gone. So has Varr."

The warrior flushed and bowed his head. "Forgive, Nobility. Cernunnos protect herd. Nobility is herd. Nobility cannot leave. Cernunnos not allow."

"A god I have barely heard of will not keep me from my children," Nialei grated and instantly regretted her tone when the warrior whined and retreated back into the herd.

A warm, heavy hand settled on her shoulder, thick, blunt fingers curling into her flesh to offer comfort. "That god is your grandsire," her father said kindly. His face showed no emotion, but his eyes warmed to a shade of gold, looking at her.

"I don't care," she replied hotly. "I will not be kept prisoner while my children fight for their lives. Fal could be dead—"

Gjafvaldr, the first son of Cernunnos and leader of his herd, squeezed her shoulder a little harder. "Cernunnos has given of his essence to shield this world from Fenrir. He has given his life to protect his off-spring for as long as he can, that we may live as we do, and die swiftly when the time comes. It is a kindness. Not punishment."

"We mean no disrespect," Saeran said humbly. "But we cannot stay here. We must finish what we started."

"Fal is not dead. If he was, the tracker would have found a body. This has Loki's cunning written all over it. And that means it can be nothing but a trick. You have raised powerful children, daughter. Have faith in what they are destined to accomplish."

It was what he'd done. He'd placed his newborn daughter into the arms of a human and abandoned her there to grow up with no notion of who or what she was. He'd trusted her to be strong enough to grow into her destiny without his interference. Nialei both loved and resented him for it. She might not have needed his help but, gods, how she wished she'd had his guidance. And now he was asking her to do the same to her children. "I cannot abandon them. I will not."

"The wards are set, daughter," Gjafvaldr said and, though his voice was kind, his eyes hardened. He spoke to her like a stubborn child who needed to be taught a lesson. "They are god-made. You will not break them while he still has power."

"By the time his power fades, it will be too late. Please, we must leave now."

He held her gaze a moment longer, then released her to approach the tracker.

The herd stepped back in deference, and the tracker bowed so low her antlers touched the ground before she rose to her full height, brought her shoulders back, and stared straight ahead.

"You have done well, tracker," Gjafvaldr praised. He held out his hand, and a large pouch appeared in it. Nialei had seen him perform this magic enough times already to know the pouch would be heavy with gold coins.

The tracker nodded and reached for her payment, but Gjafvaldr pulled it back out of reach. Her eyes sparked bright black when she met his gaze, her temper showing in a webbing of black veins that snaked from her fingertips across her hands and up her arms.

"I have one more task for you," Gjafvaldr said, holding up his free hand in a staying gesture. "And will pay you handsomely for it." As he spoke, the pouch grew larger, heavier, mesmerizing the tracker out of her ire. "The daughter of fire will need help in her brother's absence. She is a fierce warrior, but even a Dragonblood cannot oppose the power of a god on her own. You will race across the Otherlands and deliver my call to arms to each and every clan."

At this, the tracker frowned at him. "They have their own battles to fight, My Lord."

"They can spare two warriors each. Two warriors from every clan, understand?" He placed the now massive pouch on the ground before her.

"If only a tenth of them agree, the daughter of fire shall have a formidable force at her back," the tracker mused. "But not an army."

"I am aware," Gjafvaldr replied. "The final battle need not be won in Wilderheim. Only fought long enough."

The tracker cocked her head to one side. "You do not wish me to find the dragon, My Lord?"

"We already know where he is," Nialei said. "A creature of in-between has already been sent to retrieve him." If Cernunnos' wards couldn't be breached by her or Saeran, then the dragon was their last hope of escape. His blood had been powerful enough to change their clan's destiny more than once. Nialei could only pray it'd be powerful enough for one more magic spell.

~

Helheim's prison had no sun or moon. Its torches and candles never burned down, and no creatures scurried in and out of the safety of their burrows to feed. Without these things, the dragon had no way to tell the passage of time, save by the deadly floods. He'd endured two score and three of them thus far but, whether each flood translated to an hour in Wilderheim or a year, he couldn't tell. For all he knew, two score and three centuries have passed in his absence, and the worlds he had known were long gone down Fenrir's monstrous gullet.

"Are you tempted yet?"

The dragon tensed at that voice, his mouth drawing back from long, sharp fangs that ached to rend flesh asunder.

"The water has receded already, have you noticed? Do you know why?"

Hands balled into fists, the dragon pulled taut his binds, strained against them, and prayed to feel the rope strands fray and snap. Instead, they tightened around his wrists until his hands throbbed.

From the shadows at his back, a cool, pale hand brushed against his burning one. Snarling, the dragon turned his face away, and there she was, his beautiful Solveig, her eyes sad as she gazed at his bound wrists.

But her voice spoke with Hel's apathy. "Its source lies outside the borders of my realm. It feels my brother's approach and freezes into eternal winter." She looked toward the river and sighed. "Soon, the stream will disappear completely."

The dragon frowned. He could almost believe he'd heard the slightest hint of true sorrow in her words. Or was it grief?

"What is it like?" she asked, still watching the waves ripple down the stream.

The dragon refused to indulge her with an answer.

Rather than press for one, she remained silent, her head tilted as if she were listening to someone else speaking to her. Had her question been directed at him at all? "Why did you choose this shape?" When she turned her face toward him, it briefly split, Solveig's ghostly visage facing him a moment before Hel, and in that moment, before Hel realigned herself, he saw genuine surprise in Solveig's eyes. He saw her mouth open to speak as Hel took over once more. "You could have become anything. Why this?"

Having borne witness to the creation of all living beings, dragons carried within them the ability to become any of them—until they chose one. Then, and ever after, the infinite potential of shapeshifting narrowed to but one alternative: dragon, or their chosen other. In all his long millennia of life, the dragon had never understood the reason for it, until he'd met Solveig.

He'd thought the ability and its restrictions to be a secret kept by his kind alone. He'd never spoken of it to anyone. Not Solveig, or their daughter, or any of his clan. How could Hel have known?

The dragon flinched when she reached out to touch one of his horns, but she persisted, running soft, cool fingertips from one's base at his left temple all the way to the tip. "You, a creature born of infinite potential, chose *this*. Why?"

Water splashed up as he whipped his tail to knock her hand aside. Hel stepped away.

Solveig lingered a moment longer, gifting him with a glimpse of the woman she'd used to be. Her lips began to form his name, and he sucked in a breath, aching to hear it again, but she faded too soon, blowing back around Hel and settling over her until Hel once again became her. "You bound yourself in shape and form. You gave up infinity for a wizard's trick. I will know why."

The dragon bared his fangs in a vicious snarl.

Solveig's eyes closed as Hel stilled for a moment. "For her," she said. "For *love*. No, that cannot be." She opened her eyes to regard him with her utter lack of interest, even as a ghostly tear glittered down her cheek. "You must have known her fate the moment you looked into her eyes, yet still, you condemned her to it."

The dragon's scales bristled with a roiling mixture of fury, grief, and shame. He'd been selfish from the start, wanting Solveig all for himself. He'd known it from the start, too. The brave, beautiful, kind-hearted human girl had given up everything and everyone she'd ever known to be with him. It'd been a steep price to pay, and the dragon had matched it eagerly by binding himself into a shape she could love, one that could love her back.

He'd thought it would be enough to keep her safe. Blinded by his love, humbled by everything she'd sacrificed, the dragon had been loath to take away the one thing she'd retained: her freedom of choice. Solveig herself had refused the offer of his blood, treasuring her mortality as the last remaining vestige of herself and, despite knowing what the consequences would be, the dragon had honored her decision. He'd loved his mate all the more for the brevity of time he knew he'd have with her.

Yes, he had known Solveig would eventually die.

But he hadn't expected it to happen so soon.

"She forgave you for her plight, but not yours."

"Enough," he growled. "Stop this, Hel."

"It pains you to hear this." Her arms billowed with pale mist, Solveig trying to reach out, but Hel wouldn't allow it. "It pains her, as well. I feel it pressing on my chest. She cannot bear to see you like this, bound in flesh, tied like a rabid animal—and she knows you are. She can see the creature she had loved so dearly is gone. She mourns you."

"Let her go!" he roared.

"Answer me, and I'll return her to oblivion where she knew nothing of your presence here, or her own. She will be at peace. That is what you want for her, is it not? An end to her suffering."

The dragon looked directly into her fathomless eyes, sought Solveig's heart in them, sought some meaning to this madness Hel had brought him but found neither.

Hel floated closer, a current of magic twining around her form to split it into two. Hel, in her natural form, tilted her head at him, ignoring the ghostly woman hovering beside her. Solveig's eyes were closed as if in sleep, her lips leeched of color, her cheeks pale in the sunless dungeon. "Tell me why," Hel insisted. "Why sacrifice everything when this was always going to be the result?"

The dragon couldn't breathe. His entire being screamed with unbearable agony to see his beloved in such a state. And she would remain that way forever, asleep even when her eyes opened, wandering through Helheim, oblivious, lost. Alone.

"Tell me."

Defeated, the dragon dropped to his knees, bowed his head to escape the sight, but he couldn't. As if sensing his turmoil, the water stilled so completely its surface became as smooth as a silvered glass where Solveig's image floated unattainably near, glowing like a sleeping star waiting to awaken.

Then Hel's face took shape in the reflection, the smoking shadows of her dark hair hiding Solveig from his sight. His relief shamed him.

"Tell me."

"Because..." The words stuck in his throat like shards of volcanic glass tearing it to shreds until he tasted blood.

Hel sank to her knees before him, bowing her head, and he saw her in the water's surface, seeking his gaze.

The dragon looked up, not at Hel, but at his heart floating behind her, as lifeless there as the organ that lay within his chest. He'd lost all sunshine the day she'd died in his arms, and darkness had choked him every day since. "Because…" he swallowed with difficulty, clenching his jaw so tightly he thought he'd never get it open again. "The briefest moment of joy with her was worth a thousand years of torment."

Hel absorbed this in silence while the river resumed its flow. The torches briefly banked to humble embers before resuming their steady burn, and in that moment, the whole of Helheim sighed its secrets into him, repaying his intimacy with a glimpse of its vast depth. Hel had spoken true. This realm was steeped in tranquility that blanketed all who dwelled within its borders. Solveig was part of it now, if not happy, then at least at peace, untouched by the turmoil and pain of her mortal life. It was more than he would ever have.

"Without her," he confessed, "infinity would have held no meaning. She was my everything. Always. And her memory is more precious to me than my own life."

Hel turned to look at Solveig, and his beloved's ghostly form disappeared, leaving the dragon alone with his unfeeling tormentor. "This is what they call love," she said.

"Yes," he replied, though *love* felt too inadequate a word to convey the true depth of his connection to Solveig. She was a part of him, as he would always be a part of her.

"Thank you," she said after a while, and then she was gone.

For a long time, the dragon knelt there in silence, listening to the river sing its lullabies. It almost began to make sense to him. Without Solveig, he felt his fire begin to weaken. The pain of grief eased, the rage against his prison faded, and he became numb.

He didn't change positions again until the water around him had risen to his chest, and then it was with a bored sort of reluctance that he bothered pushing to his feet. It was a tiresome chore to keep his head above the surface, to hold his breath when it washed over his face again and again. What did it matter, anyway?

When the water receded, he sat with his back to the stone wall. The tips of his horns dug into the cold stone, and he raked them back and forth across a single groove, scoring it ever deeper. Liadan's ring throbbed cold around his finger, its rhythm matching the shallow waves lapping at his thighs. All he had to do was twist it on his finger to summon his clan to him from wherever they happened to be. But what purpose would it serve? Instead of setting him free, they'd end up imprisoned in Helheim along with him. No, they were needed far more elsewhere.

The dragon submerged his hand, cupped some water into his palm, and brought it up to his face. His mouth watered for a taste. One sip…

Squeezing his eyes shut, he dug deep within his soul to bring forth his fire and heated the water until it steamed. The hiss it produced sounded almost like a scream, and he took perverse pleasure in drawing it out to the last drop.

17

Fal's new Otherland, which he'd decided to name Anderheim, was a veritable playground for his mind and magic. He could shape the world into anything his imagination could conjure. But, though necessary, using magic, learning the way it moved and could be moved here was a dangerous game to play. With little enough time to waste, every moment Fal spent sitting or standing still to work a spell felt like a moment wasted. He weighed the importance of each pause and task against Sanja's life, trying to balance the scales in some way. Fal had no way of knowing where Sanja was along the path, but as long as she kept moving, he knew she'd be safe. If he failed to learn enough about Anderheim's nature and structure, he knew he'd lose her no matter what.

But the more magic Fal used, the faster it poured out, speeding up the process he wanted to slow down. He'd tried to stop it altogether, and Anderheim had struck back at him with a furious thunderstorm, demonstrating not only its strength but also its weakness.

It appeared Anderheim needed Fal's magic far more than he'd originally thought. Fal suspected its existence still depended on it and, if he were to remove it, the Otherland would not only stop evolving, it would disintegrate.

A tempting alternative, but only as a last resort. His life was currently so entangled with Anderheim, destroying it might kill Fal in the process.

Instead, he turned his efforts toward passive spells that used what was already there, rather than an infusion of his will. It felt very much like learning everything for the first time. Of all the lessons imparted to him by the dragon, his parents, and his tutors, Nialei's wisdom proved to be the most useful: "There is no separateness in the world. Everything is connected to everything else. Find the connection. It will be your conduit for change."

With that in mind, Fal sought water. As the most abundant element anywhere, it was the most powerful and the farthest-reaching. It was the source of life, flowing through every realm and connecting them all.

He sacrificed another puff of magic to find his way to a small puddle that might eventually grow into a lake. Lowering to his haunches, he gazed into the surface as he would his scrying bowl. The difficult part was patience—allowing himself the time necessary to work the magic when with each beat of his heart, he felt it slipping through his fingers. "Show me what you will," he said, making it an invitation, rather than an order.

At first, nothing happened. The water heard him and understood what he wanted, but struggled to form a proper response. Fal hovered his hand over the calm surface without touching it. As if sensing his nearness, the ripples pushed up higher, closer, with a yearning he could feel. "Show me what you see," he beseeched.

The surface stilled, reflecting his own face back at him.

Fal smiled. "Can you show me Wilderheim?"

The puddle hummed and vibrated with confusion. It shrank down to almost nothing, and Fal sensed it had retreated to its source deep underground, as if for guidance. When it welled up once more, the reflection showed him the same configuration of trees, but no Fal.

He frowned. "That's not…"

The water welled up more, insisting on what it showed him. It rippled, and the tips of its waves shone with colorful lights. He hadn't noticed them for the trees, but now that his eyes knew what to look for, he spotted swirling, roiling coils of chaos in the reflection of

Wilderheim's sky.

"Thank you," he said politely.

The waves jumped back and forth. Now that they'd found the right place, they were eager to show him more. *Ask*, they whispered without words. *Ask. Ask…*

He asked the only thing that mattered, already knowing what the answer would be. "Can you take me there?"

The waves stilled. Once more, the pool shrank down to its source. He waited for it to return, but the task he'd set it appeared to require a far longer consultation. Fal had almost given up when he felt the pool pushing to the surface again. No longer jaunty with excitement, it settled to its original level far more subdued than before.

The answer, as expected, was no. Even between two worlds directly on top of each other, the waterways were still frozen. He would not be getting back to Wilderheim that way. "Worth a try."

The water welled toward him, pushing out of its basin in an attempt to forge its own path for a stream. It reached out to him with encouragement, urging him to keep trying. It wanted him to succeed and wanted to help him do so.

Fal placed his hand flat to the surface and filled his mind with thoughts of Sanja. The wild disarray of her hair, the sparkling intelligence in her eyes, the sweetness of her smile. He gave the water his memory of her covered in wildflowers, laughing and twirling on the green with so much joy it made his heart clench with longing. He gave it her curiosity, her courage, her perseverance. The smell of books that would forever remind Fal of her love of them, the reverence with which she treated every word on every page. He gave it the feel of her soft kiss in the rain, the cool smoothness of her skin, the music of her sigh, and the sweet clutch of her hand on his. "Can you find her for me?"

A wave lapped up over his hand, pulling it down beneath the surface. It tasted his request, absorbed the image of a thin, pale girl with black curls cut short around her head. It took far more than he offered, pulling from him the searing pain of lightning melting Sanja to him, and the vision of a lifetime condensed into a single heartbeat that thumped back into him without mercy, reminding him of things that had never been, and would never be, yet hurt regardless as if he'd lost something precious he'd never known he had.

Fal shrank from the memory, presenting Sanja instead in her hair-cloth shirt and trousers, crawling on her knees up the staircase carved into Hallowed Mountain. She had to be somewhere on this path; he needed to find her. His need dispersed beneath the surface, urging the water to guide him, to show him she was all right.

It quivered away from the cold and pushed back instead, seeking out another sunny day, with the grass still green and soft, though the ground from which it grew was already freezing. It sought Sanja's face turned up to his, her eyes filled with breathless wonder as his hand gently cupped her cheek. It sent warmth up his arm and across his chest, bringing him the feel of her shivering in his arms inside the cold barn, trusting him with herself, even as her fear of him harming others pushed her away.

"What is this?" He didn't understand. His instructions had been clear: find Sanja.

As the soft ripple whispered with Sanja's voice reading from the book he'd gifted her, he realized that was precisely what the water was doing. It sought her—inside Fal. And with each memory it raised to the surface of his thoughts, his need to find her in Wilderheim grew sharper. Sanja was safe, warm, and protected in his mind, but not in the real world. With every moment he wasted here in Anderheim, she could be slowly freezing to death or suffering at the mercy of Steen's temper.

It hurt like a thousand needles scratching across his mind to force the memories aside. In their place, he filled his thoughts with the worst possible outcomes: Sanja lying on the ground, still, frozen, with the wind blowing drifts of snow to bury her in eternal winter. He imagined her bound and beaten, kneeling before Steen as he sneered down at her in victory. His heart grew shards of ice that stabbed frozen dread into his body with every beat. His breath misted as he forced the visions into the water with the understanding that it could never come to pass, else the ice in him would never melt, and he would freeze right along with Sanja.

The water keened and shrank away, then came back for one more taste of Sanja's joyous laugh, shivering as it receded again. When it welled up, it showed him the dark night sky and snowy trees swaying against it. It gave him the flickering light of a fire, the smell of smoke and burning flesh, and the sound of male voices shouting angrily at each other.

"Closer," Fal commanded with enough magic to make the water flinch and obey instantly.

Anderheim rumbled around him, pulling more magic for its own ends, but in return, it gave him fireflies to illuminate the night.

In the water's surface, he looked out through the thin sheen of melted frost clinging to a tree trunk. Skeins of black smoke rose from the ground below, and his gut clenched when he noticed the charred remnants of someone's hand amid the burned foliage.

Too big to be Sanja's. It wasn't her.

But Fal's relief was short-lived. Some distance away, the light of a torch waved back and forth. Male voices argued over something to do with a blade, and Sanja was nowhere in sight. Fal squinted to see better, but the arguing figures were too far. "Closer," he commanded again.

The water's surface quivered. It wanted to obey, but beyond that charred circle where the fire had melted enough snow and frost to liquid water, everything was frozen. The edges of his window were beginning to freeze as the chill of night descended on the scene.

No, this couldn't be right. Sanja ought to have been much farther along already. By his unreliable count, a full fortnight had passed since he'd last seen her—she only had one day left to reach the temple and earn her cleric's robes. How could she have fallen so far behind? And who were those men?

Fal pushed again to get closer, and again the water resisted. "Please," he begged, feeding more magic into the spell. "I need to see." Everything about the scene looked wrong, and all he could think was that Sanja was in danger. He needed to get to her and quickly.

Anderheim absorbed the request along with a great deal of his magic. The entire world quivered and shifted around him so fast his head spun, and, when Anderheim settled once more, Fal was kneeling in a different spot entirely. Despite the gentle glow of fireflies, the dark of night obscured his surroundings. Fal couldn't tell where he'd been

taken; had no point of reference to orient himself, but he sensed he'd
been brought closer.

"Sanja!" he slurred as Anderheim claimed more of him to feed
itself. Fal needed water, but, perversely, Anderheim denied him. The
ground all around him was completely dry, not a single droplet of
mist to be found anywhere.

Fal braced himself against a tree as he conjured orbs of light and
sent them flying in all directions in search of a reference point. One
of them halted a short distance away and flared to illuminate a rock
wall. He was almost to the staircase carved into Hallowed Mountain.

"Sanja," he called again, and when his echo returned, it carried with
it those strangers' voices.

"Think I need a knife to end one troublesome little bitch?" one of
them said. "I'll kill you with my bare hands!"

Fal sucked in a sharp breath as something raw and terrible sparked
inside him. It turned his blood hot and cold at the same time, made
gooseflesh prickle all over his arms and legs. He gritted his teeth,
felt his feet root down, drawing his magic back from Anderheim.
It coursed up his body, churned in sickening torrents in his chest,
and when it released through his voice, it made Anderheim shriek.
"*Where is she!*" he shouted, the rockface returning his voice threefold.

In the silence that followed, frost crackled into being at his feet. He
watched it spread, shivered as his breath misted in the sudden cold.
The trees turned white, mounds of snow grew at their bases. Dry
ground became churned mud, frozen into hard peaks and hollows.

Fal smelled winter on the air, distant smoke, and the reek of blood
and unwashed bodies. Like a mirage, Anderheim drew back from
him for a distance of several paces in all directions and, as it did, the
men he'd only seen from a distance before appeared in front of him.

And between them, kneeling in the middle of the frozen path was
Sanja. Her hair was wet, freezing into stiff curls and spikes. Her shirt
was filthy from sleeping on the forest floor, the trousers torn and
bloodied at the knees. She looked impossibly small and fragile, huddling close to the ground between the two men intent on killing her.

She leaned to one side, shifted the other knee forward, and drooped
lower still as she settled her weight on it. The effort came at a great

cost. Already weak and shivering with cold, Sanja was forced to pause and gather her strength as her shoulders rose and fell in great, labored breaths.

"Sanja…"

"Just drop already!" One of the men shouted at her. His legs were crusted with snow up to his thighs, and he was rubbing his hands for warmth.

The other seethed in silence, his clenched fists quivering. "She will, soon enough. She's half-dead as it is."

In answer, Sanja took a deep breath, leaned to the other side, and brought the opposite knee forward. As she did, the last of her strength seemed to desert her. She dropped forward onto her hands, her head hanging limp, and a broken moan shivered from her lips.

She was dying.

"There, you see?" the quiet one purred, cracking his knuckles. "We're almost on our way."

"Steen wants her alive," argued the other one.

The quiet one's reply never came as all sound faded into echoes. The men's figures became transparent, closing in on Sanja as the warmth of Anderheim began to creep back toward Fal once more, slowly taking the scene from him.

Fal didn't think. He lunged forward, reaching for Sanja even as whatever doorway Anderheim had opened began to slam shut.

~

She'd overestimated herself. Only forty paces along and Sanja was flagging in a dangerous way. Her legs were numb, her body shaking uncontrollably in the freezing night. Without fire, without her blanket, even Princess Liadan's gift wouldn't keep her from succumbing to eternal sleep.

She needn't die, either, only grow weak enough to faint. Dyri and Bale would finish the rest.

Keep moving forward. No other choice. She had written this ending for herself by choosing to let Jarl Steen live. *My own fault.*

If only her body would obey. Her spine was turning to jelly, her limbs as heavy as sacks of lead. She could no longer keep her head up, and staring at the ground made her yearn for but a few winks of sleep.

It took everything she had left to bring her knee forward. She had to be leaving tracks of blood in her wake, but Sanja no longer felt any pain. Only cold. Her mind was beginning to play tricks on her. It almost seemed to her like summer had returned. As chilled as she was, Sanja felt a warm breeze caress her frozen cheek with the scent of night-blooming flowers.

She heard it whisper her name…

"Just drop already!" Bale snapped. He'd failed to locate Dyri's knife, which infuriated the brothers and pleased Sanja to no end. He'd soaked himself to the thigh looking for it, and the cold was beginning to gnaw at him now, too.

"She will, soon enough," Dyri replied. He'd grown silent since his threat to her parents, keeping his voice quiet when he did deign to speak, but it was no less malicious for its softness. "She's half dead as it is."

Sanja wanted to prove him wrong. She shifted forward a little more, and her body simply gave out. Dropping to her hands, her head dangling, it was all Sanja could do not to keel over and let them have her. She tried to right herself but had no more strength left to draw upon. A weak little moan made it past her lips, her eyes stinging with the need to weep. But she had no tears left to shed, either.

It's over. This was where she'd breathe her last.

"There, you see? We're almost on our way."

Sanja felt Dyri move closer. The protective magic keeping him at bay was fading right along with her. Would she feel his hands on her before her heart gave out? Its laboring beats already shuddered in her chest. And still, Sanja would have smiled if she could. *Better than Jarl Steen's marriage bed.*

"Steen wants her alive," Bale argued.

"Look at her, brother. She's dead, no matter what."

Here it comes. There'd be no stopping Dyri now.

If only she could have said good-bye to her parents…

A large hand curled hard around her upper arm, yanked her sideways off the path. Sanja didn't have time to cry out before she struck the ground, her impact softened by a thatch of soft, dry grass.

Head spinning, she struggled for breath, struggled to move, but the lightest of touches easily overcame her efforts. Warmth surrounded her with the smell of dry earth and tree sap. Lights flickered in the darkness of her vision, and an ethereal buzz of insects filled her ears. If this was death, it was a more peaceful ending than she ever could have imagined.

Sanja sighed, letting her weight sink down into the cushion of a warm cradle.

Heat touched her cheek, chafed across her brow, and forced her eyes open. Everything was dark and blurry, swirling this way and that, refusing to let her focus.

"Sanja, can you hear me?" She knew that voice... "Hold on a little longer. You're not going to die. I won't let you..."

18

Gods, she was frozen through and through. Fal gathered Sanja in his arms. He needed to get her into water. He could restore her in water.

Anderheim hummed in its stillness. Wary after Fal's earlier outburst, it neither took from him, nor gave, waiting for his next move, and he was glad of it. Now, perhaps, the Otherland would learn to obey its creator.

He filled his mind with thoughts of his waterfall. On foot, it would take him days to reach it, but Anderheim seemed to have other means of travel. Reading his intent, the Otherland blurred, streaking around him as it had before, and in the next moment, Fal stood precisely where he'd wanted to go.

The crescent moon shone brightly above the clearing, setting the waterfall ashimmer. Where it poured into the lake, the surface churned white, throwing off clouds of cool mist. This, at last, was a familiar and most welcome sight. This was where he'd first learned to travel through water.

He offered quiet praise and thanks to Anderheim in the form of more magic. In return, the world sighed, and night birds began their song.

Fal waded into the lake, taking comfort and strength from the water's embrace as it lapped at his legs and waist. It was deep enough to come up to his shoulders when he lowered to his knees, bringing Sanja with him until she was submerged up to her neck.

He knew spells to channel the water's healing magic, but Fal dared not speak a single word of one while that terrible vortex still churned within his chest. It was wild, barely contained, and far too powerful, seeming to respond to water with an eagerness that unnerved him. If he miscalculated even a little, if Anderheim twisted his spell…

Swallowing the raw magic back as deep as it would go, he tested his voice on a whisper. "Sanja, can you hear me?"

She didn't stir.

Fal touched a gentle fingertip to her cracked, bloodless lips, dripping water between them in the hopes it would revive her a little. "You are safe now." For the moment, at least. And only if he could heal her.

How do I heal her?

Kneeling in a pool of reflected moonlight, Fal remembered a lullaby his mother had used to sing to him. It had no words, but the melody had never failed to soothe his troubled mind. Now, it teased his senses with secrets and mysteries that lay beneath its surface.

Adjusting Sanja in his arms, he began to hum.

With the first few notes, the chaos in his chest flared like a blooming flower, reshaping itself into some semblance of order. He clenched his stomach to somehow keep it contained, but despite his efforts, a delicate strain of it seeped out into his voice, weaving through the melody, shifting it into something new and unfamiliar, yet somehow comforting.

When he would have stopped, the strange magic refused to let him, commanding his voice to keep going. It wasn't finished yet; it had barely begun its work.

Sparks of light glittered over Sanja's face. Her pale skin became like snow in the moonlight, then pinkened with signs of life. Her lips softened and reddened as the bleeding cracks and fissures healed from within before his eyes.

And in the water's cool embrace, her body began to radiate a tender heat.

The melody hummed through him louder, and Sanja bowed up with a gasp, as a burst of light flared from within her. When it faded, the song's magic finally released Fal into silence, and Sanja softened against him.

Her color had improved, and her body had filled out a bit from its earlier, terrifying leanness. She looked the way she had in Frastmir. *Thank you, gods.* Whatever that magic had been, it had saved her life.

"Sanja?"

Her brows drew together in a disgruntled frown. She didn't respond, still fast asleep.

But she was alive, and she was safe here with him, where neither Steen's men nor Wilderheim's untimely winter could touch her.

Fal pushed to his feet and carried her out of the lake, drying them both along the way. Though he was loath to let her out of his sight again, he needed to gather wood for a fire and to take stock of the situation.

He could sense Anderheim's consciousness watching him. It was mollified for the moment, but a tense awareness existed between them that Fal now had the means to force his will upon the Otherland if he so wished.

Such a weapon would be formidable in his current circumstances—if he knew what it was, and how to use it. That it seemed to be somehow connected to his voice hadn't escaped him. Anderheim had drawn back on his verbal command. His melody had brought Sanja from the brink of death back to blooming life.

As an experiment, Fal held out his hand and tried to manipulate the churning vortex of strange magic out into his palm. It didn't react at all.

But when he hummed a low tone, it leaped to life, and a flower bush burst from the ground at his feet, dozens of pale white blooms flaring open in the blink of an eye. They were his creation, not Anderheim's, and he could feel the Otherland's curiosity as it responded by growing a second bush next to Fal's.

"Perhaps I'm more water sprite than I thought." His grandmother's people had carried such potent power in their voices, it could give life as well as take it. Seol had tried to teach it to Fal, but the lessons had always ended in disappointment for them both. Fal's Halfling blood had simply been too diluted. Or perhaps the limitations of his homeland and his illusions had made it impossible.

Whatever the reason, the old rules seemed not to apply in Anderheim.

"Open the doorway," he commanded. Now that he knew Anderheim could be escaped, it should only be a matter of learning how. Far more useful would be learning to travel back and forth. "I said, open the doorway."

Anderheim remained unchanged. It didn't seem to understand what he was asking.

"Do what you did before."

At once, the Otherland blurred and shifted, delivering him triumphantly back to Sanja.

Brilliant.

Shaking his head, he returned to his quest for firewood. The lessons would have to wait; he couldn't experiment with new, unpredictable magic around Sanja, and he needed to be there when she woke up.

Fal gathered as much dry wood as he could carry and returned to the waterfall. Having learned his ritual over the last few days, Anderheim warped itself to clear a fire circle for him, pulling the grass blades back underground to keep them from harm. The gathering of stones was Fal's task. Happily, the lake had plenty of them, and in no time at all, he had the makings of a proper campfire. Striking a flint stone against his eating knife, he produced a spark strong enough to light the kindling and catch the dry wood. The only thing missing was something to roast on it.

In the morning, he'd catch fish from the lake to feed them both. But for now, Fal was too preoccupied with other thoughts to concern himself with physical nourishment.

The night was so peaceful he wished he didn't have to return to Wilderheim. He had everything he needed in this place.

Everything but his family and his people.

Fal was becoming convinced that nothing would stop Fenrir from destroying anything and everything in his path. The damage had already been done the moment the great wolf had broken free. Restoring the Veil would not bind Fenrir back into his prison.

But Anderheim felt different.

Fal had spent almost a week within its borders, and no higher being had thus far made it through. With Otherlands falling one after the other, he would have expected a flood of refugees to come pouring in, but they haven't. Either they weren't aware of Anderheim's existence, or they couldn't get in.

Could it be possible, then, for Anderheim to stand strong against Ragnarok simply hiding in plain sight?

Fal rubbed his weary brow. He was grasping at straws, looking for hope in illusions.

Even if this Otherland was truly the safe haven Wilderheim needed it to be, it was still as impenetrable for him as it was for everyone else on the other side of its borders. The doorway he'd opened to get to Sanja had lasted mere moments. Enough time for him to pass through, but no more than that. It wouldn't be enough to fold all of Wilderheim into Anderheim—assuming he could open another one.

Fal looked over at Sanja's sleeping face. Still there, still safe. The tight band of fear around his chest loosened enough for him to take a proper breath. With an unsteady hand, he pushed a stray curl away from her brow, then brushed his knuckles gently across her soft, warm cheek.

She was safe.

But her parents were still in Wilderheim, as was her betrothed. She would never make it to the top of Hallowed Mountain in time, and now Fal couldn't even go back to Frastmir to sort out Jarl Steen as he'd meant to do. Every promise he'd made this girl, he'd failed to keep.

Well, there was one thing he could still do to make up for it.

She's not going to like it.

But it would keep her alive. That was all that mattered.

When sleep pulled him under, it was into dreams of storms and fire, with darkness blanketing the land, and a strange, beautiful sword cutting through it in screams flashes of sharp, bright light.

PART THREE

A New Age Dawns

19

Artairas didn't sleep a wink all the night through. The animals in the camp were agitated, horses whinnying, and dogs howling as if they felt something amiss with their world. Artairas felt it, too, like a warm wind of change blowing through their midst, altering the ground itself. It set his teeth on edge and made him clutch God's sword so tightly his fingers cramped around the handle.

When the first light of dawn appeared, he put on his boots, fastened his sword belt around his waist, and walked out. The rest of the warriors were beginning to stir as well and, though they were quiet and subdued, each had a weapon at the ready, wary of whatever unseen enemy had crept through their camp in the night.

Artairas nodded to his men in passing, then veered off to make his way up the hill. He needed a better vantage point; he needed to see what lay in the distance. God's sword quivered in its scabbard. He stroked up and down its handle as if his touch alone could soothe its restless spirit. Rather than settle, the blade responded with eagerness, humming to him louder and louder, until Artairas clutched the grip hard to make it stop. Though he didn't mean to, he found himself drawing the blade out of the scabbard and raising it before him. Then, and only then did its spirit quiet enough to let him think.

Sometimes, its power over him worried Artairas. When it became that insistent, he could no longer tell which of them wielded the other. He could now feel its influence from anywhere in the camp. If he strayed from it too far, too long, it screamed in his mind for him to return. When he failed to draw it at least once in a day, it roused within him a terrible thirst for violence and blood.

The blade was a living thing, needing to taste the air, to see the world beyond its sheath. It was a jealous, demanding, controlling mistress, as all God-made things were, he supposed. But the power contained within the blade and its promise of victory made it a pleasant burden to bear. It set his shoulders back with pride each time he wore the sword at his side. He relished the men's envious glares, as well as the deference they paid to the sword and, by extension, to him.

He ascended the hill like a king about to face his people and reached the top as the sun peeked out from behind Silver Mountains in the distance. Shielding his eyes from its glare, he frowned at something a little higher in the sky.

A star glittered there, uncowed by the sun's majesty. It shone bright, like a beacon pointing the way forward, and remained there as the sun slowly climbed up across the sky. Artairas had never seen its like before.

Nor had the blade. Faced with the glory of the morning sun, it reflected only the star, as if its cool, twinkling light were a signal for the blade, and needed to be answered.

Caught between the two, Artairas swayed on his feet. A foreign warmth started in his sword hand and crept up his arm. It turned his head with dizziness, set his heart pounding. His breath became labored as his limbs quivered, and his loins stirred with excitement and anticipation.

He licked his lips and tasted blood, but when he wiped his mouth on the back of his hand, it came away clean. Artairas licked his lips again and smiled. *It is time.*

The thud of hooves broke him out of the strange spell and drew his eye back toward the camp. His squire, Gareth, waved from the saddle, riding pell-mell up the hill. Artairas headed down to meet him and caught the horse's reins as Gareth pulled him to a stop. The squire leaped down and dropped to one knee, bowing his head. "My

Lord, the queen is asking for you."

Wasting no time with questions, Artairas mounted the horse and turned him about, riding toward the castle at a breakneck sprint, the sword still clutched aloft.

He was forced to sheathe it when he reached the castle courtyard but kept his hand on the pommel as he raced up to the queen's chambers. The pall of impending death saturated the hallway. Servants and priests scurried in and out, carrying armloads of cloth either way: in with the clean, and out with the sullied.

Artairas stopped before the closed doors, and the current of activity halted along with him. All of them stared at the soldier most improperly dressed for an audience with the queen, but none of them said a word, as aware as he was of the power now radiating from the blade at his side in flashes of blinding light they could feel, but couldn't see.

He wanted to ask them after the queen's condition, but the thought of hearing any of them speak of her nauseated him. No, Artairas would rather see for himself.

With a shaking hand, he pulled open the massive door just enough to allow him to slip inside. There were no guards on either side of it. The priests had all removed themselves into the hallway, and as Artairas entered, the last two maids ran out with quick, passing curtsies. They closed the door behind them, abandoning Artairas in the living tomb of the queen's bedchambers.

The walls had already been draped with black cloth, the mirrors covered, and all the windows shielded with thick tapestries so no hint of the morning sun could intrude. Hundreds of candles had been lit all through the chamber to make up for it. While the hearth stood cold, those candles filled the room with stifling heat, but all of them combined could not mask the sickroom stench.

Had he come too late?

Artairas approached the bed as he would a trap, stepping with his toes first, creeping in silence up to the queen's side. She was nigh invisible in her bed, with the covers pulled up to her chin, and her pallid face and white hair almost the same color as her pillows. Her eyes were closed, her mouth open. She made not a sound.

Artairas lowered to his knees and crossed himself, speaking a silent prayer that the queen might find peace in God's presence at last. "Amen," he whispered.

"Artairas," the queen said, startling him.

"My Queen."

She turned her head to face him, her eyes opening a little as her dry lips pressed together. She hummed weakly, then took a struggling breath and tried again. "My God has left me in a state," she said, attempting to smile. "But He will be back. Once His victory is secured, He has promised to restore me to strength and youth for all time."

"Yes, My Queen."

Queen Genevieve shifted, struggling to free one hand from beneath the covers. Artairas helped her, then clutched her bony hand as hard as he dared. Her grip was stronger. Such a powerful spirit, trapped in such a weak, withering shell. "He bade me tell you, the sign has appeared."

"I have seen it," Artairas replied in a discreet whisper. "A star has risen in the east. It is not banished by the sun, but shines through in the day sky."

Queen Genevieve sighed. "Then it is true. The time has come at last, as He promised."

"What are your orders, Majesty?" He expected he already knew what she would say, but his heart beat stronger, faster, waiting for her to say it.

"God wills that the armies be ready to march into battle at sunset," she said.

"Sunset? But—"

"When the day has turned to night, the star will shine the way," the queen said as if she had not heard. Her gaze was distant, her voice slurring, weakening. She spoke as if from a dream, and Artairas wasn't certain if any of what she said made sense. March to battle at night? Whoever had heard of such a thing? And how could they meet an enemy hundreds of miles away by sunset?

Yet he felt in his soul, and in the hum of his blade, that it was not the queen speaking at all. It was God Himself, using her voice as His conduit.

"The star will point the way, and the men must be steadfast in their faith that He will see them safely through to the other side." She paused for breath, clutching his hand tighter. "They must not stop or turn back a single time. Have faith in God's promise, and He will deliver you to the land of heathens."

"We will not fail, your Majesty."

"You will come upon them in the dark of night. Fight well, and by morning, their kingdom will be ours."

Even if, by some miracle, God could deliver them directly into the heart of Wilderheim, attacking in the night was a cowardly, dishonorable way to fight. "Is Wilderheim truly so strong that we must resort to underhanded tactics?"

Queen Genevieve smiled. "It is not for us mortals to question the word of God."

"Yes, but… Forgive me, My Queen, I simply do not understand. Our armies are vast and well trained. Does God not have faith in *us*? We can win this war the honorable way."

A disgruntled sound came from the queen, and she shook her head, her eyes closing. "There is no honor in war. There is only pain and death. Winning or losing. God has favored us to win, and we will do so only with His guidance." She sighed. "I am weary. I must rest. God will guide you, Artairas. Heed Him, and all will be as it should."

"I will," he swore.

He took his leave with purposeful strides, brushing away questions from the priests who demanded to know what had been said in their absence. In the courtyard, he reclaimed his horse and mounted.

There was the star, high in the eastern sky, unperturbed by the sun's bright glare. "Tell the castle guard to ring the bells for muster," he ordered the hostler. "Send messengers to each camp with orders to prepare to fight by sunset."

"Yes, My Lord. At once!"

By the time he made it back to his tent, the preparations were already underway. After waiting for so long, the men finally had purpose once more. Servants and squires ran about, gathering gear and supplies. The restless horses were saddled, weapons cleaned, and armor inspected.

Gareth had already packed all of Artairas' belongings and was in the process of breaking down the tent. His eyes were feverish, and his color was high when he took over the horse's care. "We heard the bells. Is it true?"

"Yes," Artairas replied. "We war at sunset."

"Sunset? But—"

"Don't. Do as you are told. I do not want any rumors spreading through the camp. We have our orders, and we will obey. Do you understand?"

"Yes, My Lord. Of course."

By noon, the tents were down, and a caravan of carts was making its way from the castle to the camps, carrying fresh food and gear to replace what had been lost during their long wait.

As the afternoon grew into evening, the men began to assemble into formation, a long line of mounted warriors, followed by foot soldiers bringing up the rear. If there were grumblings or rumors, they didn't reach Artairas' ears. After so long, the troops were quiet, eager to get going, and their restlessness translated to the animals. Horses stomped and fidgeted, battle dogs barked and snarled, and hooded hawks screamed, beating their wings to fly.

At the front of the formation, Artairas faced east, staring at the star which had not dimmed a single time throughout the day. Many had already remarked upon it, a few going so far as to approach him with questions. Artairas had sent them all off with a stern reprimand to keep their minds on the battle to come.

But everyone and everything hushed as the sun began to dip below the horizon in the west. "Do not light the torches," Artairas ordered as he heard flints being struck to do just that. His words carried back through the formation in a long hum, and the eve remained dark.

Then, the sun finally disappeared, and as soon as its last light dimmed, the new star flared brighter. A wave of gasps and prayers moved through the men as a shaft of its light speared down onto a place some distance away, a beacon marking their direction.

"*March!*"

Artairas set off, and the formation roused to life, following after him. The measured pace maddened him, made his entire body itch to spur his mount to a sprint, but he resisted. They would need to keep their heads about them and preserve their strength for the battle to come.

Yet as he crested a hill and saw the light shimmer in a clearing down below, the impulse became too powerful to fight. He fancied he could see Wilderheim within that shining pillar, a landscape just different enough from Synealee's to stand out against the night.

Reading Artairas' eagerness, his horse sped up to a trot down the hill, the others matching his pace.

"My God," someone cried.

"What is that?" another chimed in.

"It couldn't be…" added a third, and the murmurs spread until every man within sight of that light was praying for God to keep them safe. A chorus of metal chimes rang through the ranks as every man drew his weapon, and Artairas could feel them all brace for battle.

Their eyes did not deceive them. It was, indeed, a different world within that shaft of light, and, as the army neared, it widened like a doorway opening directly to the heart of enemy land. As Queen Genevieve had said, God would deliver them to victory.

"Ride on," Artairas ordered, "and don't look back!" Drawing his sword, he raised it high, relishing its soundless war cry as he spurred his mount on and shouted, "*In God's name!*"

And as the army streamed through God's portal to catch Wilderheim unaware beneath the cover of night, in her royal bedchamber, hundreds of candles gently blew out as Queen Genevieve breathed her last.

20

Sanja woke to the sound of bird songs and rushing water. The sun beat relentless heat into her cheek, the scent of campfire smoke teasing her nostrils. It was the latter that startled her into full wakefulness. "W-what…"

As her mind first comprehended and then accepted what she was seeing, Sanja slumped with equal measures of relief and sorrow. A puffy white cloud made its languorous way across the blue sky above her. Not a hint of those strange lights to be seen anywhere. The grass was green and lush, warm in the morning sun. Someone had built a small fire nearby, now all but reduced to embers, and Sanja herself was relatively clean and dry. She felt stronger than she had in weeks.

She was dead. The torments were over, at last. She would never again need to think about Jarl Steen and his machinations. Ragnarok would no longer be her concern. Oh, but her parents…

And Mattias! Where was he? She needed to see him, to thank him, and beg his forgiveness. "Mattias? Where are you?"

She heard a splash and then someone calling her name.

Sanja pushed to her feet but hesitated to turn and face the man who'd died because of her. *You owe it to him to look him in the eye and speak the words.*

The running footsteps neared.

Braving his reaction, she turned around. "Mattias, I—"

"Finally! I was afraid you would sleep through the day." Sanja gaped as Prince Fal dropped his catch to the ground, wiped his hands on his thighs, and grasped her shoulders, looking her over with a bright smile on his face. He pulled her into a brief embrace and, when she didn't return it, set her away again, his glittering blue gaze searching hers. "How do you feel?"

"Y-you are here…" Not only that, he was himself, in all his Other beauty. His hair was so dark it gleamed blue in the light of day. With his cloak discarded, his sleeves rolled up past his elbows, and the laces of his shirt undone down his chest, he looked so human and approachable. No more changing faces, no more illusions. His form remained his own, and he stood tall and proud, finally relieved of the burdens he'd carried all his life. He was the same Fal she knew, and yet nothing at all like the crown prince of Wilderheim.

A lifetime in a kiss…

"Are you dead, too? But that means… Is it over?"

His smile dimmed, and he looked as if he wanted to say something but then thought better of it. Bending over, he retrieved two long sticks, each with three lake fish skewered on them. "Let us sit down. We have much to talk about."

"Where is Mattias?"

Prince Fal winced. "Sit, please." He waited for her to sink back to her pallet, which she now recognized as his cloak before he added more wood to the fire, set the fish to cooking, and picked up a small, sharp eating knife to fiddle with. Anything but tell her what he so clearly wanted to. Bad news, then.

"I am not dead, am I?"

"No," the prince confirmed.

"And Mattias isn't here because…" She had to swallow past the lump in her throat to recover her voice. "He *is* dead."

"I found you on the path near Hallowed Mountain in difficult circumstances."

"Yes," she murmured, "I remember." Dyri and Bale, and the freezing cold she couldn't escape. She'd been so close to dying, had expected it at any moment. And then—"You took me away from there."

"Yes. I brought you here and—"

"How much time has passed?"

"You have slept through the night and half the day." Guessing at the unspoken question, he added, "The last day."

Sanja couldn't breathe. Her gaze lowered from Prince Fal's to the ground, and then to her toes curling into the grass. *The last day.* Any hope of her making it up Hallowed Mountain was gone forever. Without the magic of Journeyman's Sanctuary to counteract the contract, there was nothing left to protect her from Jarl Steen.

"Sanja, are you listening?"

Nothing but a dream. And, gods, how it hurt.

When the sun set, she would officially fail the wager. Her blood oath would compel her to return to Steen if she had to walk her bare feet bloody to get to him and, oh, he would be so much worse than the brothers. He would hurt her until she begged for death, and no one would help her.

"Sanja…"

It was his fault. The prince had promised to help her, and instead, he'd stolen her last chance of escaping the Jarl. He may as well have handed her to Steen himself. "You should have left me there to die."

"No, you don't mean that. Listen."

But she didn't hear. She couldn't think or hope anymore. She could only see Jarl Steen's face turn red with fury, his ham-sized fists slamming into her again and again. With each imagined strike, she flinched a little more, breathed a little faster, a little harder, until she couldn't take it anymore.

When Prince Fal reached for her, Sanja ducked past his arms to the knife he'd stuck into a piece of wood on the ground. Her aim was off, and she caught it by the blade but catch it she did. Its bite hardly registered at all, and she shifted her grip to the handle and tugged it free.

"Sanja, no!" Prince Fal snatched her around the waist, rolled her away from the fire, and caught her hands on the knife.

"Let go, curse you!"

They grappled back and forth. The prince was twice her weight. He would easily overpower her if she gave him a chance. Not about to be stopped, Sanja kicked and flailed to keep him from pinning her down. If she could turn the blade enough…

Prince Fal cursed, curled his hand over hers on the knife, but his hold slipped, right down the blade. Rather than pull back, he squeezed her wrist with one hand and wrenched the knife from her grip with the other.

"No!" She reached for it again when he tossed it away, and he caught her hand in his, bleeding wound to bleeding wound. Sanja gasped and stilled.

Prince Fal growled, disentangling his legs from hers so they could both sit up, but he didn't release her hand. His expression thunderous, he yanked the lacing free of his shirt and wound it around their clasped hands before her mind caught up with what he was doing. When she would have pulled the lace free, he swatted her hand away, then caught her chin to make her meet his gaze and bit out, "Two as one, now unto always, and evermore."

A tingling heat began in the palm of her hand, spreading up her arm to her shoulder. Confused, Sanja shook her head to clear some of the dizziness, but it wouldn't go away. In her mind, she saw the lightning's vision, a sun-filled meadow, and the prince smiling down at her. Against that dream of happiness, love, and ceremony, this was a farce.

"Say the words," Prince Fal commanded.

Sanja blinked the dream away, but the waking moment didn't feel any more real. "What are you doing?"

"Breaking your contract," he replied impatiently and repeated, "Two as one, now unto always, and evermore. Say it, Sanja."

"Two as one"—the tingling intensified tenfold—"now unto always…"

"And evermore," he supplied.

"Now unto always, and evermore."

The heat flared until she felt like she was holding onto a burning ember, but just as quickly, the sensation cooled and, when at last Prince Fal untied the lace and released her, a thin line of an old scar graced her palm where a fresh, bleeding cut ought to have been.

A lifetime in a kiss…

"We could have avoided the battle had you let me explain, rather than try to throw yourself on a blade," Prince Fal grumbled, retrieving his knife.

"Was that…?"

"A marriage ceremony. The uncivilized, heathen version of one, anyway."

Sanja traced her new scar. "We are married?"

"Yes, Princess Sanja, we are married. Congratulations, you are officially free of Jarl Steen for all time."

"Why would you do that?"

"Because I had to," he replied simply.

It wasn't the solution either of them had wanted, but it was the only thing Fal could have done to keep her alive and safe. He didn't expect dramatic displays of undying gratitude, but a simple "Thank you" might have been welcome. He had just solved all her problems, after all. Whatever debts Master Carver had managed to amass would be wiped clean. Sanja and her parents would move to Castle Frastmir and never again need to set foot into that ramshackle cottage they called home. Mistress Carver would have an army of servants at her beck and call, and Sanja herself would one day become the queen of Wilderheim.

All things considered, Sanja ought to be dancing for joy.

Instead, she sat there, staring at the scar on her hand as if she couldn't quite comprehend what'd happened. Her wound had healed instantly, and Fal wondered whether it was a part of the binding spell, or whether his blood had changed her on an elemental level. And if the latter, how great was the change, and how long might it last?

"You bear no responsibility for my decisions," she said.

"I should have let you kill yourself instead?"

"Why not?"

Fal wiped off his knife and sheathed it back into its scabbard on his belt, furious that she would even consider taking her life in the face of another possibility. "What a little hypocrite you are. You would not have Steen's death on your conscience, but you would have had me carry yours? Does your own life truly mean so little to you?"

"My life," she snapped, "would have meant nothing at all, had it remained in any way tied to Jarl Steen. My only thought was to remove myself and my parents from his hold the surest way I could think of."

"And it never occurred to you that marriage to me would do the same?"

"No! Why would it?"

Her immediate answer, delivered with equal measures of affront and ridicule, enraged him beyond words. "Were it not for me—"

"Steen's men would have done unspeakable things to me in Frast-mir," she said without mercy, making him shudder at the chill of her words. "And if they did not kill me after that, I would have done it myself, rather than let my parents see. I would have suffered briefly, but at least I would have been free of Steen, and the world at large would not have suffered in the slightest for my absence." Her anger brought a little color to her cheeks, but the gleam of tears belied her indifference. "I may be an idealist, Highness, but I am not a fool, and neither is Steen. He knew his men would bring me to heel. You may have bought me time with your rescue in the barn, but nothing else. Their involvement ensured I would have died sooner or later, by their hand or mine, and no one, save for my parents, would have mourned me."

"*I* would have."

Sanja was about to say something but, taking a good look at his face, seemed to think better of it. In a more cordial tone, she allowed, "Perhaps. But not for long." She rubbed the scar on her palm, then held it up for him to see. "You have done yourself no favors with this. Nor me."

The fish were beginning to burn. Fal repositioned the skewers away from the strongest flames and turned them to cook the other side while his temper flared hotter than the sun. Fal had never considered himself particularly proud, but for her to dismiss him so easily, as if he were no better than Steen, offended him on a level he wouldn't have thought possible.

"You don't deny it," she noted.

"What would be the point? You have already decided that death would have been preferable to marriage to me. I'll be damned if I waste my breath exulting my virtues after that." He sounded like a sullen, spoiled child.

"Your virtues have never been in question."

Fal snorted with derision. "Haven't they? Admit it, you still think
of me as the Prince of Deceit. As you said, I saved you from those
men in Frastmir only to set you on a path of suffering. I promised
you aid and wasn't there to give it. And after everything you have
endured, when you had your chance to escape forever, I pulled you
back instead and locked you into marriage with a man you haven't
chosen." He flushed at his own words, realizing too late the enormity
of his actions. Intentionally or not, Fal carried no small responsibility
for the pain she'd suffered.

Gods, what a fool he'd been. He never should have listened to Liadan—never should have made promises he'd been in no position
to keep.

But his gut still told him he'd done the right thing. No matter that
it didn't seem to have made either of them very happy.

Sanja shifted to her knees and pulled out one of the fish skewers.
The top fish was burnt, but the other two would be just right. Using
one of the sticks he'd carved into a simple fork, she removed the fish
and placed them side by side on the large piece of bark he'd stripped
for a platter. "We both know that, had the situation been anything
other than what it is, you would never have chosen someone like me
as your wife."

"We most certainly do *not* know that."

"Please, let's not lie to each other."

Fal straightened in his seat, his hackles up to be called out for deceit,
but he bit his tongue against a harsh response. His words had been
spoken thoughtlessly, for no other reason than to contradict her. He
hated how calm and rational she appeared after what she'd said when
his heart was still pounding at the thought that, had he been but a
little slower, Sanja might have been dying in his arms now, instead
of taking care to arrange their rustic supper just so.

Their roles seemed to have reversed. Where before Sanja had been
all restless chatter to his cool rationality, she now appeared to have
no trouble at all delivering a cogent argument, while Fal struggled to
form a single coherent thought.

The change felt so out of place Fal broke one of his most resolute
rules. Without her knowledge or permission, he reached out to her

mind, telling himself it was for her own good. He only did it to make certain Sanja was truly as calm as she appeared; that he wouldn't need to sleep with one eye open, fearing she'd do him or herself injury in the night. She'd already proven herself more than capable of it, after all.

What he found was akin to a lake after a storm—calm on the surface, but murky with churned up mud. The remnants of her torments might have been safely contained, but they were by no means gone. Basking in the fire's warmth, she still felt ice chilling her from within, shards of it lodged in her hands and feet, so cold Fal shivered and curled his own fingers into his palms to warm them.

He saw her memories of Mattias, the jolly, fair-haired giant who'd kept her company along her Journey. His bearded face shifted between a good-natured, happy smile, and a grotesque mask of swollen, bleeding bruises. She would never again separate the two. The tainted memory of her friend would always squeeze her heart with the smell of burning flesh and the knowledge that she'd been the indirect cause of his demise.

He saw her tormentors, too. Dyri, Bale, and Alfrec, their faces dark and demonic, their voices slicing at her with vicious threats as sharp as Dyri's blade.

All of it, she'd endured alone, walking her knees bloody along the frozen path, as her hope of making it to the temple had slowly withered to but one wish: to repay her pain in kind and die before Jarl Steen or his men could get their hands on her. She'd known she'd lose her wager, but she'd kept going, anyway, because every moment she'd spent continuing her Journey had meant a moment more of safety from Steen and his men. A moment more to live. A moment more for them to suffer.

Fal's chest ached for the torment he felt inside her. He wanted to pull her into his arms and make the bitter cold go away. More than anything, Sanja needed the warmth of an embrace that asked for nothing more than it gave. But as much as she craved such contact, she feared it. If she allowed herself the briefest show of emotion, admitted the smallest moment of weakness, any need for comfort or support, the dam would break, and she would drown.

Simply, Sanja was calm because she had no other choice.

Suffused with guilt and helplessness, Fal withdrew quickly and refocused on what she was saying.

"...poetry where it belongs—in books. People like me don't get dashing heroes riding to our rescue. We must make do with what we have."

The connection with her mind was severed, yet he still felt a chill he couldn't shake. Breathing into his hands for warmth he ought not need, Fal made his face neutral so she wouldn't suspect the liberty he'd taken with her mind. But he couldn't keep the bitterness out of his tone when he said, "My choice would have been irrelevant. As the royal heir, my wife would have been chosen for me for the benefit of Wilderheim."

Sanja nodded, her point proven.

But, though it was the truth, it was far from complete, and Fal was not inclined to let her believe otherwise. "Matters of state aside, I am still Other, and ever at the whim of more powerful forces—my illusions among them. I might not have had the chance to marry at all, if not for you. It is also quite possible you were always meant to be mine, regardless of my—or your—current thoughts on the matter." Fate had a way of manipulating its outcome, and only a fool chose to oppose it.

Sanja absorbed everything he said, and from the shift of her gaze, he knew she was gearing up with all sorts of arguments in opposition.

He forestalled all of them by saying, "But, were I completely free to choose, I might well have chosen someone like you." When she would have replied, Fal held up his hand to silence her. "You asked for truth. That means you don't get to ignore the parts you don't want to hear."

"Fair point," she allowed and set the task of supper aside to give him her full attention.

Perversely, her calm gaze made the words harder to say. "The truth is, you charmed me from the first. Your spirit, your wit,"—he grinned, rubbing at his temple—"your aim with unconventional weapons."

She blushed, but couldn't duck her head fast enough to hide a quick little smile he was most relieved to see. Despite everything, Sanja was not broken. Her trials might have transformed her, but she was still there, underneath it all.

"You don't balk at taking me to task." If he were to be honest with himself, as much as it frustrated him, Fal enjoyed the challenge. "I like that you are not afraid of me. I like that you are too clever for your own good. You are honorable to a fault and more beautiful than you seem to realize. I would be proud to have you by my side as my queen."

Without looking at him, she returned her attention to the fish, breaking them into thirds. For a moment, Fal was afraid he'd gone too far, said too much. But, though her hands shook a little, Sanja didn't run or cry. Instead, after a deep breath or two, she replied, "Nevertheless, your family would not—will not approve."

Fal grinned. As far as arguments went, that one was weak, at best. She was running out of objections. Accepting the bark platter when she offered it, he took one more risk. He pulled her to sit beside him and placed the platter over both their laps, then picked out a fluffy piece of fish and held it up to her lips. "You underestimate them greatly."

Sanja frowned, but as he continued to wiggle the morsel enticingly before her, she opened her mouth and accepted it. "How so? Your father married for political reasons."

Fal shrugged, feeding her another piece of fish. She was literally eating from his hand, not seeming to realize the small show of trust spoke far more than words ever could. He soaked up the light scrape of her teeth on his fingers with relish. "The first time, yes," he said in answer to her question. "The second, he married for love, and scandal be damned." His father's decision to take his wizard and right hand to wife had caused dissent among their people at first. Many had feared that having to obey her royal husband's wishes would prevent Queen Nialei from standing up to him when needed for the good of the kingdom. It had taken his parents years to quell that fear, but in the end, they'd earned their people's trust and proven their loyalty to Wilderheim beyond all doubt.

"But your sister's marriage was one of state, to forge an alliance with the Imarah tribe of Aegiros."

He laughed, taking a piece of fish for himself before feeding her another. "So the official story would have you believe. The truth is, I very much doubt Wilderheim was in her thoughts at all when she ran off to Aegiros in search of adventure. She, too, married for love. The resulting political alliance was merely a happy byproduct."

"And your parents did not object?"

He considered that. "By the time they found out, there was nothing they could do about it. But no, I do not believe they begrudged Liadan her happiness for a single moment. It had been too hard-won for that."

Sanja grew quiet, turning away from his next offering, so he ate it himself. A sparrow flew overhead, and a woodpecker drummed out a rapid rhythm somewhere in the trees. The day was warm, the rush of water lulling. Sitting there beside a fire, with fish cooking over the flames and Sanja pressed against his side, Fal felt almost content. He could happily while away his days this way and count himself a lucky man, indeed.

But when she refused his next offering, he grew worried. "What are you thinking?" he asked, resisting the temptation to see for himself. He needed her to trust him enough to tell him of her own accord.

She gently pushed the platter fully into his lap and got up to remove the second skewer from the fire. This one, she placed on the ground and sat back on her heels, facing away from him. "They all married for love," she said. "But you did not. You married me because it needed to be done, you said so yourself."

Fal winced. "I did say that, didn't I?" And, naturally, she had given his words the worst possible interpretation.

"Do you deny it now?"

He frowned, unsure of how to answer. "No." He chose his next words with care. "I would do it again without hesitation." He would have done anything to keep the blade from plunging into her heart. "But it was not only an act of necessity."

She faced him with obvious reluctance, waiting for him to say more.

But what could he say? She couldn't expect a declaration of love. They'd known each other for so short a time, all of it fraught with so much, he hadn't had an opportunity to analyze the connection between them. Nevertheless, a connection was there, and Fal did feel *something* potent enough to make the prospect of Sanja's death unthinkable.

With the perils of Wilderheim out of reach and Sanja safe in Anderheim, Fal at long last had a moment to take measure of the situation. And, ever the scholar, he tried to look at it objectively. He liked Sanja a great deal and couldn't deny a deep attraction. Their first kiss had been seared like an invisible pulse into his lips. As he recalled it again, he felt the same sensation of an impending lightning strike yet, at the same time, being in Sanja's company felt like the most natural thing in the world—effortless, guileless, and comfortable.

The feeling was in no way similar to what his sister felt for her husband. Theirs was a love as fiery and intense as Liadan herself. Nor could he say it was like the connection his parents shared, which went deeper than the heart all the way to the soul.

Having ruled out those possibilities, Fal was at a loss. He hesitated to mention it at all, not wanting to give Sanja false hope, but neither could he dismiss it outright. "Ours may not have started as a love match," he said, "but that doesn't mean we can't still make a good life together. I know I haven't given you much reason to trust me when I say this, but I will be a good husband to you, Sanja."

She studied him so intensely for so long, Fal almost suspected she could see into his thoughts the way he'd peeked into hers. He wished she could; perhaps she might make sense of it all. "I believe you," she said, the words themselves spelling the surprise of her new realization.

"You do?"

Sanja nodded.

"Why?"

She hesitated, appearing to consider several responses before announcing, "Well, you could hardly be worse than Jarl Steen."

Fal grinned. "If that is the standard against which I am to be judged, we are off to an excellent start."

Sanja chuckled but sobered quickly. "Thank you for not taking offense. I may make light of the matter, but please believe I am aware of where I would be now, if not for you." Her gaze lowered to the eating knife at his waist, and he tensed, waiting to see what she'd do next. Seeming to come to some sort of decision, she nodded to herself and said, "I am grateful to you for saving my life. And I would like the chance to spend it with you. You are right. We can still make a good life together. And perhaps, in time, there may come affection. It would be more than I have ever dared to hope for."

Me, as well, he thought, and the unknown feeling within him swelled a little more.

21

Me, as well.

The sentiment whispered across her mind in the prince's voice, startling her. Sanja blinked at him. Had he said it aloud? No, she'd been watching him, and his mouth hadn't moved. She must have imagined it.

And yet Sanja was certain she hadn't. As certain as she'd been a moment ago that he'd spoken the truth. She'd felt it in him, somehow.

Fal looked away first, shifting forward to awkwardly poke apart a splitting log. "You have not asked me yet where we are."

The sudden change of subject caught her off guard, breaking whatever strange connection she'd thought she'd felt a moment ago. Now that he mentioned it, she was curious about the lack of swirling colors in the sky. And since he said they weren't dead, "Where are we? And why isn't your face changing anymore?"

"Because everything else has changed. We are in an illusion made real. An Otherland directly on top of Wilderheim, in every way the same, and completely separate."

"How can that be?"

He began to speak, then winced and said, "I don't know."

"That is hardly encouraging."

"I know we are safe for now. I know we have everything that exists in Wilderheim, except its people and its troubles. The war there will never touch us here; nothing can go in or out of Anderheim, and I think... I think it can keep us safe from Fenrir, too."

Nothing in or out? "We are stuck here?"

The prince flushed. "More or less. Temporarily," he rushed to assure her. "I got you through, did I not? So it follows that passage back and forth is possible. I just need time to learn how."

"Time." Sanja looked up at the sun marking its slow progress across the sky. Time was the one thing she didn't have. "Before we get to that, there is something else we ought to address." And the mere thought of it made her palms sweat, and her tongue stick to the roof of her mouth.

"Yes?"

His patient gaze sought hers, soothing and encouraging, making her throat too dry to speak. Gods, she couldn't even bring herself to say it.

"Sanja, you need never be afraid to tell me anything. Whatever it is you need, it is already yours. Remember, you are the future queen of Wilderheim."

Oh, she remembered. That was the problem. Her face burned. "The handfasting," she ventured, hesitating. "It is only the first step."

"Ah," Prince Fal cleared his throat and, when she dared a peek at his face, it was as red as hers felt. "Normally, you would be correct. The handfasting is meant to be a promise that must be consummated to keep." He shifted in his seat, drew his knees up and rested his forearms on them. Not quite hiding, but almost. Well enough for him to speak the words of a marriage vow but, apparently, the marriage itself was as awkward for him as it was for her.

"But...?"

He toyed with one of his golden cuffs, keeping his gaze averted. "It is the physical commitment that must be confirmed with... And, you see, under normal circumstances, it would have only been the holding of hands and a piece of string but..."

Sanja traced the scar on her hand. "Our hands were cut. We shared blood before the string was tied."

Prince Fal nodded. "And, as you know, blood binds all things."

Sanja considered this. The bond would be irreversible and everlasting. And, for an Other whose lifespan might well stretch across several millennia, *forever* was a very long time. Then another thought occurred to her. "You had a good grasp on my hand when we fought. But you let go and cut yourself in the process."

He ducked his head.

But this was too important for either of them to hide from. If he was mistaken or, gods help her, lying, her life was still in danger. "Did you do it on purpose?"

Without looking up, he mumbled something under his breath.

"What was that?"

Prince Fal hunched his shoulders up to his ears, then let them drop and looked off to the side, his mouth twisting as if it could keep him from having to respond. Finally, he faced her and admitted, "I had my reasons." That appeared to be as much as he could bring himself to say on the matter.

"I see." But she didn't really. The Other prince had bound himself to a human girl for all time; he had to know there would be repercussions. Was that why? With the physical requirement satisfied by a blood bond, "Did you intend for us to never share a marriage bed? Ever?"

"If necessary."

Sanja steeled herself not to flinch or look away. He was resolute in his decision—fatally so. Sanja felt the tide of his will wash over her in a silent command to let it go. Don't ask questions, don't look for answers. Accept what is and don't want more. "We are to have a marriage in name only? What about the line of succession?" Did he consider her so undesirable he would give up legitimate heirs to avoid lying with her even once?

"Liadan and I are Halflings, Sanja. The line will end with us no matter what."

Sanja gaped. "But then—"

"Truth, yes? That is what we agreed. The truth is, I may be more water than fire, but I am still a Dragonblood, and the risk of conception might still be there, even if the child doesn't survive to be born. And it would likely kill its mother from the womb as it died. I refuse to do that to any woman, much less my human wife."

Sanja closed her mouth, absorbing this news. So much fear and dread concealed in that short speech. A lifetime of it, as if he'd always known, or been taught to be wary of his own desires. Part of her wanted to tell him it wasn't his choice to make. Having faced death once already, Sanja felt reckless and defiant of Fate and Destiny. But she remembered the stories she'd heard whispered across the market square every year on the prince's birthday. "There are rumors about Queen Mari." King Saeran's first wife was said to have died under mysterious circumstances while pregnant with their first child. Some had connected this to Saeran's mother having died in childbirth and said the royal line was cursed.

Prince Fal nodded. "All true. Any human woman would meet the same fate, were it possible for me to give her a child. Only dragon's blood can birth a Dragonblood."

"I suppose your mother survived birthing twins because she is Other." Something Sanja most definitely was not.

"I am sure that was part of it. But there was also my dragon grandfather's involvement. He offered Nialei three drops of his blood to protect her."

Sanja held up her hand. "What do you mean, your *dragon* grandfather?"

He flushed. "I, uh… My family is called Dragonblood. You knew we were descended from dragons."

"Yes, but centuries ago, not…" Gods, the look on his face. "But no one has seen a real dragon in over six hundred years."

"And therefore they no longer exist?"

Sanja gaped. "Do you mean to tell me there are still dragons in the world?"

"I only know of one. But that is not what I—"

"Dragons are massive. If they were still alive, would we not have heard of them by now?"

"You certainly would not have heard of this one. He is my father's grandsire. If he does not want to be known, it is our duty to keep his secret. A dragon's blood is so powerful it can change a person from within. Can you imagine how dangerous it would be if people learned a true dragon dwelled just north of Wilderheim?"

"The dragon lives north of Wilderheim?"

"I should not have told you—"

"A real, live dragon? Just north of Wilderheim?" There was nothing north of Wilderheim except mountains and snow. Hallowed Mountain was one of the southern peaks of its range. How close had she gotten to the dragon's lair on her Journey? Did the clerics know? They couldn't. If they did, they'd be compelled to share any knowledge of its existence—

"Focus, Sanja. You can never tell anyone about the dragon, or he will die. Do you understand?"

"Yes." Having seen the levels of depravity some men were capable of, she could well picture what they would stoop to for but a scale from the dragon's tail. "I understand. I will keep his secret." If a single dragon still lived, the last thing Sanja wanted was for people like Steen to make a sport out of hunting him down.

Her answer seemed to mollify Fal somewhat. "What I am trying to explain is that without the dragon's help, my mother would not have survived birthing me and Liadan. It is the nature of our bloodline and the curse of being a Halfling. It is why I will not risk giving you a child. Had circumstances been different, I would have prevailed on Grandfather to protect my wife the same way he had my mother. But he appears to have gone missing, along with my parents. Not that it would have made a difference here." With a belligerent wave of his hand, he indicated the clearing around them.

"Is there no other way to keep me from conceiving? Surely there must be some herbal concoction or a spell."

"No witch's brew or wizard's spell would work—they never do. Theoretically, an Other ought to have control over such things, but I have always considered the risk too great to experiment." He flushed at his own admission, and, with an annoyed huff, pushed to his feet to add more wood onto the fire. "In any case, I have told you, the need for physical communion was satisfied with our blood bond. It is not necessary for us to do any more than that."

"Yes, well, forgive me for being skeptical, Your Highness, but you have told me other things in the past as well, and not all of them have been strictly accurate." To put it mildly. "We can live the rest of our lives chastely, if you wish, but this one thing I must have. I must be certain my contract with Jarl Steen is well and truly broken."

That it might not be all but sent her into another bout of panic. Despite Prince Fal's assurance that the sharing of blood finalized their marriage, she still felt the dread of her former betrothed like a blade at her throat. She dared not move or take a breath too deep, while it threatened to cut her. Sanja needed to finish it, consummate the union as it ought to be, so there was no question of its validity.

"What precisely are you suggesting?"

Sanja steeled her spine and clutched her hands together to stop them shaking. "An act of necessity." When the prince scoffed and cursed, she flushed. "It is not how I would have preferred it to happen, either," she admitted. "But I cannot afford the luxury of waiting for it to be right. I cannot risk our being wrong about my contract. Not after everything I have been through." By sunset, it would be too late. "Surely it must be safe *once*." She'd known couples who'd tried for years before conceiving a child. Some never did, at all.

"Sanja, you do not know what you are asking."

"I am asking to be your wife."

He looked at her sideways, and she saw in his eyes all the things he dared not share. Anger at his own nature, and at her for demanding he risk her life. Fear of what it would mean for both of them. Yet, despite all that, Sanja was surprised to see a spark of heat in his gaze as it traveled down her body and up again to clash with hers. It lit up his eyes like jagged sparks of lightning, and she remembered as if it had happened mere moments ago.

A kiss sealed by a lightning strike, a lifetime inside a heartbeat of joy so pure it'd almost made her weep. It was a long ago dream of countless beautiful impossibilities, all of them contained within the press of his lips against hers. The searing heat, the blinding pain, and the unspeakable pleasure of a secret embrace. It had been real.

And he remembered, too.

A lifetime in a kiss. And it hadn't been a dream.

Despite her humanity, and all the risks involved, Prince Fal had wanted her then, and he wanted her still.

Sanja found herself responding. A wave of warmth spread across her body as she boldly held his gaze, knowing in her soul that this man would never cause her a moment's pain if he could prevent it. She would never have cause to fear his temper or his touch; she would never be lonely for companionship with him by her side. Somehow, by a stroke of divine luck, Sanja had married a man who put all those romantic poems she'd read to shame.

"Please," she said on an unsteady breath. "Let me be your wife."

At length, his jaw twitched as he dipped a slow, meaningful nod. "As you wish," he answered, then turned and walked away.

Stunned, Sanja pushed to her feet. "Where are you going?"

"To think."

"To *think*?" They didn't have time for that! What in the world did he have to think about, anyway?

But he was gone before she could ask, leaving her alone to pace around the fire and watch the sun slowly crawl toward the west.

The shadows grew longer while she waited. The day's heat cooled, and a light breeze began to blow. Sanja added more wood to the fire, ate more of the fish to fill her empty belly—anything to stave off memories of freezing nights without any food or shelter at all.

Whenever the wind blew stronger, she shivered, inching closer to the fire. With every hiss of movement in the grass, she flinched, seeking enemies about to descend upon her without mercy. Out in the open, she was completely exposed, and without the prince's voice to keep her grounded, fear raked its icy claws down her back, scoring it clean through to her spine.

Desperate for any kind of distraction, she dashed off toward the trees, intending to gather more firewood, but came to an abrupt stop several paces before the tree line. Too many shadows. Too many places for an enemy to hide. Despite her determination to do something of use, her feet slid backward in retreat.

An owl swooped down from a tree in front of her, and Sanja cried out, covering her head with her arms as her right foot slid back another step. When she calmed enough to peer into those woods again, the owl sat on a high branch, its overlarge eyes watching her.

Is this how I'm to live my life now, afraid of birds and shadows in the trees?

What a wonderful queen she'd make.

Closing her eyes, she tilted her face up to the sky and breathed in deep of the evening air. Summer nights had always been her favorite. She loved the scent of warm earth and flowers; she loved being able to taste the sunset and feel life thriving all around her. Simple pleasures in a small, simple life. It'd been so safe before Jarl Steen, with never a worry too deep to overcome.

Now, all Sanja knew was worry and fear. They maddened her, these enemies within, for she had no way to fight them back, no weapon or shield to use against them. Sanja would rather have met Dyri face to face. A physical opponent, at least, she could confront.

She needed a weapon. No matter that she wouldn't know how to use one, anyway, she'd feel much safer just for having one. A knife, a club—a large stick would do. When Prince Fal returned, Sanja would ask him for his eating knife.

He won't give it. Not after she'd tried to stab herself with it and, out here that left her at the mercy of his protection alone.

The light dimmed, and she opened her eyes. This close to the trees, she could no longer see the sun, and its light in the sky was beginning to fade. Her time was running out, and the prince still hadn't returned. Should she look for him? But what if she left the clearing and he came back to find her gone?

She ought to go back. But not with empty hands. Sanja searched the ground around her, gathered a few stray sticks, then dared to walk farther along the forest's edge to collect a few more before rushing back to the fire. Already, her heart was beating too fast. Her hands were so cold her fingernails had started to turn blue. She held them up to the fire's warmth, willing herself not to imagine Mattias' body lying there in place of a woodpile.

"Prince Fal," she called, hoping to hear him answer.

He didn't, but Sanja sensed something from the direction where he'd gone. No more than a little twitch of new awareness, like a soundless beacon waking to her call, unfamiliar, but not menacing. Sanja felt drawn to it. In her mind, she imagined its location not far from where she stood. It beckoned to her, and Sanja found herself following its lure away from the safety of the fire.

The waterfall at the northern edge of the clearing spilled into a sizable lake—the apparent source of her supper. It was pristine and so beautiful, burnished in pale gold by the setting sun.

A cold breeze brushed her cheeks with delicate mist that ought to have chilled her. Instead, Sanja felt it like the sun upon her skin, warm, comforting.

She imagined the water sang to her in ethereal melodies that swept away her fears and worries and wrapped her entire being in the comfort of an invisible embrace. It swayed her on her feet in a slow, gentle dance, loosened her tense spine. As the sun dipped a little lower, swarms of fireflies took to the air, filling the meadow with flickering lights.

What a beautiful, magical dream this was. Sanja never wanted to wake up.

She came to the water's edge, sensing her beacon's approach. The surface bulged up at the other side of the lake, the protrusion silently gliding in a straight line toward her and, as it reached the height of its endurance where the water shallowed, the smooth barrier broke, and Prince Fal rose up before her.

He was shirtless, water running down the valleys of his body in rivulets and, oh, how beautiful he was. Unlike Jarl Steen's bulky, intimidating form, Prince Fal had the body of a lean warrior, encased in smooth, golden skin, sheened with the merest hint of pearlescence. Sanja saw a mystical glow about him, the coolness of water and the fire's heat mingling together in his being and radiating magic strong enough to banish the chill of approaching night.

He was the same prince who'd pulled her from the freezing winter, the same one who'd sat with her by the fire and fed her pieces of flaky fish, yet he seemed a different being altogether; an Other being, gazing at her from his watery demesne with eyes like glowing sapphires.

Without a word, he held out his hand, beckoning her forward.

Sanja froze, suddenly nervous at the prospect of his touch. "The water is cold."

"I will keep you warm," he promised, his deep voice causing heat to pool deep in her belly.

Still, she couldn't bring herself closer than the water's edge. It lapped gently at her toes as if to draw her in. Its welcome called her home.

"Don't be afraid," the prince said, waiting patiently with his hand still outstretched.

Sanja looked over her shoulder. The sun was already halfway hidden behind the trees.

This is what you asked for.

No, she'd asked for an act of necessity. This felt so much bigger, more dangerous. The Other Prince was asking her to trust him with her body, but Sanja felt an insistent tug at her heart as well. The two would go into his keeping hand in hand, and what if she never got them back?

"Come to me, little love."

The endearment brought her gaze back to his face, and Sanja was struck by a sense of connection she hadn't felt before. Its gentle, relentless pull drew her ankle-deep into the lake, close enough for him to reach, yet he remained still, waiting for her.

Another step brought her off the rocky ledge into waist-high water. She gasped, reached for his strong shoulders to steady herself, and he caught her by the elbows, holding on while she found her balance.

Sanja shivered as warmth suffused her entire body, from the toes of her feet to the crown of her head. She blinked, and her hair shirt and trousers were gone; she was bared completely to the prince's gaze. Blushing, she pressed herself against him to hide and felt him suck in a harsh breath, his heart thumping hard, drawing hers into the same, rapid rhythm.

His arms came around her, and he sank back, pulling her along into deeper water, buoying her safely near the surface. His hands caressed her back, her sides, over her rump and thighs, gently guiding her legs around his waist. Wherever he touched, the sensation lingered, multiplied by the lapping waves until Sanja felt her entire body being petted by countless hands.

"Will you kiss me, sweet Sanja?"

Overwhelmed into an almost drunken stupor, Sanja lifted her heavy-lidded gaze to his and nodded. His lips brushed hers, one of his hands cradling the back of her head, anchoring her to his searching kiss. He teased her and tasted her, and Sanja responded with timid enthusiasm, feeling the intrusive pressure of his manhood against her core.

"Fal…"

His name on her lips shuddered through Fal, nearly sending him over the edge. Already, he hovered there for the pleasure of having Sanja in his arms. She fit to him as if made for him, and he never wanted to let her go. "Trust me?"

"Yes," she said.

With a hard thrust, he rent through her maidenhead, taking her cry into his mouth. He felt the water draw magic from him as it swirled in a lazy current around them. It didn't take for itself, but for her. It soothed away the pain he'd caused, brought her pleasure in its stead. Fal waited until he felt her relax once more in his hold before he moved again.

With the lake buoying them softer than a mattress made of clouds, they floated and kissed and loved, straining together as one. Fal's awareness of the outside world narrowed to the woman in his arms. Her gaze held him captive. Her heartbeat set the rhythm of his, and, as he felt himself nearing the endless precipice, the two synchronized for a beat.

And another.

And one more.

At the last moment, he pressed his palm flat against the small of Sanja's back, called up a thin barrier of water to contain his rising seed, and prayed it would be enough to keep her safe.

And then there was only the blinding light of pleasure and the breathless wonder of it echoing through Sanja, and back to him. Light enough to brighten the falling night. Heat enough to bring steam up from the lake's surface. A connection so complete, he shuddered when their heartbeats fell out of sync once more, each returning to its own unique rhythm, leaving a lasting echo in the other. He would know Sanja anywhere now. Deaf and blind, he would find her by the feel of her heart in his.

Slowly, reluctantly, Fal came back to himself, to the water's chorus singing a sweet lullaby. Sanja clung to him, shivering, and nothing had ever felt so good, so right as the feel of her skin against his. "Mine now, wife," he said. "And the sun's still in the sky."

He floated them around so she could watch the sun's final ray disappear behind the tree line in the west. The glittering blanket of night descended on a soft sigh, countless stars shining above. They reflected on the lake's surface all around Fal and Sanja, creating an illusion of them floating unfettered in the night sky.

"Magic," Sanja whispered.

Yes, he thought. *You are.*

22

He dreamed of battle. A great army rushed the empty field, their weapons raised high, but their voices silent. They came in the night, with only the bright Otherlands above to shine their way. And they came in droves.

The ground shook with the beat of their gallop. The wind screamed as it wove among their blades. They were the sounds of an approaching storm, and this one would end them all.

Fal dived down and became someone else.

A lone sentry on patrol heard the noise. He squinted into the night sky, seeking thunder clouds and, when he saw none, turned his gaze lower. Fear tightened like a noose around his neck; he couldn't find his voice to shout a warning. For too long, he stood frozen to the spot, watching a sea of armed warriors flood toward him.

His torch shone the target for their arrows. They missed, but their clatter against the wall at his back roused the sentry into action. He dropped the torch and ran for the tower, tripped and fell so many times his body was bruised and his face streaked with tears by the time he reached the bell. Wheezing sobs echoed off the stone as he gripped the hammer and swung.

Over and over, he beat the bell, desperate to hear an answering gong from the other towers before the army reached him. An arrow pierced his neck as the first response rang out, and he smiled as he fell. The alarm had been sounded.

Fal left the man's dying body, hovered there a moment with the entire world open to him, before he was drawn away, pulled to another place, to become another man.

In the next tower, two sentries had been placed in charge. The one remained to continue sounding the alarm, but the other had a different task. Torch in hand, he ran down the tower stairs, across the field to the other tower, where a great pyre stood ready to be lit.

The princess' instructions repeated in his mind as he thrust the torch into the pile: "Light a fire large enough, and it will call to me. I will come at once."

As the dry wood caught, the sentry watched the night swarm with soldiers. They came out of nowhere, soundless, but for the beat of horse hooves. They carried no banners, but their white tabards were emblazoned with a bright red cross.

He watched the first tower fall, its bell already silent for some time. Soon, they would reach the second. He wanted to run for his life. Clan Steen had never answered the crown's call to arms. There were no soldiers stationed here, only sentries charged with sounding the alarm, should anyone think to sneak up on them from behind. They'd expected perhaps a score of men, not legions.

In the end, when the second tower's bell fell silent, fear got the better of him. The fire had just started to consume the pile of straw and wood. It would burn on its own and had no need of more tending. The sentry dropped his torch and ran.

A spear through the gut ended his escape halfway down the staircase, and by the time he tumbled to the bottom, the soldiers had already run up and doused the pyre. The sound of thousands of booted feet marching past drowned out his wailing moan of despair as his soul fled its dying prison, expelling Fal along the way.

He flew far up into the sky once more, gazing down at death creeping through the night. The rush of feet, the drum of hoofbeats came to him in waves like great, growling breaths of Fenrir's approach. Icy mist followed in their wake. It concealed deep furrows in the ground, invisible claw marks none but he would ever see.

With a shudder, Fal turned his gaze in the other direction.

Only a stretch of open fields and forests remained between the army and Castle Frastmir. Their path, it seemed, lay open to seize the seat of the crown but, overeager and overconfident, they made a mistake.

Someone in their ranks ordered the fields to be burned. A series of flaming arrows shot into the sky and landed true, lighting a wild blaze that flared across the landscape and sparked an unmistakable alarm.

With the fire's roar to sound their advance, they gave voice to their fury and screamed a chorus of war cries so loudly they never heard the wildfire flare behind them as high as the castle wall, spewing forth a creature of nightmares.

Instantly, Fal became the dark, silent being who soared over the army to head them off. She flew, and flew, seeking an edge to the sea of troops, and found none. Were she anyone other than who she was, the Dragonblood princess might well have panicked at the sight.

But Liadan had faced far worse in the past, and she knew that succumbing to fear would spell defeat before the battle had even begun. Baring her fangs in a snarl, she beat her wings harder to gain more speed. She could see the front lines now, almost to the castle's outer wall.

Liadan allowed them to reach it, let them corner themselves, and then let loose a massive stream of fire. Men screamed below her, but she was already gone by the time they turned their gazes to the sky, flying along the wall to burn as many of them as she could reach.

There! The army did have an end. Liadan veered along the edges of the formation, the weak point where those who bore witness to their comrades burning alive grew afraid enough to run. She cut them off with her flames, framed the formation in glorious, golden fire.

There were too many to burn all at once; she knew she'd never get them all this way, but she needed to kill as many as possible, weaken their ranks, and give Wilderheim's forces time to muster.

The dragon would be furious with her if he knew how badly she'd miscalculated the enemy's intent. He would never forgive her for leaving their flanks so exposed.

But he wasn't there, and neither were her parents or her brother.

Liadan was on her own, facing a threat more massive than any of them had anticipated.

All of them had failed, and if she couldn't make it right, all of them would die for their failure.

Catching a favorable wind, she let it carry her higher so she might better see the battle. Frastmir's soldiers were streaming up to the battlements, ready to face the enemy. Inside the castle, everyone trained for battle was busy at work preparing weapons and vats of oil. Servants carrying armfuls of linens rushed into the great hall, which would serve as their infirmary. Anyone too old or too young was being evacuated.

Unsettled by the surprise attack, Liadan took a chance and abandoned the fight to soar over the city. The streets were dark and quiet, not a soul out of doors. The sounds of battle hadn't reached them yet.

Liadan threw a fireball into a pile of hay, and another at a stack of firewood, and one more into the middle of the green. It was all the warning she could give the people, and she prayed it would be enough.

The wind shifted, bringing with it the scent of burning flesh. It called Liadan to return to the fight, but she resisted, drawn toward the west by a sense that she had overlooked something.

Beyond the city of Frastmir, the countryside was peacefully asleep as far as her eye could see. Still, something about it felt wrong. Liadan flew on, trusting her instincts more than her sight. She flew so far, the battle for Castle Frastmir seemed an entire world away, and all the while, her gut clenched with dread.

Almost to the town of Crossroads, Wilderheim's central point, Liadan stopped, hovering aloft to get her bearings. A ringing started in her ears, high pitched and relentless. It speared into her mind, confusing her sense of up and down. She lost control of her flames and they cracked fissures across her black scales, turned her hair to living fire.

Liadan clutched her temples, shook her head, stabbed her talons into her scalp, but nothing would make it stop. She flipped over in the air, lost the wind, and tumbled headlong toward the ground.

As she fell, a sparkle of light nearby tore the world open with the flash of a strange, polished sword, admitting another wave of mounted troops.

Liadan struck the ground, writhing in agony as flames flared out of her in uncontrollable bursts. She crawled her way to a creek and doused herself in it until the smoke that usually accompanied her transformation from one shape to another congealed into sludge. Fully human, unarmed, and disoriented, Liadan lay still in the stream as the sky spun madly above her.

She heard screaming as soldiers murdered their way through the town. They would find her soon and, in her current state, they might succeed in killing her. Liadan turned to her side to ease her way up to sit, but the world tilted, sending her back into the creek.

The relentless noise filled her skull to bursting. It was the sound of metal, a blade forged to thirst for blood. It screeched with madness and cut without mercy. Guardsmen and soldiers died by that blade, and more would have, were it not for the hand of its wielder turning it forcibly away from women and children. But the blade's metal kept screeching, demanding its due and growing more powerful with each drop of blood it absorbed. It would not keep obeying for long. Liadan squeezed her eyes shut to somehow keep them from popping out. The scent of blood reached her, and she realized it was her own. Liadan's mouth opened on a soundless scream as her body began to turn against her.

Desperate to get away, she tried one more time to rise.

A cold, wet foot slapped against her shoulder, pushing her back down. Liadan opened her eyes just a little to see something standing over her. It had two legs, two arms, a torso, and a head—a human shape, but made entirely of water. Though the undine had no discernible eyes, Liadan could feel it watching her. She sensed it was angry, and Liadan was helpless to defend herself against it.

The undine lifted its head to look away, then turned back to her. Faster than Liadan could react, it slapped its transparent hand over her face and submerged her head in the creek.

She fought to surface but, though she felt no binds on her limbs, they wouldn't move. Her fire flared to the surface of her skin only to be instantly doused by the water. Without air, she couldn't burn to defend herself. Mud churned up around her as she thrashed, rendering her blind, hiding her from sight as a stampede of human feet shook the ground.

Her lungs burned with the need for air until she could bear it no longer. She inhaled and let the stinging, muddy water burn deep into her lungs. Heavy pressure on her chest kept her submerged, pushing her deeper into the mud as she coughed and drowned, until the mud encased her up to her neck.

But she wasn't dying. Water rushed in and out of her lungs, alien, painful, terrifying, but it wasn't killing her. Heavy footfalls stomped her legs and torso, an army rushing across the creek. She felt them, but they never saw her. And, as she gasped in lungful after lungful of murky muck, she noticed something else. Her head no longer hurt.

The water cleared above her, forming the shape of a translucent head as the undine held a watery finger to its nonexistent lips. It was helping her?

Suddenly, the creature was gone. The pressure keeping her submerged disappeared, and the water in her lungs became deadly without the Undine's magic to protect her. Buried in the mud, Liadan thrashed as hard as she could to get free. She only needed a little give, a hand's width to reach the surface—

~

Fal's own shout startled him awake, and he bolted upright out of a stream. He was soaked through, and nowhere near where he'd laid himself to sleep the night before.

He stepped out of the stream and crawled up the grassy bed to level ground. The town of Crossroads spread out before him, every house and roadway as he knew it from Wilderheim. Here, it all stood empty, not a soul to be seen, not a single animal scurrying about.

By the location of the sun, Fal guessed it to be a little before noon. How had he gotten there?

Sanja was probably looking for him by the waterfall, no doubt imagining all sorts of nightmares of Fal having abandoned her again. The need to return to her burned so badly within him it turned water into steam, drying him in an instant.

But he must have been brought here for a reason, and until he discovered what it was, Fal couldn't risk bringing it back with him to put his mate in danger.

"I dreamed."

But *what*?

Though the fear he'd felt remained, shivering through his limbs at odd intervals, Fal couldn't remember anything else from his dream. It had been vivid. He knew that much. And, as he walked through Crossroads, he remembered the odd detail here and there. A sparkling light, accompanied by a ringing sound, a flash of fire, and a blade screaming for blood.

He didn't like this. Being alone in nature was one thing, but Crossroads felt alive and dead at the same time, like a burial ground full of ghosts watching him from darkened doorways and closed window shutters. Fal's skin crawled in the echoing silence; he needed to get away from it.

Offering more magic to Anderheim, he pushed to be transported elsewhere. Anderheim responded eagerly and, through a blurred stream of its particular mode of travel, delivered him into the courtyard of Castle Frastmir. It was as empty as Crossroads, and every other town Anderheim had copied from his memories, turning the castle's structure into a massive bell reverberating with echoes of a long-ago strike. He felt those vibrations in his bones; expected at any moment to see the walls begin to disintegrate beneath their silent force, but they remained standing, tall and proud. He didn't know what to make of it.

There were pitchforks and gear beside the open stable door and barrels by the kitchen. This version of Castle Frastmir appeared to be as equipped as the original in Wilderheim. Better still, his tower library, destroyed in the original, was whole and untouched in Anderheim. It gave him hope its contents would be there as well.

Eager to find out, Fal stepped up to the great front door but stopped with his hand a finger's breadth from making contact. The last time he'd been here, everything he'd touched had disintegrated into water. But Anderheim had been little more than an illusion then. Things might be different now.

Taking a chance, Fal pressed his palm to the door and pushed. The great portal groaned a loud complaint that echoed through the hall. Stepping across the threshold, Fal felt like a tiny ant walking into a cave.

"Hello," he called to relieve the yawning silence. He didn't expect an answer.

In the great hall, his parents' thrones stood on the dais, illuminated by a shaft of light coming from a high window. They glittered with magics imbued in the wood with symbols as sharp and fresh as the day they'd been carved.

Fal ached to see his parents seated there. He craved the comfort of their presence and the guidance of their knowledge. He missed them both, as well as his sister. Never had he yearned for Liadan's presence in his mind as much as he did now, in this new, empty world.

Turning his back on the dais, he went to his tower library in search of answers. All the books and scrolls he'd collected over the years greeted him when he arrived at the top, and Fal breathed in their familiar scent. There, among those pages, lay the answer to his predicament, he was sure of it.

He sought one tome in particular, an old, leather-bound volume with iron clasps and a meticulously stitched spine. He remembered the title embossed on the front: *The Origin of Worlds*. He remembered setting it aside, at the time more interested in the ending of worlds than their origins. Considering Fal had somehow managed to start the birth of a new world, the book might prove useful now.

Where had he put it?

Aha! At the top of a stack of books on the topmost shelf. Out of reach and out of the way of more important research material. Three more books fell from the stack when he extricated the one he wanted, but he didn't care. With fingers so eager they shook, he unlatched the iron clasp and opened the book onto the first page.

It was blank.

He turned two more pages, then fanned through the rest of them, but all of them were completely blank. Anderheim had known to recreate a book Fal remembered seeing, but it couldn't reproduce words Fal had never read.

Setting the tome aside, he picked up another and leafed through it. This one was a treatise on elemental magic he'd read in search of a cure for his illusions. The copy in his hands was filled with passages he remembered, but the writing faded to illegible stains in parts he'd only skimmed, or hadn't read at all.

He wouldn't find anything here he didn't already know.

But the library was still shielded with spells Fal himself had devised to keep his experiments contained. He would find no safer place to test his limits within Anderheim. Offering up a puff of magic, he sent the Otherland a silent request for a window.

Anderheim accepted, but not as eagerly as it had in the past. Sometime between Fal's retrieving Sanja from the path and now, the Otherland's formation had completed fully. It had become its own thing, separate and no longer dependent on Fal, and the magic he offered became no more than part of a transaction. In return, Anderheim physically shifted several stones out of the tower wall to create an opening large enough to pass for a window. It smoothed the edges, formed a sill along the bottom, and sent the remaining rocks tumbling away.

The window opened to the east, overlooking fields and forests. Far beyond the horizon in that direction was the demesne of clan Steen and, beyond that, the Ravetian border. Fal took in the sight, savored its tranquility for a moment longer before he began his work in earnest.

It may have quieted while he'd slept, but the water sprite magic still roiled in restless eddies inside his chest. Fal sensed it like a sleeping beast. If and when it awakened, he wasn't certain he could keep it from overwhelming him.

New magic was dangerous magic, regardless of who wielded it. Water sprites were born with an innate understanding of the power they held and learned nuance as they matured. To come into possession of so much of it so late in life put Fal and everyone around him in peril. He could bring the entire tower crashing down simply by voicing the wrong melody.

But more power could also mean a way out of Anderheim. It was another straw for him to grasp. With Sanja safely away at the waterfall, now was the time to try.

Fal closed his eyes and focused on the churning magic within him. Like a flower in the sun, it bloomed and flared, tickling his throat to be released. There lay the lock to keep it contained: the magic could only work through his voice. As long as he remained silent, it would be safe.

Fal took a moment to center himself. On his next inhale, he thought of home, and when he exhaled, he gave the thought a melody. He sang softly, at first, uncomfortable with his voice and unsure of how it would affect Anderheim.

He felt the Otherland quiver in reaction. It didn't like this new magic. But it wasn't being hurt, and so it held as steady as it could while the spell built upon itself. Fal's voice grew louder, folded back on itself in endless echoes, and the melody begot layers, growing more complex.

As it turned into a chorus of several voices singing along with Fal, he felt the boundary beyond which he would no longer be able to pull it back. It was so close at hand it frightened him, and he stopped at once, his eyes snapping open.

His tower, a moment ago whole, now looked destroyed. Fal stood on what felt like solid stone, but when he looked down, he saw nothing under his feet but a long drop to the catacombs below. A chill wind brushed the back of his neck, turning his gaze to the east.

The peaceful scene from Anderheim was no more. Before him, the fields and forests of Wilderheim were aflame, thick smoke obscuring the sky. He could not hear a thing, but he saw enough to force a terrified cry from his throat.

At once, the vision slammed shut, closing him away in the safety of Anderheim. But the sight of a sea of warriors spilling over the castle's outer walls remained seared into his mind's eye.

Fal stumbled back, fell over a chair, and slammed his head against the bookcase. His mind seized with terror, and his body shook uncontrollably.

Castle Frastmir was under attack.

Spurred into action, he shoved to his feet, stumbled his way down to the great hall and, through it, to his own chambers. In the far corner of his dressing room stood an old, ornate chest he never expected to have cause to open. Now he had no choice.

Fal changed his clothes and boots, then knelt before the chest and, with shaking hands, opened it. Pulling aside the embroidered wrap, he began to take out the contents one after the other—leather padding, arm and leg guards, chain mail, body armor, a helmet. He didn't put on any of them, save for a leather jerkin trimmed with embroidered protection spells.

Despite having trained with Wilderheim's soldiers from a young age, Fal was a mage, not a warrior. He didn't need heavy armor weighing him down; he needed speed and freedom of movement to work his spells.

But there were a few items in the chest he couldn't afford to leave behind.

First, the sword and dagger Liadan had forged for him in the dragon's fire. Light as a feather, stronger than any steel made by man or Other, with grips fashioned for his hands alone. Liadan had forged many weapons under the dragon's tutelage, but these were the first she'd ever parted with, a gift he'd treasured more than any other. He strapped them both to his waist, grateful to have their protection at hand, should he need them.

From the bottom of the chest, he retrieved a pendant on a long, thick chain. The image of a dragon in flight was etched into its round face, chips of diamonds marking his fangs and a glowing ruby forming his eye. It had been a gift from his parents, the same design worn by his father. The charm protected its wearer with the dragon's magic from both physical and magical assault. As soon as he put it on, he felt his grandfather's fire fuel the water magic inside him and knew instantly that the dragon was alive and well somewhere out there.

Good. They'd need all the help they could get.

Fal pushed to his feet and rolled his shoulders back, preparing himself for the battle to come. He was ready, and the path stood unobstructed. It was time.

Only when he reached for his new magic to open another portal did Fal remember he'd left Sanja at the waterfall, and he faltered. With one hand over his heart where hers beat alongside, he couldn't bring himself to voice a single note. *More than a wife.* She was part of him now, and it brought him equal measures of peace and dread. If he got hurt, she would feel it. If she felt sorrow, Fal would grieve with her. Their lives would be so closely linked neither of them would ever be alone again.

Last night, when he'd held her sleeping in his arms, the knowledge that he'd have a lifetime of such nights ahead of him had filled him with such happiness it had bordered on relief.

Today, faced with the prospect of having her life cut short in an awful, violent way, made him sick to his stomach.

She'll be safer in Anderheim, he told himself. At least here, none of the ugliness and death could touch her.

But she would be alone, in an unfamiliar part of an unfamiliar world, with no magic of her own to aid her. She would think he'd abandoned her.

Fal couldn't take her with him, but at least he could put her in more familiar surroundings. Yes, he could do that. He would not leave her with only a dying campfire to keep her safe.

Decided, Fal sang once more. This time, his voice was steady and strong, his intent clear and focused. He would accept no other outcome but what he was after, and Anderheim dared not oppose his will.

As he sang, he watched the world ripple, felt the doorway opening before him. And it was a doorway. Unlike the brief wound he'd torn open to retrieve Sanja and the window he'd created in his tower, this opening felt as steady as a portal. Anderheim wasn't fighting him anymore. It had taken what it'd needed from Fal. Its existence was no longer bound with Fal's, and so it no longer cared whether he came or went.

Fal altered the melody, forging roots for the portal, anchoring it in place. He sang three more portals into being—one at the waterfall, one in the heart of Crossroads, and one more in the mountain pass between Wilderheim and Lyria. He anchored them deep into the earth and locked them all so no one but Fal could open them. Once he stepped through to Wilderheim and let the doorway close, Fal might lose all sense of the Otherland. He would need another way back.

With his task complete, it was time to go.

Though it looked much the same on the other side, Fal knew he no longer saw Anderheim through his bedchamber doors. He heard sounds of battle; he smelled smoke and felt the fear and pain of his kingdom saturating the cold air. His heart beat faster in response, wavering his resolve, but he pushed his fear aside. His people needed him, and he could not abandon them.

With one hand on the grip of his sword, he stepped up to the portal. Goose flesh prickled all over his skin, and his breath misted in the cold as he stepped through to Wilderheim. As the portal began to close after him, he sent one last bolt of raw magic back to Anderheim with the image of a small, cozy cottage on the western side of an empty copy of Frastmir and an order it wouldn't dare refuse: "Send her home."

He prayed Sanja would understand.

And, if he never made it back, that she could find it in her heart to forgive him.

23

There were shadows and, from with their prison, a copper-haired Halfling god stepped out into the night, this time for good. He breathed in deeply of the cold as he surveyed the vastness all around him. Stars watched him in silence as among them multitudes of worlds lay naked, exposed to eyes that ought never have beheld their mystery. The wild dervish of their fear filled the silence with a melody of soundless screams, terror whispering on the dark wind.

All of them sang their own end.

The Trickster closed his eyes to better savor the anticipation, hands flexing at his sides and sharp teeth bared in a snarl. Freedom had never tasted so sweet.

His Shadow prison swirled around him one last time, trying in vain to pull him back into its depths, but Loki barely felt its cold caress as it turned to mist and faded away completely.

Triumph, rage, vengeance—all of them had long ago melded together within him into something new and dangerous. Loki felt it coursing through his veins, crawling beneath his skin, and swirling 'round and 'round in his mind, a madness that gave him strength, a weapon that would rend Asgard asunder. He would feast on Woden's bones and drink of his lovely wife's blood anon.

And he couldn't wait.

The void between worlds shuddered with a howl not heard but felt.

Loki turned his gaze in its direction and watched darkness grow in the distance, swallowing light after swirling light as Fenrir neared, devouring everything in his path. Loki launched himself forward to meet it halfway.

What a beautiful monster his son had grown up to be. The great wolf, they called him, for they lacked the words to describe the true shape of him.

He had none.

Fenrir was hunger itself, ever empty, ever ravenous to fill the void inside. He could never be sated and, in the end, would devour himself, as well.

But not yet.

Loki drew on his essence, extending his being through his arms to shape a pair of swords. They tore away from him, then slammed back into the secure hold of his reformed palms. Like the sword he'd given the ancient queen in Synealee, they were imbued with not only his power but also his will, his madness, and his thirst for the blood of his enemies. And they would never be sated.

The queen would never know the magnificence of the gift she'd received. Whoever wielded the sword would slay anyone who stood in his way and win any war he deigned to fight. The blade would bring him power and glory for the price of his precious soul. Those who stood with him would sing his legend for centuries to come, and none of his enemies would live long enough to hate him.

But the blade would have its way in the end. It would infect his mind until right and wrong became life and death. He'd spend his life trying to build a kingdom with the glory and mercy of his god, for fear of burning in his eternal wrath after death. And the harder he tried, the more he would fail, and the deeper his madness would root inside him, forcing him farther along his path to damnation. He would come to loathe the weapon with every fiber of his being. But it would never release him from its hold.

Divine magic always came with a heavy price. Had the queen not been so intent on her revenge, she might have thought to ask. Then again, had she not been so intent, she wouldn't have needed his gift at all.

Humans. Never had another species entertained Loki more. He might miss them in the end. But, for now, he had more than enough games to keep him occupied.

The blades in his hands were as cold as ice and, when they sliced the void, they left gaping wounds. He scraped one sharp edge across the other to produce a screech that stopped Fenrir in his tracks.

The yawing darkness turned on Loki, howling for nourishment. It recognized its maker—for now.

Now was all Loki needed. "Our time has come at last," he said, gazing into the heart of his monstrous progeny. He could feel Fenrir's anguish brimming the endless abyss of him and steeled himself not to fall into it. "Soon, we will have our vengeance on everyone."

Fenrir bayed furiously, displacing the stars as they shrank away, dimming to hide from his seeking gaze. To be seen was to be no more.

Loki's feral smile stretched wider, his lips dragging across the sharpened tips of his fangs. He tasted his own blood, and it fueled his burning wrath. "We claim Wilderheim as our first prize." Cut off all possible paths of retreat; destroy any chance of the Dragonblood clan restoring the gods to their full strength. Then there would be nowhere else for them to hide.

As Fenrir thrashed, eager to set off once more, Loki turned to the line that served as both an anchor and a border between Wilderheim and Mitgard. The border was so thin it was nigh invisible, but Loki felt the power weaving along its length, fortifying it with millions upon millions of whispered prayers. It moved so quickly back and forth it appeared as an unbroken ribbon of light. Only when it stopped, its task complete, could Loki perceive its true shape.

A new god had risen in Mitgard, a fiercely territorial being, willing to sacrifice anything to lay claim to his faithful. And they were very faithful. The old gods had their champions, but their numbers were few and scattered, each paying tribute in their own way, to their own god, diluting the collective strength of their faith. This new god had but one path of worship, and he never shared. With each prayer and offering, his power grew so vast, all the gods of Asgard combined—

even Fenrir himself—could not match it.

Wilderheim was but the first casualty of his wrath, sacrificed to Loki and his machinations to wipe out all of Asgard. Once it fell, the new, nameless god would turn his sights onto every other kingdom, and every other god, until only he remained to reign over Mitgard unopposed. Whether the other gods knew it or not, the age of many was fast coming to an end. And only part of its demise would lead down Fenrir's insatiable gullet.

The lines had been drawn. The light of the fledgling god's essence flared bright behind the safety of his impenetrable border, an acknowledgment of Loki on the other side of it, and a reminder of their ultimate bargain. He'd already played his part, paid his price by sacrificing the souls of his oldest, most devout regent follower and legions of her warriors to Loki's war in Wilderheim.

Now it was Loki's turn. *Pay up, Trickster.*

Loki nodded, clutching his swords. "As agreed."

Then he filled his lungs with borrowed power and let it loose on a roar that sent Fenrir into a frenzy, racing straight for Wilderheim.

24

The water came up to the dragon's chest, languishing there a moment, its waves lapping at his heart on sorrowful sighs. The dragon braced his feet against the wall at his back and pulled steadily, twisting his wrists and chafing his skin off against the coarse ropes. He felt blood seep out of the wounds, but it never dissolved. Rejected by the water, it coalesced into heavy droplets that sank to the floor and rolled around like marbles until, with more deep sighs, the water slowly ebbed back into its basin.

When his cell had dried completely, the dragon regarded the crimson orbs with dispassionate interest as they levitated off the stone floor to hover in the air before him. Without saying a word, he waited for his tormentor to announce herself while she played with his blood, making the drops swirl in the air, then coalesce into one larger orb, then break up into hundreds of minuscule specs before coalescing them once more.

"Does it hurt to bleed?" Hel's disembodied voice questioned.

The dragon refused to answer.

Having shaped his blood into five little spheres, she moved them into a circle and conjured lines of soft green light to form a pentacle. "Gods have no blood," she remarked as the pentacle reformed itself into another, more complicated shape. "We have no hearts, no stomachs, no lungs. Our forms are arbitrarily chosen to give physical shape to our essence, but they are a lie. We are very much like dragons in that way."

She paused, no doubt waiting for him to speak his mind. The dragon remained silent, keeping a watchful eye on his blood. Nine droplets now shaped a sphere of webbed light, then the lines twisted into a flat weave of knotwork in the shape of a dragon.

"It is whispered that the first god who chose to take a physical form went too far and fell into living flesh. It is said that he became the first dragon, and the curse of his mistake is why his descendants can only ever choose one shape to escape their own."

The knotwork dragon reshaped itself into a human man with horns and a tail. The figure bowed its head to look at its own hands, then dropped to its knees as though in anguish.

"When a god dies, she first loses her ability to coalesce into a body. Bodies are useful things, such practical vessels for our power. Hardly any effort at all to manipulate. Take it away, and the power begins to scatter."

The shape collapsed into a ball of light with his blood at its center. Its bright glow dimmed by slow degrees, dispersing light into nothing until only his blood remained.

"We die by disintegrating into nothing, our power redistributed throughout the worlds in such trifling quantities as to be impotent. We become part of everything, and can never again rebuild ourselves whole."

"You are dying," the dragon surmised. Why else would she bother telling him all of this?

He didn't expect her to respond but, to his surprise, she did. "Yes. Like the waters beyond those bars, and the wards of this world, and every other." She didn't sound particularly distraught at this development. "The Other blood that formed the Veil drained away when it shattered. Without it, all the gods are dying. All except one."

"Loki."

His blood suddenly dropped to the stone floor, absorbing into it, and a moment later, Hel coalesced before him like a ghost. "My father lied to us. He sacrificed us all to save himself."

The dragon sneered, baring his fangs. "Did you expect anything else of him?"

"No," she said with what might have been a shrug. "Familial ties hold little meaning to us. But he isn't all bad. After all, he left me a parting gift. A mighty Other of my own."

As he comprehended what she was telling him, the dragon's fury stoked an inferno inside him. He yanked on his ropes, felt them strain even as they tightened further, cutting into his wrists. Every drop of blood that fell to the floor fed power to his prison, strengthening his binds, turning him into his own jailer.

"As long as I have you, I, and all of Helheim, will persist."

"My blood will not keep you alive forever."

"It will keep until the war is over, and Fenrir has had his fill. Then, perhaps it will be my turn to strike a deal with the new god." She looked around. "Helheim can grow as large as it needs to be. It can change as much as it must to please him. After all, the dead must go somewhere."

"And if I drink before then?"

Her pale lips formed something like a smile, though it carried as much feeling as her voice. "And what if you do?"

If he did, he'd die.

Or so she'd led him to believe.

"You lied?"

"My father's idea. He said the greatest torment that can be wrought upon a soul is its own hope of redemption. Perhaps that is why the new god likes him so well." She spoke as though reciting a practiced speech. The inflection of her voice and the expression on her face felt like a performance fabricated for a specific purpose: to anger him. The dragon knew this, and still, he couldn't stop himself rising to the bait.

Fire sparked in his palms and spread to glove his hands and arms up to his elbows, burning his wounds whole. He would not give Helheim a single more drop of his blood if he could help it. If he had to remain burning for the rest of his eternal life, he would, if only to see Hel wither and die. Wrath added fuel to his flames, and soon they covered him from horn to tail, scorching black marks on the cold stone floor.

Hel watched him, her head tilted at a bored angle, but her gaze strayed from his eyes to the ropes tied at his wrists, and the dragon caught the faintest hint of a scent: smoke. Startled, he followed her gaze to see the tiny fibers fraying from the braid turn black and wither into the whole. The rope didn't weaken in the least, but the small damage was enough.

When the dragon faced Hel again, his smile was as dark as his wrath. "Shall we say our farewells now?"

"How about a bargain instead?"

In answer, the dragon's flames flared hotter, turning blue, scorching the ropes black. Yet, writhing as if in pain, they refused to set him free.

Through the blue haze, he saw Hel's form flicker and grow fainter. "Dragon, you have not considered the full consequences of your actions."

"I starve you, you disintegrate, and I go free."

"And Helheim disappears forever. Along with everyone in it."

In the next instant, his flames were gone, and he shivered with cold dread.

"Do you understand now? If you starve us, you will never see your beloved Solveig again. Her soul will die, never to be reborn. That is why you have forced yourself to carry on this long, is it not? Somewhere in the depths of your burning heart, you hoped to meet her again one day, in another life, another body. You have kept yourself alive, waiting for the day when you would see her again, so you might right your mistakes and save her. You would have waited an eternity for that."

"Curse you." He couldn't deny it. Seeing Solveig again, even as a slave to Hel's whims, had only made his yearning deeper. Hope was, indeed, the cruelest torment Hel and her wretched father could have wrought upon him.

"What would you do to be with her again?"

Anything. But if he gave in to Hel, she would repay his sacrifice with nothing but more pain. He would never be free of her. But how could he go on living knowing he'd left Solveig to die?

"All I want is to live," Hel said, drifting closer. "Give me that, and you can have her."

"What would you have me do? Bleed myself dry so you can build a body to contain you?"

"Yes, a body for me, and enough energy to convey you to her. Here in Helheim, her soul is as immortal as you are. She can never sicken, get hurt, or die. You could be with her forever."

"As long as we stay," he clarified bitterly. "I would be your prisoner for the rest of eternity." He would have to give up the clan he'd sired to their fate in Wilderheim. They might all die for his selfish need for his mate. Oh, but to see her again, hear her voice, touch her skin, and feel its vibrant heat…

"Say, rather, you would be allowed to stay. Still, a small price to pay for the gift I offer in return." Hel looked around as a soft mist filled his cell. It carried sunshine, and birdsongs, and green grass on a dream so enticing his eyelids drooped heavily. "And it need not be in this cell."

A figure moved through the mist, indistinct, yet painfully familiar. He watched Solveig stroll through the tall grass, oblivious of being observed this way, and if he could have torn off his own arms to free himself and go to her, he would have.

The rope bit deeper. Helheim claimed more of his blood, and its mistress solidified beside him. "I offer you an eternity with your woman for but a little bit of blood."

At the sound of her voice, Solveig turned to face them, and the hazy vision sharpened a little more. All it cost him was another drop of blood.

The dragon forgot to breathe, staring at her. Her eyes widened in surprise, and he could hear her gasp as if she was right there before him. When her lips shaped his name, the dragon's throat constricted until it hurt.

She smiled.

"Does she know?"

A faint scratching sound made his ear twitch, but with Solveig's tearful gaze on him, the dragon dared not let her out of his sight to seek out its source. Hel traced the seam between the ropes and his skin, taking his blood directly from him. He shuddered when her form condensed enough to restore her scent. The queen of Helheim smelled like mist and cold, and death. "Which answer would make your choice easier to make?"

The dragon growled, shuddering when the sound echoed back from somewhere else. Not an echo. A response.

"She knows enough," Hel said, her hair whipping at his arms when she briefly turned toward the source of the sound, then back to the dragon.

Solveig started toward him slowly, hesitating. She knew. And she understood how impossible a choice had been put before him. Too many paces away, she came upon some invisible barrier that would allow her no closer. Placing one hand on it, she brought herself as close as she could and touched her other hand to her heart.

"Sol," he whispered.

"You have but to say the word to be with her. Give me what I want, and you shall have what you so desperately need."

The dragon was so focused on his Solveig he didn't notice another presence invading his cell until he felt its approaching snarl shudder the ground at his feet.

Solveig gasped, backing away from the barrier separating them, and only then did the dragon tear his gaze from her to see Hel, too, had retreated as far as the cell's confines would allow. Though she showed no fear on her face, the dragon could smell it.

A deep, rumbling growl rendered the wall at his back liquid. Massive ripples deformed the cold stone slabs as a large, lupine snout pushed through, followed by the rest of his head and torso. In the bowels of the withering Helheim, the beast was as big as a small horse. Head canted low, hackles standing on end, the wolf glowed as he faced off with Hel.

Yet, instead of smiting the creature where it stood, the goddess of Helheim appeared to weigh her choices. Surely she didn't consider herself unequal to the battle. Then again, if her state was so desperate that she needed a dragon's blood to survive…

Braving a sideways glance, Hel noticed the dragon watching. She placed her hand on the wall at her back, and the dragon felt a disturbance as the cell walls expanded, retreating to give her more strength. Her body filled out, becoming heavier, more solid, and she raised her chin in defiance. "You cannot have him—"

The wolf snapped his fangs in her face, silencing her with a snarl so vicious the dragon shifted sideways to place himself as much between the beast and Solveig as his ropes would allow.

When Hel would have raised her hand to strike him down, the wolf growled a low warning and pressed his snout to her chest. "He is *mine*," she insisted. "He chose to stay. He chose her."

The wolf's next growl reverberated through the cell and struck fear into the dragon's heart—for Solveig's sake, not his own.

The wolf's body shook with the force of it. —*Liar*— he accused. —*You will not dare!*—

Hel quieted, pressing herself as hard as she could against the wall without escaping through it to safety. With his enemy backed into a corner, the beast turned to the dragon.

"Varr?" The wolf Nialei's magic had inadvertently brought back from death had been her faithful companion ever since. He was not alive and so could not die, but neither was he dead. As a creature of in-between, he had an inexplicable ability to move between realms with ease and defy any attempt to keep him restrained. The dragon almost smiled. "What took you so long?"

Varr huffed his displeasure, wordlessly communicating a deep dislike for this place. Ignoring the vision of Solveig altogether, he turned around to sniff at the dragon's ropes.

"You cannot break them," the dragon said. "They have withstood my fangs, my claws, and my fire countless times."

One large, milky white eye focused on him with what might have been amused indulgence. Opening his maw, Varr took a rope between his teeth and bit down. Lightning crackled along its length, biting back at both Varr and the dragon, causing the wolf to flinch and retreat.

"Helheim will not release him," Hel said. "It needs him too much. And he needs her."

On the other side of the barrier, Solveig spoke the dragon's name. She was wary of the wolf but drawn to the dragon as he would always be drawn to her. "She said we could be together again."

The dragon nearly went to his knees. Starved for the sound of her voice, he silently begged her to say more, unable to speak himself.

Varr answered for him. —*He is needed elsewhere.*—

Though he'd spoken as softly as a creature of his size could, the force of it still caused Solveig to flinch. "Ragnarok," she whispered in response as she hugged herself, shivering. "I can feel it coming. It's cold and dark. No place for a dragon and his kin."

"I could stay here," the dragon said at last.

The wolf stomped his front paw, claws curling down into the seam between two stones, and then, with a growl that made the dragon's fangs ache, bit down once more on the rope, yanking back so hard it tore free of its moorings.

The wolf had no magic of his own, but he was immune to it. His very being would not suffer the binds of a prison, even if they weren't his own. The rope had withstood the dragon's fury, but it couldn't hold out against Varr's.

The dragon heard its dying squeal, watched it flail like a snake with its head cut off, fighting desperately to live until all fight drained out of it. The loop around his wrist loosened, and he shook it free of his arm. He came as far as the remaining rope would allow, to the place where the metal grate ought to be. Now, instead of keeping him from the water on its other side, it marked the invisible shield keeping him from Solveig.

With another powerful bite, Varr severed the remaining rope, freeing him. *—It's time. Your clan needs you.—*

Ignoring Varr, the dragon shoved at the barrier and repeated, "I could stay." His fire all but split him in two, one half yearning for his mate, the other needing to return to Saeran and his family. He still had the ring; he could stay and bring them all here as well, all together and safe from Fenrir and Loki's mad machinations.

"Oh, my love, how I wish you could." Solveig came to him, pressing her hands against his. "I wish with all my heart and soul that I could feel your arms around me one more time."

From where she cowered, weakened back to her ghostly translucence, Hel said, "You can. Give me your blood, dragon, and I will take you to her right now. You could be together forever, and nothing would ever tear you apart again."

All the while Hel spoke, Solveig shook her head. "I have loved you with all of myself, every moment of my life, from the moment we first met."

"Sol, all that I am is yours. I missed you. Gods, how I missed you."

She smiled, even as glittering tears spilled down her cheeks. "And I you. But our time is past, my love. No matter how much we wish it, we can never have it back again."

"We can!" he insisted.

"You know better," she replied.

"No—"

"Things do not *live* in Helheim," she said without mercy. "They do not feel or love or cleave. Seeing you now, alive, I remember what it felt like to be loved by a dragon, and I feel your fire warm my blood. But it will fade just as you will if you stay. Things do not *live* in the land of the dead."

"I cannot keep her here much longer," Hel warned, her form now all but invisible. "Alive or dead, you would still be together. She died for you, dragon. Are you not willing to do the same for her?"

The mist began to fade, Solveig's beautiful face blurring.

—*We must go,*— Varr growled, nudging him away.

"He's right," Solveig said, stepping back.

"No, Solveig!"

"Our clan needs you. Go to them, and give them my love. Let it be your strength and shield you against what is to come."

Varr closed his maw over the dragon's shoulder, pulling him back from the mist, which was already losing all color as Solveig faded away.

"Sol!"

"My love with you, my heart. Always…"

With one hard yank, Varr knocked the dragon off his feet and swung him onto his back, then took off running. Darkness swallowed them as Varr leaped at the stone wall and through it into the in-between. Worlds blurred as they raced ever onward, and soon the searing pain of losing Solveig dulled to the familiar old ache. The dragon became numb, hollow, as the flowing aether stole his tears and scattered them into the darkness like glittering stars that would forever mark the path to where Helheim lay dying.

Varr ran, and ran, for how long the dragon didn't know. But the farther they went, the smaller Varr shrank, as if shedding his fierce warrior's shape until he was once again his normal size. By then, the dragon had run out of tears and pushed back the pain of loss enough to turn away from Helheim and toward Wilderheim.

He could see its shining borders flicker up ahead and, with a bend of his will, burned his human shape into that of a full dragon. Taking Varr gently into his claws, he beat his great wings and flew headlong, racing the ravenous darkness hurtling toward his clan.

And he prayed to whatever gods were still alive to hear that he would not be too late.

25

As soon as he stepped through into Wilderheim, the doorway closed, and Fal shivered with cold. No torches burned in this part of the castle; no fires had been lit to relieve the chill. In the dark silence, screams and wails echoed from the great hall. Fal conjured a swarm of lights to fly ahead and show him the way but, as they spread out before him, the sight they revealed drew him up short.

A long, shallow creek wound its way down the center of the floor. Tall grasses swayed on either side with little yellow flowers bobbing atop long, sturdy stalks. The walls he knew to frame the path on either side had disappeared, giving the impression he was walking through a nighttime forest.

His illusions were back.

No time to think about it. Fal was needed on the battlements.

He splashed along the creek to the staircase and down to the great hall to first take measure of things there.

So many wounded already. Healers and servants rushed from one to the other, slipping in puddles of blood. The dead and the dying side by side, because those charged with their care were too busy tending those who still had a chance.

The sounds they made tore at him.

Fal clutched the grip of his sword, grateful to have illusions blanketing the bloody floor with visions of soft grass and piles of sweet, dry hay. He forced himself to look into the eyes of the dying, watched their cries quiet, and their eyes grow big with wonder to behold the world changing around them. Many wept. Still more looked at him in awe, whispered prayers as he walked past them.

The healers and servants tending the wounded looked little better than their charges. They nodded their greetings and thanks but kept their attention on their work. Fal did his best to keep out of their way.

Near the dais, he knelt by a man whose bloodied face was half-covered by bandages. He'd been badly burned and couldn't stop shaking. Fal laid a hand on his shoulder, called on the healing powers of water to soothe his pain. When the man calmed, Fal asked, "What happened?"

"Gods all bless, milord," the man mumbled, delirious from shock. "Gods all bless ye an' keep ye…"

"Tell me," he tried again, but the man was already fading into an exhausted sleep.

"They came in the night."

Fal pushed to his feet to face the speaker and steeled himself not to react. Councilor Braith had always been a force unto herself, with boundless energy despite her advanced years, and a glib tongue that had refused to blunt for anyone, including the king himself. Now, her hair was a disheveled mess, her pale face flushed and stained with blood. Her bleary eyes and stooped shoulders bespoke of a long day of endless labors, and her bedraggled, bloody clothes said those labors had been torturous.

"Clan Steen abandoned us," she said. "They never answered the call to arms."

Frost tipped the grass at her feet. She was too weary to notice, but others did. Whether or not they understood the reason for it, to the last they drew back as far as their cots and pallets would allow. Shards of ice crackled and groaned beneath Fal's skin as his fury grew. He should have expected this. Liadan should have expected it. "Why was our flank left exposed?" he demanded, his voice colder than he'd intended. "Tarben should have known better."

Braith rubbed her brow, smearing dirt across her forehead. "Tarben ordered the bulk of our army to the south." Her tone made it clear what she thought of his decision. "He was convinced Synealee would march through Aegiros to reach us. Princess Liadan did not like it, but she was outvoted. Even Kvaran said…" Braith stopped on a deep sigh as if to catch her breath. As if it was too painful to speak of. "They are dead, you know. Kvaran bedded down that night and never woke again. Tarben, the old fool, was the first to climb those battlements. He took an arrow for one of the men and threw himself over the wall."

Fal staggered. "And Liadan?"

Braith shook her head. "She burned a good number of them, woke the city, and sounded the call to battle. But she has not been seen since."

"She is not dead. I would know it if she was."

Braith's gaze turned distant. "The Others are holding the line for us now. No human troops left to defend us. All we can do is wait and pray."

Others fought to defend Castle Frastmir? "How did they get here?"

Braith shrugged. "The gods only know. They started appearing at sunrise. All different sorts. But there are too many soldiers."

"Then we will need every warrior armed for battle."

Braith waved a shaking hand to encompass the great hall. "You are looking at them, Your Highness."

Fal balled his hands into fists at his sides. The creek running through Wilderheim's gardens was closest. It carried a fair amount of blood, but its source was still pristine. Agonized with the violence spilling over its banks, it answered his call at once. He caught hold of its strength with one hand, sent it blanketing the great hall in preparation of a much larger undertaking. With the other, he reached out to the river flowing along the outer edge of Frastmir. Its responding roar of fury flooded him with strength, and Fal channeled both into a wave that swept across the great hall, feeding it no small amount of his magic as he hummed the same melody he'd used to heal Sanja.

The sound pulsed and bounced off the stone walls like ripples traveling back and forth, the one building upon what the other had begun in cycles that swept away pain, melted broken parts whole, and cooled burns in turn.

Screams quieted into moans, then rose again into cries of aston-ishment. One by one, the men sat up, pulled away bandages to reveal

wounds fully healed. The servants and healers sighed as their weary
bodies restored themselves to full strength.

And Fal hadn't even strained himself unduly.

"Gods all bless," Braith said, appearing stunned, and at least a decade
younger. She clutched his arm tight and nodded, her eyes bright with
fighting spirit. "Go. Teach those fools they ought never have dared
set their sights on Wilderheim."

An answering shout echoed through the great hall and, within
moments, Fal had five score men in full vigor marching out the door
behind him.

Where they split off to arm themselves with discarded weapons
and armor, Fal ran through the gardens for the battlements. Already,
he saw several beings lining the top of the wall. Their attention was
turned outward but, as he topped the staircase, the closest speared him
with a quick, sharp, golden glance. Her skin was as blue as the sea, her
hair composed of gray, bladelike fins. She looked none too pleased to
see him. With a growl, she launched a volley of invisible blows into
the swarming army below, knocking them over like children's toys.

Beyond her, a giant covered in black fur swept a massive paw along
his part of the wall. His claws, as long as Fal was tall, hooked on ropes
and ladders, yanking them from their anchors, along with the enemy
soldiers climbing them. Some let go right away, plummeting to their
deaths below. Others held on, and the creature spun, swinging them
in a great arc before he released his hold. The force of his throw sent
his victims flying clean across the bailey to slam into the outer wall.
As if angry with his accomplishment, the creature snarled and shook
himself.

Still farther stood a tall, thin creature, like a sliver of a star-filled sky.
Fal couldn't see it move at all, but he sensed its magic grow outward
like a bubble, forcing the soldiers below into retreat. At a certain
point, the magic reached its limits and burst, allowing the army close
once more until the shield rebuilt itself and forced them back again.

The creature appeared to be working in harmony with another down
below. As the bubble pressed forward, flashes of light along its edge
cut across the barrier, slicing into the enemy. When the bubble burst,
that spear of light spiraled up into the air out of harm's way until the

battlefield was cleared enough for it to descend and resume its carnage.

"At your leisure, son of water," the blue woman growled through several rows of sharp, pointed teeth.

"Who are you?"

"Talk later, fight now." She nodded toward the outer wall, where more soldiers spilled into the bailey. "Have they circled fully 'round?"

"Yes," Fal confirmed. He'd felt them in the river. "Frastmir is overrun. They have cut off all paths of retreat.

"Best start making yourself useful, then. Hear tell there are more of them in the south. Your army's holding its own at the borders, but your people farther in are dying."

"Whatever happens, hold the castle," he ordered.

The female scoffed. "I take no orders from you. I protect the blood, not your pile of stones."

So that was why they'd come. The Other blood Nialei had collected over the last two decades was a source of untold power, and it lay hidden beneath the castle. The Others would sense it and fight to keep it out of mortal hands while the threat was imminent. Would they try to take it for themselves if or when an opportunity presented itself?

Every Otherland was in danger of destruction. The blood represented a chance for their survival. No matter that no one seemed to know how to use it, it was still a beacon of hope for them all. And now a deadly liability for Frastmir if its prince failed to protect it.

"Move!" The female shoved him hard, and Fal felt an arrow whiz past his ear before he tumbled headlong down the staircase, back into the gardens.

He righted himself in time to see her swat arrows out of the air. She caught one and dropped for cover as a cloud of them darkened the sky above. Not one of them made it to the ground. The shafts burned up in the air as a new Other appeared on the battlements, a tiny fire sprite no larger than an ember, but no less powerful for its diminutive size.

Braith had been right. There were too many soldiers for the Others to hold back on their own. Fal needed to improve their odds—and quickly.

With his jaw set and his thoughts dark, Fal marched back up the staircase, working magic into his palms as he went. The mad vortex inside him roared, ready to be released, but he held it back. *Not yet.* He might only get one chance to make a lasting impression. He had to time this right.

At the top of the staircase, the blue female took one look at him and stepped out of his way. The furry giant sensed his approach and whined, shaking his head violently. He jumped off the wall, holding on by the claws of one paw to allow him passage. By the time he'd reached the center, Fal's body hummed, and illusions of water spilled over the battlements.

In the bailey below, the sight of so much water made soldiers wary. They paused in their assault, stepped away from their ropes and ladders. Already, they could see water bursting out from chinks in the wall like a great dam about to break.

Fal made sure they saw him, too, with his ever-changing shape, and the blue light of his magic glowing around him. He used their fear against them, gave them the display they expected to see. Raising his hands high, he tipped his head back and shouted to the sky. Behind him, a wall of water rose well over his head, causing panic down below. Its roar drowned out desperate calls for retreat as soldiers turned to run. The bailey was enclosed on all sides by a wall three stories high. They were trapped.

Fal brought his hands forward, sent the wave crashing down on them. It swept them to the outer wall, crushed them against its barrier, and churned wildly, forcing them under so no one could escape. Those atop the outer wall watched their comrades drown and froze in place, their assault forgotten. Many disappeared down the other side. Those who remained bore witness to hundreds of men floating dead up to the surface of an enclosed lake that hadn't been there a moment ago.

Fal sensed their gazes turn to him, their horror a palpable thing. He picked out one man and met his gaze across the bailey, then let his hands drop to his sides, releasing the great illusion. The water filling the bailey shimmered out of existence, leaving the ground dry, piled with bodies no less dead for his deceit.

He stared the survivor down a moment longer, reading visions of a dark, cloaked bringer of death in his mind. Fal reinforced the image, carved it into the man's memory with a deep stroke of an invisible scythe so he would never forget what he'd seen this day, so he might tell everyone he came across about Death reaping mortals without mercy.

He felt a shudder rake through the man, leaving a soul-deep chill in its wake, and he made sure the rest of them saw him as he turned and walked away, dismissing them offhand.

"Where is Liadan?" he asked the blue creature gaping at his approach.

"Crossroads," she replied as he passed her without pause.

Fal nodded, heading down the staircase. "I trust you can handle things from here."

"Aye," she said, and though he didn't turn back to acknowledge it, he heard a feral smile in her voice. "Remind me to never get on your bad side, Reaper."

By the time he'd reached the ground and glanced up, the Others were gone, removed to the outer wall.

He ran back around to the castle's front gate, traced the wall to the left of the main doorway with the flat of his palm. Between one stone and another, the wall turned soft. Making sure no one was watching, Fal pressed through the illusion, opened the door, and stepped into the dark, winding stairwell.

His mother's magic was strong. It drew him deeper, yet at the same time created a heavy barrier against his descent. It felt as if the stairwell was filled with sand, and Fal had to swim his way through it to get to the bottom. He didn't recall it presenting this much of a challenge before.

Then again, he'd been halfway to Anderheim when the vision had shown him the way.

At the bottom, the selfsame candle still burned in the center of its table. The selfsame books lined the shelves, whispering their secrets into his ear. Fal struggled his way to the nook, confirming the glass container was still there, swirling with Other blood. It was safe—for the moment.

But the kingdom was not.

He returned to the bookcase and started pulling tomes from their shelves. Battle spells, healing spells—each book contained enough magic within its pages to make his skin tingle. His people would need them all. With his arms full, he turned for the door, but a quiet whisper pulled him up short.

One small, delicate book remained on the closest shelf, leaning against its edge, its black spine pulsing relentless shadows into the dark chamber. For all that it was the smallest tome there, its magic sent a chill down Fal's spine. Its leather was so soft, its pages translucently thin. It couldn't contain more than a single spell.

Fal shook his head hard to break its hold on him. Tucking the volume into his belt at the small of his back, he raced for the stairwell. The same magic that had hindered his progress coming down now all but shoved him back up the stairs to the courtyard.

He emerged into the light of day and turned his gaze to the sky. Before his eyes, a swirl of red faded away. Another Otherland dead and gone. Dark, foreboding clouds gathered from the north. He could sense a great storm's worth of rain in them. Heart pounding with dread, he ran for the great hall.

"Braith!"

She came to him at once, relieving him of his leather-bound burden. The councilor had magic in her. Not much, but enough to work a spell or two. "What are these?" she asked.

"Reinforcement. Gather everyone who can read and everyone with a spark of magic in them. A book to a wizard, no more."

Tearing her gaze away from the arsenal he'd handed her, Braith raised her chin and nodded, her eyes blazing with intent. As he knew she would, she turned her back on him at once and began shouting for people, sorting them into groups, and handing out tomes and orders. Councilor Tarben would have been proud of her.

Fal left her to it. With men once more engaged in the castle's defense, Others holding back the enemy, and wizards at the ready with magic at their fingertips, the castle was as safe as Fal could make it.

It was time to find his sister.

26

A gust of cold wind woke Sanja with the faraway sound of angry voices and the smell of frost and blood. Startled out of deep sleep, she sat up on the pallet, her heart thrashing as she searched the clearing for unseen enemies. They were there; she could hear them.

But they weren't. The echoing screams had already faded back into a forgotten dream, and despite the chill making her skin pebble with goose flesh, the day was as warm as it had been yesterday.

There was no reason to fear, yet the shivers wouldn't stop. Sanja felt exposed and chilled to her core.

"Fal," she called.

Another breeze stirred the grass, and in its hiss, she imagined she heard the screech of metal against metal. It forced her to her feet, her shoulders hunched as she hugged her middle, and curled her toes down into the dirt.

No one around.

"Fal, where are you!" He ought to be there. Unless she'd imagined him, too.

No, there was his cloak, and his eating knife laid out beside the uneaten fish from the night before. It hadn't been a dream. She truly had married the crown prince of Wilderheim. She was safe—from Jarl

Steen, his henchmen, and anyone else who might think to do her harm.

So why could she not make herself believe it?

The sun was at its zenith, hot enough to warm her despite the cold sweat on her brow but, as a dark cloud passed overhead, the ground beneath her feet turned to ice, and her skin pulled tight over her bones as if she'd stepped from summer straight into bitter winter. And then, just as quickly, the cloud moved on, and the sun embraced her with its comforting warmth once more.

Something was wrong.

"Fal, answer me! Where are you?"

The silence echoed back at her, making her suddenly hollow body reverberate with the rumble of a coming avalanche. She dared not move a muscle for fear her bones would crumble into dust where she stood.

Breathe, she ordered herself, forcing air in and out through her tight throat. Each breath became a tremulous wheeze while her jaw clenched so tightly it ached. And no matter where she looked, Sanja couldn't make herself unsee invisible soldiers locked in a terrible battle.

Breathe! Squeezing her eyes shut, she pressed her hands against her ears to block out the silent screams and fought to calm her racing heart. It was only her mind playing tricks on her, nothing more. Fal had brought her to a place where nothing could intrude. Nothing could harm her here, he'd said so himself.

Gradually, the oppressive chill of imagined war passed, and she opened her eyes. The fire was going out. She loosened her limbs enough to take two shuffling steps toward the pile of wood Fal had gathered for them. Her spine creaked as she bent over to grasp one of the sticks in her numb hand and add it to the fire. Shivering all the while, she stoked it higher, pretending not to hear a child crying in the woods, pretending not to see the ghostly apparition of a woman in a bloodied dress wailing wretchedly, not fifteen paces away.

Sanja turned her back to the visions, hunching closer to the fire as another wintry gust of wind turned the ground around her feet momentarily white with frost.

Ignore it.

It wasn't anything she hadn't experienced before with her new husband's illusions. What she saw and heard might be different, but *how* she saw and heard it remained the same. Was Fal casting the visions from a dream somewhere? Being no stranger to nightmares herself, Sanja knew how tightly they could tether a body into sleep. If Fal's dream was as bad as what she was seeing, it could have made him act on it, respond in truth to what was playing out in his mind.

He could be anywhere, fighting those terrible soldiers all on his own.

A man shouted at the lake.

"Fal?" She took off without thinking, abandoning the safety of her fire.

Had he called her name?

"*Fal!* I'm coming!"

Diving heedlessly into a thatch of reeds, she ignored their sharp lashes, fighting her way through to the other side. Fal was in pain; he needed her; she couldn't let him suffer his nightmares alone. But the merciless plants refused to clear a path for her. With each step, they swayed toward her, scratching her, tripping her, stealing the sun from the sky, and turning the mud beneath her feet cold with ice.

She could no longer see where she was going. Fal's weak voice became her only guidance in the darkening maze. She thought she heard him say something...

Send her home?

No, that couldn't be right. He wouldn't send her away without a word farewell, not after everything he'd done last night.

He couldn't.

Her vision blurred, and her breath misted in the cold, but she kept going. Even when the ground swayed beneath her feet. Even when a wrenching shift stretched the world into endless streams of color.

With her next step, the vortex spat her out into darkness, and she fell to her hands and knees onto the wooden slats of a familiar floor. With the entire world tilting violently this way and that, Sanja stayed there, breathing as deeply as she could until it settled and the urge to vomit had passed. Then raised her head to look around.

Her father's cottage hardly looked the same anymore. The chairs were overturned, the table shattered. The floors were covered with dirt, the walls smeared with dark stains. With the shutters closed and barred and no fire in the hearth, the cottage was dark and as silent as a grave.

This was no dream.

Shaking, Sanja righted herself and squinted through the darkness. He'd done it. He truly had sent her home.

She'd believed him when he'd said they could make a life together, and the next day, her new husband had washed his hands of her.

Fal, how could you?

An insidious voice inside her taunted, *Did you expect the Prince of Deceit to keep his word? What use does the crown prince of Wilderheim have for a lowly merchant's daughter?*

She might have listened to it a week ago. But now, after everything she'd endured, everything Sanja had become rebelled against that voice. *I am not useless.* Fal wouldn't have bothered saving her, much less marrying her, if she were. He must have had good reasons to send her back to her father's house, and as soon as she found him again, she would ask him about it.

But for now, she needed to get herself together. Her home wasn't what it should be. Something was wrong, and she couldn't sit there and wait for disaster to find her.

"Da?" she called softly. "Ma?"

But, of course, they didn't answer. The cottage was closed up; they must have left for Lyria when Sanja hadn't returned. Good; they'd listened to her and removed themselves to safety. She was glad. Her only regret was not having had a chance to wave them off.

Running footsteps rushed past the front door. She heard whimpers, soft cries nearby, hushed by urgent whispers. Heavier footfalls followed, accompanied by the clang of metal.

An angry voice speaking in a foreign tongue elicited rough laughter in response.

Sanja crawled back against a wall, watching shadows move across the floor as the figures passed by. They stopped not far off, and in the heavy silence, Sanja counted her heartbeats and prayed.

When the screaming started, she slapped both hands over her mouth to keep from joining them and prayed harder.

Slaughter. That's what she was hearing. The wet sound of blades slashing through flesh, the tear of cloth and a woman's wretched howls, abruptly cut short. She turned her face away, made herself as small as she could, hoping it would somehow make her invisible, wishing she could melt through the walls and fall back into the world from which she'd been exiled.

She didn't look up again until the men had left, their footsteps fading into silence. By then, her entire body had cramped, and the smallest movement caused pure agony. Sanja gritted her teeth against making a sound and slowly pushed to her feet.

Painfully aware of Death prowling the streets, she measured each step and tested the floor with her toes first before committing her weight to it. At the staircase, she stopped, torn between running for cover and braving the outside to offer what help she could, but as the silence stretched on, she realized there was no one left to help out there. Though her heart ached, she made herself turn away and quietly sneak up the stairs to her room.

She found it in the same disarray as the kitchen below, her bed-clothes torn to shreds, the furniture broken, but the stack of books and parchments in one corner had remained curiously untouched.

She reclaimed her dress from a haphazard pile and changed out of her haircloth shirt and trousers, layering another dress on top of the first, and a sheepskin vest on top of that. With thick wool stockings and her winter boots restored to her cold feet, Sanja's shivers subsided enough for her to move more easily.

A crash near the front door startled her. She held still and waited, but in a moment, the sounds grew distant again.

She was safe. At least for now.

Shoring up her courage, she sidled up to her window. Like the ones downstairs, this one, too, had been shuttered and barred, but there were gaps large enough for her to slide her fingers into and, with a careful, creaking snap, she broke off a piece to take a peek outside.

The swirling colors in the sky, obscured by wafting clouds of thick smoke, confirmed that she was, indeed, back in Frastmir.

And, like her house, the castle city looked nothing like the place she remembered.

Princess Liadan had told her on the eve of her Journey that Fal was preparing for war.

Well, war had come, and it had ravaged her home without mercy.

In the streets beyond the next cottage ahead, lights flickered where thatched roofs had caught fire. Streams of smoke rose up toward the sky, choking the air yet, despite so many flames, it was still bitterly cold.

The screams were the worst. Higher off the ground where nothing stood between her window and the sky, the dulled hum she'd heard downstairs became a cacophony of furious war cries mingled with the clash of weapons and the sound of women and children dying.

In the distance, the castle echoed with massive booms of noise. Its banners had been torn down. The towers were reduced to rubble. Beyond the main keep, the sky flared with fire from below where the battle still raged on. The invading army must have caught the city unawares. Else it never would have fallen so quickly—and fallen it had. There was no more fighting; only stragglers prowling the streets, exterminating anyone left alive.

Only the keep remained. The kingdom's warriors would fight to the death to defend it, not only as a symbolic seat of political power in Wilderheim but as the beating heart of its magic. Wilderheim was so much more than its land or its castle city. If Castle Frastmir fell, it would be the end of everything.

This was no dream or illusion.

This was Ragnarok.

That was why Fal had sent her here. He'd kept his promise and saved her from Jarl Steen. Now it was her turn to do what needed to be done and help him stop the end in its tracks.

Sanja dived for the stack of books, shoving loose parchments aside and tossing ancient volumes left and right to get to the one she sought. She'd only gotten through half of the contents of Fal's journal before starting her Journey, and that half had been so dense with ancient lore and modern interpretations it had overwhelmed her. The rest would be no less difficult, but she needed to learn it and quickly if she was to help him in any way.

"Aha!"

Clutching the journal tightly, she shifted closer to the window, but the broken shafts of weak sunlight stabbing through the shutters, weren't enough. Sanja set the journal aside, grasped the bar her father had nailed across her shutters, braced a foot against the wall, and pulled with all her might until the bar ripped free, sending her sprawling.

The shutters flew open, admitting a cold blast of wind that lifted scraps and sheets of parchment into the air. The pages flew up and circled around in a funnel, and Sanja stilled. For a brief moment, the pages had aligned, and sunlight had shone through them just so, that a brilliant spark of epiphany struck Sanja dumb.

"They do fit!"

Scrambling to her feet, she snatched at the pages still wafting in the air, while trying to gather all the ones still on the ground at the same time. Her arms were filled with a mess of them when one of the shutters slammed against the wall as a frigid gust sent the remaining two sheets flying.

She caught one at the windowsill, but the other slipped out of her reach. As she watched it flip end over end in the air, her gaze shifted to the rolling waves of darkness coming toward the city from the north. Never before had Sanja seen clouds so thick and black. They swallowed the swirling colors, obscured the horizon, and, though she knew it couldn't be, Sanja felt them baying with a terrible, silent hunger that devoured her cry.

The wind snapped her page up and sideways, over three rooftops, and a ways off before letting it drop out of her sight.

Sanja didn't stop to think. Crumpling her stack of parchments together to keep it safe, she raced down the stairs and out the door into the cold.

27

With no time to waste, Fal needed the quickest way to Crossroads. The waterways were too dangerous. They'd already started freezing over before he'd disappeared into Anderheim. The gods only knew what condition they were in now. A horse would take too long, and there were no Others around to convey him such a distance.

But he might have one other way.

It would have to be meticulously executed—if it worked at all. What better way to test pathways into Anderheim?

Fal ducked out of sight in the courtyard and churned up the vortex inside him. His connection to Anderheim was still there at the core of his illusions. It wove through his ever-changing face, through the visions of grass and flowers that spread out around him. All he had to do was channel it into a doorway. The song it required was the same one that had brought him out of Anderheim. He forced himself to slow down, focus, and do it right. Any mistake could be disastrous; he couldn't afford to take any chances.

He sang, and the doorway opened. With the song still humming from his lips, he sent his request to Anderheim ahead of his crossing, and it responded with such eagerness Fal stepped through the Frastmir doorway directly into a streak of blurred scenery and was expelled forcefully through another doorway in Crossroads.

Fal stumbled to his hands and knees, the mud rippling beneath him until he feared he would pass out. As the ringing in his ears cleared into the clang of weapons, he shook his head and squinted at the battle raging around him. Anderheim had delivered him straight into the thick of it, with no armor and his head spinning like a top.

He fought to stand, only for a heavy foot to slam into his back. "Stay down!" Liadan barked, and a moment later, a stream of fire blazed over his head, scorching a trio of soldiers into dust. In the short lull that followed, Liadan hauled him upright, grinning brightly. "It's good to see you, brother."

Fal took in his sister's condition and found her to be roughed up around the edges but, on the whole, hale and strong. Covered in the gore of battle, she held her head up high and smiled in the face of death.

He'd seen her like this before, hadn't he?

Liadan's gaze flicked sideways over his shoulder, and she shoved him away to meet a soldier's blade. She, too, wore only leather armor, which made her faster and more nimble than the enemy's heavily armored knights. She used their ungainly weight against them, tripping them and shoving them into one another.

"Don't just stand there—fight!"

Fal drew his sword, put his back to Liadan's, and fought.

But all the while, every face he saw looked familiar; every attack felt as if he'd seen it before. He reacted from memory more than instinct, anticipating each move as if he'd rehearsed it. There was the one with the cracked spear. Fal shifted to the side, brought his sword down on the shaft to break it, then whirled a swing to take off the soldier's head.

Stepping over his fallen body, he met swords with another, whose gap-toothed snarl he knew so well he'd already counted the remaining teeth. This one was strong, but he'd braced his foot in mud, and Fal was able to shove him sliding back into another man's blade. They fell together, and Fal was so certain they wouldn't get up again, he turned his back on them to move on to the next.

He fought until he couldn't feel his sword in his grip anymore. His body went through the motions while a dream-like haze mired his mind, keeping him going when lesser men would have dropped from exhaustion. Vaguely, he noted that Others fought alongside Wilderheim's men. Fal saw so many of them he lost count; stopped bothering to identify their kind. He was simply grateful they were there.

And in the midst of it all, Liadan shone with strength and courage, fighting as well with her blades as the berserker tearing through enemy ranks not far off. She was a thing to behold, using her fire as a weapon without marking herself a target with it.

And *he* fought better for having her at his back. They worked in tandem, guarding each other's flanks and keeping each other safe.

But soon, the tide of battle began to turn against them. Fal cut down a soldier and behind him saw an Other disappear before his eyes, followed by another to his left, and one more farther on the right. Without those allies to hold off the enemy, the soldiers came at him and Liadan.

"Did you see that? They're gone, the cowards."

"They're dead, Liadan." He felt the empty void the Others had left behind. "Not just them, their entire worlds."

Liadan tensed at his back, then swore and hurled a fireball at two men charging her. Their tabards provided eager kindling, flaring up in an instant. As they stumbled into others, the flames jumped, and soon a dozen enemy soldiers were flailing on the ground, screaming as they cooked in their metal shells.

Fal's stomach clenched as he met another attack, anticipating something terrible he couldn't remember. He glanced up at the sky, saw it darken with storm clouds, and grimly turned his attention back to the battle at hand.

He turned with Liadan and rammed into a man's midsection as he brought up an ax. They fell together, and Fal stabbed him through, quickly jumping back to his feet to meet another blade.

By then, not even the dragon amulet could keep exhaustion from weighing him down. Picking up a shield someone had dropped, he reclaimed his place by his sister and willed himself to hold steady, but despite overflowing with magic, he couldn't harness it to give himself more physical strength. His legs shifted heavily, and his sword swung slower. Evening would soon be upon them, but the battle wasn't waning in the least. If anything, it was heating up.

"Liadan," he called, needing her to restore him.

She didn't hear, locked in battle against three soldiers at once. They pushed her farther from him until he lost sight of her altogether. Taking advantage of the situation, more soldiers poured into the gap between them, pushing them apart, and Fal didn't have the strength to go after her.

Liadan lived and breathed battle every day, but this was Fal's first, and he didn't know what to do, other than fight the next man coming at him. He needed his sister's guidance and strength. The farther she went, the weaker he felt until his chest ached with each tired beat of his heart.

Fal blocked a speartip with his shield, his feet slipping on a fallen tabard as the enemy forced him back. He twisted the shield, snapping the tip off the spear and ran the soldier through. The grip of his sword was drenched with blood. More of it dripped down his face. He adjusted the chipped shield on his arm and wiped his wet cheek on his sleeve.

Time seemed to slow as he looked at the carnage all around him. The battlefield was littered with hundreds of dead soldiers already, their bodies trampled into the mud by hundreds upon hundreds more.

Just as he'd seen in his dream.

As if reliving it again for the first time, he sought Liadan's fire amid the chaos, but far too much of it already blazed left and right, and the din of screams disguised her battle cry.

At his feet, the ground had turned to dark mud, pools of blood reflecting the sky back at Fal. It hurt like a long needle stabbing into him to witness each light going dark. He had no time to mourn them when his own world was dying. Thunder rumbled above, threatening a storm, and fear knotted his insides. He looked up once more, hoping it had only been a fluke, but a fat raindrop splashing down onto his cheek confirmed his worst fear.

Fal had to retreat. Already, the air felt thick, and flashes of another battlefield miles away obscured his sight. Shadows flickered all around him, a brightly polished blade cutting down his soldiers. He sensed magic in it again, as he had in his dream, yet when he sought its wielder's identity, he met with dark shadows that only cleared enough to reveal parts of the knight's body and never his face.

Another soldier came at him, the red cross on his tabard no longer distinguishable beneath the muck of battle. His mind weary and his body weak, Fal blocked the soldier's battle ax with his sword, rather than duck out of the way. The impact forced him to his knees. He gritted his teeth, pushing back with all the strength he had left, to no avail. He couldn't hold out much longer. That ax would cleave him in two.

Suddenly the solder spit up blood as the tip of a curved blade forced its way out through his chest. Wide-eyed, he tipped sideways, taking his ax with him.

Liadan grasped Fal's arm and pulled him to his feet.

She'd changed. Her eyes now blazed with fire behind a braid that had fallen over her black horn-crown. Though she had yet to unleash her wings, her tail slithered back and forth with a mind of its own, and her feet had grown long, curved talons that dug into the soft mud. Her entire being glowed with fierce strength, smoking, on the verge of burning up into her Other self. "Wilderheim will not die on its knees," she snarled at him through the sharp fangs filling her mouth, reminding him so much of their dragon grandfather. Her grip fed strength into his exhausted body, but nothing would shield him from the madness the rain was about to bring.

As Fal recovered, still connected with his sister, he felt within her the tiny, bright spark that had turned his dream into a nightmare, and his body grew cold with dread. "Take to the sky," he ordered. "Now!" Away from the armies, beyond the reach of their weapons. Against all odds, his sister had managed to conceive. If there was any chance for the child to survive, Fal had to get her somewhere safe.

"And leave you to die?"

"Liadan—"

She shoved him aside to meet another enemy soldier head-on, her curved blade making quick work of him and his three comrades. The two coming for her from the back met with Fal's sword and fell in short succession.

Liadan retrieved her other sword and put her back to Fal's. They were surrounded.

"You must go!" Fal tried again. "For the child's sake, if not mine."

He felt Liadan tense at his back. "Won't be the first time I've lost a child. Or the last." She tried to make it sound careless, but Fal wasn't fooled. Her grief was a living thing, coiling inside her like a snake, biting at her heart—and now at his.

A vision of women running through a nearby raided village blinded him just as the soldiers attacked. He gave a shout, bringing up his shield to block a thrust and slashed sideways. Between rapid blinks, he saw his enemy again, then Liadan's, then another place entirely.

"Oh, no," Liadan whispered as a few random drops turned into a heavy downpour. She looked back at him, her eyes dimming anxiously. Then a furious snarl turned her face into something beastly, and she faced her enemy once more and screamed, bursting into flame, scorching their foes to dust where they stood as she transformed.

Within moments, the thick mud at their feet turned into pools and creeks, the earth already soaked with too much blood to drain the rainwater away. Fal became blind and deaf to the world around him as everything the water touched flooded into his mind. He saw everything, heard everything for miles around. He felt a thousand deaths, smelled smoke mixed with blood and bile, and tasted hopeless prayers on his tongue, knowing there was no one left to answer them.

His sister's voice echoed through the madness: "Wake up! *Wake up!*"

It was too late.

Imprisoned by his own weakness, Fal's mind was already gone, scattered as far as the storm stretched. His body became weightless in flight, and then, with a sickening capitulation, the remaining physical sensations faded away, and he ceased to exist.

28

The storm swept across the whole of Wilderheim and, where it touched, Fal saw, and heard, and felt. Scattered among countless raindrops, he ceased to be himself and became everything at once.

Seven portals speared up toward the sky, bright, screaming cuts into Wilderheim that had admitted hordes of enemy soldiers all throughout the kingdom.

In Frastmir, a girl wearing sheepskins cautiously stuck her head out into the storm, then ducked under an overhang. A moment later, she was out, racing down the muddied street, hugging a small, flat bundle to her chest. She pulled her large hood down low against the rain, turned away from the bodies littering the ground, and ran on.

Two portals had cut off the passage to Lyria only recently and were still spewing mounted riders to trample over fleeing families, pushing inward to force the rest into retreat.

A group of five soldiers in soaked white tabards strolled through the city, laughing at a lame woman trying in vain to get away from them. Her fear tasted like bile, and her skin felt slick as she flailed back and forth like a fish out of water at their approach. She didn't get far…

Two more portals had appeared in between camps of warriors sent to guard the Aegiran border. True to their honor, even outnumbered five to one, Wilderheim's forces were holding their own, but they could do nothing for those being slaughtered farther inland.

An old man somewhere in Crossroads wailed over his young son. "My boy!" he cried, his heart breaking over and over as he hugged the boy's lifeless body up from the muddy ground, rocking him back and forth. "I curse you, dogs! I curse your blood and the blood of your offspring!" His poisonous spell slithered from him on noxious green smoke, splitting and racing toward every enemy soldier he could see. It wound up their legs and bodies to shackle their throats. They would never know it, but madness would forever stain their bloodlines, forcing men to turn on their wives, children to cut down their siblings—

To the east, two shafts along the Ravetian border flickered weaker than the rest. These had been the first, admitting the flood of knights who'd attacked Castle Frastmir. Clan Steen was no more. Those who'd managed to escape the carnage were scaling down the walls of the ravine to cross to its Ravetian side.

Rain pelted down heavily there. It poured over old women with gnarled hands and aching backs, over screaming babies swaddled in soaked linens, over armed men with wide eyes whose blades had never left their sheaths, and over the man leading them all—the traitorous jarl himself.

As the river swelled outside of Frastmir, its rage spilled over the banks, knocking soldiers off their feet, washing over them. At its shallowest, the flood was still high enough to drown a man held to the ground by his heavy armor. He kicked uselessly, held his breath as long as he could, but the river wouldn't release him. It felt the pain he'd caused, mourned the lives he'd taken, and it wanted to repay him in kind. It rushed into him, swelling his body. In his last moments, the man looked up toward the surface and the sky beyond, his lips moving in prayer before his stained tabard floated over his face, closing his eyes forever.

So much death. So much rage, and fear, and agony. It carried on the blood of the fallen, soaking deep into the ground, poisoning it. The earth shuddered with disgust, rejected it all, crying out for help that was nowhere to be found. In its absence, it woke the trees to life.

Roots tore free of their anchor to lash outward. They knocked riders off their mounts and twisted them up in unbreakable wooden binds that tightened until armor warped and bodies crushed beneath the pressure.

Jarl Steen ran onward, his gaze trained on the rope ladder that would be his salvation. He dared not blink and would not answer anyone who called his name. His men-at-arms stood his guard, keeping the clan back, but as they neared the ladder, they, too, lost their heads to fear. Abandoning their master to the panicked herd, they raced ahead to begin their climb, fighting one another, jerking the ladder back and forth until one hard yank snapped it out of its moorings and sent the whole of it tumbling down.

The last portal stuck out of the very center of Wilderheim in Crossroads. There had been no fighters to meet the soldiers there, only farmers and merchants, families sleeping innocently in their beds. This had been the one to herald the shining blade so thirsty for blood it drove its owner ever eastward.

The girl in Frastmir reached the market, a muddied ball of parchment clutched in her hand. She could go straight toward the castle or right toward the library. Her beloved city was now black, stinking of death and wet, scorched wood. The ground quivered with explosions of magic. Everywhere she looked, her neighbors lay dead or dying, and she hurt for each and every one of them. But she could not stop. She turned her muddy boots to the right, pulled her hood lower over her face, kicked up the soaked hems of her dress, and ran on to the library.

A forest nymph stepped out of the shelter of her tree in Frastmir's glen. Her large brown eyes gazed out over the carnage and wept. She saw the group of soldiers approach, their tabards still pristine with red crosses emblazoned on white fields like virgin blood staining the marriage bed.

They were laughing. But they fell silent as she came into view.

She blinked her doe eyes at them, reaching out her delicate brown arms in welcome. She smelled their excitement but kept her expression soft and innocent.

They came to her at once, dropping their weapons, shedding their helmets, unbuckling their belts. She let them come, floating backward, deeper into the glen. Their breath stank of death; their hands were sticky with sweat and blood.

The nymph smiled at them, caressed a cheek here, brushed a hand there. Her touch whispered over them, making their hearts beat faster, their thoughts churn slower. Her spell kept them docile as they sank to their knees.

It kept them quiet as their bodies began to dry out. It made them smile as vines slithered over them, drawing them into their graves before they'd breathed their last. The nymph smiled bitterly and set out to seek more.

As Others lay waste to the enemy where they could, the shining blade continued on, never allowing its owner a moment's rest. Already, he was crossing the bridge into Frastmir at a breakneck pace. His horse's strength gave out, its legs buckling. The blade drove its wielder onward on foot, directing his gaze where it might taste more death.

It cut down straggler soldiers armed with swords and ordinary men armed with scythes and pitchforks but, unlike the others, its wielder turned it time and again away from women and children. He spared the old, too, and any who ran from the sight of him.

But already, the blade screamed louder, shone brighter, ravenous for so much more than he could give it.

To the north, impenetrable blackness opened its yawning mouth, slowly crawling toward Wilderheim. It swallowed all sound, yet its insides screamed. It robbed the air of warmth and burned the land with frost.

Those who fled along the Journeyman's path in hopes of seeking shelter in the cleric's temple took one look at it and turned the other way. Safer to chance a mortal's blade than the void of that terrible, nameless nothing. They were right to fear.

Though the storm stretched well into that blackness and beyond, where the void encroached, Fal's consciousness slammed into a barrier that forcefully expelled him back and scattered him.

To the south, Wilderheim's soldiers were pushed out all the way to the Aegiran border, cornered and fighting not for their kingdom, but for their own lives. Though no physical barrier stood between them and the relative safety of Aegiros, they remained in Wilderheim, unable to escape.

To the east, a flash flood raced down the ravine, washing away the last remnants of Clan Steen and anyone else foolish enough to have followed them. Some washed up far downstream. Others caught on rocky outcroppings and ledges. None survived for long. Jarl Steen's body caught on a rocky hook. The current had already washed the blood from his clothes, but it could not hide the tears in his flesh or the odd angles of his broken limbs. The churning waters flopped him like a rag doll onto his back. With one eye missing, his jaw all but severed, the jarl was recognizable only by the markings on his scalp.

The man who'd defied his king and abandoned his people had died not as a warrior but a coward, drowned, broken, and dishonored.

To the west, beyond the mountain range, King Ulrich's men stood at attention, awaiting orders. To enter the narrow pass would mean certain death, and not even Ulrich's love for his royal cousins could compel them onward. The rocks echoed with the sounds of Wilderheim being torn apart, and all they could do was stand faithful watch, herd the small handful of terrified refugees toward safer ground, and prepare for the war to come for them next.

The clerics' temple to the north was gone, swallowed by the void. The city of Crossroads was razed to the ground. The Dragon lakes gleamed red with blood, dead things floating along their surface.

And in a crude, makeshift tent, surrounded by countless other tents in which the wounded rested their weary bodies, Prince Fal twitched with feverish visions that wouldn't abate. He could neither see nor hear his sister calling his name. He couldn't feel the warm fire blanketing him and drying the rain from his clothes and skin.

A guard rushed into the tent, rainwater running down into the open cut on his face, tracing his mouth as it formed frantic words. *We must retreat!* He received a quiet response from the princess as she stared at a small, incongruously heavy black book in her hands. Humming with the need to act, the guard stomped deeper into the tent. His wet hand hissed as it closed around Liadan's arm, and he pulled back, momentarily stunned. In the face of her fiery glare, he repeated himself with low, growling words that rumbled out of his throat.

A raindrop made murky with mud caught Liadan rubbing the torc around her neck and shaking her head as she replied into silence.

Dismissed to his own devices, the man ran back out and was struck down by an arrow not two paces from the tent.

The girl with her bundle had reached the library. She struck the barred portal with her small, pale fist, fearful of making so much noise, but having no other choice. Three soldiers were heading her way from the east. Two more on horseback had heard the noise in the south and were already turning their mounts in her direction. In a dark alleyway, the last of five soldiers shoved away from the woman who'd long ago gone still and silent. He drew his dagger and slit her throat for good measure, leaving her ravaged body sprawled where it lay as the group moved on, drawn by the sound of the girl's voice.

She pounded harder at the door, shouted louder, begging to be let in. At last, it opened, and she was pulled inside. By the time the first soldiers came into view, the door was once again closed and barred.

The hungry blade had run out of blood to spill. Its tip gleamed clean and bright, not a scratch upon its surface as it leaned left then right, seeking, seeking...

It turned its wielder left and pulled him along through the market to meet the other soldiers gathered outside the library door. One of them had already tied a rope around the handles and lashed the other end to his saddle. He sat his horse and waited for the other to do the same. Between the two of them, they would rip the entire portal off its hinges, and those on foot had already drawn their swords, eager to storm inside.

Their excitement caught up the blade, and it screamed pleasure-pain up its wielder's arm infecting him with the selfsame zeal. With his lips drawn back in a snarl, he tasted the rain, and, though it couldn't see him, it could taste him in return. It tasted hunger mixed with righteousness, hatred muddled with pride, and bitter darkness enshrining it all, hazing his vision and slowly silencing the voice of his conscience.

There were innocents in the library; he couldn't slay them.

But the others could.

The rope was lashed; the riders kicked their mounts; the library door groaned, cracked, and finally gave way.

29

In the absence of golden candlelight, the library was a dark and sinister place. The bookshelves transformed into looming walls filled with nooks and crannies where feral creatures lived. The sweet smell of old books had taken on a musty, rotten undertone more akin to an abandoned cellar than a reverent place of learning.

"Hurry," Brother Erik urged, "this way."

He took Sanja by the arm and led her past writing desks already covered with a layer of ash and dust, past the display tables where precious illuminated tomes of magic lay spine up with their thick pages haphazardly crumpled underneath. Quills were strewn all over the floor, bottles of ink shattered and bleeding dark stains into the polished wood. There was no one left to look after it all. The library had been abandoned to its own fate, and Sanja felt its sorrow weep down the candlesticks in frozen rivulets of melted beeswax.

She would mourn its memory later. For now, Sanja followed the cleric all the way to the back, where a humble wooden door opened on a dark stairway leading down. Brother Leif stood on the second stair with a torch in hand, waiting for them to precede him. It seemed he and Erik were the last of the cleric brotherhood. The rest of them would have made their escape at the first sign of trouble, hopefully taking as many volumes with them as they could carry.

"They are right outside the door," Brother Erik reported.

"The others are almost to the end of the tunnel," Brother Leif said, wide-eyed. He had one foot on the next step down, anxiously looking back and forth between the escape tunnel and Brother Erik. "We ought not have tarried this long."

Brother Erik didn't argue, merely pulled Sanja along, eager to make his own escape.

"No, wait!" Sanja pulled free of his hold. "We can't leave. I have to find Prince Fal."

Brother Leif huffed with impatience while Brother Erik shook his head, baffled. "My girl, haven't you heard? The prince is gone." He said it with the weight of regret, the way people always delivered news of death.

They wouldn't know about the realm Fal had created. Sanja didn't know how long Fal had been missing, but it must have been long enough for his people to assume the worst—that he'd either died or abandoned them to their fate. But they were wrong, and Sanja didn't have the time to explain.

"He is somewhere in Wilderheim, and I must find him."

"Sanja, he's dead."

"He is not!" She could feel his heart beating next to hers. He was alive and fighting for them all, and she had to give him what he needed to finish it.

Brother Leif's torch swung down into the tunnel, then back up. He'd already gone two steps deeper down the stairway. "Brother, we must go."

Acknowledging him with a wave of his hand, Brother Erik approached Sanja as he would a wounded animal. "The city has fallen. If we don't leave now, we will be trapped." He tried to herd her toward the door, but Sanja rooted her feet.

"I know how to stop it."

"Stop what? The war?"

"The war, Fenrir, all of it." The song of worlds had woven the first Veil to keep the realms separate, yet connected. If Fal could sing it again, he could forge a similar connection with the Otherland he'd created. He could fold Wilderheim into it and effectively move the entire kingdom out of Fenrir's path.

"Brother Erik!"

"Please," Sanja begged, fumbling the bundle in her arms, "you must help me, or it won't matter where we run; we will all die anyway." Pieces of parchment spilled over the floor, and she dropped to her knees to gather them together. "The directions are all there in pieces. I only need to shape them together into a cohesive whole." Then Fal would have everything he needed to save Wilderheim. He'd only need to open the doorway once. It would take an awful lot of magic, but he already had that, and more. It could be done. There was still hope!

Brother Erik sighed. "Brother Leif, go."

The other cleric took off so quickly his torchlight faded in moments, leaving Sanja alone with the last of their brotherhood. As she frantically picked up page after page, folding them where the symbols cut off, she felt him staring at her and glanced up to see sorrow in his eyes. "I can do this," she insisted. "I swear. I only need help. This page…And this one—no, this one. Yes, and this one here." One after the other, she matched them together, but they wouldn't fit perfectly laid out on the ground. She picked up three of them, matching up the symbols as best as she could. "They fit together, I swear, I just can't—"

A groaning sound echoed through the empty library. The cleric laid his hand gently but firmly over both of hers, stopping her movements. "Sister," he said, addressing her as one of his order, as if she'd earned the honor. He thought so highly of her. Sanja couldn't bring herself to meet his gaze and tell him he was wrong. But she felt his gaze on her; felt him squeeze her hands, urging her to look up. "We must go."

Desperate tears blurred her vision. She needed time, a safe place to put it all together; more hands than her own two to hold the parchments aloft in the spherical shape it was all meant to have. Had she any magic in her, she could have floated them in the air with ease, but her cursed human limitations cost her precious time none of them had to lose. And the cleric would not—could not—help her.

The main door groaned again, a loud crack making her flinch. She'd run out of time.

A shaft of sunlight briefly broke through the clouds, spearing through the narrow window high up by the ceiling down onto the floor beside her. Dust swirled lazily through its beam, and the polished wooden floor gleamed with dreams lost to misery. Sanja stared transfixed at a small triangle of darker wood that had been inlaid into the design. It fit seamlessly with every other piece it touched. Its surface had been smoothed to a shine, but she could still see the lines of its natural grain veer around a dark, almost invisible eye. She imagined it winked at her, and in that moment, her path became clear. "The knowledge must be preserved." No matter what happened to her, to the clerics, or anyone else down in that stairway, those mystical symbols had to be kept safe for Fal. He was the only one left who could use them to save Wilderheim.

Another groaning crack. The door would give way soon; she had to move.

Swiping the parchments together again, she quickly bundled them up and shoved the whole lot of it into the cleric's arms. "Take these. Keep them safe. Prince Fal will need them, and you must swear to me you will place them in his hands, and no one else's."

"Child—"

"Swear it, Brother, or all is lost."

Compressing his mouth into a tight line of displeasure, he gave a single nod.

"Tell him they fit together in an unbroken sphere. That's how he must read the spell. Find the centerpoint and sing the symbols in a spiral along the sphere."

"I don't understand."

"It doesn't matter. Only tell him exactly what I told you." The pattern was so obvious, once she'd seen it take shape. Fal would already know the symbols by heart; he'd be able to put it all together instantly, and all would be well, but he still needed to be told. "Go, run as far from here as you can. I will lead them away, give you time to escape."

"They will kill you!"

"They will have to catch me first," she replied recklessly, then pushed and shoved him into the stairway and closed the door behind him.

A tall bookshelf stood not three paces away. Filled as it was with heavy tomes, it took everything Sanja had to rock it out of balance. But she had to bar the doorway to give the clerics a fighting chance. She'd seen those men prowling the streets; they were scavengers looking for easy prey and would be more likely to chase her than bother with what looked like a privy door. She pushed hard, rocking the shelf forward, then let it fall back toward her before pushing again as it tilted away. Sheer force of will gave her enough strength to nudge it past the tipping point just as the front door tore outward, and both crashed at the same time.

She saw foreign soldiers running up the outer stairs. They spotted her. Spinning on the balls of her feet, Sanja took off as fast as she could toward the opposite wall, weaving through the familiar maze of bookshelves back toward the main entrance. She was much faster than them. If she could reach the main door undetected, she could slip out into the storm and disappear. But if they chased her into plain sight outside, Sanja wouldn't stand a chance.

Ducking into a narrow passage, she slipped around a pillar and tiptoed into the shadows, skirting the wall all the way to the front entry. It was clear. The soldiers were busy rampaging inside the library, pushing over bookshelves to root her out like a rabbit from its burrow.

Sanja wanted to smile. How much easier it was to evade evil men when she wasn't bound to her knees in the snow. *Useless? Ha!* They hadn't seen anything yet. They had horses outside. She could loosen the saddle straps or send them running altogether. Weapons set on the ground? They were as good as hers; none of the soldiers would ever find them.

Sanja might not be a fighter, but she had her wits, and there were infinite ways in which she could make those soldiers' lives unbearable without ever coming near them. Frastmir was her city; Wilderheim was her home. She would do her part to see it safe and sound if it was the last thing she did.

Sounds of fighting registered in her ears as she pushed away from the wall and raced for the storm outside.

She ran straight into the thick of it.

~

A sea of red crosses had overrun the camp, tearing tents from the ground, dragging wounded men from their beds. Shouted warnings came too late and cut too short. It was a massacre, and the rain saw and felt it all.

As they neared the farthest tent, a circle of fire flared up from the ground around it, stretching high up into the air. Its flames changed colors from red to yellow, then flickering blue, burning so hot the rain couldn't douse it.

Stopped in their advance by that impenetrable veil, the soldiers didn't see the strange, black-scaled creature step out of the tent on its other side. They couldn't see her fiery eyes, the flowing flames of her hair, or the massive black wings flaring and folding restlessly at her back.

The rain did. It saw the small book clutched warily in her claws, felt its chill turn her scaled hands cold with powerful magic, heard her shuddering gasp of revulsion, and mourned the way her claws clutched the tome all the harder for it.

The creature gazed up, her eyes pleading for the clouds to part, for the rain to abate—not for her sake, but her brother's. But she knew she couldn't make them move, and her brother was in no condition to try.

And that left her only one choice.

Already knowing her call would go unanswered, she rubbed the torc around her neck yet again, sending out one last wordless summons to the only creature who could sway the tide now. Then she turned her attention to the fiery barrier, listened to it sing to her of the many armed men standing at the ready on the other side, of their bloodied weapons and their savage faces, and their hushed voices chanting soft prayers up to the sky. It knew their hearts and warned they could not be reasoned with. Nothing would compel them to mercy, or retreat. They would keep fighting until the battle was won and, if they fell, more would be sent in their place.

The Dragonblood princess shuddered as the book's cold voice slithered through her mind. Her palm pressed to her belly, and she closed her eyes for a moment to feel the life of her unborn child glowing inside her. No matter what she did, the princess knew she couldn't save that precious life. It might survive the war and Ragnarok unscathed, but in the end, Liadan's own nature would burn it out of her, as it had the two before.

She would never give her mate a son. But she still had a chance to save her clan and her people. The spell was their last hope, and the child's life was the price she had to pay for it.

She missed her mate; wished with all her heart to see him one last time.

In answer, the flames called her name and showed her a great open chamber with ceilings so high they almost reached the sky. They showed her a dark-skinned man with golden adornments woven through his hair, standing at the window. It gifted her with a waft of sweet, desert air, and the scent of fragrant oils. She whispered his name softly, willing him to face the flames.

But as he turned his head to the side, a blade came flying through the flames. She caught it on reflex, but the damage was done. The vision had shattered, and all she had left were her flames, and the book in her hand.

Pulling back her shoulders, she called heat into her hand to melt the foreign blade and flicked molten drops of metal from her fingers with disgust. A crude weapon, hammered in haste without care or delicacy. Its metal had had no voice of its own, just like all of the others—except the one.

Even from miles away, the Dragonblood princess still heard that one screaming for death. Soon, nothing would be able to stop it. Not even her.

As the flames warned of more weapons about to be thrown, the princess mercilessly pushed back her fear and sorrow, shut out all awareness of her brother lying senseless on a crude pallet nearby, and pretended she couldn't hear him shouting incomprehensible warnings to the empty tent. The rain saw her, so she knew he would, too.

He would hate her for what she was about to do, but at least he'd be alive to do it.

She stepped into the flames and, with shaking hands, opened the little book. Impervious to fire, neither woman nor book noticed the heat licking over them. But with its ancient pages at last laid bare to open air, the book bled from every word she read aloud, red-black ink running down the page, rushing her through the text before it was rendered illegible.

The torc at her neck burned white-hot, its metal warning her to stop before it was too late.

She didn't listen. Her breath misted as her spell poured heavily to the ground outside her flaming circle and spread outward with a life of its own.

The shapeless monster slipped beneath booted feet, shod hooves, and bare, bloody paws. Every creature it touched instantly turned rigid, its soul sucked down and devoured by a black magic that cared nothing for distinctions between friend and foe. Animal, human, Other—everything outside the protective circle for miles around paled and died on an eerie, echoing sigh, and little by little, the battlefield fell silent.

But the spell wasn't finished. The words kept pouring out, forcing their way off the page, severing it free of its parchment prison and loose of its caster's control. Having tasted freedom at last, the black magic turned up its nose at mortal fare and raced instead toward a heartier meal: raw power in the shape of seven open portals. It poisoned the ground in its wake, sowed the seeds of weakness and malady everywhere it touched. When it reached the portals, it paused as if in awe to whet its appetite and then, with a massive boom that shook the ground all throughout Wilderheim, gobbled up all seven of them at once.

With the last word on the last page spoken, the book's black magic was free, off to seek its next repast. It had no sense of scale and knew nothing of pecking orders. It sensed the darkness in the north and hungered for a taste, recklessly racing toward its own doom.

The Dragonblood princess snapped the book shut. Despite its spell being done and gone, the tome retained enough of its stain to curl her claws around it, refusing to let go. She cringed as tainted ink dripped over her hand, burning her like acid that somehow seeped into her blood and made her feverish with stinging frost.

Forcing her hand to straighten, she released the book at last and let it drop into the mud at her feet. Instead of burning to ash, it sank down and disappeared in the muck, a black heartbeat throbbing malice through the earth.

Her knees quivered, and her arms felt too heavy for her body when she banked her flames and faced the destruction she'd wrought. The battlefield reverberated with silence. There was no one left alive for miles around. Men, women, human or Other, all of them lay dead where they'd stood, and she was to blame for it all.

But the portals were no more.

The ravenous void spreading from the north had met the spell and slowed, pausing for a while to feast on the power it had consumed, destroying it little by little before it could do more damage. For the price of innocence, the princess had bought the rest of her kingdom a little more time.

A dull, burning pain started in her belly, growing more intense until it doubled her over, and she dropped to her knees. Fighting the darkness, she raised her gaze to the sky, fancied she could see a dragon's shadow against the flash of a lightning bolt. If only it were real.

But if the dragon hadn't answered the hundreds of summons she'd sent out every day since the Veil had shattered, he would not have answered this last one. Fal would be on his own. Liadan had done all she could to help him, but she had nothing left to give. "Wake up, brother," she whispered through numb lips. *Wake up, the kingdom needs you…* Darkness closed in on her, swaying the ground beneath her. "Wake up…"

A strong downward wind buffeted her upright just long enough for her to feel the heat of fire against her skin. She embraced its comfort for the beautiful dream it was and gave herself up to it, hardly noticing a pair of strong, hard arms closing around her as she collapsed.

30

They came out of nowhere, peasants with farming tools and creatures such as Artairas had never seen before. They rushed the square from all sides on rising war cries, attacking with the single-minded abandon of a people who knew they were running to their deaths.

An elderly man came upon Artairas from the back, wielding a pitchfork. It took no effort at all to send him to the ground, but right on his heels, a hissing red creature with slitted green eyes jumped high into the air, its clawed hands and feet aiming for Artairas. He fell back and rolled with the creature until he had it pinned to the ground. Raising his sword high, he stabbed the demon through, savoring the shock in its eyes before they dimmed in death.

Two women jumped onto his back, their little eating knives aiming for his heart, scraping against his armor. He shook them off, his arm itching to swing the killing blow, but at the last moment, he changed the sword's aim to miss them by a hair's breadth. They screamed and ran, leaving Artairas shaking with the need to go after them and finish them off.

With great difficulty, he turned his sword to the two men who'd managed to fell one of his soldiers with a scythe. They were no match for him, and the blade shouted in triumph when their heads toppled to the ground.

But in the next blink, the blade fell silent, quivering in his grasp. The ground roiled beneath his feet in a massive shudder that stopped everyone in their tracks. The fighters tripped off balance; the mounts screamed and ran.

Everyone in the square gazed around warily, waiting for whatever had caused the ground to shake to come bearing down on them. When nothing did, the peasants picked up their crude weapons and attacked in force.

God's blade roused instantly and screamed with renewed vigor, causing his arm to cramp. The blade clutched his fingers around the handle, directed his movements to defend against creatures he never saw coming. Rather than fight its control, Artairas gave himself up to it, thanking God for keeping him safe from those savage demons.

They fell one after the other, their eyes dimming, their claws turning to ash, and with each one slain, he felt more strength flood his body. The weight of his armor was nothing to him; the fatigue of battle was banished by a feverish zeal. He bared his teeth in a snarl, something akin to joy taking hold of him as he moved, flowed, danced through the fight.

More bodies poured into the square, and he reaped them down in quick succession. He didn't see their faces, didn't hear their shouts. All he saw were moving targets and the shining blade cutting them down.

And he loved every moment of it. His heart raced with excitement, the blade singing in his grasp, sending zings of pleasure through his arm, down to his loins.

He felled a knight, watched his mouth open on a shuddering gasp as his wide-eyed gaze shifted to something behind Artairas. Pulling his sword free of the dying man, Artairas brought it around in a flash. His aim was perfect; the blade stabbed into a soft belly before his mind had located the target.

It was the gasp that broke through his battle haze.

With the blade still buried in its victim, Artairas froze. His focus returned slowly, registering the sounds of battle before the sights. He blinked and blinked again, finding himself staring into a pair of large, green eyes. The pale face went blank as baffled as Artairas, plump, red lips opening and closing soundlessly.

A woman. A young girl with cheeks stained pink by the cold and hair cropped so short it made her look like a child.

Artairas shouted, releasing his grip on the sword as he backed away from her. The sheepskin had already begun to turn dark with her blood as she dropped to her knees. Artairas was only vaguely aware of the silence around them, so focused on the girl, he didn't notice the fighting had stopped.

She sat back on her heels, shuddering, and Artairas shuddered with her. He couldn't feel his body past the thud of his heartbeat. His mind refused to comprehend what he was seeing. No, this couldn't be. He wouldn't have slain an innocent—the queen had expressly forbidden it.

The girl swayed where she sat, tipping her chin up to stare at him with those doe eyes filled with confusion and fear. She wasn't breathing, but Artairas could still hear the soft whimper quiver past her lips as she slowly tipped over. With her hands around the blade, she gasped a breath, then another as she curled in on herself and changed. Like frost licking up from the ground, her body became gray and stiff, turning to stone before his eyes, the sword sticking out like an accusing finger pointed directly at him.

Artairas couldn't move. He couldn't look away, frozen to the spot, an easy target for the most inept of peasants.

But no one was fighting anymore. They all stared at the girl sealed in stone, holding the sword inside her as if she would never let it go again.

"My Lord," someone said.

Artairas moved his numb lips, managing to speak a single word: "Retreat."

31

The dragon carried Liadan into the tent with Varr brushing against his legs and sniffing at her. "She will heal," he assured Varr.

In response, the wolf keened a frantic, high pitched whine, pressing close as the dragon laid his granddaughter on the spare pallet. She was cold, her hands and clothing stained with black sludge that tainted the veins beneath her deathly pale skin.

On the other pallet, Fal lay panting and twitching, but silent, as if he waited for news of his sister. As long as the rains continued, the dragon could do nothing for his grandson. He needed to focus on Liadan.

He called fire into his palms but, before he could begin, Varr pounced on Fal with a sharp whine-bark as the boy gasped and turned rigid.

"Fal!"

A sheen of cold gray stone quickly spread over Fal's body. It turned him into a statue up to his neck, and only a broken whisper of, "Sanja," made it past his lips before the stone crept up over his face to encase him fully.

The dragon quickly banked his flames. Stone had no give. Too much heat, and it would shatter.

While Varr whined and paced frantically back and forth between Fal and Liadan, sniffing each of them in turn, pawing at them, nuzzling them, the dragon stabbed a claw into the base of his ring finger and twisted Liadan's ring 'round and 'round, using his blood to power its spell. He cast the summoning far and wide, adding the strength of all his will to bring Saeran back. Where the king of Wilderheim went, his queen followed, and right now, Fal needed his mother's magic more than ever.

A curious sound brought him back to Fal's pallet. He put his ear to the boy's chest to hear better. Strange, it sounded as if two hearts beat within him almost perfectly synchronized. As their rhythms separated more and more, the gray stone slowly faded back to living flesh. Fal sighed and went limp, and his breathing settled into the rhythm of deep sleep.

The dragon laid a cautious hand on his forehead, seeking his grandson's mind. He found it scattered in the breadth and depth of the rain. Safe, but lost to the tumult of the storm.

The dragon couldn't force him whole without causing irreparable harm. Without Nialei, all he could do was wait for the storm to end so Fal could find his own way back. "Keep an eye on him," he told Varr, then turned his attention back to Liadan.

The vibrant girl who danced with flames now lay as one dead, still holding the stain of the dark spell inside her. He called fire back into his palms and laid both of his hands over Liadan's abdomen. His flames licked along her body, seeped down through her skin, seeking out every last remnant of the dark magic's corruption.

Burning it away was the easy part. Far worse was the damage it had left behind. Black magic was an insidious thing, warping anything it touched in ways no one could predict. Liadan's veins were melted closed, and her heart was rotted like rusted iron. All of these things would heal with fire and time. But no amount of time would heal the sorrow and pain in her mind. No amount of fire would bring the child in her womb back to life. And no amount of magic would reform Liadan's wounded soul to the way it used to be.

Like a bad break, Liadan would mend into something altogether different. Stronger, more powerful and resilient, but different.

A warm hand on his shoulder brought him back to himself. He looked up to meet Saeran's questioning gaze. "I could not save the babe."

The king of Wilderheim blinked back the tears in his eyes. "You saved my daughter," he said fiercely. "It is more than I could have done."

"And Fal?"

Both of them turned to watch Nialei work on her son. A faint blue aura glowed around her where she knelt beside Fal's pallet with one hand on his forehead, the other over his heart.

Varr crawled over to Nialei and carefully laid his chin on her knee. Saeran took his place behind her, putting his hands over hers to lend her his strength.

The dragon left them to it. He encased Liadan in a shroud of blue flames to help her heal, then stepped out of the tent.

The rain had eased to a soft drizzle. As far as he could see, the land around him was dead aboveground and below. Mist covered the field of battle, blanketing thousands of dead bodies, but it couldn't mask the smell of death.

Taking a knee, the dragon once more called up his flames. He stoked them white-hot and sent them racing over the earth, scorching the remains to soft ash, razing the empty town of Crossroads to the ground. All of it would sink down into the earth and turn the valley into a lush, verdant paradise in the years to come.

If Fenrir didn't destroy it first.

The dragon cast his gaze to the north. There in the distance, the stain of eternal hunger hovered at the base of Hallowed Mountain. It had stopped to feast on the dark spell and all the powers it had absorbed. Divine powers—a delicacy not easy for it to digest. The dragon sensed Fenrir gnawing away at it a little bit at a time. He was grateful for the short reprieve. Though his fire had warmed the earth for now, it could not banish the frost of Fenrir's approach completely. Another storm was brewing over the mountains, and this one would cover the kingdom in eternal snow and ice.

Night fell without fanfare. In the sky above, Otherlands twirled their dance, a beautiful spectacle he'd witnessed in all its glory before the Veil had fully formed. Back then, the sky had been on fire with a riot of colors. The dragon had watched them clash and reform anew. He'd spent centuries visiting each Otherland, watching its dominant species evolve and rise to power. He'd learned politics from the shadows of the Sidhe court and warfare from Ice Fey battlefields. He'd known that ever-changing sky like the back of his claw.

This one was little more than its skeletal remains.

Saeran joined the dragon outside the tent, and the two of them sat together, watching the sky in silence. "What happened to you?" Saeran asked after a while.

The dragon couldn't begin to explain. "I was…away. Your grand-mother sends her love."

Saeran turned to stare at him. "You saw her?"

"For a moment too brief." And one that would never happen again. The dragon turned away from the thought.

Thankfully, Saeran didn't push for more. "What do we do now?"

"I do not know." With all the knowledge he'd collected over his end-less millennia of life, the dragon had no solutions to offer. There was no spell to stop a void as ravenous as the one bearing down on them.

"Is anywhere safe from Fenrir anymore?"

"Not within Wilderheim's borders," the dragon replied. "Do you feel the new barrier?" He huffed out a plume of smoke, and inside it showed Saeran a vision of blinding white light. On one side of it, Wilderheim's soldiers battled an army of invaders. On the other, foreigners from each bordering kingdom looked on in silence. They couldn't see the barrier but sensed its force pushing them back. No one could cross it from either side. "I do not know if it is strong enough to stop the Wolf, but it is more than strong enough to stop us escaping him."

Never one to back down from a fight, Saeran balled his hands into fists, ready to face off with death itself if need be. "Can Fenrir be killed?"

The dragon sought the void and found its meal reduced the slightest bit. Another day or two, perhaps three before it moved on to the rest of the kingdom. Fortified by the Divine powers, it would make short work of Wilderheim and everything in it. "If he could, the gods would have done it long ago."

Saeran nodded his grim acceptance. "Don't tell the others," he asked. "At least not yet."

A scream-gasp behind the tent's flimsy curtain brought both men to their feet and back inside. Liadan sat up on her pallet, pale and shaking. She was panting for breath as her body smoked, and her wide eyes burned bright orange.

"Liadan?"

"It stopped raining. Where is Fal?"

She looked to them for an answer, then followed their gazes to Nialei, still working on Fal. With an incoherent cry, she rolled from her pallet and fell to her knees beside Fal, taking his hand in both of hers. "No, no, no, it should have been me." Errant flames flared out of her back like ethereal wings that couldn't quite coalesce. "It should have been *me!*"

Saeran and the dragon pulled her away, embraced her shaking form between them to keep her erratic fire from burning down the tent. "I cast the spell. I paid the price," she sobbed. "Why won't he wake?"

"Hush, child," the dragon crooned. "It will be all right."

"I paid the price," she repeated over and over. "I did the right thing!" Then, on a broken whisper, "Didn't I?"

"He won't die, Liadan," Saeran said. "I swear to you we will not let him die."

But she didn't hear, fighting them both as her flames flared out farther and farther. Neither of them could reach through the chaotic haze in her mind to make her calm, and so the dragon did the only thing he could. He sent Liadan into a deep sleep.

Her fire banked in a rush, and she went limp. Saeran caught her against him, rocking her back and forth, his face pressed to her shoulder.

By Fal's pallet, Nialei sighed and sat back. Varr scrambled to his feet immediately, licking her face and whining his concern. Nialei endured his attentions for a moment, quietly assuring him she was all right. When at last she managed to push him away and face the rest of them, she looked utterly drained. "I did what I could," she rasped. "The rest is up to him."

~

Scattered into millions of raindrops, Fal plummeted from the sky, washing over a kingdom drenched with blood. He slid down chipped blades and torn flags, washed over open wounds and dead, sightless eyes. A small, quick current carried him down city streets, past enemy soldiers retreating into huts and haunted people huddling in fear of them.

Little by little, his essence coalesced back together, guided by a warm, blue light. But before he could be made whole, the current splashed into a boulder, scattering him over its surface and straight into the blade sticking out of it. It cut him through, and the current moved on, spinning him end over end into the black void of a rabbit hole.

He fell, and landed, and seeped through to fall deeper still until drop by drop, he dissolved into an underground well. There, at last, his mad dervish stopped. Fal coalesced into consciousness, cocooned in darkness and silence.

He sighed, basking in a moment of much-needed peace.

The water echoed his sigh with sorrow and the crackle of growing frost.

Where am I? He needed to get back to himself; his kingdom depended on it.

Another sigh was his answer. The water had no answer for him. It only collected the drops that seeped like tears from above, each one carrying tales of horror, and pain, and suffering.

I want to stop it.

There will never be an end to ending, it replied. *Fenrir cannot be stopped.*

Can he be contained?

Fenrir cannot be stopped, the water repeated. *Fenrir will devour the worlds and then itself, and it will expel the dregs of what it has devoured, and bits of it will birth themselves into all that was once immortal, and there will never be an end to ending.*

Everything that had once existed would be forcefully altered into a different state of being, the water related without words. Not once, but again and again. The water accepted this. It was the natural order of things, after all. Water froze to ice and melted back to water, or boiled into steam. It was as it should be. The elements knew this; all of Nature knew this, but only some higher beings accepted it.

Change is the only truth.

The water perked up at those words. *Yes,* it agreed, pulsing in the rhythm of a heartbeat that echoed inside him. *Like her.*

Cold, sharp spikes of frost scraped along the edges of his consciousness. *What do you mean?*

The water swirled him about, pushed him back up to the surface, reversing his flow. He emerged into the night and splashed up over the selfsame boulder with the sword sticking out of it. The blade sliced through him, and he poured down over a surface far too smooth to be simple stone. He gathered sensations drop by drop and collected them all together in a pool at its base. From there, he gazed up at a boot shoved against the stone, hands clenched tightly around the sword handle. The soldier pulled and strained, but couldn't free the sword.

The woman it had impaled wouldn't let him.

Fal gasped, suddenly finding himself elsewhere, staring at a familiar tent roof. His head pounded, and his chest ached with each breath. Moving at all felt impossible, so Fal remained still, clutching at the heartbeat echoing his own as the only steady thing in a world gone mad. She was alive. Her heart still beat as strong as ever. She was alive, and that meant he could heal her.

She's alive. He repeated to himself against the flood of furious panic that threatened to drown out all lucid thought. She wasn't dead, merely sleeping, and he had to focus on that because if he didn't, he'd shatter. And Sanja needed him at full strength and thinking clearly so he could wake her.

How is she here? He'd left Anderheim with a clear order to—

Gods…

He'd told the Otherland to send Sanja home, and it had. To her real home in Wilderheim during the middle of an invasion. And now she was stone.

No, she's alive. Fal set the rhythm of his breaths to the beat of her heart and pushed everything else from his mind until the cold noose around his neck loosened, and he could breathe normally. *She's alive, and I can heal her.* And once he did, he would find whoever had brought that sword to Frastmir and make him pay.

His next breath puffed out cold mist. Icy crystals of magic rattled in his throat, demanding to be set loose. He swallowed them back, wincing as they cut him up on the inside. Rather than ground him, the pain increased his fury tenfold, and above him, the tent roof froze into intricate patterns of white frost.

Cold stone anchoring her to the ground. Drunken men crowding around. Reckless hands yanking on the sword, jarring it inside her. Filthy boots shoved at her for leverage.

The ice inside him spread, cramping his fingers into grotesque claws as snowflakes wafted down from the tent ceiling.

They'd kicked at her. They'd spat on her.

The ice grew so cold he couldn't feel it anymore, and he welcomed it, let the wrath consume his fear until he felt nothing but hate.

"Fal?" Nialei appeared beside him with Saeran and the dragon close behind. She placed her hand on his shoulder, allowing her magic to flow over him, warm and soothing, the epitome of maternal love.

He didn't want to give up his wrath and desperately fought her gentle healing. But she was relentless and the ice inside him began to melt. Fury gave way to anguish so deep it cut his soul to shreds, but his mother's light mended it back together, stitching him whole until he could heal on his own. His wild magic settled back into place, leaving him alone with his grief.

"You are not alone," Nialei told him. "We are with you now."

Yes, he had his family back.

Lush green grass sprouted from the cold, muddy ground at his feet, spreading through the tent as his illusions returned. He no longer bothered to pull them back. Instead, he welcomed the wildflowers blooming here and there as a reminder that all was not lost.

But all was not well, either.

He sat up, lightheaded, but relatively sane. "Where's Liadan?"

"Resting," his mother replied, shifting aside so he could see where his sister slept.

"She became frantic when you wouldn't wake after the storm passed," Saeran added. "She will want to see you when she wakes."

"The child?"

Their collective silence was answer enough.

The flowers at his feet sprouted thorny vines that choked off the blooms. "I saw it coming," he confessed. "I tried to make her leave—"

"This was not your fault."

"What bloody good is seeing the future if I can't change it?"

"I used to wonder the same," Nialei said, her gaze on Saeran. "I used to fight the will of Destiny and paid for it dearly every single time. But eventually, I came to accept that what we see is not meant to be a challenge, but a gift. We're not meant to change what is to come, only prepare for it, come to terms with it, and help others do the same."

Fal shook his head. "Not this time." He would not stand by as everything he'd ever known froze and died.

"Son, you can't fight Fenrir," Saeran said.

White frost adorned the tallest blades of grass and weighted the flowers down among them. "Perhaps I don't need to."

Anderheim called to him, eager to take him back. All Fal needed to do was find a way to fold all of Wilderheim into it. "I can save us. All of us. Everyone in Wilderheim, and any Others still alive out there."

"How?"

"We have a drop of blood from almost every clan. We can use it to summon them." The magic was the same one Liadan had used when fashioning the dragon's ring. The blood would call to its kind. He merely needed to feed it enough magic to reach everyone still alive. And, at the moment, magic was the one thing he had in ample supply.

"And then what? There is still no escape from Wilderheim."

No, but Anderheim lay directly on top of it. If Fal could create the doorway, no one would need to escape anywhere; the Otherland would simply enfold them all where they stood. "I'm certain there is a way, but I will need help to find it."

Nialei cupped his cheek. "Fal, you are grasping at a dream."

Perhaps he was. "But haven't you noticed, Mother? Our dreams have a way of coming true."

Hope surged within him on a rush of renewed strength. The grass all around them burst into a riot of dandelions and bluebells, and he felt them solidify in truth, a small part of Anderheim encroaching on Wilderheim, carrying its soundless call. For a moment, he could almost see the border between the two worlds misting around his family.

They noticed, too. The vision caused King Saeran to reach for his sword, while his queen looked about her in wonder. She met her son's gaze with something akin to awe. "Oh, to walk among such giants," she whispered, her eyes glinting with tears.

Fal pushed to his feet, eager to get started, but he tempered his excitement before approaching Liadan's pallet. The dragon might have cleansed the stain of the dark spell from his sister's body, but Fal sensed the turmoil it had left behind. Plunged deep in dreamless sleep, Liadan's fire still roiled inside her in a wild vortex of sparks too scattered to coalesce into a coherent flame.

He took her hand into his. As his mother had done for him, he left his body in search of his sister's soul, gently guiding each spark back into the whole. He took his time, left nothing to chance—Liadan was too important to all of them. When at last the final spark was corralled back into place, Fal drew back to behold his handiwork, and the sight of it shocked his consciousness back into his body.

Liadan's soul was altered. Instead of the wild, flaring inferno of golden fire, her core was now a small orb of blue flames so intense he dared not get too close. By breaking apart, Liadan had reformed much stronger than before. Like dragon's fire tempering a blade, Liadan's pain had seared away any remaining human weakness and forged her into an Other whose magic could change the world.

She was beautiful. Inside and out.

And, after Wilderheim was safely folded into Anderheim, he might never see her again.

Fal gave her hand a squeeze to wake her from her slumber. Despite the softness of his call, Liadan woke with a startled gasp and arched up to sit. Her magic pulsed with each frantic beat of her heart, sending waves of heat over the entire tent. When she met his gaze, Liadan's eyes were as blue as his own, a physical representation of the flame that would never bank again.

"You feel different," she said. Noticing the flowers around her pallet, she reached down with her free hand and plucked one of them. "You *are* different." Her discerning gaze raked over him in a thorough examination and came to a halt at his chest. Liadan pressed her hand and the flower in it over his double heartbeat then, with a curious tilt of her head, she turned his hand in hers palm-up to reveal the thin scar of his handfasting.

Fal attempted a smile but couldn't quite manage it past the thought of his mate trapped in stone. He needed to get to her and see firsthand the damage the sword had done. He needed to heal her before the echo of her heartbeat drove him mad. The grass dried around them, and the flowers froze to ice mid-sway. What little calm his mother had managed to gift him was already freezing away at the thought that Sanja might remain trapped in stone forever.

Liadan noticed. When she met his gaze once more, he felt her seeking through his memories, and what she found made her eyes glow like stars. "The same magic fashioned the blade and tore Wilderheim open to admit our enemies at our backs."

"Yes," he confirmed. Summoning a puddle, he wove an illusion across its surface to show the others. He conjured the glowing blade as it cut down their soldiers from the shadows. Liadan supplied its unearthly metallic scream.

"It cuts from shadows," Nialei noted.

Saeran swore viciously. "Loki. It must be."

Fal showed them what the rain had seen of the man wielding the weapon, but looked away himself before its final stroke.

Nialei gasped to see Sanja fall.

Saeran moved in for a closer look as she turned to stone. "The blade died with her?"

"The blade died," Liadan agreed, watching Fal. "The girl lives."

The dragon laid his hand over the surface, taking over the vision to make the blade its only subject. His magic filled the tent as he pulled a simulacrum of the sword from the puddle and turned it in the air. One by one, he removed all the symbols etched into its blade, then broke apart the handle to reveal its shining core. "No, the blade isn't dead."

Fal frowned. "What is that?"

"Divine power," the dragon answered. "A piece of a god's physical form refashioned into a weapon. Which means it cannot be killed, save by an act of the Divine."

"Get rid of it," Liadan growled, squeezing Fal's hand so hard his knuckles creaked.

Nialei grasped the vision in a tight fist and shoved it back through the puddle. Its scream carried on long after it disappeared.

"When the girl rouses," the dragon said, "the blade will wake again, as terrible as ever."

"A clever trap for whoever pulls it free," Saeran sneered. "I would have expected nothing less of Loki."

"I'll pull it out," Fal declared.

"You will do no such thing," his mother snapped.

"She's right," Liadan chimed in. "That privilege will be mine."

Saeran drew his sword and stabbed it into the center of the puddle. "Enough! Nobody will touch the sword until we know how to do it safely. Do you understand?" He stared down Liadan until she flushed and bowed her head in a nod. Then he moved on to Fal, demanding the same obedience from his son and heir. When he got it, the king of Wilderheim turned to his wife and queen. "That includes you too, love. Don't think I don't know how your clever mind works. Swear to me you will not go near the thing."

Nialei raised her stubborn chin. "I swear I will not lay one finger on Loki's cursed sword."

Saeran narrowed his eyes at her.

"In your place, I would accept it, Father," Fal quipped. "A better compromise will never pass her lips."

Saeran's mouth twitched in a smile despite his thunderous scowl. They all knew Nialei too well to expect her to keep her distance altogether.

Liadan pushed to her feet and removed herself to the far corner of the tent to stretch. Her joints creaked and crackled like old firewood as she realigned herself. Small blue sparks danced along her fingertips. She caught them up and molded them into a sphere, watching it spin in the air above her palms as the rest of them looked on in wary silence. "Two days it took me to do this in the desert," she said with a wry shake of her head.

Fal exchanged a silent look with his parents and the dragon. As unpredictable as Liadan had been before, she was now a thousand times moreso. That small blue flame burned so hot Fal felt its sting clear across the tent. If she lost control of it…

But Liadan handled the orb with such ease, it seemed to bore her.

She played with it for a moment, let it weave among her fingers and dance up her arm to her shoulder, then caught it with her opposite hand and stifled it in her fist. And she did it all as if she was handling a ball of yarn. "In the morning," she said with calm gravity, "we will return to Frastmir, reclaim the castle, and take back the girl. But tonight, I think it's time for Fal to show us where he's been for the last three weeks."

32

In a cold, dark hut, Artairas sat at the remains of a shattered table, his head in his numb hands. Men came and went, bringing news of the siege, but it was General Gawain who received them and issued new orders. Everything they said passed through Artairas without acknowledgment. Every question directed at him went unanswered. Artairas was lost to the world at large, his mind mired in memories of the girl's face, the shock in her eyes.

He recalled the smallest details again and again. The way her lips parted, the sound of her soft cry. The way she collapsed so slowly, like a weightless feather wafting to the ground.

The bloodstain spreading over her sheepskins. A lamb slaughtered before her time.

Artairas hadn't felt a single moment of doubt before last night. Now, doubt was all he knew. If this was what God had wanted, why was Artairas so ashamed?

Dawn had come and gone.

Sometime in the night, the storm had broken, leaving in its wake a miserable chill that refused to yield to their hearth fire. His men had taken over abandoned houses in the castle city, burning whatever was available to warm themselves.

"My Lord."

The fifth address. Or was it the sixth? Either way, Artairas didn't move to acknowledge it.

"My Lord, the sword."

A good man, Gawain was. Despite his misgivings, he remained true to their cause. His faith hadn't wavered a single time, even after what he'd seen, fighting side by side with Artairas. Even after the girl.

"We sent men to retrieve it, but no one can budge it from the stone."

No one ever would. It belonged to the girl now. She'd bought it with her life.

Artairas shuddered, ducked his head lower, and curled his fingers into his hair, tugging hard.

"My Lord, it is the symbol of our cause," Gawain insisted.

"What cause?" he muttered. "What has Wilderheim ever done to God that He would send us to destroy it?"

Gawain flushed and jerked his head to send the others out. "God's will is not for us to question. You are tired, My Lord. You have not slept or eaten a proper meal since we got here. You know not what you say."

The man was right. Artairas had fought through the night and day without cease. He'd slain so many he couldn't remember any of them, except the last. The girl. "We trespassed where we were not meant to go."

"We were sent by God to cleanse this heathen land in His name."

"Were we? Or was it the Devil whispering in an old woman's ear?" He'd been there the day they'd burned Sir Arnaud. He remembered the man's last words and the whispers that had spread through the castle about Queen Genevieve.

Gawain shot to his feet and took two angry steps toward Artairas before he stopped himself to rein in his temper.

"Do you not have even a whisper of doubt?" Artairas challenged. "After all we have seen here, do you not wonder?"

A muscle twitched in Gawain's jaw as he fought valiantly to hold onto his temper. Rather than answer, the general chose to change the subject. "The siege towers have been abandoned on the east side of the outer wall. I have ordered them to be moved to the south. The moat has been drained, and we have men digging through the mud to undermine the wall on the north side. We appear to have struck a tunnel there, which may be our way inside, but the stones are too tough for our weapons."

Artairas shook his head. "We are at the heart of it all, Gawain. There is magic in everything around us, and it will not yield to chunks of metal for our asking."

"Happily for us, we have a supply of masonry tools made right here. They seem to be holding up well enough."

"How many men have we lost on the east side?" It must have been a significant number for the siege towers to have been abandoned altogether. "And how many dead everywhere else?" He'd caught random words of a report here and there. In the south, the dead numbered in the thousands. The western front had failed to send a report with their blood-stained pigeons. Artairas could only assume their forces there were lost. "Would God lead us all to slaughter like this?"

"Yes," Gawain answered. "His glory demands sacrifice, and it is our honor to have been chosen to bleed in His name."

Artairas scoffed. What a wretched waste of life.

"You speak of devils in Synealee, yet you refuse to see them screaming you in the face right here. You have slain enough of them yesterday to know our cause to be true, yet now that we are so close to victory, you falter? Then it is as I suspected. All of your courage lies in the sword. And if so, then God be my witness, I shall get it back in your hand if I have to reduce the stone to rubble!"

"You will fail." Dozens had already tried; he'd heard them out there all through the night. After the girl had turned to stone, after the fighting had stopped, the sun had set with such quiescence that for a while, Artairas had believed himself to be stumbling through the darkness of purgatory.

But food and drink had eventually been brought forth. The men's spirits had been revived, and they'd flooded back out to the sword to test their strength against it. By midnight, their cheers and laughter had echoed through the streets, setting Artairas on the razor-sharp edge of impending disaster, and that's where he'd been ever since.

Sunrise had come and gone. The sun had reached its zenith and passed it. Night would be upon them again soon, and still the men were out there, taking turns trying to free the sword from the stone—the girl.

Artairas was exhausted in mind as well as body, ready to embrace the endless sleep of death, yet the cursed blade still called to him, and it was all he could do not to stalk out there and fight each and every one of his men to claim the weapon for himself. Some ancient, mystical awareness told him he could do it. The blade had been given to Artairas by God—he was the only one who could free it from the stone.

He knew precisely where to brace his feet and how to take hold of the handle. He knew how hard to pull, and he could already feel it giving way in his grasp; hear the scrape of metal against stone turn into the wet sound of the blade slicing free of soft flesh.

Artairas shuddered, his stomach heaving as he turned away from Gawain and the open doorway behind him. A shame he couldn't turn away from his own mind. In it, he smelled the blood seeping from the girl's gut. He saw it pooling at his feet, staining his boots. He saw it running down the center of the blade, over the handle, and onto his hand. It was cold, sticky, and Artairas would never be clean of it.

A desperate sob escaped him as he frantically wiped his hands. He prayed for mercy, for forgiveness, for peace.

When he came back to his senses, it was to find Gawain before him, staring at him with horror. "You've gone mad."

Artairas almost laughed. If only it was that simple.

"Stay here," Gawain ordered. "Rest. You will see sense again after you have slept. I will find a way to retrieve the sword, and in the morning, we will take the castle. Then everything will fall into place."

"You overstep, General. I give the orders here."

"You are in no condition to lead us!"

Artairas merely sighed. "The sword is dead."

"Dead or not, you'll still carry it into battle tomorrow." Turning on his heels, he marched out, snapping orders at the men outside. No one was to enter the hut without his permission.

Artairas dropped his head into his hands once more and prayed for God to guide him back into His grace.

33

Morning dawned on the sound of a battering ram slamming into the castle's massive gates. It bounced off harmlessly, only to be propelled forward once more. On the battlements, bleary-eyed sentinels stood silent watch. The humans clutched little books in their hands. The Others paced restlessly, watching the archers below ready their bows.

Outside the walls, Synealee's army stood in formation, weapons in hand, waiting for a path to open for them to storm the castle.

Inside the courtyard, humans and Others waited for something else.

Word had spread of the prince's return, and the great blow he'd stricken against the invaders with the ease of an afterthought. Rumors whispered on the breeze of a dragon flying across the sky, breathing great plumes of fire through the clouds. Though many had fallen during the first wave of attack, those who'd seen their crown prince bring a hundred dying men back to roaring life stood tall in the face of Ragnarok, knowing their rulers would not abandon them.

The ram slammed into the gates, leaving behind the shallowest of indentations. It had barely come to a stop after its recoil when the general shouted, "*Forward!*"

As the north wind kicked up, its whistling rush grew louder, carrying an unearthly chorus of baying howls. No time to sound a warning.

The screams spread southward as a pack of ferocious befurred beasts tore through the ranks. Their claws rent metal with ease; their fangs crushed bones like dry tinder. Six of them cut a wide swath through the army, distracting a third of their forces away from the siege. No arrow was swift enough to catch them, no blade sharp enough to cut through the Ulfhednar's thick fur.

Atop the battlements, the humans opened their books and began to read. Magic poured from them, tearing up cobblestones from beneath the soldiers' feet for ammunition, turning the frozen ground to quicksand that sucked enemy forces down faster than they could run.

When arrows began to fly, aimed at the wizards, the Others plucked them out of the air, sending them back to the archers coated with fire and poison. For each fallen archer, two more stepped up. One arrow hit its mark, killing a woman mid-spell. She tumbled off the wall onto the mud giant taking shape in the moat below, and both collapsed back into the muck.

The Other left behind shrieked a volley of barbs at the soldiers below, felling ten of them into the selfsame moat. But with that blow, he himself collapsed and was no more.

The wizards spread out farther, ducked low to make smaller targets of themselves, but they couldn't retreat. To strike a blow against the enemy, they needed to see it.

In the south, ghostly apparitions of beautiful women with pale skin and bloody eyes wove through the ranks. Their hands wafted like mist over a shoulder here, a hand there. Their mournful sighs whispered across dry lips cracked by the cold, and everywhere they went, death followed. Soldiers' faces turned gray in their helmets, their eyes widened, and their mouths opened as they wheezed for breath.

This time, the warning spread, but mist could not be cut down. And when the wraiths keened, weeping tears of blood, the soldiers began to drop like flies.

And the siege towers never touched the wall.

The steadfast ranks fractured outside the walls while in the court-yard, Wilderheim's soldiers stood their ground. A shield on one arm, a sword in hand, they beat the one against the other in a steady rhythm, watching the gates bow inward each time the ram slammed forward.

One hundred strong and fifteen fledglings all ready to lay down their lives.

A dull thump joined the chorus of clangs. A scrawny waif with mud-stained cheeks and wild brown hair had joined the ranks. Twelve years old, if she was a day, she defiantly stared up at the soldier shooing her away and banged her little eating knife against the wooden barrel top she'd tied to her arm.

Sheathing his sword, the soldier swooped up the brat and endured her screaming fit as he carried her back through the kitchens into the pantry. He made sure to lock the kitchen door behind him as he returned to his place in the formation.

Others had joined them while he'd been gone. Giant creatures with furry, hooved legs as long as he was tall, swarthy torsos, and thick antlers on their heads. A shield and a sword each, they added their much louder beats to the rhythm.

Two knights in thin golden armor winked into being at the front. Their spears were made of light, their shields like translucent frost. A male and a female with no helmets to cover their long, snow-white hair. The ram's next blow cracked the bar securing the gates. The pair turned to one another. Pale blue markings covered their dark brown skin, their fierce black eyes flashing a wordless message.

They smiled a challenge at each other when the ram rolled forward and, when it shattered through the gates, wordlessly rushed into battle, leading the charge. They managed to push Synealee's soldiers back far enough for the hooved Others to get out and join the fray, but even with all of them standing between Synealee's soldiers and Castle Frastmir, too many still managed to slip through the gates. They were met by Wilderheim's steel.

Outside the gates, the cold wind became a gale, and the sky rained shards of ice over the city, blinding anyone foolish enough to look up. The battle was thickest around the castle gates, but weapons clashed as far west as the river with Others converging from all sides to herd the invaders in for slaughter.

Those on the bridge saw it first—a great shadow gliding through the clouds. When it roared, all of Frastmir shuddered.

That roar was the only warning the warriors would get. Every Other who heard it disappeared, taking friendly humans with them and abandoning the invaders to their fate.

The great shadow swooped in from the west, emerging from the clouds with a stream of fire that incinerated an entire streetful of soldiers in a single pass. It banked left and returned for another pass one street over, systematically cleansing the city of its infection from the outside in.

Those quick enough to escape the dragon's flames ran straight into the clutches of its progeny. On one side, a black-scaled creature with a horned crown and fiery hair used her flames to pen them in by the dozens. On the other, a human with massive black wings swooped over them, taking heads with his flaming sword so swiftly, the bodies ran on for ten more steps before collapsing in fits and spasms.

The survivors ran toward the keep, some to seek safety in numbers, others to shout for crossbows and catapults. At first, they rejoiced to see water spilling down the streets as a respite from the flames. But the water grew, thickening the mud to calf-depth, and on its heels came a heavy mist that obscured everything beyond arm's reach, and then the cold deepened, freezing the mud solid around their legs.

They called to one another as they struggled to free themselves. Their voices, dulled by the thick mist, didn't carry far. Word of the Reaper in their midst spread too slowly, dogged by the swish of his cloak and the soft whistle of his blade as, one by one, the soldiers fell silent.

Water spread through the streets all the way to the library, where Others had cornered Artairas and Gawain's battalion. The ground turned into a shallow lake, and as the thick blanket of mist descended over them, the sounds of battle grew silent.

Though they couldn't see it, the dragon had reached the keep and perched on the battlements. Its roar resounded across the city, and its flames briefly illuminated the mist.

"Stand fast, men!" Gawain ordered.

Artairas put his back to Gawain's. "We're surrounded." He felt the noose pull tighter and tighter as the enemy closed in unseen from all sides.

"My Lord, the sword!"

Artairas shook his head, already too tempted by its soundless call to need any further urging. That sword spelled damnation. He couldn't risk laying another finger upon it.

Gawain grasped his arm. "If anything can save us now…"

But Artairas wasn't listening anymore. His attention snared on a whisper of a sigh somewhere nearby. His breath caught as his mind filled with visions of a beautiful woman with pearlescent skin calling to him from the depths of a lake. His legs were knee-deep in water, but the surface was perfectly smooth, undisturbed by the falling hail. It reflected his face back at him, but also something else. Something he couldn't name.

The sigh became a whispered word of command, and the ice raining down upon them froze mid-air as if time itself had come to a silent halt. Artairas watched a clear glassy ice crystal come to a stop on the surface of the lake, balancing there on its tip, spinning slowly to reflect weak sunlight at him. He looked up to find thousands more suspended in the air like a sea of stars glittering in the mist.

It humbled him to supplication, and he wasn't the only one. All around him, his men lowered to their knees right along with him, bowing their heads. The mist parted, and the creature he'd imagined a moment ago emerged from its depths.

She was beautiful beyond words, her golden hair aglitter, her flawless pale skin sheened with pearlescent perfection. She glided forward over the water's surface, her bare feet neither disturbing it nor sinking through. The ice crystals moved out of her way to allow her passage, showering her with loving kisses of reflected light.

"The Lady of the Lake," men whispered at her approach.

She glanced at each of them in turn, and they crossed themselves in gratitude for her blessing. Her presence overcame even the steadfast Gawain, whose forehead kissed the water almost despite himself.

But the Lady wasn't alone. A great white-eyed wolf followed on her right, and on her left, a cloaked figure of chaos matched her footsteps, carrying a bloodied sword in one hand and a great, curved scythe in the other. Where his booted feet touched down, the water froze solid and cold mist swirled outward.

The company came to within four paces of Artairas and stopped there. He felt the wolf's hot breath on his face, expected at any moment to feel its fangs tear into him, but they did not.

He chanced a look up and found his gaze snared by the Lady's silver one. "Move aside," she said, and it was only then he realized they hadn't come for him, but for what was behind him.

The sword in the stone.

Artairas moved.

The Lady's gaze shifted to her cloaked companion. "Are you certain?"

The man tossed aside his bloodied sword, made the scythe melt into mist, then pulled back the hood of his cloak. He looked human enough, but Artairas felt magic pulse around his cloaked figure in waves so powerful they almost bowled him over. He overflowed with so much of it Artairas could hardly breathe in his presence, and he knew it was but a fraction of what the man held contained within.

He imagined this had to be what it felt like to stand in the presence of a god. A god, not the God. Then the man looked at him, and Artairas knew it was not a god, but Death itself staring frost straight into his soul with eyes of pure blue ice.

"Be ready," the Lady of the Lake warned. "I don't know how much time we will have."

As the man knelt before the sword, he reached out to touch the girl's stone cheek with the gentlest of caresses. "Hello again, little mate."

"As soon as she is free, take her to the other keep. She will be safe there."

"Father's still at the green and Liadan's miles to the south. Someone sent up a beacon."

"Whoever it is," the Lady said dryly, "I hope for their sake they called her for something important. Or something bloody. Are you ready? My spell will not hold these men forever."

Gawain raised his head, and just as quickly bowed it once more. But his honor would not allow him to remain silent. "My Lady, you cannot take the sword."

"I respect your courage, knight, but I would prefer your silence." Turning to Artairas, she waved her hand and forced him upright, holding him entranced with her gaze. "King Arthur, it is time to claim your legacy."

"I—cannot."

Her serene silvered eyes turned fierce. "I was not asking."

As gently as she delivered the words, they carried the force of a magical command that gave Artairas no choice but to obey. His feet turned him to face the sword while Death's icy, hate-filled glare watched his every move. Artairas' fingers curled tightly around the sword's handle. As he'd imagined the night before, his feet braced just so, and he pulled just hard enough to loosen the blade. The sound of metal scraping against stone shuddered through him with the first tingles of the sword's waking hunger, and as the blade pulled free from soft, living flesh, its whispering voice roused to a blood-curdling scream inside his mind.

Artairas stumbled back, shaking from head to toe, the hateful sword clutched in his grip. He watched through the blur of unshed tears as the cloaked man scooped his felled maiden into his arms and disappeared.

"Please," he whimpered to the Lady of the Lake. "Take it with you." He wanted to fall to his knees once more to offer her the blade, but its power wouldn't let him bend a knee. Instead, it gripped him tightly and squared his stance, raising the tip to the Lady's neck. "Please, I beg you."

She looked at the blade, then met his gaze with her unfeeling one. "No," she said, killing his hope with merciless efficiency. "This is your legacy, King Arthur. This sword will build your kingdom on a foundation of the blood and bones of all it has killed. Your realm with endure for generations and your faith will do your god proud. In the end, you will all have what you wanted: a world without magic and the Other creatures you find so repulsive. And until your dying breath, you will not walk a single step without the regret of it bearing down on you."

Artairas whimpered, blinking away his helpless tears as the old thirst for blood once more tensed his limbs for a battle he no longer wanted to win.

Between one breath and the next, the Lady of the Lake was gone, as was her wolf, and the mist, and the lake she'd brought with her. The ground was covered in snow, his men kneeling deep in it. As they roused and pushed to their feet, entranced by the tableau of ice crystals suspended in mid-air, the dragon roared from the castle's battlements, breaking whatever spell had been placed upon the scene. The storm resumed its chilling fury, and from all around them, creatures of nightmare attacked in force.

No time for prayers and regrets.

The war was only just beginning.

34

Fal appeared in Anderheim's waterfall lake with the healing melody already humming from deep within his power's core. Sanja's injury ought to have been a quick thing to mend, but the sword that had stabbed through her had not been an ordinary blade. The wound closed slowly, fighting his spell every inch of the way, draining as much blood as it could before Fal's healing overpowered it.

It left behind a scar inside her womb that refused to heal any more than it already had, no matter how Fal altered the melody. The human body could only absorb so much magic; Fal had already brought Sanja back from the brink of death once before, and she simply couldn't take any more. Her body was healed, but it would never conceive a child.

"Thank you, gods." He bowed his head in gratitude. The possibility of his child draining Sanja's life from the inside had tormented him ever since their handfasting.

Sanja groaned, frowning before she'd opened her eyes. "You didn't tell me when you married me that I'd have to wake in water every morn."

He chuckled. "I suppose her Royal Highness would prefer a bed of goose down."

Nothing had ever looked as beautiful as her smile. But then she gasped, flailing out of his hold to right herself.

"Whoa, easy!"

She sank, pulled down by her soaked clothing, then came up sputtering and shoving her wet hair out of her eyes. "The parchments," she said, coughing. "Did the Brothers find you? Did you sing it? Is it over?"

Fal pulled her from the lake, dried them both with a thought. "Take a breath. What are you talking about?"

"The puzzle, the song of worlds, don't you remember? I solved its shape. I know how it needs to be sung. But I… The soldiers chased me out of the library. I gave the parchments to Brother Erik and told him to find you."

"That must be who sent up the beacon for Liadan."

Sanja looked around. "We're in Anderheim."

"Yes, it's all right, Sanja, you are safe now. I will not let anything happen to you again."

"No, we have to go back. There is so little time left."

Sensing her rising panic, Fal kept his voice low and spoke slowly to calm her. "Tell me what you solved. I will go back and sing it."

She was shaking her head before he'd finished. "You cannot do it by yourself. I have to go with you."

"I am not taking you back to Frastmir. It may have slipped your notice while you were getting stabbed with a mystical sword, but there is a war going on there."

"Did creating Anderheim cure you of your illusions?"

He flushed. "No, not as such."

"Then you have to take me."

"Sanja—"

"You said if all I do is hold your hand, it will be a gesture far more powerful than any spell you could ever speak."

Fal gaped at her. "How in all of Anderheim can you remember my exact words from a month ago, but not recall that you almost died—*twice*?"

"There is far more at stake now than my life, Highness. You may get one chance to save everyone. Only one. If you cannot control your illusions and sing the song at the same time, they will all die, and you along with them."

Fal opened his mouth to argue but found he had nothing to say. If the song was somehow the answer to everything, then she was right. He couldn't sing it with his voice changing on every line, nor could he do it from within his illusions and halfway in Anderheim.

Still... "The song itself only creates a Veil—"

"It creates a connection and a doorway," Sanja corrected. "That is what the Veil has always been. To keep realms separate, something has to exist between them, and that something will always connect them. Humans could never see it without magic, but it was always there, and you can build it again and bring everyone across."

"Then the blood can be the key that locks Fenrir out."

Sanja frowned. "What?"

Fal took her face in his hands and kissed her. "Little mate, I have just come to a wonderful realization."

"What's that?"

"I married someone much smarter than myself."

Sanja's laughter carried them all the way to Anderheim's version of Castle Frastmir, and through to Wilderheim. All at once, the heat of summer turned to bitter winter. High up in the remnants of Fal's tower, there was no shelter from the frigid wind that lashed them with sharp hail. With Sanja tucked into his side, Fal carefully chose his steps along the inner wall, far away from the broken edge of the floor.

"Don't look down," he warned.

Sanja, being Sanja, didn't listen. She whimpered and clutched him tighter. "It's all gone. The fields, the forests—everything."

Fal followed her gaze to the east, where the fire had leveled everything the armies hadn't trampled into dust. Outside the castle's walls, the earth was scorched black, slowly getting covered in a layer of snow. Between the inner and outer walls, the ground was piled with dead soldiers wearing the red cross of Synealee's mad monarch.

"What are we doing here? We have to find Brother Erik. He has the parchments."

"He has the copies, remember?" Fal gently pried Sanja's arms free of him and pushed her all the way to the wall where the bookcase would provide some shelter from the winds. "Don't move."

"Where are you going?"

"I took everything that survived the lightning storm to my chambers, but the book containing the song wasn't there. That's why I gave you copies. The book itself must still be here somewhere. I have to find it."

"But Brother Erik—"

"Isn't here, and we don't have time to wait."

He had a point, "But do I have to be here while you search?"

Fal shrugged. "You wanted to come with me. At the moment, this is the safest place in all of Frastmir. The castle is under attack. If the soldiers get inside, they will raid the entire keep and kill anyone they come across."

"But no one will bother with a tower that's teetering on the brink of collapse."

He grinned. "Precisely."

Sanja glared.

"Not to worry, princess, I spelled this tower to withstand far worse. It may look unstable, but trust me, it's as safe as can be."

"Oh, just hurry up, will you?"

Sanja sank down and made herself as small as possible, watching her mad husband in the shape of a long-haired, dirty hermit rummage through piles of rubble in the stairway. The wind stole her breath away. Her face was numb from the cold, and the tips of her fingers were beginning to turn blue. She tucked them underneath her sheepskin tunic and shivered.

She was glad Mattias didn't live to see Wilderheim come to this. "Do you th-think we could find my p-parents somehow?" she called to Fal through chattering teeth.

"It's not here. It must have fallen down in the collapse," Fal called ahead as he clambered back to the top. Were it not for the familiar blues of his eyes, Sanja would have shrieked. He was swathed in the illusion of an enemy soldier, his dirty tabard flapping in the wind.

She did shriek a moment later when a dragon dropped from the sky and roared at Fal. The sheer force of it shook the tower, knocking Fal off balance and shattering half of the remaining floor. Sanja scrambled for purchase on the last two stones left beneath her feet. She reached out to the bookshelf, but it tipped away from the wall and tumbled off the edge.

Sanja tripped sideways. Her foot slipped off the edge, and she screamed as she fell, landing hard a short way down. Her relief was short-lived as her saving perch moved, raising her up to a giant golden eye.

"Too bloody close!" Fal snapped in the voice of a shrill young girl. "What were you thinking?"

"I was thinking," the dragon rumbled, "that the enemy had managed to get past my watchful eye. Did you know, boy, that your illusions also change your scent now? I smelled Synealee and reacted."

"Never mind. It's good you are here. I'm looking for a book that is probably buried down there beneath the rubble."

The dragon scowled fiercely. "Is this really the right time for books?"

The face and voice of an old Aegiran crone gave Fal's answer gravity beyond the words themselves. "It is if it happens to be our only hope of surviving Fenrir!"

The dragon turned his golden gaze on Sanja and shrugged. "Fair point." He gently handed her down to Fal, now an old warrior with a scarred face and missing eye, then let himself fall down below.

"T-that was…"

Fal took her hand in his and swirled his cloak around her, pulling her into the warmth of his embrace. "My great grandfather," he said in his own voice.

"He's en-n-normous." Her teeth chattered so hard she couldn't speak properly, but she couldn't keep quiet, either. She'd just met a dragon!

"Is he? I hadn't noticed."

Sanja would have kicked him, were she not so cold. "W-where's he gon-n-ne?"

In answer, a loud rumble of rock exploded up from below them, massive boulders flying up to hover in the air. Among them, books in various stages of destruction spun slowly, stray pages wafting left and right.

The dragon climbed back up the tower until his muzzle was level with them. "Which one?" he asked, the gentlest puff of his breath slamming them both against the wall at Fal's back with a blast of much-needed heat.

Sanja squinted at the volumes. There were so many, at least half of them damaged beyond repair. What if the one they needed was missing the pages they were looking for?

"That one!" Fal pointed to a sizable tome bound in thick, dark red leather with a bronze clasp holding it closed. One corner of its back cover was bent up, the last few pages crumpled, torn, and darkened with soot.

The dragon gently plucked it out of the air with two massive claw-tips and handed it to Fal. Then he turned his paw palm up and, to her dismay, Fal shoved her ahead of him into the dragon's grasp. His claws curled up around them into a living cage, encasing them in too much heat, but Sanja was glad for it. Then everything the dragon had raised from the pile below dropped back down as he pushed away from the tower and crawled around and down to the front courtyard, using one of his wings as a shield against the storm.

"You couldn't have saved the books?" Sanja shouted before she could bite her tongue.

The dragon's chuckle reverberated in her chest and made her bones rattle. "I like her," he said, sounding pleased. He set them down in the courtyard but couldn't join them there himself, as large as he was. Instead, he perched on the wall over the gate, seeming not to notice the shower of arrows that bounced off his scaled hide. "Pardon me a moment."

With catlike agility she wouldn't have expected of a creature his size, the dragon pulled in his wings and pivoted around on the relatively narrow wall.

"Duck!" Fal shouted, tugging her down as the dragon's massive tail swooped over their heads and curled around the remnants of another tower. Sanja heard him take a breath, and through the open gateway, she watched his stream of fire scorch three hundred soldiers at least.

The volley of arrows stopped.

Fal straightened and took her hand in his once more. Immediately, his illusions fell away, and her husband squinted against the driving wind, shouting to make himself heard. "Where is everyone?"

"In anticipation of your return, your parents are in the great hall," the dragon replied.

"And Liadan?"

"On her way, I presume."

A blast of frigid wind blew in clouds as dark as night. Sunlight dimmed, the temperature plummeted even lower. Sanja, already chilled to her bones, felt her skin pull tight across her face. Her eyelashes frosted over so quickly, when she blinked, her eyes almost stuck closed.

"Hurry, Fal!" the dragon urged. "I can hold off the soldiers, but I can't stop that."

Fal pulled her into the keep. A pitiful little company awaited them in the great hall. Survivors, both human and Other, huddled together, scrambling to add more wood to the giant hearth fire. Chairs, tables, tapestries—they fed the fire anything they could get their hands on, and still the flames faltered.

"Fal!" A beautiful, golden-haired woman who could only be Queen Nialei rushed to meet them. Her husband, Sanja presumed, shouldered his way to the hearth and revived the flame with a blast of magic that momentarily filled the great hall with heat and light, but the fire refused to burn on its own.

"Mother, this is Sanja. My mate."

Mate. Not wife, but *mate*.

The queen, too, noticed his deliberate choice of words. She swept her gaze over Sanja in a perusal at once critical and loving.

Painfully aware of her haggard appearance, Sanja pulled on a short curl, wishing she'd had more time to make herself presentable. This was not the way to meet the queen.

But Queen Nialei merely smiled. "Well met and welcome, Sanja. We have been waiting for you both. Come, there is no time to waste. Tell me what you need."

They followed her to the dais where four giants with hooves and antlers stood guard over a small glass cauldron swirling with colorful lights.

It was so beautiful…

"I need Liadan's summoning spell," Fal said. "Where is she? Has the dragon added his blood to the cauldron?"

"Not yet," the queen replied. "But we added ours."

"Father, we need that flame much higher for her!"

At the hearth, the fire blazed so high its flames licked the top edge and scorched the stone wall there. The small crowd drew back from its heat, but not too far. The rest of the cavernous chamber was still freezing.

"I can't hold it for long," the king called back.

"You won't need to," Fal said to himself.

The fire blazed outward, forcing the survivors farther back. Then with one more flare, it spat out a ball of fire that rolled across the floor. It unfurled on the shape of a woman who emerged from it running, her hair still on fire. "The clerics sent this," she said, thrusting a burned stack of parchments at Fal. "I saved what I could, but—"

"And this is why we needed the book," Fal told Sanja. To his sister, he said, "I have it. You and Mother start on your spell." He squeezed Sanja's hand. "Are you ready?"

Sanja nodded.

"Then tell me what I need to do," he said, already pulling her toward a clear corner where they'd have more room to work.

A man who might have been the king's twin stepped into their path. His gaze raked over Sanja. "You still look cold, child," he said with the dragon's voice. "Have some mead to warm yourself."

Sanja looked at the wooden cup he offered in his clawed hand. Its contents were too dark to be mere mead. "Maybe later," she said politely.

Fal squeezed her hand, pulling her back when she would have walked away. "Go on," he said, his voice low and intense, his eyes steady but grave. "Take it."

"But the spell—"

"We have time enough for this," he insisted.

He wouldn't let her refuse, and suddenly Sanja felt as if everyone in the great hall was watching her. Fal blinked, and she looked away, only to have her gaze snared by the dragon's. In the depths of his eyes, she saw so many things, light and shadows, love and pain, endless memories from an ageless existence stretching back farther than anyone but the gods could remember.

Sanja found herself letting go of Fal's hand to accept the cup. The moment she touched it, she felt its magic like a flame neatly contained in liquid. It seeped into her skin, warming her up to her shoulders, and she wanted more of it, still shivering in the cold. But a flame that strong wouldn't warm her; it would burn her alive.

"It's a gift," the dragon said. "A drop of fire, so you will never be cold again." His voice was low, soothing, and threatening at the same time.

A gift. The same one he'd given to Fal's mother? Sanja didn't know what to say.

Fal put his arms around her and whispered at her ear, "Drink, little mate. To the last drop."

"It will hurt," she said with absolute certainty. "But I have already endured far worse." She'd endured snowstorms in nothing but haircloth. She'd been stabbed through and turned to stone, and still walked away in one piece. Whatever else this cup had to throw at her, as long as she had Fal holding onto her, Sanja knew she could survive anything. She'd gladly take a drop of fire over the piercing ice in her bones.

Raising the cup to her lips, she tossed the contents back in one large gulp.

It burned going down, but the pain was nothing compared to the inferno it ignited in her belly. Her breath caught on a scream that never made it past her throat. Her knees buckled, but Fal held her fast. Liquid fire exploded inside her, pouring into her veins, melting through her bones, searing her mind with things no human should ever have to know, but she dug her fingers into Fal's bracing arms and held on. She didn't fight the fire; she embraced it, gave herself up to it, and let it do with her what it would.

And it hurt in ways she didn't have words to describe.

But it also made her stronger. It reshaped her somehow on an elemental level so that when she felt her husband's heart beating next to hers, she also felt his magic. She heard his thoughts whisper across her mind. His strength poured through her limbs and fortified her spine, and Sanja felt invincible.

When the fire eased to a soothing warmth, Sanja braced her legs to stand on her own and looked around with new eyes. Everything she saw had a glow of magic around it, and nothing moreso than the dragon. His essence filled the great hall to bursting, and he'd just given a little piece of it to her. She bowed humbly. "Thank you."

"Would that I could have done it sooner."

A shrieking howl echoed outside. The ground shook under them, and dust rained down from the rafters.

Fal released her to pry at the book's bronze clasp. "We're out of time. Sanja, the spell."

She brushed his fumbling hand aside, and deftly worked the mechanism. The latch popped open, and the strap fell off. "The pages fit in an unbroken sphere," she told him quickly, leafing through the volume to find the pages with symbols on them. "You must find the centerpoint and sing the symbols in a spiral."

She found the section and began to tear out one page after the other, careful to preserve all the symbols. As each one fell away, Fal caught it with his magic and raised it into the air. The edges folded down along the proper seams, and he fit them together.

With the sphere completed, the symbols began to glow. They separated from the parchment that was no longer needed to contain them, and the pages wafted to the floor.

Sanja watched the last one drop into the water and warily lifted her foot out of a puddle that was growing into a lake around them. "Fal…"

He hadn't noticed, still holding onto the book as he studied the sphere of symbols. "It's a perfect sphere. Where is the starting point?"

"Fal, I need you to pull it back." She groped at his shoulder, but his hands were busy with the book, and she couldn't find his bare arm beneath the folds of his cloak while also keeping an eye on the chaos reigning around them. His illusions were manifesting in reality. Water spilled across the great hall in a flood that swept everyone off their feet. It poured down the walls into a lake that filled the chamber and began to freeze over. The streaming waterfalls froze to icicles and broke off into deadly sharp spears.

The dragon had joined the rest of the royal family on the dais, where Princess Liadan was performing some other kind of spell with whatever was in the glass cauldron. He grimly surveyed the rising water and said something to the princess, who nodded in answer without looking away from her task.

"It doesn't make sense!" Fal leafed through the book, barely glancing at the pages. The water rose faster the more agitated he became, and within moments it was up to her waist.

She was still groping along his sleeve when someone opened a door. "I found it!"

"Fal!" The fabric slipped through her fingers as her feet went out from under her.

"Sanja!" The book fell from his hands as he reached for her, too late. The current swept her away from him and through the open doorway into a dark, narrow corridor. She managed to catch hold of a tapestry, but it tore off its moorings. Sanja screamed as she went under. Her skirts tangled around her legs; she couldn't tell up from down. In the cold, churning darkness, all she could do was hold her breath and pray.

Something lashed around her wrist, pulled her back to the surface. She came up sputtering, never so grateful for the ability to breathe. She traced the thin red tail wound around her wrist up to its owner, a small red creature perched on the rafter above with black hair and silver horns. It hissed at her, then took off on all fours, dragging her against the current all the way back to Fal.

He caught her hand, and the waters stilled into a placid lake, but they could no longer be undone, and the frost was already spreading across the surface.

She laced her fingers through her husband's and held on for dear life. "Sing, Fal!"

The first notes lifted them both clear of the water. Fal sang, and the melody filled the great hall with raw magic that stretched it at the seams. It pounded inside Sanja's head, constricted her chest until she couldn't breathe, but she held on, refusing to let go.

One chance. That was all they'd get.

The sphere spun faster, commanding Fal's song to follow along. He matched it, turned it to his will, and molded it into something bright, and warm, and sweet. Sanja smelled clovers in the air; she tasted honey on the tip of her tongue.

Then, all at once, everything dropped. Sanja broke through the surface of the lake and sank down into its impossible depths. Up became down, light turned dark. She wanted to laugh, and cry, and scream, as chaos tossed her about, and her only anchor was the hand holding fast to hers.

~

The tide of battle was turning in their favor. Artairas could feel it in his bones. They'd cut across the city and left a path of destruction in their wake. The heavens had turned dark and brought them a terrible snowstorm to hide their advance. The frigid wind cut deeper than any sword, but Artairas and his men had God on their side. Their purpose propelled them on toward the castle seat of this heathen land.

It was guarded by beasts of legend, but he already knew none of them would be a match for his Holy sword. Not even the dragon. The Lady of the Lake had said so herself. She'd anointed him King Arthur and told him his kingdom would be built on the victories he would win here. She'd returned to him the sword he'd thought lost to evil magic, and it was even now guiding him true.

The storm clouds coming in from the north were as black as night. He dared not stand against such might. When the storm reached the city, Artairas would have to sound retreat.

But not yet.

"*Charge!*" he roared, meeting an opponent at a dead run. He slashed through the soldier's leather armor with ease. Cold made them all slow and clumsy, but not him.

He cut down three more in quick succession, grinning at Gawain fighting at his side. The two had become nigh inseparable, gathering more loyal men along the way. Percival fought bravely to his left, a man called Galeas not far behind.

As they neared the castle, the battle intensified. Gusts of wind-born snow obscured his vision. He attacked anything that rushed him, be it human or other. Beasts with silver claws fell at his feet. Things with green skin disintegrated into slime when he pierced them.

Tristan's shout sounded a warning moments before one of the great, unkillable beasts slammed its way through the ranks. It reeked of rot and death. Its crazed eyes never stilled. With a severed limb still clutched in a monstrous claw, it tore open throats with its fangs and tossed away dead bodies like discarded toys.

Gawain caught his arm, already pulling him away. "My Lord, this way!" He had to shout to make himself heard over the roar of the coming storm.

Artairas shook him off. "I will not cower before a mindless beast!" He wiped the melting snow off his brow, spat blood onto the snow, and ran at the monster holding Sir Marrok in its clutches.

With a mighty war cry, he charged, God's sword clutched tightly in his grip. He slashed at the beast and scored a mark, a thin cut across its thickly furred arm. The beast tossed Marrok aside and snarled at Artairas, a drop of bloody saliva pouring from its maw.

Artairas' blood boiled. This was a worthy opponent. Strong, fast, and deadly. One wrong move and it would rend him in two. He grinned, savoring the spicy thrill of danger. With black clouds darkening the sky overhead, and the deafening roar of the storm crashing down on him, he charged the beast. His sword glinted in the dying light as it cut the air itself, aiming true for the beast's neck.

But the strike fell empty, and Artairas stumbled to his hands and knees in the snow, with nothing to show for his bravery.

The beast was gone.

The storm died down with a suddenness that brought his head up, and as sunlight broke through the receding clouds, he looked out across an empty landscape of snow and distant trees.

The snowdrifts moved, spewing out his men one after the other, including Marrok, torn and bloody, but alive. Gawain stumbled up to Artairas, helped him to his feet, but said not a word. Percival crossed himself, his wary eyes gazing around in disbelief. All of the men looked as baffled as Artairas felt, searching for an enemy that was no longer there.

They'd fled.

No, not fled, disappeared into thin air, along with the entire God-forsaken city, leaving nothing but a level patch of ground where the castle ought to stand.

As far as the eye could see, Artairas and his men were surrounded by land covered with snow and completely devoid of life.

35

The water spat them out onto hard stone, exactly where they'd been a moment ago. Only it wasn't the same place any longer. The great hall was dry and neatly appointed, with all its furnishings returned to pristine condition and a strong fire crackling merrily in the hearth.

Fal groaned as he sat up. "Did it work?"

"I don't know," Sanja said. "But, I am not cold anymore."

Rather than risk letting go of her prematurely, Fal pulled her up to stand and drew her with him to the courtyard outside. A beautiful clear blue sky greeted him above. The ground was warm, with flowers blooming in their garden beds. The gate that had been shattered moments ago was now whole and opened to admit visitors from far and wide—and there were many. Humans, as well as Others, filled the streets, bedraggled, wounded, but very much alive.

"This is Anderheim." Fal whooped and caught Sanja up in a spinning dance around the courtyard. "We did it! We saved everyone! I can feel them, Sanja, hundreds of thousands of them. We are going to need more space. I will have to expand the Otherland farther out to fit them all in."

Laughing, Sanja pushed to be set back on her feet, and he obliged her. "First, I want to see my parents. Can you take me to them?"

Fal searched through the many minds filling his new world, but as far as he could reach, he found no sign of Gerhart or Olga. He tried again, and again, and one more time, but came up empty. "They... Sanja, I'm sorry. They are not here."

"Don't be silly. They have to be. We saved everyone, remember?"

Gods, how he wished he had a different answer to give her. Fal wished he didn't have to say the words that would break her heart, but he owed her the truth. "Liadan's spell summoned everyone still alive in Wilderheim with its magic inside them."

Sanja's bright smile dimmed. He felt the pain of loss stab through her, and it nearly brought him to his knees. It hurt all the more to know how hard she was fighting to stay strong. "Y-you're saying they're dead."

Fal pulled her into his arms. Sanja didn't return the embrace, so he squeezed her as tight as he dared, needing her to know she wasn't alone, and never would be again. "I'm so sorry."

"B-but they were on their way to Lyria. They could have made it through the pass in time."

"Yes," he said for no other reason than his mate needing to hear it.

She shuddered, sniffling back a sob as she put her arms around him at last. "Thank you for lying to me."

He pressed a kiss into her hair and squeezed her a little harder.

Princess Liadan burst out of the keep, calling out, "Tir! Tirasdunh al Dhakir, answer me right now!"

Fal swore.

"*Tir!* Where is he, Fal? How bloody far south do I have to fly to get him? Because he is sure as shite not anywhere in this Frastmir. I called the dragon's blood—that means he has to be here somewhere, too."

Behind her, the dragon emerged slowly, followed by the king and queen, side by side and hand in hand. The dragon placed a hand on Liadan's shoulder. "Do you remember the barrier along Wilderheim's borders with Mitgard? It kept us in and others *out*. Tir isn't here, child, because your spell never made it past Wilderheim's borders. He is still in Aegiros."

"He's safe?" Liadan asked through gritted teeth.

"Yes," the dragon confirmed. "I sensed the storm coming from the north before we left and felt it strike the barrier to our east. Fenrir claimed Wilderheim, but he was not allowed into Mitgard."

Later, when the dragon's words have had time to sink in, Fal would revisit them and wonder what could have stopped a creature so powerful all the gods of Asgard couldn't keep him contained. For now, his worries were much more immediate.

Liadan's eyes blazed blue, and her skin took on a faint glow. "Then let's go get him."

"We can't," Fal said. "The doorway is shut to keep Fenrir out. I might be able to open a small window briefly, but whoever leaves will never be able to come back."

Liadan shook her head, her entire being steaming as her fire rose, only to be doused by her tears. "No, I will not believe that with all the magic contained in this courtyard alone, no one has the power to bring my mate to me."

"And if we could?" the dragon asked. "His tribe would be left without their leader, vulnerable to attack again when they have barely found their footing back in the First Valley. They need him. His place is with them."

"And mine is with the clan," Liadan replied bitterly. "Is that what you are telling me, Grandfather?"

"I am telling you the time has come for you to choose."

Liadan gaped at him, speechless.

Nialei and Saeran reached out to her, but she shook them off and launched into the air, burning into her Other self, and she flew as fast as her wings would carry her, heading south.

"I should go after her," Saeran said.

The dragon sighed heavily. "No, give her time. She needs to come to terms with this, and none of us can do that for her." The last, he said to Fal, but whatever silent message he tried to convey with his inscrutable eyes, Fal didn't understand.

~

Night descended gently on a chorus of bird songs and cricket chirps. Those Others who chafed in close confines removed themselves to the farthest reaches of Anderheim. The rest spread out across the

Otherland to begin building new homes for themselves. The cities they left for humans. Fal had done what he could to bring as much of Wilderheim with them as possible to ease the transition. What the people lacked, Anderheim could easily provide.

Nialei and Saeran took over organizing a new council and getting their new kingdom on its feet. Fal, meanwhile, closed himself off in his chambers with Sanja.

Beyond exhausted after the day's trials, Fal wanted nothing more than to sleep, but Sanja's grief ached in his mind long after she dozed off. Without trying, he saw her thoughts churning over the last time she'd seen Olga and Gerhart before her Journey. Her father had been adamant about staying put until Sanja returned. They never would have left Wilderheim without her.

When her dark thoughts pulled Sanja into bad dreams of faceless monsters hunting her in the night, Fal couldn't stand it any longer. He put his forehead to hers and closed his eyes. Reaching into her dreams, he brought sunlight to her night and turned the dark woods into a meadow filled with wildflowers, birdsongs, and music.

Tables laden with food appeared on one side. A group of musicians picked up their instruments on the other. Fal's clan, Sanja's parents, and her friend Mattias shimmered into being around them, and then the meadow filled with nobles and villagers, all cheering for their happiness.

It was the feast they should have had to celebrate their wedding. Fal could never give her a real one now without her parents, and so he filled her dream with as much warmth and happiness as it could hold until it became as real as a memory. Then he let himself sink into it, too, and forget it had never been real. It was the most beautiful dream Fal had ever dreamed, and the most restful sleep he'd ever slept.

But when dawn broke, and Liadan still hadn't returned, worry over his twin dragged him away from the warmth of Sanja's embrace to the window.

"You look dashing in the morning light," Sanja said from the bed. She was smiling, rosy-cheeked, and deliciously rumpled. Just awakened from their shared dream, the shadows of grief had yet to catch up to her, and the beauty of her spirit sparkled across their connection directly to his heart.

Fal welcomed her momentary happiness, let it distract him from his own heavy thoughts. "And does that please her royal highness?"

"Very much," she purred, stretching beneath the covers. "I like you very much without your illusions and cloaks."

"I feel weightless without them." It was an odd feeling but a pleasant one.

Sanja slipped out of bed to join him at the window. Her thin arms came around him, and she pressed her front to his back, kissing his shoulder. "Don't worry. I will keep your feet firmly on the ground."

Fal chuckled, bringing her hand to his lips. "Did you sleep well?"

"Well enough." He followed her thoughts to her dream and, through it, to the memory of her parents. The heartbreak he'd begun to heal while she'd slept reopened, but she didn't say a word. Instead, she raised up on tiptoes to look over his shoulder out the window. "Any sign of Liadan?"

"Not yet."

Sanja wasn't ready to face the loss of her parents, and Fal wouldn't press her. There were other, gentler ways to help her. Sensing her persistent chill, he left her embrace to stoke the embers in the hearth and added more wood to it. Despite Anderheim's summer heat and the dragon's blood warming her from within, he knew Sanja would always need a fire burning nearby. He would never let her be without one. "What did the dragon mean about her having to choose?" Sanja asked, slipping back under the covers.

He sighed, searching the skies for any sign of his sister. "One trip, no way back. If Liadan decides she wants her mate more than all of this, it is possible I could still send her to him. But once the window closes, I may never be able to open it again."

"What if she chooses to go, anyway?"

The fire flared in Fal's hearth, admitting his sister. "Then she would be trapped in a foreign land forever, the only Other of her kind among mortals who fear her magic," she said. "Never to see her beloved mountains again, never to embrace her parents, or call her brother a bumbling idiot."

Fal snatched his sister into his arms. "Would a bumbling idiot have saved an entire kingdom from destruction?"

"No," she replied softly, then turned them to wink at Sanja. "But his brilliant mate would."

Fal scowled at them both as Sanja burst into helpless giggles in their bed. The gods had smiled down upon him the day they'd put him into her path on the green, and he would be forever grateful.

"Rest easy, brother. I have made my choice. I am staying here, with you cantankerous lot." But her eyes turned gray like ash when she said it, and despite her irreverent grin, he sensed the heartache underlying her words. She was saying what she thought he wanted to hear. "I came to you only because I would like to see Tir one last time. I tried to scry for him, but it appears my flames don't reach beyond Anderheim's borders."

"Of course," he said without hesitation. "I will need a few things. Sanja?" Only yesterday, she'd lain bleeding in his arms. He found it difficult to let her too far out of his sight.

She smiled softly, but he saw shadows of unease gathering in her eyes. "Go, I will be all right on my own for a little while." Sanja wouldn't say anything, but he felt the way her heartbeat sped up. She didn't want to be alone any more than Fal wanted to leave her.

He nodded. "I won't be long."

He took Liadan to his tower library. Fully restored to its original glory, it now had a window to let in the morning light.

Liadan hesitated at the threshold. "The last time I stepped in here, half of the chamber was gone. The time before that, it was filled with water." She shook her head with wonder. "You never fail to amaze, brother."

"So says the woman who burned a horde of demons to ash and restored water to her desert people."

She answered his smile with a wan one of her own. "How long will this take?"

"No time at all. I just wanted to have my wards around me when I muck about with the fabric of my Otherland." Without any further ado, Fal placed the flat of his hand on the stone wall and sang a sweet melodic command to open it. The stone rippled like a mirage, and when the center cleared, the desert night stretched out before them.

They were looking at the First City, nestled in a verdant valley that a few short months ago had been a barren desert.

Liadan joined him before the window, her face lighting up with wonder. "Can you bring us closer?"

Fal tilted his head, and they raced across the sands to the riverbank, over the bridge, and into the heart of the city. Fal opened the window wider, watched his sister's face closely as the scent of jasmine and oil lamps filled the room. Her eyes closed dreamily as she took a deep breath. That was all it took for the sallow pall of her skin to recede beneath its natural golden glow. Liadan came to life at the merest glimpse of the desert.

With tears spiking her lashes, she opened her eyes so she wouldn't miss a thing as they followed the main thoroughfare through the market to the palace with its towering spires and arched windows. They found Tir in the royal chambers, sitting at the edge of a fire pit, so close his billowing pants were beginning to singe. He didn't notice, staring intently into the flames.

"He is looking for me," Liadan said miserably, hugging her middle. "I told him I would never be more than a call away, that as long as he kept a fire burning bright, I would always come back when he called. Fal…"

"I know, Lia."

"I can't stay here."

"Nor could I." If he were the one standing there, looking at Sanja across an eternity, knowing he'd never be able to touch her, hear her voice… The thought of it made his throat close up. He would no more keep Liadan from her mate than he'd want her to keep him from the woman he strongly suspected he was beginning to love.

Liadan had helped him find his way to Sanja; he owed it to her to get her back to Tir. Even if it meant he might never see his twin sister again.

"But I cannot leave you, and our parents, and the dragon—"

"We will never be more than a thought away, sister. And who knows? Perhaps one day I will find a way for us to visit without undermining the foundation of an entire Otherland."

She launched herself at him, hugged him so tightly his ribs creaked.

"Careful! If I lose the window, it will be gone forever."

"I love you, Fal. You will always be the other half of my soul."

"Live long and rule well, Liadan. The hearts of your clan go with you."

She released him, wiping her nose on her sleeve. "Don't let Father's head get too big for his crown. He may be king, but Anderheim is your world. And keep an eye on the dragon, will you? He puts on a brave face, but he needs his kin more than he will ever let on." Touching her forehead to his, she added, "And don't you dare let that girl in your bed slip through your fingers."

"Never," he swore. "I will miss you."

"Always, brother."

With those final words, the Dragonblood princess, *shensari* of her people, and the other half of Fal stepped back through the rippling wall to her beloved mate. The disturbance caused Anderheim to squeal in pain, fighting to heal the wound Fal had opened, and the window rippled closed, leaving behind nothing but a long crack across the stone wall of his tower library.

Fal took a deep breath and let it out slowly. "Fair winds and farewell."

He stayed there for a while longer, imagining the life his sister would have in Aegiros. It would never be easy, but Liadan had never liked easy. She wouldn't have her family to advise her, but she'd never taken their advice, anyway. The only thing his sister truly needed was to have her mate by her side, and Fal was fairly certain that after Liadan told Tir all about the war, and Ragnarok, and how close he'd been to losing her to Anderheim, Tir would never let her out of his sight again.

The scar of her departure retained the desert's heat and, if he leaned close enough, Fal could almost smell the heady scent of jasmine and hot sand lingering around it. Liadan would thrive in Aegiros. Now Fal had to make sure everyone in Anderheim did, too.

The castle gates were open. Soon, the great hall would fill with people come to petition their royal majesties for whatever they couldn't live without. His presence would be required, no doubt. He'd spend the next year at least stuck in council meetings and royal banquets, or roaming the lands to mend whatever got broken during his spell. People would look at him and truly see him, and they'd tell him how grateful they were for their new home, and how they'd love it so much more if only they had this or that. And once those conversations began, they would never end.

Fal would be expected to teach wizards the ways of Anderheim's magic, and the Others would keep him so busy creating unique landscapes for them he would never again lack for an outlet for his magic.

In short, his days of solitude and study, of hiding from his people and fearing his magic were over. His only solace of peace, if not quiet, would be measured in the moments he spent with his lovely, brilliant mate, who would always have wildflowers in her hair and a book in her hands, and whose heart would forever beat right next to his.

Fal smiled.

It was good to be the prince.

AUTHOR'S NOTE

Many, many moons ago, in a dark, abandoned corner of a girl's mind, there once was a story. In 2007, I had this silly idea of turning a long-ago dream into a short story, never expecting it would turn into something as epic as this series. I never expected to be sitting here, with the final draft of the last revision of the third book in my hands, hesitating to write *The End*. Those two little words don't just mark the end of the story; in many ways, they mark the end of an age for me.

Every writer crafts their stories with bits and pieces of their soul, and I'm no different, but this particular story is far more than even that—it's personal. The Dawn of Ragnarok series has become something of a time capsule for the life I lived inside my mind as a child, where magic sparkled through my day, and the wind hissed with gossip from faraway lands; where fairies danced in the woods behind my grandmother's house and every bridge hid a troll or river spirit underneath.

And here I am, at the dawn of a new age, misty-eyed and nostalgic for those carefree days when everything still seemed so easily possible. I don't want to write *The End*. I don't want to say goodbye.

But I do want to say thank you.

To my amazing editors, Victoria Miller, Kimberly Grenfell, and Allie Beckman, for combing through hundreds of pages of these books to make sure all their gremlins were in line and behaving.

To friends who have stood by me, encouraging me every step of the way to write more, write faster, displaying more enthusiasm for my yet-to-be-written words than I do for a pizza delivery. There are too many of you to name, but you all know who you are, and I hope you know how much I love you and how much your love of my books means to me.

To you, dear reader, and all readers out there who have been so incredibly patient, waiting for me to finish this series. I'm not sure I would have had that much patience if I was in your place. Your eagerness and obvious love for these characters and their worlds have been the light at the end of this winding tunnel for me. I am humbled by your support throughout the years.

To my parents, without whom I literally wouldn't be here. But seriously, if you hadn't decided to up and move us all across the Big Blue Ocean, I wouldn't be the person or the writer I am today. You've given me everything I ever could have needed. You've been my tireless champions through good times and bad. For that, for a billion other things, and for no reason at all, I love you both more than words can say.

I offer one final thank you to Loki, who's been a constant gnat in my ear since he first stepped out of his shadows in The Royal Wizard. In true Trickster form, you haven't lacked for imaginative ways to push me along to the last page, using fair means and foul. It's done now. I hope you're happy.

And now, with these last few words, I want to bid farewell and fair journey to the Dragonblood clan who never knew I secretly adopted myself into their midst, if only as a faint whisper on the breeze. It's truly been a privilege.

Love always,
Alianne

ALIANNE DONNELLY is an avid lover of stories of all kinds. Raised on a healthy diet of fairy tales in a place where they almost seemed real, she grew into a writer who seeks magic in the modern age and enjoys sharing a little bit of it with the world through every story she writes. Her books span the spectrum from fantasy to science fiction with varying degrees of romance sprinkled throughout. Alianne now lives in California, where she spends her free time reading, writing, and daydreaming. To find out more about her books and works in progress, visit her website at aliannedonnelly.com.

CPSIA information can be obtained
at www.ICGtesting.com
Printed in the USA
LVHW011551071220
673553LV00001B/156

9 781948 325189